Suit filled the doorway, blocking us from the open yard and the unnatural lake beyond. His vacant head and shattered skull didn't keep him from lurching the glistening blue steel revolver up towards us.

Kipuka Blues

Michael Warren Lucas

Tilted Windmill Press

Kipuka Blues
Copyright © 2016 by Michael Warren Lucas. All rights reserved, including the right of reproduction, in whole or in part in any form.

Published in 2016 by Tilted Windmill Press.
Cover art copyright ©2016 by Ben Baldwin.

Editor: Richard Jones
Copy Editor: Dayle Dermatis
Proofreading: Amanda Robinson
Cover Design: Ben Baldwin
Interior Design: Tilted Windmill Press

ISBN-13: 978-0692674970
ISBN-10: 0692674977

This book is a work of fiction. Names, characters, places, and incidents either are products of the author's imagination or used fictionally. Any resemblance to actual events or locales or persons, living or dead, is merely coincidental. This book is licensed for your personal enjoyment only.

Tilted Windmill Press
www.tiltedwindmillpress.com

Acknowledgements

My gratitude goes to the folks who helped me with this book: Kelly A. Harmon, Richard Jones, Alex Kourvo, Kate MacLeod, Mark Moellering, Juliet Nordeen, and Rob Rowntree.

I also need to thank the people who read Immortal Clay and demanded I immediately (if not sooner) write a sequel. This book wouldn't have happened without your encouragement, bribes, and threats.

This is for Liz.

Novels By the Same Author

Immortal Clay
Kipuka Blues
Butterfly Stomp Waltz
Hydrogen Sleets

Immortal Clay

Michael Warren Lucas

What Came Before

THE ALIEN chewed its way out of Antarctica, devouring every living thing it found and spitting out exact duplicates. Even the duplicates didn't know they were human ghosts, clothed in alien flesh. The alien's infiltrators in schools and subways and office towers transformed into tentacled horrors in less time than it took to drain a boil, engulfing entire cities in its relentless crawl north. Humanity fought, hard, eventually using nuclear missiles to turn Australia into glass. Four months later, they cauterized South America and sub-Saharan Africa. The alien subverted the oceans, using those secret depths to crawl around the globe in plankton and dolphins and squid, shrugging off explosives and poisons.

Surviving nations turned everything against the invader. Cities became armed bunkers, every resource conscripted for defense. Toxic plutonium dumped in the seas was a problem for tomorrow, if it could help buy today. Today was about escaping extinction, even as the alien crept to surround the northern continents.

At the end, the very end, with the alien surging up every waterline in the world to nibble on the last remnants of the human race, police detective Kevin Holtzmann snatched his wife and daughter and fled from the eastern shore of Michigan out into the western United States.

They almost survived. They never had a chance. Any hope was a doomed, desperate delusion. The alien, incarnated as a murderous psychopath Kevin had put away years before, trapped them in the wastes of Utah.

Kevin shot his wife and daughter before the alien could torment them, allowing them the dignity of a quick, painless death before turning the gun on himself.

But he was too slow.

The alien ate Kevin alive.

Once it devoured every living thing and grunted out duplicates of it all, once the alien owned the world, *was* the world—it set Kevin's copy and every copy near me free to live in a remade land.

If I don't watch myself, I forget I'm not Kevin. I remember killing my wife and daughter to keep the alien that calls itself Absolute from eating them alive. I still have a blister under my chin, from when Kevin jammed the savagely hot barrel of his Springfield XD under his chin and tried to pull the trigger.

I am not Kevin. He murdered his family. Not me.

Like everyone else in Frayville, I'm a copy.

Our world has changed. Despite being clothed in alien flesh, people remain people. Which means, even with the new rules, some people will break the rules for their own gain. I plan to be the guy who puts a stop to that.

Kevin is dead. I have his memories, but this is *my* life. I'm going to be one of the good guys.

Whatever that means.

And Absolute, a genocidal alien many times over, that murdered Kevin, the human race, and the world?

Some way, somehow, I will make it pay. And pay. And pay.

No matter what it takes.

Chapter 1

THREE YEARS ago this place had been a treasured showpiece sparkling along Frayville's Lake Huron shore. Dark-red brick walls mortared in gray. Broad aluminum-lined eaves to block out Michigan's summer heat without screening the weaker winter light streaming through vast picture windows. Wrought iron railings along the roofed concrete porch, separating the padded chairs and the creaky iron glider from the sidewalk. A roof angled to the south, allowing the silver-trimmed solar shingles to gobble and convert every scrap of energy.

Three years ago, I'd never have made it to the front door without flashing my badge and, even then, it would have been close. Now, I walked up to the front door like I owned the place. Because my badge was about as useless as most things these days.

All I was concerned about was that it looked up to code and probably wouldn't burn easily. Probably.

I really wanted to get through today without torching any buildings.

The cool brass latch in the windowless stained-wood front door clicked when I squeezed the thumb slat. At my touch, the unlocked door eased from its frame and glided a few inches open.

Behind me, Eric coughed. He'd eaten something spicy for breakfast. With onions. Eric wasn't the smartest guy I'd ever worked with, but he knew every water and power junction in the city and could shut down a house in a quarter of the time I'd need.

It was one thing if we torched a house. Houses burning accidentally was a problem.

Besides, I remembered being a cop. The man I had been knew better than to hunt people alone.

Ex-people.

Whatever we were.

Stop. Focus on the job. Do not lose it. Again.

"Ready?" I said.

Eric nodded, shifting his shoulder against the weight of the angular, rust-dotted metal toolbox dragging at his hand. The brisk mossy breeze off the unspeakable lake had brushed the heat away, but a single line of sweat ran down the side of his blocky brown face just in front of his ear.

After yesterday's disaster, I couldn't blame him. My palm itched to hold a sidearm, but a gun would only anger whatever we found.

A seagull screeched somewhere behind us. No, not a seagull—something made to look like a seagull. A *copy* of a seagull. Never forget that.

Seagulls: Taken. Taken grass.

Taken people.

I tapped the heavy wooden door. It gently swung the rest of the way open.

Someone had spent a lot of money remodeling an old house. They had to have been from out of town—nobody who worked in touristy Frayville could have afforded this place. A crystal chandelier shattered the sunlight into a million tiny rainbows, splattering their color across stark white walls. Overlapping footprints and streaks of dried mud and sand smeared across the pricey, black-marbled white tile floor. Someone had made a weak attempt at cleaning the floor near the entryway to a living room, swirling and diluting the dirt before surrendering to it. Sandy footprints faded away towards the dining and family rooms. A family portrait, two adults and a horde of kids, hung opposite the door, its silver frame making it even more obviously askew. A black crushed-velvet chair with wooden claw feet sat just inside the door, its seat host to a grimy blue crumpled windbreaker.

"Police!" I shouted.

Silence.

"Kevin Holtzmann, Frayville PD!"

I bounced the door off the wall of the entryway. Nobody hiding behind it. No silhouette shadows in the living room or down the hall. No nervous scuffle of feet, no click of a pistol safety.

A seagull-creature screeched.

A distant motor roared. Sound carried for miles in this silent town.

I shuddered only a little as what felt like adrenaline threw a dance party in my muscles, and took a deep breath to steady myself.

The stench of burned, rotting meat punched the back of my throat. Party's over.

"What the hell?" Eric whispered.

My stomach knotted around the sure memory of that stench. "A body," I said.

You never forget the reek of a corpse, especially when it comes laced with the scorched-pork smell of electrocution.

Chapter 2

WE COULD have followed our noses straight to the cooked corpse. Eric tried, but I held him back, motioning for him to follow me so we could sweep the house for living people first.

The people who owned this place must have been important even three years ago, after humanity discovered Absolute eating Australia and nuked the entire continent to glass. On a solid oak dining room table big enough to seat twelve, I found bills and catalogs addressed to Jerome and Tabitha Morpeth of ritzy Bloomfield Hills. This had to be their summer home. The roomy kitchen featured stainless-steel cookware and wooden-handled knives dangling from chrome ceiling racks. Food crumbs and spots of dried mustard and ketchup marked the island. Something sticky had spattered the gleaming white, ripple-textured Pewabic-style tile backsplash, and smeared grease marred the chrome refrigerator handle.

On the white-speckled black granite kitchen counter I found a bunch of thick comb-bound books from Building the Future, the federal group that had supposedly helped people prepare for the aftermath of burning Absolute out of the world. A bunch had white covers: *Nuclear Winter Preparations. Greenhouse Management. Core Electrical Grid Decentralization Plan*, version 5.2. I remembered seeing version 6 a week before Absolute's final attack. In blue covers, *Employment-Based Dietary Allotments* and the detested *Gasoline Rationing Index*. Kevin had wondered which of those last two books people had hated more.

Two thick books, in heavy, blue cardboard covers and stamped "For Official Use Only," dominated the countertop. A shiver of remembered disgust rippled through me. Kevin had hated these books, hated what they stood for and what they would have meant for him. Books that had appalled Kevin even though he'd never needed either. *Duplicate Detection and Destruction. Martial Law Procedures.*

At the bottom of the stack of books I found one in an unfamiliar black cover, the title stamped in blood red. *North American Cauterization Plan.*

From the kitchen library, it seemed pretty clear one of the Morpeths was supposed to help people prepare for Absolute's invasion. Or deal with humanity's failure to stop it.

Had the Morpeths been rich before the bombs flew, or had they been among those bastards who turned civil disaster preparations into profits?

And what kind of person did their whole house in black and white?

I left the books where I'd found them. If I ever needed kindling—worthless, useless leftovers of a vanished past—I knew where to get them. Not that I'd needed kindling recently. These days, things had a tendency to explode into flames around me.

We cleared the sumptuous main floor, finding it empty, so I led Eric up the broad spiral staircase to the upper level. The plush padding beneath tightly knit zebra-print carpet swallowed the sounds of our steps. Eric moved quietly for such a big guy, but his massive toolbox clanked at each tread.

Upstairs, the stench of scorched carrion thickened into an almost visible fog filling the hallway from gleaming white wall to empty gleaming white wall. My lungs rebelled against each breath, and I felt instantly glad we'd skipped lunch.

The spacious guest bedrooms featured queen beds with soft, thick mattresses and too many shams and lacy comforters, all in stark black and white, and each window tightly closed and locked. I couldn't imagine anyone hiding in a room with gelatinous air that tasted of rancid meat, but things were different now, and what I could imagine didn't cover half of what was happening. I flung open closet doors and Eric glanced under the beds before we headed through the abandoned master bedroom to the private bath, the stink growing stronger with every step.

The bathroom must have been designed to make the rest of the house look like a down-market Detroit No-Tell Motel. Iridescent tile in blues and reds gleamed from the floor and walls, except for the frosted glass walls of the two-person steam shower and the floor-to-ceiling mirror beside the sparkling chrome sink. I almost didn't see the lavishly appointed room, my attention immediately dragged to the mirror and the words scrawled there in bright red lipstick: *I CAN'T DO THIS.*

I knew *exactly* how the writer had felt. I stepped further into the room, glancing to my right. An octagonal window with tinted one-way glass looked out over what had once been a wonderful view of nature. Instead, the window faced the horrible green, choppy muck saturating Lake Huron, a constant reminder of the new world.

A thin strand of desiccated jerky ran around the window.

My gaze followed it down to the raised platform supporting a sunken triangular tub.

And in the tub, something that had once been human. Ish.

Maybe.

The malformed body had stretched thin and flat, hugging the inside of the tub as if squeezing away from the oily water that still filled the bottom of the tub. I couldn't tell if it had been male or female, but the toilet seat stood upraised, so I assumed "him" until proven otherwise. Rivulets of dried corpse tracked across the area where once they crawled from the tub, leaving behind dried riverbeds of flesh. One thinned and elongated arm flowed up the wall, detouring around the octagonal window to end in a flattened hand, stretched fingers curled to dig into the grout between the tiles. The other had stretched across the room towards the sink, only to collapse in a skeletal rigor a foot short.

His head balanced on the edge of the tub, mouth impossibly stretched in an agonized scream so wide that it jammed the man's nose up between his imploded eyes. The scalp had pulled away from the jaw, partially swallowing the short blond hair and pulling his ears towards the crown of his head.

A thick orange extension cord ran from a hall outlet and into the bathroom, where it plugged into a dark black cord snaking into the tub. The rancid, oily sheen on the water revealed only the shadow of some cube-shaped device. Probably a toaster—most people who chose to die this way used a toaster. The dead man's abdomen reached from the side of the tub towards the dark cube, partially covering it, as if the man's flesh had tried to safely encapsulate the appliance before he died.

Eric grunted, deep and sharp, his breath caught between sounds.

Years as a detective in Detroit had taught me to take in the whole body immediately. If I looked away, I'd never look back. I focused on the leg that had flowed out of the tub towards the steam shower. "Go outside if you're going to spew."

"'m fine," Eric said. The toolbox clanked to the floor, followed closely by the sounds of Eric's shoes pounding towards the stairs. The front door—already open from our entrance—slammed against the wall and stuck there. From outside, I heard the muffled sounds of gagging.

I covered my ears for a moment, allowing the sound to fade slightly. I already wanted to puke up everything I'd ever eaten, and listening to Eric would push me over the edge. Instead, I made myself hammer the scene into my memory. Kevin had been a cop. I was a civil servant, sort of. Besides, if I didn't deal with this, nobody else would. I'd known fire could kill us, kill what we were now. I'd hadn't known electricity could too.

The police department, as part of the defense preparations, had trained Kevin how to use a flamethrower. Why hadn't they mentioned the electrical thing?

Probably because nobody made lightning throwers. And how much extension cord could you drag around behind you?

The corpse wore a black cotton T-shirt, stretched into shreds by the body's transformation but still gently cloaking the chest and forearms. I peered through the water, and…maybe, those might be shorts under there.

Someone had written *I can't do this* on the mirror. This poor bastard had ample reason to write that—but maybe it hadn't been him. The way it looked was, after writing, he climbed into the tub, fully clothed. And pulled a radio or a toaster or something in with him.

Open and shut, really, no matter what I told myself. The only thing that made this different from a dozen scenes I remembered from before was the absence of paperwork. Or a coroner's team. Well, that and the body smearing itself all over the bathroom. One of those fingernails had become a six-inch stiletto, sticking straight out from the wall up near the window.

Frayville had no government. No civil authority. Those of us Absolute had loosed did whatever needed doing to keep things running. Eric and I were trying to reach anyone in Frayville who might have been too afraid to leave their home. That meant visiting every single house. Every. Single. Damn. House. This was the first successful suicide in the two weeks since we'd started knocking on doors.

I didn't want to think about the other suicides. The ones that weren't successful.

Eric dragged himself back through the bathroom door. "Opened the back door. Found a fan, plugged it in."

I nodded and jerked the extension cord out of the wall. "Thanks." I'd grown acclimated enough to the stench that I was able to breath more deeply. Before going home I'd have to hit the pharmacy and grab a bottle of Vicks for the next time this happened. I let myself look away from the body. I didn't remember getting acclimated to that distinctive decomposition stench so quickly when I'd been at other sites. Before.

Eric's Mediterranean features had acquired a greenish-white undertone, but his jaw was set.

Opening the bathroom window would air the place out faster. I'd have to kneel on the raised platform around the tub, reach over Mister Crispy, and move the misshapen elbow away from the window crank. Nothing to it. Sixty seconds and done.

I gritted my teeth. "Let's open a window in the hall. Get some air in up here. And get the hell out."

Eric lumbered ahead, but I kept my pace carefully even as I walked back downstairs. I made it a rule to not run from crime scenes. Once you start running away, you never stop. Thankfully Eric's new cross breeze had already swept the worst of the stench from the first floor, but I knew that my hair and clothes had soaked up that reek. I'd need an extra-long shower and new clothes before I saw the girls. Or anyone.

The mossy lake air cleared my brain. Maybe that's what let me notice the floor.

Given the white tile and pristine white carpeting throughout the main floor, the previous owners must have taken off their shoes every time they came in. Dried sand and dirt marred the tile entryway, and sandy footprints trailed through the dining room and family room. Mister Crispy hadn't bothered to kick off his shoes.

But one section of the tiled entryway floor was clean. No, more than clean. That little section between the front door and the family room, in front of the coat closet, gleamed like new.

Years of experience suddenly hummed in the back of my brain. I'd seen that clean patch when we opened the door, but the corpse's punch to my nose and the search for living people had claimed all my attention. Now that I could breathe, my instincts screamed that I'd missed something.

Out on the front walkway, Eric said, "What's up?"

"Hang on." I dropped to my knees on the dirty tile and bent to look more closely.

The tile wasn't really clean. It only looked clean next to the surrounding tile. Someone had swirled the mop over the ceramic and left faint swirls of dirt behind. Whoever had cleaned it didn't know how to work a mop properly—they'd swabbed but not scrubbed.

This house was built on dirt, but the sandy beach was only a few steps away. The sand was a pale tan, almost gray.

Amidst the beige of the beach sand, I saw faint brown hints that didn't belong. The sand had formed in tiny ridges, but the brown was more streaky. Like a dried liquid.

I wished I could smell the tile. I wished I could smell anything except scorched corpse. Instead, I got to my feet.

"Wait here," I said before heading farther back into the house. "I need to check something."

The kitchen trash overflowed with empty frozen dinners and sticky, filthy cans of prepared pasta. The bathrooms' trash cans were empty.

A big plastic trash can half full of plastic wrappers along with dusty cans and sharp bits of metal that really should have gone to recycling sat in the corner of the echoing, empty two-car garage. I carefully reached down and shifted the top layer of detritus, exposing a massive wad of paper towels.

They were stiff with clotted blood. Too much blood to be a simple cut. The towels hadn't yet acquired that petrified texture so distinctive of drying blood, so it wasn't more than a day or two old.

Mister Crispy hadn't committed suicide.

This was murder.

Chapter 3

THE OPEN air outside felt even more oppressive than the closed air of the dead man's house. Too much familiar life surrounded us, every scrap of it alien. The trees. The grass. The seagull-creature squawking for food in the distance. Walking down the center of the sun-scorched asphalt road towards the tool-filled pickup truck Eric had liberated from the abandoned Consumers Energy building, every living thing we saw was made of alien stuff.

Lake Huron had once been a beautiful gray and green and blue. Now a turgid neon green sludge, choked with deformed plankton and misshapen weeds and who knew what else, covered the surface. Too thick to form proper waves, the water surged and ebbed in slow, moss-scented respiration. The Great Lake smelled of deep forest. It smelled *wrong*.

The few yards of sand between the water and the road were free of driftwood and debris. The lake had always washed trash up from Canada or Chicago or Cheboygan, but today's pristine sand held only shallow, surf-sculpted dunes. Where seagulls had once darkened the sky, now only two white-and-gray replicas poked among the crumbling black spars of the incinerated wooden boardwalk.

Without the summer's teeming tourists and autumn's hunters strewing half-eaten bags of chips and spilling fresh-cut fries, perhaps Frayville could support only two seagulls. Or maybe just Absolute hated winged rats, like every human I knew.

Houses hugged the lakeshore road, front porches and stoops right against the wide sidewalk. Most of these had been summer homes for rich people from down around Detroit or Lansing, intermixed with battered party rentals. The street should have been full of obnoxious tourists and the buskers who loved separating them from their money through the sheer power of amusement. We hadn't found a single inhabited home down this stretch. Nobody wanted to live next to that roiling, badly sketched memory of a once-great lake, drawn in alien colors by alien imperative. Nobody wanted the reminder that we'd lost a war against Absolute, that we weren't human.

Nobody was fool enough to face that every day. Almost nobody. I still hoped to talk Ceren, one of the two girls I'd adopted after doomsday, out of it.

None of the houses had lawns, though. That was a plus. The thought of walking on alien grass still creeped me out, even when I wasn't running for my life over it. I couldn't help imagining it changing form, twining around my feet to yank me beneath the ground.

Eric stayed his usual quiet self, possibly using the time to think, definitely giving me time to think.

I'd seen the black-and-white house's set piece before, many times, in my tenure as a detective at Detroit PD. There's a fight. Someone gets killed—pushed down the stairs, whacked upside the head with a lamp, something like that. The panicked killer gets clever and stages a suicide, forgetting that coroners treat every suicide as suspicious.

These days, Frayville housed a hundred, maybe a hundred and fifty people. We didn't have a coroner, and suicide felt pretty much the same as natural causes. We had a whole group of people who'd directly or indirectly committed suicide. Instead of having the decency to sprawl out and decompose, they kept walking around and being far too supportive of each other, their very minds somehow connected over distances. "Acceptance" is what they called themselves. Collectively. Acceptance worried me, when they didn't terrify me.

Before Absolute, Acceptance would have terrified me. People only have so much terror to go around, though, and mine was spread pretty thin these days. Alien grass. Group minds. What we would do when the canned food ran out. What other time bombs the alien Absolute had left for us, or *inside* us, and what would happen when we triggered them.

Mister Crispy pushed all that to the back of my brain. I—*Kevin*—had been a detective. I had all Kevin's memories and skills and heartaches and passions. I'd become a cop because I wanted to help people, because I wanted to make the world a better place. Accidental death was bad. Manslaughter was worse. Conscious, premeditated murder beat all that.

But we were hard to kill. Two weeks ago, I'd been shot through the heart by an Olympic target shooter and recovered. We had people walking around who had lost their heads—literally—and their bodies had survived. Not their minds, but their bodies.

Killing someone now demanded more than passion, more than simply losing control. If you wanted to put someone in the ground so they didn't get back up, killing *required* premeditation.

On my second pass through the black-and-white house, when I knew I was looking for hints, I found them easily enough.

Grab the victim. Drag him to the bathroom. I'd found a few drops of blood on the stairs and sunk deep in the upstairs hall's white carpet.

Run a tub of water. The chrome faucets held a couple drops of blood dried into smeared smudgy fingerprints.

Grab an appliance. Find out the cord wasn't long enough. Hunt up an extension cord. I didn't know what the appliance was. I wasn't looking forward to reaching into that greasy pool and prying misshapen flesh out from around it to find out.

Then throw the appliance into the water with the victim.

Most of the frantic improvisers who try this sort of scene forget one crucial detail. The circuit breaker will blow as soon as the appliance touches the water. After a bit of searching, Eric found the reason this one hadn't. Someone had yanked the breaker, replacing it with a few inches of heavy-gauge copper wire instead. The current had stopped only when the wire melted.

This wasn't a momentary whim, a moment of anger and a flash of violence. This killing had taken ten minutes, maybe half an hour to set up. Thirty minutes for the killer's conscience to prey on them, to whisper about right and wrong.

Someone had rigged that house to kill an unconscious man.

I imagined the shadowy killer standing in the bathroom, holding a toaster in their hand, looking at the victim sprawled in the tub.

And deliberately tossing the toaster into the water.

Watching sparks fly, standing by while the victim flailed and stretched until the power failed.

Murder.

The first question I needed to answer: Who was the victim? Anybody could find an empty house and move in. Absolute hadn't restored the whole population of Frayville, just a few scattered people here and there. Someone had wanted a nice house and moved into the Morpeth place, but lacked the habits or discipline to keep mud off the carpet and crumbs off the counter. Had the killer been the new tenant, or a visitor? I couldn't ask the neighbors. Nobody lived near the lake. You'd need something a little wrong with you to walk out your front step and face the churning goop of Lake Huron every day.

Then again, anyone who didn't have something wrong with them after being murdered, copied, and released into a dead city…had something wrong with them.

I absently rubbed my chin in thought, the way Kevin used to. At the stab of pain, I jerked my hand away. The blister had been there for a month, ever since Absolute freed us, and I was beginning to think it would never heal.

Kevin had earned that blister when Absolute had trapped him and his family in the desert. He'd killed his wife Sheila, and his daughter Julie, before the alien could eat them alive, then tried to blow his own brains out. He wasn't fast enough.

His memories. His life.

My pain.

But the best way to deal with heartbreak, or maybe to avoid dealing with it, is doing something. The bathtub scene put a familiar pull in my chest, a fishhook tugging at my spirit.

Someone had gone through a lot of effort to commit a crime. Not just a crime…*the* crime. The stewed lake, my secondhand grief, the alien grass that might change shape and rise up to eat me again, the worries about survival and my two adopted daughters and all the million horrible things that might go wrong, all seemed distant now.

We had no laws. No juries, no judges. And no one who really cared. No one but me.

I could wallow in grief.

Or I could find and punish a killer.

Chapter 4

ERIC DROPPED me at Ceren's, where I grabbed a quick shower and change of clothes. Once I'd washed off the corpse stink and dropped my death-infused outfit in the washing machine with extra bleach, I walked the empty residential streets to Jack's to meet the girls for dinner.

Kipuka Blues

The low ceiling at Jack's, with its looming square wooden beams stained walnut-dark, makes it seem smaller than it is. On the white stucco walls, neon signs advertising brands of beer we'd never see again cast red-and-white shadows across the gleaming wood tabletops. Jack had yanked the jukebox to make room for another table, but left the dart board at the back near the restrooms. The evening crowd had just started to trickle in, and Jack was in his usual place between the long wooden bar and the mirrored wall. The shelves in front of the mirror that had once held dozens of bottles of liquor now stood empty and wiped clean. The mirror reflected only the room and the dozen or so people sitting in tight clusters around the bar's tables. Eric and Vince usually played bouncer, but it was still early for them, so I walked right in.

I missed the jukebox, but it had streamed everything from the Internet. Those services were gone. Music had gone from ubiquitous to completely absent. Eric and I had found a few old CDs in some of the houses, but nothing any good—mostly techno or pop.

My absent Julie and Sheila were only the worst ache in my heart. Music was another—I missed my grandpa rock: the Stones, Blue Öyster Cult, Black Sabbath. I would have cut someone for an hour of Pink Floyd. I missed relaxing in the evening with a beer and an old TV show, but all that had come from the Internet too. I missed absent friends and even the damn cat videos Julie always wanted to show me.

I missed my daughter's enthusiasm, Sheila's unfailing optimism.

I missed my friends. All the ties that made me human.

I hoped it wasn't the flesh that made me human then or now, but the connection to others around me.

I had Alice and Ceren. Great kids. They said that they'd adopted me, but I had the feeling that they missed their families as much as I did.

If I kept musing, though, I'd plummet straight back into bottomless depression. I went straight to the bar, carefully sitting three empty stools from the black-veiled Rose Friedman. "Jack," I said.

"Sheriff," Jack said, ambling to stand right before me. Jack had once been a heavier man, but now his face seemed to drape off his skull. He'd lost his two front teeth in a bar fight years ago, and Absolute hadn't restored them.

"Not the sheriff. Don't go giving people the wrong idea. You have any Stroh's left?"

Jack smiled. "Been saving the last six for you."

I nodded. "Thanks. One, please."

I don't know what Jack had done before, but I guessed he'd studied at the Bartender Ninja School. The cold can materialized in front of me before I could take another breath. "Rough day?"

"Unpleasant surprise." Stroh's isn't the best beer Jack still has, but the strawy taste makes Kevin's life flash through the back of my brain. Dinner on the patio with his wife and daughter. Birthdays and holidays. A cooler on the sun-scorched beach, while little Julie worked with a tiny plastic shovel to dig a hole she'd want to bury him in.

Everything that had made life worthwhile and now made my throat clench harder. I forced down another swallow of Stroh's.

All I had left of them was my wedding ring. And a home I couldn't bear to enter.

I set the can back on the counter. "You hear of anyone missing?"

Jack blinked. "Everyone."

I raised my eyebrows at him and kept silent.

"Ah, crap." Jack grimaced. "You found someone."

"Yeah."

"Who was it?"

"If I knew, I wouldn't be asking."

"What about a picture?"

"Wouldn't help."

"Damn." Jack shook his head. "I hear anything, I'll let y'know."

"Thanks. Use the walkie-talkie I left you." I took another sip and made myself ask, "Any other news?"

Jack shrugged. "There's some folks meeting up at the Big Boy by the Winchester for dinners. Someone ought to go take a look. The Perlstein guy you sent came by this afternoon."

"Good. Glad he made it." Eric and I had found Hans Perlstein yesterday. Like the rest of us, he'd awoken a month ago, terrified of the outside world. He'd barricaded himself in his one-bedroom house. Eric and I had spent an hour talking to him before he'd shifted the upturned couch from the window and let us glimpse his pale, gaunt face. Like most of the others we'd found, he only needed a few kind words. *You're not alone. There's hope. We need to help each other.*

Perlstein had run out of food the day before. He eventually cracked a window and accepted a protein bar before we headed to the next house.

Everyone we found got a protein bar. While people had raided the grocery stores and hoarded the cans, nobody before me thought to pillage the health food store. We didn't know how long it took for one of us to starve before we began burning our brain as fuel, but we knew how badly things went when it happened. A protein bar would at least buy the person a day to overthrow their terrors. Hopefully, knowing that we were all out here, and all rooting for them, would help.

I'd festered in my—Kevin's—house until Alice rescued me. She rang Kevin's doorbell. I answered.

"You going up to the Big Boy?" Jack said.

I shook my head. "I'm doing the house-to-house. Someone else can go say hello."

Jack nodded. "Fair 'nuff. I'm sure that Mista Woodward will be happy to go shake hands."

"Dammit." That jerk would be all too glad to go tell another group of people that he was in charge. I slammed a mouthful of Stroh's, then cursed myself for forgetting to savor it. *Five cans left.* "All right, I'll go up tomorrow."

"Someone's gotta," Jack said. "Better you than him."

"I thought Absolute only brought back the useful people," I muttered.

Jack snorted and looked over my shoulder at the door. "Yours."

I turned just in time to see Alice trot through the door. She had a fourteen-year-old's energy, and today it bubbled over into her thin hands and pale face. "Kevin!" she said, skidding to a stop only a couple feet from me. "You'll never guess?"

Alice had been one of Julie's friends. Ceren had been Alice's neighbor. We were living in Ceren's house until I found us a better home to call our own. "You cleared Legacy from the game store."

She shook her head. "I cracked it."

I froze, then carefully set the half-full can on the cool bar. "You got into Legacy?"

Before releasing us, Absolute had grown a giant, organic-looking computer in Winchester Mall. Alice couldn't keep away from it, spent her days working with a couple other people trying to extract useful information from it. Absolute had wanted us to find it—it had left two words echoing in everyone's mind, and the word *Legacy* was one of them. The moment I'd seen the giant green bubbles, I'd known they were called Legacy.

We still had no clue what *Immanence* meant. I felt completely confident everyone would know it when we saw it.

But If my adopted daughter had cracked the alien library Absolute had left for us, I'd need that beer and more.

"Almost." Alice flapped both hands, shaking enough to set her tight brunette ponytail bobbing. "There's a pattern. The signals are grouped into packets. It's not, like, Ethernet, but it's a frame-based protocol." Her voice raised at the end of each sentence as if she was asking a question. I hoped she wasn't, because I sure didn't have any answers. "Each frame is a few terabytes, but it's definitely frames. Steve is building a machine big enough to collect the frames so Brandi can do some math."

I smiled. "You cracked it." Pride shivered in my chest, a tiny sliver compared to the pride I'd taken in my own Julie, but I nursed it. Alice was my responsibility, and I wanted to help her turn into the best person she could be. I also wanted to remind her to stop ending each sentence like a question, but this wasn't the moment. "Good work, kid."

"There's a lot more to do," she said. "But it's like finding the corner pieces of a puzzle. You have to start somewhere."

Alice hopped onto the stool next to me. "Steve said to ask you to keep your eyes open for computers. He needs some big ones. Really big ones."

I glanced over Alice's head at Rose Friedman. The veiled woman hadn't stirred other than to lift her drink. "I can do that." I had a notebook in my pocket for writing down interesting things Eric and I discovered. I hadn't thought to list *murder victim* in there, but I doubted I'd forget. "Let's get a table while we can. Hey, Jack, any chance you have a cupcake for my smart girl here?"

"I'll make you one tomorrow," Jack said. "Hey, Alice. I got no idea what you just said, but it sounds pretty good."

"Thanks." A white, toothy grin split her face. "Brandi actually smiled at me."

"Wow," I said. Brandi and her husband Steve normally only had time for their struggle to untangle one of the mysteries Absolute had left us. Steve seemed pretty mellow, but Brandi's fierce intensity bordered on mania.

"I know, right?" Alice said.

Jack said, "I'll put this day on the calendar."

"Oh, don't do that," I said. "You ruin Brandi's rep, she will come for you."

"You'll watch out for me," Jack said.

"You think I'm getting between Brandi and anything?" I said. "Tell me, Jack, what's it like walking around without a survival instinct?" I half suspected that one day I'd have to sit on Brandi, Frayville's digital Valkyrie, but Alice's success and a moment of banter shoved away the memory of a smeared body and a badly cleaned pool of blood.

Contentment never lasts. An annoyed voice from behind said, "What the fuck is *wrong* with you?"

Chapter 5

CEREN STOOD in the doorway, silhouetted by summer evening light pouring from the street. Where Alice was thin and porcelain, Ceren looked like she could grow up to be a linebacker. For the men's team. If there were any men left. I hoped her growth spurt would end soon, for her sake. Ceren wore a loose black T-shirt with the words *The Birthday Massacre* splattered across it in lurid purple, denim shorts, and heavy leather hiking boots. Her hair was dyed a neon electric blue. I wouldn't have guessed that Ceren was a TBM fan; they were a few years before her time. Then again, I like Pink Floyd, and that's grandpa or even great-grandpa music.

I had a flash of an alternate future, one where Absolute hadn't taken over the world. Ten years from now, Ceren might have been hanging around this same bar, slipping between the wooden tables to the glossy counter to demand brain death in a bottle. But she might have ridden a motorcycle to the door. She'd probably have tattoos and scarred knuckles. And Police Detective Kevin Holtzmann, a little heavier, a little grayer, a little slower, hoping to survive those few years left until retirement, would have shown up to sort out the trouble after some jerk had tried to grab her and wound up on the pool table in a puddle of personal pain.

That Ceren would never grow up.

Just like that Kevin would never retire.

"I waved," my Ceren said. "You could have stopped. Given me a lift."

Alice fluttered her hands up to her face. "Ceren! I'm sorry, I didn't even see you. Brandi offered me a ride down, and we were talking, and—"

"It's fine." She waved her hand. "Fine. I made it. What's dinner tonight?"

"Pork stew," Jack said. "With rice."

"Stewed leftovers," Ceren said. "Grea-a-at. Leftover leftovers, made with leftovers. You running out of ideas or something?"

Jack raised his eyebrows. "You all can cook for yourself any time you like."

I had this mental picture of Ceren in a onesie, deciding she wouldn't spend her life taking crap from anyone. And she'd held to that vow every day since. When other girls got teary, Ceren grew fangs. But this was harsh, even for her. "What's going on, Ceren?" I said.

"I'm fine," she said. "Stew is fine. Let's get a table."

"It's not ready yet," I said. "We're early."

"Well, let's get a table while we can," she said.

Nobody could emote like a teenage girl. And she wouldn't tell me anything until she felt ready. I tried to keep the frustration from my voice. "Fine."

We snagged the small, square table that had replaced the jukebox. Ceren flung herself onto the blocky lacquered wooden stool. Alice sat herself more delicately on her stool, her bubbling cheer intimidated into silence. I studied the girls for half a second, then took my seat and said, "Someone giving you trouble, Ceren?"

"What? No, nothing like that." She waved my words away. "Someone crosses me, I'll feed them their kidneys. I'm fine."

"I broke part of Legacy's coding today," Alice said.

Ceren nodded but didn't smile. "Cool."

Teenagers. You don't get a manual, and they don't let you use a club. The rules might have changed, but I wasn't about to break that one. Time to try a new subject. "You notice anyone missing?"

"Missing?" Alice said, looking around the bar.

"Not from before," I said. "I mean, missing now."

"No," Alice said. "Should we?"

"If you do, let me know," I said.

"Sure," Ceren said.

The uncomfortable silence resurfaced. Kevin had used silence as a tactic when investigating crimes. I hated having it used against me. It took me another moment to realize that I had news. "I found a house I think might work."

"Up by the mall?" Ceren said.

Alice perked up.

I shook my head. "Eric and I went down part of Lakeshore today."

Ceren's mood inverted. "The lake?" A grin shattered her face. "Sweet!"

Alice made a face. "The lake? But—"

"I know," I said. "I don't like the idea of the lake either. But Ceren looked at a couple places we liked. And this place fits everything we said we wanted."

After I'd handled the mess with Alice's father, after Alice and I were almost sucked into a four-part group mind, and after Rose Friedman put a bullet through my heart, the girls and I had agreed that it might be a good idea for us to make a home together. I thought the girls could use some kind of parent, even a nonbinding one. I wasn't sure what "parental rights" meant anymore anyway. And after a week of all-night teenage parties, Alice and Ceren seemed to find having an adult hanging around the place an annoying relief.

But I couldn't face going through my—*Kevin's*—home and getting rid of Sheila's and Julie's belongings to make room for them. Alice's house had the room, but she wouldn't go back in after what happened to her dad. I didn't blame her.

So I crashed in Ceren's guest room, while the girls slept in Ceren's room. We kept her parents' bedroom door closed.

If we were going to form any kind of family, though, we needed a place to make our own. Somewhere with space for the three of us, without any painful memories. Alice and I wanted somewhere downtown, while Ceren insisted that she wanted something on Lake Huron.

"It's four bedrooms," I said. "Used to be a summer home. It's got full solar, a nice big family room, really good insulation. Might be too big, though. Fireplace and a woodpile you won't believe. Eric says it's in great shape. And Alice, it's got the computer plugs you wanted. Everywhere."

Best of all, the owners had left only a couple changes of clothes. A few paintings, but no photographs. No trophies or mementoes. We wouldn't have to scour away someone else's life to build our own.

"Sounds okay," Alice said.

"Eric says it's all low-voltage," I said. "Even the fridge."

"When can we look?" Ceren said.

"I already told Eric I'll be late tomorrow," I said. "Alice, are they expecting you early?"

"I'll get there when I get there," she said. "But the water..."

"We're just looking around," I said. If it were up to me, I'd put us as far from the lake as I could get. While I was the adult, Alice and Ceren weren't tied to me. They needed guidance, but I couldn't play Father Knows Best and swing my weight around. I had to persuade. And part of persuasion is listening to people, even if they end up persuading you instead. "Ceren came along and looked at the places you liked. And maybe this place will work for all of us. It's right at Lakeshore and Lagrange. Tomorrow, first thing."

"Sure," Ceren said, whatever annoyed her forgotten.

Alice looked dejected. "I guess." Her gaze flicked around the room, hunting. "Hey, Bill just came in."

"Yeah?" Ceren glanced over her shoulder. "Oh, that Bill." She turned back to look at the table. "I don't know what you see in that guy."

"He's funny," Alice said.

"Funny wrong," Ceren said.

"He's just shy," Alice said.

For Alice to call someone *shy* was practically a professional opinion. I raised my eyes without moving my head, and glimpsed a husky, blond-haired teenage boy just inside the door.

"We should invite him next time we have a party," Alice said.

"You can have your own party, then," Ceren said.

"Ceren," I said, "is there something about this kid I should know?"

"What?" Ceren's eyebrows bent in puzzlement for half a second, then her eyes went wide and she shook her head. "Oh, geez, no. No, he's just such a dork. He thinks he's funny when he's really just being stupid. He's, like, the most annoying person in the world."

"I see." Teenage Ceren had no idea what annoying really was. "You know—"

Behind me, the second most annoying person in the world said, "Kevin! Glad you're here tonight!"

Chapter 6

DANNY GERVAIS, professional lickspittle, stood behind my right shoulder. I'd like to say he was just the type to sneak up behind me, but the clatter and rattle of Jack's increasingly crowded bar would have drowned anyone's footsteps.

But still: he'd snuck up. Even if he hadn't.

Danny's small enough that he was able to wedge himself between two blocky, square wooden tables behind us. He wore heavy work pants and a dark blue polo shirt, as if trying to say he worked for a living, but I remembered him as one of the Building the Future crew from the years before Absolute's final attack. He wore his black hair combed straight back from his forehead, wore slim gold rings on each finger, and carried his own personal cloud of expensive cologne everywhere. Danny would smile and fawn to your face. Turn your back, and you'd learn he knew exactly which ribs to slip the knife between.

"Mister Woodward wants to talk to you," Danny said. There's nothing objectively wrong with his voice, but it still set me on edge.

"Then he should come talk for himself," I said. "But I don't know any reason to."

"He's got a lot of people to see."

"Then he should go see them. I'm talking to my girls."

Danny stepped up beside me and lightly dropped a hand on my shoulder. "There's no need to be like that, Detective. We don't have a lot of time to get organized."

I looked at his hand. I looked up into Danny's eyes.

Danny looked back.

I kept my face carefully blank. "We don't have detectives any more. Or leaders. The only future we're building is our own." I doubted that anyone more than three feet away heard me over the clatter and babble of the people quickly filling the bar. "I would still advise you to keep your hands to yourself, Mister Gervais. Someone might take offense."

Danny tried to keep a cool, level gaze, but in a heartbeat he flinched and snatched his hand back.

"You have a nice day now," I said.

Danny scowled. "What is it going to take for you to listen? Some big disaster?"

I turned back as he walked away.

"Who was that?" Alice said.

I said, "His name's Danny Gervais. He's one of Woodward's yes-men. And he thinks that everyone should jump as high as he does for his boss."

"Boss?" Ceren snorted. "How's he paying him?"

"Who knows?" I shrugged. "Some people think that someone should be in charge. We'll need to sort that out some day, probably soon. We can't let anyone just put themselves at the top, though."

"I know someone like that," Alice said.

"I'm sure you do." I made myself relax. "You can't let those people push you around, either. So, Ceren, how did your day go?"

Ceren said, "Okay." Her eyes flashed over my shoulder, fixing on something.

I had a good idea what—or *who*—she saw, and self-consciously relaxed as I glanced that way.

"Kevin!" Lyle Woodward stood over our dinner table, precisely far enough away that I couldn't quite punch him in the junk.

Not that I make a habit of that. Just a corner-of-the-eye observation.

I didn't look up. Surrounded by heavy wooden tables and padded vinyl stools and chairs and illuminated by neon beer signs, his crisp blue suit looked completely out of place. The paunch fit right in, though.

"Woodward," I said, without taking my eyes from Ceren. He wanted me to look up. It's a psychological trick, looming over someone to "assert dominance." Not looking up was the best counter. "I'm eating dinner with my girls."

"Dinner's not ready yet." Woodward had the thick, rich voice of a news announcer or professional preacher.

"You never heard of small talk? It's what holds a family together."

On my right, Ceren leaned back and offered Woodward a cool, level stare. Opposite her, Alice set her jaw and stared up at Woodward. They'd never met the man, but they took their cues from me like champions.

"You've been ducking me for days," Woodward said.

"Avoiding you would mean that I cared," I said. "I don't. Care, that is. I have important work to do."

"I heard," Woodward said. "Dragging people out of their homes."

Woodward wanted a fight. I wanted to talk to Alice and Ceren, but I'd have to shut him down first. Scooting my chair back, I rose to my feet before turning to face him.

Lyle Woodward is an inch taller than me, with silver hair, a practiced smile, and an oily, unctuous charm. He has the kind of bulk that comes from hard work, with the couple inches of the overhanging gut that comes from not needing to work hard anymore. I'd seen him flip into rabid rattlesnake mode at a wrong word, and back to ice-cream sweet just as quickly. He showed up in Frayville as the federal Building the Future lead two days after the first nukes flew at Australia, immediately starting to throw that weight around. Mostly he annoyed and frustrated everyone until the end. It looked as though he wanted to keep at it, right past the end.

The new Woodward had shown up at Jack's a week ago. In a crisp, tight, dry-clean-only suit and tie. We had as many dry cleaners as we had coroners, but still, he wore a suit every day.

I met his gray eyes. "We're doing a house-to-house search. Checking for traumatized people. Making sure that everyone knows that there are other people out here, before they starve."

"Yes, yes," Woodward said. "Very worthwhile."

"It is if we don't want to lose any more people," I said.

"Nobody wants to lose anyone," he said. "Is that you and—Eric, is it?—marking empty houses with the warning tape?"

"Yes, we are."

"Great! That's good to know. And we're going to need a census. Do tell me you're writing down names."

I didn't want to agree with him, but I wouldn't stoop to lying. "Of course."

"I'm glad you're checking on them. I'm glad it's not like I heard."

He wanted me to ask what he'd heard. "It beats breaking out the flamethrowers."

"That's actually what I wanted to talk to you about," Woodward said.

I waited, not inviting him to speak.

"We have some big problems coming up," Woodward said. "There's lots of food now, but it'll run out some time. We have solar, and Brockett's done an exemplary job getting the main power back. But we'll freeze this winter, or starve, unless we get things organized."

"And you're just the man to organize it."

Woodward gave that politician's smile again, the kind where his warmth and mirth never made it past his nose. "I ran the county's invasion preparations. I know everything about Frayville, what our resources are, how everything's connected, and what skills we have. Who else?"

"Have fun getting people to listen to you," I said.

"Part of that is doing the work," Woodward said. "I have a fine team of volunteers checking warehouses and stores, building an inventory of what we have. I went to the police station today."

I'd been to the station, and found its littered halls and slack-doored offices unbearably sad. "There's nothing there to interest you."

"Someone changed the access code on the police armory," Woodward said. "Added an extra lock."

"So?" I said.

"I need to check what's left. Can't have those weapons lying around loose."

"They're not loose," I said. "I locked them up."

"We had enough equipment here to fight a small war," Woodward said. "We might need them for defense."

"We fought that war," I said. "We lost."

Woodward's smile dissolved. "We're getting things back in shape around here. Have to make sure people don't go hungry this winter. Have to be sure we can defend ourselves against whatever Absolute throws at us next."

"Tell me, Woodward," I said. "Have you ever heard of fire discipline?"

"Of course."

"The armory still has firearms, yes. Serious firearms. And explosives. And flamethrowers."

"That's why we need them. So we can train a militia."

"And who is going to train them?"

"I have someone—"

"No, you don't," I said. "You have a couple of retired soldiers who know how to shoot rifles. A flamethrower is totally different. Do you have any idea what can go wrong with one of those beasts?"

In the edge of my vision, Ceren's face flushed. She kept her eyes on Woodward, though.

"We will need them," Woodward snapped. "One day, you'll be out going door-to-door and some dreg will come into town."

"Dregs," I said. "How many of these *dregs* have you even seen?"

"That's not the point."

"That's exactly the point, Woodward," I said. "I've burned down three houses this week. To kill what was inside. Something that had been human, but wasn't anymore. Something that I couldn't let out into the streets. While you've been trying to convince everyone that you're still in charge, I've persuaded a couple dozen terrified people to leave their homes and eat something so they don't go the same way." My voice grew sharper than I intended. "I'm the one who's taking care of what needs doing. So don't go telling me I'm not doing my job."

"You're not the only one," Woodward said through bared teeth. "We have—"

"You want those vets trained? Sure. Send them to me. If I think they can handle it, I'll work something out. With them. But I'm not going to hand out that gear to any yahoo and let them burn down half of Frayville."

"And in the meantime, you're the only local cop," Woodward said.

"I'm not a cop," I said. "I'm a *copy*." I stared into his eyes. "Exactly like you."

Something behind his eyes cracked. For just a second, I saw past Woodward's veneer of normality, glimpsing the screaming, gibbering terror behind it. I recognized that terror—it showed up in my own face every time I tried to sleep.

I caught motion at the bar. "Jack's ready for us. I'm going to get dinner now," I said. "I suggest you go find yourself a table and let my girls and I eat in peace."

Alice's chair scraped the floor. "I'll give you a hand." For the first time tonight, she didn't sound like she was asking a question.

"I'll hold our spot," Ceren said.

I nodded at the girls, then glanced at Woodward. "You have a good night, now."

Before he could speak, I turned and let Alice trail me to the bar. When we returned, weaving our way through the crowded tables carrying trays stacked with stew bowls and fresh-baked rolls, Woodward had retreated to his customary booth at the back of the bar, where his lackeys insulated him from us *no*-men.

Jack had cooked the meat until it fell apart at the touch of a spoon. You couldn't tell it was last night's roast pig, which had been recycled from the previous night's barbeque. The bread was his usual fine, fluffy domes of pure carbohydrate goodness. There wasn't any butter, but I tore off a chunk of roll and stabbed it into the thick, savory, vegetable-laden pork broth.

I'd eaten an entire roll that way when Alice said, "So, who was that?"

I swallowed. "His name is Lyle Woodward. You two did good with him, by the way."

Ceren nodded. "We've got you covered. Now that he's out, though, can you tell us *why* I was giving him the death glare?"

I drained an inch of water from my tall, clear plastic tumbler and set it back beside my aluminum spoon. "He—his original—was the local Building the Future rep. Washington sent him out here after the Australia bombing, even before we glassed South America. They sent someone to every county in the United States. He was supposed to get us ready for whatever came next."

Alice looked at her stew. "Absolute." I barely heard her fear-softened voice over the surrounding hubbub of conversations.

I nodded. "And he did the job. We built greenhouses before the weather carried the ash up here, got us through those cold summers and nuclear winter. Mined the beach. Water sterilization. Decentralized power and water. We got the official vehicles switched to diesel, clamped down on the gasoline supply to limit the scope of panic. It took three years, with winters lasting extra long and Absolute creeping up on us everywhere. We were as ready as we could be."

"So what's the problem?" Ceren asked. She kept her voice even quieter, but by choice rather than Alice's fear.

"The problem is…" I sighed. "The problem is that he enjoys being the man in charge. And everything that comes with it. He not only had a gasoline card, he got himself one of those big SUVs to use it in. Said he needed it for official business, then showed up at restaurants with a girl half his age on each arm. He lived in this big house overlooking the Sand River. Everyone was putting in energy efficiency, spraying foam insulation over inside walls if nothing else, and he had these huge picture windows. We had families with thermostats set to fifty degrees in February, and he's lounging around in his outdoor ten-person hot tub and throwing parties."

I looked from Ceren's intent face to Alice's widened eyes. "It's okay to come in and be the bad guy. It's okay to be in charge. But you don't eat steak every night while the people you're supposed to be helping are trying to figure out how to stretch that box of mac-and-cheese to feed four kids."

Ceren said, "He needs to have an accident. We'll swear you were with us the whole time."

Alice made herself smile. "I'll bring the shovel."

I snorted. "No, it's not like that. You can't let those people get their hooks into you, or next thing you're either stuck out in the cold or helping him rip off someone else." I lifted my spoon. Jack's stew wasn't as spicy as last week's, but it had a rich, mellow flavor from long cooking. Was he running out of peppers? "You can't try to get along, you have to let them know where they stand before they even start." I dug my spoon back in. "And if this isn't a fresh start, I don't know what is."

I'd just filled my mouth with shredded pork and carrots and broth when someone shouted "Help!"

A gawky, bony man in pristine mechanic's overalls stood inside the front door. His hair was a shock of red, his eyes wide. "Is anyone a doctor? Please!"

"Stay here," I said, jumping to my feet.

As far as I knew, we didn't have a doctor. I'd had first aid training every year as part of my police training, but I didn't know that first aid would do anything for us.

I bulled my way through the crowd. "Reamer," I said.

Sweat ran down Ian Reamer's gaunt, pale face. "In the truck."

Chapter 7

EVEN AT almost six o'clock, June sunlight still poured heat down from the spotless blue sky. The weather had been unseasonably hot, and promised a scorching August. Not that "unseasonably" meant anything, after years of fallout and then the fires of humanity's last futile fight against Absolute. The concrete sidewalks and asphalt road radiated heat back up at us as we dashed out of Jack's.

Reamer had pulled a massive, sparkling blue diesel pickup truck up over the curb, stopping the front wheels on the sidewalk next to Jack's front door. The engine still ran, and the driver's door hung open. A massive willow loomed over the far side, its leaves, boughs, and incongruous, dangling hard-rind melons crushed against the side of the cab and shading the truck bed.

I grabbed the driver's side door and peered into the cab.

Reamer bolted past me. "Bed!"

I hopped down to the road and rounded the truck. An elderly, dumpy woman sprawled sideways at the end of the plastic-lined truck bed, kept from sliding forward by four heavy rubber tires. Blood soaked her gray hair. Her eyes stared emptily across the lowered tailgate, and her irregular breath rattled.

Blood dripped from her brow to her eyelid. She blinked.

"Shit," I said, hopping up to kneel on the tailgate.

"Mom," Reamer said.

"Go inside," I said. "See if Jack's got a first aid kit. If not, get some towels. Ice—no, there's no ice. See if either of the firemen are here." They couldn't be, or they would have been out here before me. But it would keep Reamer busy for a moment.

"On it," Reamer said. Half a second later, he was shouting at people to get out of the doorway.

I took a deep breath and touched the woman's bloody chin to turn her head.

A sickening indentation crumpled the left side of her head, up near the crown. Blood matted the tightly curled gray hair and trickled down wrinkles in her slack skin to her bright blue cotton T-shirt. The last time I'd seen an injury like this, it had involved an aluminum baseball bat and a literally killer dose of meth.

"Shit," I said quietly.

We had an empty hospital, but Absolute hadn't reincarnated a doctor, a nurse, anyone medical. I would have taken a second-semester PA right then, or an experienced candy striper.

Her mouth twitched. "Ian?" she said.

"He's coming right back," I said, keeping my voice level as I fumbled in my pocket.

"He's not coming back," she said. "He's in prison."

"He's out," I said. "He's coming. He's on his way right now."

Ian Reamer had been the worst kind of villain in pre-Absolute Frayville, back when the town served as a sleepy home base for outdoorsmen. He'd supported his drug addiction by dealing, including to children. I'd put him away. He'd cleaned up in prison, and seemed remorseful.

And even if Reamer hadn't shown a scrap of contrition, I couldn't have told this dying woman anything else.

A white toolbox with a big red cross on it hit the tailgate beside me. "Got it!" Reamer said.

I fumbled in my pocket again. "She's not good," I said.

"I know," Reamer shouted. "I know."

"Hold her hand. Talk to her. Try to keep her with us."

Reamer's scrawny fingers looked even bonier around her plump hand. "Hi, Mom."

"Ian?" she said.

"I'm here."

"Ian?" Her voice was fainter.

"I've got you, Mom."

"Ian?"

She'd lost a whole mess of brain function. Was it blood loss? Or shards of bone in the brain?

"There's no doctor," I said.

"I know that!" Ian said.

"I've got one idea," I said. "It's not great."

"Ian?" she said.

My idea wasn't *not great*. It was much worse than that. Much, much worse than the hideous tangle of guesswork that had festered in the back of my brain since the night I was set on fire.

"Do it," Reamer said.

I hopped out of the truck and trotted around Ian to the willow.

Willow trees grow almost everywhere in Frayville. They suck water out of the ground, and are the only thing keeping the town from devolving back into a festering swamp. Absolute had restored the willow trees, but covered them in fast-growing melons.

When I'd been burned so badly that I'd lost rational thought, when my body had started eating my own brain to survive, eating a willow melon had brought me back from the edge and healed my body. I hadn't tasted one since.

I grabbed one of the melons in both hands, wrenched it off its stem, and slammed it onto the tailgate beside Reamer. I yanked the multitool from my pocket, flipped it open, and plunged the blade into the rind.

A sweet, rich smell reminiscent of peaches and watermelon rose around us, carrying a faint hint of roast meat. Sticky juice swelled around my fingers as I yanked the knife through the rind.

"Ian?" she asked again.

"I got you, Mom," he said. "I'm here."

I yanked a slab off the melon. The seedless, pink-orange flesh went all the way into the core. I flipped it over and slashed the rind off. Why was this happening?

I'd seen two people who had slashed their own wrists, only to watch as the wounds oozed over and healed. Why wasn't she healing? What would happen if she totally bled out?

I leaned over her head, a slab of melon flesh melting in my hands. Sticky drops of juice bombed the blood pooling on the tailgate. "Here," I said. "Eat this. Reamer, what's her name?"

"Nat. For Natalie."

I tore off a morsel of melon, struggling to keep it from slipping slickly between my fingers. "Nat, come on." I touched it to her lips. "Take a bite."

Nat said, "Ian?" Her lips brushed the dangling melon, then latched onto it and sucked it off my fingers.

"What is that?" Reamer said.

"When I was really hurt," I said, "this stuff seemed to heal me."

Her lips smacked. I slipped another piece between her lips and watched her listlessly chew.

"Far as I can tell," I said, "this stuff is some kind of mega-food." My mind flashed back to my final encounter with Alice's devolved, brainless father, who had stopped to eat melons rather than devour Ceren and myself. "It lets you heal."

I nudged her lips with another sticky, slippery chunk. "Maybe she can heal herself." I'd healed myself from a bullet through the heart, but it had left me ravenous.

Reamer's face was even paler. "Okay. Mom, you got this. Eat. You can do this."

Healing a heart was one thing. Could a melon help heal a damaged brain? "Talk to me, Reamer. What happened?"

"I came home," Reamer said. "Been staying with Mom. Can't leave her alone. Not now. Went inside. Found her." His voice choked. "On the floor. Kitchen floor. Like this. Ran here."

"You did good," I said.

Nat twitched, sucked in a deep breath, and raised her mangled head a critical inch to snatch the next lump from my fingers.

"More melon, Reamer," I said.

Reamer dropped Nat's hand and attacked the melon with my knife. I tore my last piece in half and got it to Nat's mouth. She chomped down, almost taking my fingers with it.

"Don't slice it," I said. "Just get a slab."

Reamer started mass-producing bite-sized chunks of melon as quickly as I could ease them between his mother's lips. "I found one thing," he said.

"What?" I yanked my fingers back before Nat could gnaw at them.

"A message."

My heart skipped a beat.

"It said…" Reamer took a deep breath. "Number one. This hash mark, the number one. Big black marker. On the fridge."

Number one? A count, or a signature? Whichever, it meant nothing hopeful.

Nat devoured about a quarter of the melon. Sticky melon juice kept the blood on her face from drying, giving her a streaky, gooey red-and-yellow mask.

"Oh my God," Reamer said.

The side of Nat's skull pulsed like a heart.

"Keep it coming!" I said.

Reamer passed me another slab. I pinned it between my slick fingers and got it to Nat's mouth just as she finished the previous chunk.

A pulse of fresh, hot, coppery blood spurted out of Nat's wounded head, shooting a foot into the back of the truck bed. A second, narrower pulse shot further, as if squeezed through a smaller hole. Then, with a chorus of snaps like breaking bones, her skull heaved itself back up.

"Oh my God," Reamer said again.

Nat lifted her head off the tailgate and bit at the melon.

"Don't stop, Reamer! She needs energy. Food."

Reamer attacked the melon with huge, frantic sweeps.

A few mouthfuls later, Nat stopped devouring the fruit and sank back to the truck bed. Her breath turned slow and regular.

Reamer said, "Mom?"

"Ian?" Nat said.

"Mom, you're going to be okay," he said.

My own breathing had stopped.

It had worked. We'd saved her.

I hoped.

"Ian?" she repeated.

"I'm here," Reamer said.

"Ian?"

My hope turned to a bulging knot in my throat.

"Ian?"

Reamer's face turned white again. He looked at me.

Nat's voice grew fainter. In another moment, she was asleep.

I quivered with angry tension.

"Is she going to get better?" Reamer said.

I shook my head. "I don't know."

The original Nat might have died before she could get to the hospital. Or she could have died in the hospital. Now, I'd saved her replica body thanks to our alien flesh.

But her mind—everything that made Nat Reamer herself—might have died when someone broke her skull.

Why would someone brutally attack a feeble old lady like Nat Reamer and write *#1* on the refrigerator?

The only answer that came to mind was: for terror.

To scare people.

I didn't feel scared.

Immobile rage shook my every muscle. The sweet stink of melon filled my head from the sticky juice covering my hands, my forearms, and my shirt, all mixed with spots of red blood. The sun's heat slowly distilled the mixture to tarry gum.

I suddenly noticed the sea of faces around us. The whole restaurant crowd stared into the pickup bed. In the front row, Alice looked ready to puke.

Reamer wrenched his gaze from his mom's vacant stare and pleaded with his eyes. "I want—"

I nodded.

"You got no reason to help me."

"I know," I said.

I'm only a copy.

But after two vicious attacks in the last couple of days, Frayville needed something that only I could give.

I jerked my chin at Nat's prone form. "So I'll promise her. I'll find who did this."

Chapter 8

"WOW," ALICE said.

The place had *not* been a beach cottage. Centered on the sprawling lot at the inland corner of Lagrange and Lakeshore, its wings stretched north and south from the huge main building. The garage had three separate vehicle doors, and was connected to the south wing by a narrow, glass-walled breezeway. Pale blue siding covered everything except the broad, darkly reflective windows. The roof gently sloped from south to north, giving the solar shingles solid sun exposure. A few sticky pine trees stood between the house and the Lakeshore

Road sidewalk, creating an illusory barrier between the house and any passersby. A tangle of overgrown, thorny hedges formed an impenetrable barrier along four-lane Lagrange Road.

Not that anyone came down Lakeshore any more. Or Lagrange. A big red van sat at the side of Lakeshore, but I didn't see any other cars other than my police cruiser, parked behind us. The road was almost comically empty, an asphalt no-man's-land between the homes and the beach running along Lake Huron. The wind off the lake felt a little cool over my bare arms this morning, with the sun maybe a third of the way up the sky. The green scum choking the lake reflected emerald from the viscous waves sluggishly gnawing at the sand and wafted a rich, peaty smell over Ceren, Alice, and me.

The ragged, uncut lawns looked normal, the rich spring-green grass fading towards June pale. The pines and towering maples looked normal. Even the melon-bearing shaggy willows were more surreal than scary. I almost might have forgotten it was all made of alien cells. But Lake Huron's thick green slurry slipped slivers of ice into my spine.

I deliberately turned my back on the clogged lake. It wasn't going to hurt us. At least, it wasn't any more likely to hurt us than Absolute's copies of trees and grass. As far as I knew.

Of course, Godzilla could rise out of the water at any time.

But Absolute could raise him from the lawn just as easily.

And I had to admit, the house was pretty nice. The master bedroom was on the south end, near the garage, while the kitchen and family room and great room stood between that room and the other three bedrooms. The owners had built the place about six months before the nukes flew and the economy spasmed into doomsday gear. It had the latest of everything. The greatest, the best of everything the innocent, ignorant human race had ever made.

Or would ever make.

I couldn't help remembering house hunting with Sheila. We'd taken turns carrying Julie papoose-style through a dozen houses all around Frayville, desperately aware that we only had a few weeks to pick a place and get our offer accepted. We'd finally settled on one because it was the best compromise we were ever going to find and the owners could do the deal before our lease ran out. It hadn't offered space for the woodshop I wanted, and the kitchen had needed a lot of work that Sheila hadn't wanted to do. We'd grown to love the place, not in spite of its flaws but because of the life, the memories we'd grown there.

They weren't my memories. They only hurt like mine.

But maybe I could think of the lake as a particularly slimy woodshop.

"Hey," Ceren said, raising her hand.

I thought she was pointing at the tiny clapboard cottage on the opposite corner, across Lagrange. *I found us a mansion, and you want a shed?* Then I saw him.

What was left of the man walked with a loose, shambling gait. His arms hung limp at his sides. He wore a repulsively filthy dark blue business suit, utterly drenched with long-dried blood.

Where his left eye and temple should have been was only empty air. I could see through the open space in his skull to the cedars behind him. I'd seen him around town, and knew that the whole back of his head was gone. Most of his skull was an empty cavity. His jaw hung open, a little too wide for anything human.

After Absolute released us, more than one person attempted suicide. Frayville is hunting country, there are guns everywhere. Small self-inflicted wounds, like a razor through the wrists or a handgun to the temple, healed themselves. Most of the failed suicides had gotten sucked into Acceptance. I'd rather get set on fire again.

This guy must have thought he'd found a better solution. A large-bore shotgun, maybe, or something explosive. Fresh skin had stretched across the inside of his cratered skull but his brain, his mind, was still scattered all over a ceiling somewhere.

His body lived. His mind was gone.

He got what he wanted, I guess.

I hoped.

I hated the word *dregs*, but couldn't think of a better one to describe this guy and the half-dozen others like him shambling around town. I'd given each a private name, and tried to make it as kind as possible. This one I called Suit.

And Reamer's mom was probably one of them now.

I couldn't help wondering what Suit ate. How he ate. Dregs went mad with hunger, and attacked anything for food.

He must eat the same way he walked. However that was, without a brain.

"That poor guy," Alice said.

Suit's remaining eye seemed to focus us. He started ambling in our direction.

"He was a coward," Ceren said.

"You don't know what he remembered," I said, not unkindly. Nobody remembered what happened in the few days between Absolute's final attack and his release, between our death and our rebirth. I didn't *know*, but I was almost certain Absolute had shoved its hand up all our asses and used us as meat puppets. I got fragments, sometimes, in my sleep. Those were the nights I woke up screaming. "And not everybody's as strong as you are."

Ceren swiveled her head to glare at the lake's turgid surf. "Come on. Let's check this place out."

I tugged at my belt and followed. I'd fought my weight my whole life—well, Kevin had. And I'd somehow put on a few pounds since the end of the world. If you're extinct, shouldn't you get to not to worry about your spare tire?

The wide front door still had the yellow CAUTION tape stretched at waist height across it. I pulled one side free and set it aside. "I had Eric leave the main breaker and the water on. If we don't like this place, we need to pull them before we go."

"I like it already," Ceren said.

Alice's jaw clenched as she deliberately kept her back to the unnatural lake. "The house looks nice." She sounded even more uncertain than usual.

I seized the knob. "The inside is better than the outside."

The scene of yesterday's murder had been pretty swank. This place was swankier. Pink marble tiles, veined with black, spread from the door into a grand hall. A broad staircase swept up to the mezzanine and balcony, all railed in dark, gleaming wood. Archways beneath the mezzanine led to a great room on one side and a dining room on the other.

"We could have a bonfire in here," Alice said.

I shut the door behind us, blocking out the lake. "You have a bonfire in here and we'll have words. Bonfires go in the fireplace. It's big enough."

"So where's the swimming pool?" Ceren asked.

Nobody dug a pool down here. They walked to the lake. "There's a couple *really* big bathtubs," I said.

"Isn't this a little big for us?" Alice said.

"We might need the space," Ceren said. "Just because we have the old man hanging around, doesn't mean we won't want to have parties now and then."

"I'm not cleaning up after you and your crew," I said. "Remember, I saw your bathroom."

Ceren looked abashed for maybe a second, then strode into the great room and went right to the thick white interior shutters covering the front picture windows. She didn't just pull the slats open, but swung the whole hinged shutter out of its frame to let the morning sunlight flood over her and the clusters of elegant couches and chairs set about the chamber. "Is that one-way glass?"

"One-way solar," I said. The news had promised everyone transparent solar panel windows for decades. They'd finally hit the market a couple years before the war began. "Whoever built this place had more money than they knew what to do with, but you can run every appliance in the place on solar."

Alice walked up beside Ceren to stare out at the beach and the unnatural lake. "How can you not be afraid of that?" Alice said.

Ceren shook her head. "I am *not* afraid. I'm just not."

I suddenly understood. Ceren wasn't merely afraid of Lake Huron. She was utterly terrified of that thick green sludge. And when something scared Ceren, she charged in to fight it. She'd live by the lake, staring at the lake, just to prove that it couldn't intimidate her.

And if Absolute dragged Godzilla out of the water, Ceren would rush in with a baseball bat and give the big guy one hell of a painful toe. Before he squished her.

The world needs brave people. More than ever, now.

But bravery can break people. Looking at Ceren hurt me. I knew I had to protect her, somehow. And I couldn't.

Alice's pale skin flushed at any excuse. At the moment, she looked almost as green as the lake.

"For now," I said, "let's keep the shutters closed. We can argue about them if we decide to stay."

Ceren glanced at me, then at Alice. "Oh, all right." She carefully swung the shutters back in place until the magnetic latch clicked.

Alice looked better as we trawled through the luxury kitchen with the eight-burner electric stove and the double oven. The bedrooms looked like vacant hotel rooms, with thick mattresses sitting naked in the frames and dressers with drawers open an inch to keep them from growing stale. Softly murmuring ceiling fans kept the stale air moving.

"Who would own a place like this and not live in it?" Ceren said.

"Someone who has to impress people?" Alice said. "Probably some rich downstater, who invited his buddies up for a weekend every year just so he could show off how much he had. It's like Patty when she got her credit card."

They'd known a teenager with a credit card? "Could be someone who had to move away, and couldn't get what he needed to for the house," I said. "Just be glad we don't have to get a mortgage. You're the computer expert, Alice. Why don't you go boot up the City Hall systems and see what the story is on this place?"

"Once I finish with Legacy, sure," Alice said.

We wound our way back downstairs, towards the basement door in the naked kitchen. "The rumpus room downstairs has a pool table, a big television. That's where you want to have your parties."

I flung the basement door wide.

A two-headed spider the size of a cow clattered up the stairs at us.

Chapter 9

STANDING IN an unfurnished kitchen that cost more than Kevin's house, the girls and I stared slack-jawed at the abomination charging up the basement stairs.

Even as my guts screamed *Spider! Giant doomsday spider!* I knew that it wasn't actually a cow-sized spider. It had the right number of legs, sort of, and it hugged the ground as it scuttled straight at me, but it wouldn't squeeze into the mental slot labeled "spider."

Then my brain figured out what my eyes were reporting, and I wished for the giant doomsday spider.

Take a man and a woman, lying down, face-to-face. Wrap her legs and arms around his body, exactly as people have done for hundreds of thousands of years.

Then squeeze them together.

Tighter. Until their hips and gut flow into one another.

The woman on top? Make her arms a little longer. Swivel her hips so her legs come out the side and she can crabwalk along, dragging him along like a bulging egg sac, his dangling back swaying a couple inches above the stair treads.

The guy on the bottom gets his legs bent a little, so he can help propel the whole monstrosity forward. One of his arms goes into the air, palm-up, elongated fingers scrabbling at the stairwell's white drywall. The other wraps around her back, fingers up to the second knuckle plunged into her spine, holding his upper body off the ground.

Bend the upper torso just a bit so the two heads can peer forward, one chin asymmetrically beside the other. His head is upside down and at an angle, but so what?

Sandblast every scrap of sanity from all four eyes.

Sharpen all the teeth.

Widen the jaws.

Make it stink of old sweat and spoiled lunch meat.

And launch it up the basement stairs at three stupidly silent and still morons.

For half a second, I stared. Scattered thoughts sparked through my brain. I remembered Teresa writhing naked beneath me. My hand sticking to her abdomen, our skin flowing together. Jesse's lips burning on mine.

That monster could have been me.

Ceren shrieked.

My hand crashed the hollow-core door back into its frame and I set my shoulder against the thin wood. My hands scraped the splintery barrier as I braced my feet on the textured linoleum. "Get out!"

Alice whirled, rubber-soled shoes squeaking against the kitchen linoleum.

Ceren retreated two steps, putting her back to the granite counter.

My fingers groped the doorknob. Not even a lousy push-button lock.

We didn't have much in the way of weapons. A flimsy aluminum fry pan sat on the sparkling blue granite counter, next to half a dozen mismatched plates and place settings. A cutlery block next to the sink,

but a knife fight is a good way to stab yourself. A card table and chairs, all folded and neatly stacked beside the wood-framed crankcase windows. The place smelled of old bleach and scouring powder, without any hint that it had ever been used as a kitchen.

Bleach could be a weapon. Had they left a jug under the sink?

No, I'd seen the bleach yesterday. In the basement. Next to the washing machine.

Right past the, the, whatever they were. Not possible.

They—it—hadn't been down there yesterday. Where had it come from?

It crashed into the door.

Through my shoulder, I felt the door's hollow core crunch and collapse under the impact. The force knocked me back, the door lurching a foot open.

If they hadn't been climbing the stairs, they would have bowled me over. They were *strong*.

I slammed my shoulder back into the door to shut it again, but it bounced to a stop a few inches shy of the frame.

The door and the frame trapped a woman's wrist. Her hand gouged at the linoleum, struggling for traction. The skin on her stubby fingers looked thick and tough, as if she'd started evolving towards pads or hooves. Long, fractured nails held slashes of bright red fingernail polish. A plain gold band circled her ring finger, but the finger itself had bloated around both sides of it.

In perfect, unpracticed unison, they screamed. Both voices carried an inhuman, machinelike metallic rasp that sent tremors down my spine.

Terror propelled a flurry of plans through my brain. Even if I had a sidearm, bullets would only annoy this critter. I had a flamethrower, in the police cruiser, but I'd never get it out and ready before the creature was on me. Was it hungry? It looked kind of plump, but maybe I could lure it to a melon tree the way I'd done before and distract it until I could burn it?

I couldn't even lock it in the kitchen. The doors were hinged to swing freely, both ways, so that caterers could easily carry trays of food through the rest of the house.

The front yard didn't have any willow trees. I'd have to outrace it, through the front door, slam the front door behind me, buy a few seconds that way, but this thing would probably crash through without noticing, but if I could maybe make it to the intersection, and across the street to the melon willow, maybe.

Maybe Ceren would throw—

No, Ceren was still in the kitchen.

Charging towards me.

"What are you—" I started.

Purple flashed metallic in Ceren's hand. She plunged the brightly colored, high-end carving knife in a great circle from over her head straight toward the creature's trapped limb.

The blade slammed through the back of the woman's hand, stabbing between the metacarpals into the linoleum beneath.

She—they—*it* convulsed, screeching in surprised pain, and wrenched the hand free of the door, knife still transfixing the palm. The door thrashed again, almost knocking me off balance. I threw my weight against the door, and this time it slammed into the frame.

Ceren swapped the other knife, a long blue flensing blade, from her left hand to her right. "Let's go!"

Damn kid. Not smart enough to listen when I tell her to run.

At least she hadn't gone for the flamethrower. This time.

Ceren crashed through the double-swinging kitchen door into the living room. After the kitchen's sparseness, the scattered clusters of pristine expensive furniture made the room seem crowded.

Alice stood just inside the arch leading to the entrance hall, her back to us, very still.

"Alice, go!" I shouted as Ceren and I darted around an overstuffed couch.

Alice didn't move. She stared at the open front door.

I'd shut that door when we came in. Had something actually come out of the lake?

Another crash from the kitchen. The monster's scream carried pain now, and twice the rage.

I grabbed Alice's shoulder as I came to the door, and skidded to a halt before we moved another yard.

Someone stood in the open door.

Suit. The dreg.

From a few feet away, his emptied head resembled a half-shattered jack-o'-lantern. The edges of the ruined skull spread outward in an echo of the blast that had removed his brain. This close, I saw new-grown skin covering the edges of the wound. It seemed to wrap around inside the vacant cavity of his head. Blood and gore had geysered over his already filthy blue business suit, dried, petrified, and broken into pea-gravel scales.

He stank of rotted blood and festering meat.

One empty eye stared at Alice, then rolled to me.

His arm ratcheted up like a machine with a stripped gear.

But this machine had a greasy, wood-handled revolver in its hand.

His thumb fumbled at the hammer.

Chapter 10

DREGS DON'T have functional brains. That's what makes them dregs.

But Suit filled the doorway, blocking us from the open yard and the unnatural lake beyond. His vacant head and shattered skull didn't keep him from lurching the glistening blue steel revolver up towards us.

Dregs don't have minds. They can't cooperate.

The poster children for Worst Sex Ever erupted from the kitchen door. Both disjointed heads swung from side to side in perfect synchronization, scanning the room. All four eyes locked onto Alice, Ceren, and me at the same time. It gave a little growl and stalked towards us.

Charging a gun is a great way to catch a bullet. Standing still while a giant spider-thing eating for at least two charges closer with plans to eat you for breakfast is even more stupid.

I threw myself at Suit.

His hand couldn't twitch, couldn't move fast enough, but it tried.

I slammed into his arm, shoving the revolver aside. Fast enough.

The revolver fired. The bark stung my ears, but the bullet flew into the living room, away from the girls.

Another step and I had Suit's arm pinned between me and his body. I grabbed his gun arm with one hand and his shoulder with the other, pushing him back a couple steps. The stench of old blood and dried brains clotted in my lungs, and the prickly filth of his tailored suit coat smeared greasily over my arms and button-up shirt.

One of Suit's feet came down on the concrete stoop outside the front door.

"Get out!" I shouted.

Suit spasmed with a thousand disconnected almost-twitches. At each jerk, specks of dried blood showered off his jacket into the air around us. His one eye was inches from mine, uncannily still in its socket. His breath against my face felt like a stinking draft.

Alice bolted past me, running for the sprawling front lawn, one hand latched into Ceren's, towing the larger girl in her wake.

The people-spider gave a double scream, only a few feet behind me.

My left hand, gripping Suit's forearm, slid down to wrap over his grip on the revolver. Kevin had practiced this same technique hundreds of times. *Grab his right hand, hard. Pivot on your right heel, drag his elbow under your armpit, wrench his hand backwards. Peel the perp's grip from the weapon.*

Through my ribs I felt Suit's elbow snap. He didn't scream, didn't even gasp in pain as his overstretched fingers lost their grip on the weapon. The revolver's wooden handle, made even greasier by the filth of Suit's hand, slipped against my fingers, but I clamped down on it before the revolver could fall.

Back through the doorway, only a dozen feet away, the creature charged closer.

I stepped backwards blindly, hard, knocking Suit off my shoulder as I fumbled the revolver.

The creature didn't look so spiderlike on the polished marble floor. The woman ran on her hands and feet, but the long legs that had been an advantage when she charged up the stairs made her awkward now. Her head wrenched impossibly far back, her eyes staring straight into mine.

I knew those eyes. I'd seen that face before.

The man hung beneath her, his upper torso swaying with each step. His free hand waved towards me, fingers clawing blindly at the air. The other hand hugged him to the woman, suspending his shoulders a fraction of an inch above the floor. His inverted head remained twisted aside, eyes rolled back to glimpse me from the corner of his vision. Her hips engulfed his, their flesh comingled at the waist. I glimpsed his feet kicking at the ground behind them, trying to push them faster but only unbalancing her charge.

He still had his socks on.

Both heads glared at me with insensible rage.

I jerked the revolver towards them and worked the hammer. The weapon kicked against my hand, the bang making me grimace even harder.

Blood blossomed from the woman's shoulder, making her arm collapse. She shrieked in agony, and tumbled to the side.

Another shot went wild, but the third bullet sprayed gore from the man's ribs. Only a yard from the door, they collapsed in a screaming heap.

A bullet through the heart hadn't stopped me. I hadn't felt sure bullets would even slow this thing down.

Suit listlessly bumped my back. His hand groaned into my field of vision.

I shifted my weight and planted an elbow in Suit's sternum. In the corner of my eye I saw him stumble and stagger, step off the concrete deck, and spill backwards onto the plush lawn.

I grabbed the knob and slammed the front door, trapping the creature inside.

Could it still work a doorknob?

Suit lay on his back beside the front walk, arms weakly flailing at the air. Anyone else would have gasped for air, but his chest placidly rose and fell and rose again.

A hundred feet away, the girls had the police cruiser started and the rear door open for me. I dashed around Suit and bolted for the road.

Behind me, something slammed against the door and screamed.

Chapter 11

I SLAMMED the cruiser's rear passenger side door shut behind me half a second before Alice stomped on the accelerator, throwing me against the thinly padded vinyl backseat as we rocketed down Lakeshore. The open windows carried the smells of moss from the alien sludge filling Lake Huron, easing the stink of rotten blood that still threatened to gag me.

I rolled in the seat, and grabbed the metal grille partitioning the cruiser for balance. Beside me, the flamethrower rattled in its mount. A line from the Department policy manual flashed through my mind: *vehicles are to be equipped for flamethrowers or for passengers, but not both.* It had seemed like a good idea, before, but after I'd adopted the girls I'd removed one of the flamethrowers to make room for a backseat passenger. All three of us fit in the front seat, but barely.

From the front passenger seat Ceren said, "You okay?" She sounded more angry than concerned.

"I'm fine. You two?"

"Yeah," Ceren said.

The cruiser weaved as Alice tried to keep the car centered on Lakeshore's double yellow line. I'd given the girls a few driving lessons and set them up with a little electric buggy, but the cruiser had many times the torque of their little puttermobile. Hugging the yellow line wasn't a bad idea. "Easy, Alice," I said.

Alice's thin hands gripped the leather-wrapped steering wheel so tightly that her knuckles shone white against her flushed skin. She sat at the front edge of the seat, back straight, so she could reach the pedals with a good view over the dashboard.

I sucked in a few breaths, trying to flush Suit's rancid funk from my lungs. The lake's mossy taint smelled healthy in comparison. Water shouldn't smell of ancient forests and untouched grasslands. But at least the breeze carried the smell of life. It didn't reek like something that should have lain down and died.

Houses flashed by us on the right. We'd already passed out of the big lots into the tiny cramped rentals. "Slow up, girl," I said. I looked over my shoulder at the empty asphalt road. The house was already out of view. "They aren't chasing us, we're okay."

The motor eased from a roar to a growl.

"Sorry," Alice said.

"Don't be," I said. "You two did good. I just don't want you to drive us off the pier." Lakeshore ran down to the marina. Every summer, some drunken idiot kept going straight down Lakeshore, missed the final turnoff, broke through the chain across the pier, ran straight down it, and plunged into the small bay at the mouth of the Sand River.

"What was that?" Ceren said.

"Damned if I know," I said. Ceren should have run when I told her to, but I wasn't going to say that right now. We'd talk about that later, in private.

The cruiser's diesel growl faded to an idle, and the cruiser started to slow. Alice must have taken her foot off the accelerator.

"You're doing fine, girl," Ceren said. "I told Kevin we could handle a real car."

"It's the seat," Alice said. "I'll drive anywhere you want. But we *have* to pull this seat up."

"Don't mess with my seat," I said. "I can never get it back just right. Stop and I'll drive."

"The buggy has programmable seats," Alice said. "It knows which one of us is driving and adjusts everything the way we set it. You need a better car."

"You're right, my ride sucks." The cruiser had the same feature. I'd turned it off right after we adopted each other. Their little electric did about forty miles an hour downwind. The cruiser's speedometer went to a hundred and sixty.

Alice let the cruiser glide to a halt against the inland curb. The central console gearshift looked too big for her hand, but she wrenched it into park. Only then did she release a big breath.

"So," Ceren said. "What were they?"

"They used to be people," I said.

I opened the door. "Let's swap."

Alice opened the driver's door. "I'll scoot over."

"No way," Ceren said. "Not enough room."

The three of us had ridden in the front before, right after I'd been shot, and while it hadn't been spacious, we'd done fine. Teenagers' personal space fluctuated between zero and intercontinental, though.

Alice glanced nervously back down the street, but slipped into the rear seat I'd vacated and fastidiously fastened the belt.

I glanced into the rearview mirror. The lake still turgidly surged and ebbed, but the road stood empty.

I carefully emptied the two remaining cartridges from the revolver and dropped handgun and bullets into the glove box. "Okay," I said.

"We need to take care of them," Ceren said.

"I know," I said.

"We passed a few melon trees. Stop and get some, I'll throw to distract them, you burn them down."

I grimaced. *That was one time. And I'm not taking either of you into that again if I can help it.* "It's not that simple this time."

"We should—" Alice started.

"I'm supposed to meet Eric in a few minutes," I said. "I'll drop you off, grab him, and we'll handle it."

"I can do it," Ceren said.

"I know you can," I said. "I do." Ceren looked so different from my own daughter, Julie, but that familiar defiant pride plucked at my heart. For a split second, my jaw clenched so tightly, the blister under my chin ached. I would *not* let anything happen to these girls. "But I have something more important for you to do."

"Bullshit."

"Not bullshit." I needed to do something about Ceren's language, somehow. "I checked that house *yesterday*," I said, making my voice harsh. "Eric and I searched it. We checked the attic, the basement, everything. I searched extra, once I figured on bringing you two in. The place was empty. I shut the door behind us. How did that—that dreg get in there?"

Alice looked thoughtful. Ceren still looked pissed.

"And they cooperated," I said. "It wasn't much of a plan, but it was a plan."

"Pumpkin-head doesn't have a brain," Alice said.

"No, he doesn't," I said. Pumpkin-head was a better fit than my own name for Suit. But crueler. "I saw him yesterday crossing the street two miles from here. He's never done anything except grab a melon. How'd he get here? And with a *gun*?"

Ceren frowned.

"And exactly when we were coming to look at that house," I said.

"Someone set us up," Ceren said.

Anger flashed in Alice's eyes.

"And I need to figure out who, and why." I nodded at Ceren. "That's why I want you to stick with Alice today."

"I don't need a babysitter!" Alice said, without a trace of questioning.

I shifted to look at her more directly, the vinyl seat creaking beneath me. "I've watched you work. You stare at that computer screen and the whole world goes away."

Alice grimaced. "So?"

"You've done a lot with Brandi and Steve," I said. "But they're just like you. A brass band with a drum corps could parade into Winchester Mall and if you had your teeth in a problem, none of you would notice."

"Steve and Brandi can fight," Alice said.

"Sure," I said. "If they *notice*." I turned to Ceren. "Keep your eyes open. Check out Winchester, but stay in hearing range. Sight, as much as you can manage. You see anything weird, you yank them out of their coding comas and get the hell out."

"Fine." Ceren still didn't look happy. "All right."

"I can't go where I have to if I'm worried about you two," I said.

"Where are you going?" Alice said.

"To the people who see all," I said.

Surprise shattered Ceren's scowl. "You can't go there alone!"

"I won't," I said. "I'll take Eric."

"Fine," Ceren spat. "I'll watch her back."

"We'd be okay," Alice said.

"You cracked Legacy." Ceren turned to Alice. "I couldn't. But I can watch out for you."

I started the motor and dropped the car into gear.

Drop the girls off. Grab Eric. Check out the house again, although I knew Suit and what-the-hell would be gone. And then off to see Acceptance.

"So," Ceren said. "What with all the bullet holes, I don't think that house is quite what we're looking for. Keep looking?"

Chapter 12

I DROPPED the girls back at Ceren's place and swung by Jack's to grab Eric. Usually we took his utility truck, but today we convoyed. We might have to split up, in a hurry. As I suspected, though, Suit and the creature had abandoned the house, leaving only scattered bloodstains. I tried to linger around the scene as long as possible, hoping they'd return, but that damn sense of duty that had me hunting monsters eventually sent me off to commune with one. Sooner than I hoped, we parked at Saint Michael's.

Frayville's oldest church sits between a grimly vacant schoolyard and a chain drugstore. When I first left Kevin's house, I'd seen a decrepit pickup straddling the drugstore's smashed front window, rear tires on the sidewalk. Someone had pulled the pickup out to the curb, nailed plywood over the gaping hole, and swept up. Shattered slivers of glass still sparkled on the sidewalk.

Kevin wouldn't have been surprised by that. Cleaning glass out of a pitted sidewalk was an art. A lost one, it seemed.

The church itself was made of massive stone blocks in shades of red and brown, with a steep roof and an actual bell tower holding a real bell. Sheila's ancestors had built it to last until the Second Coming, which it had. Too bad the wrong thing came this time around.

The asphalt parking lot had picked up heat from the midmorning sun, casting a pleasant warmth on my bare calves. Khaki shorts and a short-sleeved shirt was a good outfit for searching houses on a muggy, hot Michigan June day, but every time I came near Acceptance I itched for full body armor and my own air supply. It wouldn't have helped, but it made me feel better about the whole thing.

I wondered who Acceptance would be this time.

Eric is a big, placid guy. Nothing bothered him, it seemed, until now. He looked a little nervous.

"You want to wait out here?" I said.

Eric gave a faint nod. "Nah. Going with you."

"Okay then." I'd rather not have gone at all, but that wasn't an option. Having someone watch my back beat going in alone.

Shallow troughs curved down the broad limestone steps, eroded by two hundred years of feet going in and out. Antique bricks propped the church's dark wood front doors open. I had the feeling they were supposed to symbolize that the church welcomed everyone. To me, it was a trapdoor with a spider lurking beneath. I took a deep breath and walked through the tidy vestibule into the main hall.

The church cradled the night's cool. Sunlight streamed through towering, intricate stained glass windows depicting the life of Jesus, casting red, orange, and yellow patches across the antique but sturdy polished dark wood pews. At the far end, above the pulpit, a massive gilt cross glittered in ambient light. The oak floorboards creaked at my every step, occasionally echoed by Eric's heavy, slower tread.

"Detective Holtzmann!" called a woman from an incongruous swiveling office chair up near the pulpit.

"Miss Boxer," I said. I kept my voice and my steps firm and confident as I strode up the aisle.

The creature that had once been Veronica Boxer wore a pale green pantsuit with a navy blue blouse and black leather flats. Every finger bore a gemstone ring, seemingly chosen for its ability to sparkle and cast shattered light. Her black hair, granted its own life by the climbing humidity, would have hung past her shoulder blades if she hadn't shackled it in a ponytail. A few strands lay plastered to her forehead, as if she'd been sweating. Did she work out in the church while awaiting visitors?

Boxer held out her hand.

I ignored it.

Veronica Boxer had been an elementary school teacher. Absolute had taken her in her sleep, eating the original and creating this copy. He'd commanded the duplicate Boxer to take other people.

When Absolute set all us copies free, Boxer remembered what she'd done. In Absolute's name, she'd taken twenty-two of her students. Against their will, she'd infected them with alien matter and set them to attacking their loved ones.

The moment Absolute freed everyone, Boxer, sickened that she even existed, grabbed something sharp and opened her wrists to the bone. Before she bled out, the wounds knit themselves shut. Absolute did not permit us to kill ourselves so easily.

Horrified, she'd followed the sound of a gunshot and found a man in the street, a gun in his mouth and the base of his skull filling itself back in.

At a touch, they'd connected. They felt each other's pain. Boxer understood that Absolute had taken the man's free will. He understood that Boxer had no choice. Neither of them could accept what they'd done, but they were able to accept for each other. And support each other.

Even when they stopped touching.

They found other people who couldn't live with what they'd done, and couldn't destroy themselves. Together, they became Acceptance.

Last I heard, Acceptance had almost two dozen members. Each had joined during a slough of suicidal despair. Each knew where all the others were, all the other times. Each constantly comforted all the others, accepting what others couldn't.

The idea of accepting everything revolted me. And you could join them at a touch, in a flash. Say *yes* once, be joined to them forever. They didn't say it was forever, but how could you accept everything and want to change anything? How could anyone accept Absolute?

I couldn't look at Boxer without remembering a machine pistol bucking against my hand as bullets blew my wife Sheila's head apart. I remembered the rounds punching into the base of my daughter Julie's skull. I remembered scrabbling for the Springfield XD Julie dropped, my service automatic, needing suicide, needing the absolution of death more than anything.

I remembered being too slow.

If I hadn't murdered them quickly, Absolute, incarnated as a man I'd arrested for multiple rapes and murders, would have devoured them slowly.

That was my pain, dammit. Julie and Sheila deserved it. Even that stubborn, stupid bastard Kevin deserved someone to mourn him. And I wasn't about to surrender that pain just to make things easier for me.

So I ignored Boxer's hand. "Veronica. You must like church duty."

Boxer smiled. She didn't let my rejection dampen her day—she accepted it, just like Acceptance accepted every damn thing that happened. "And Eric. Good morning!"

Eric didn't smile. "Ma'am."

"The Church has always been my home," she said. "I belong here."

"Absolute didn't bring back a pastor," I said. "You might as well."

Boxer chuckled. "We've talked about what to do if a pastor comes back," she said. "There's a couple other places in town we could use. It doesn't matter where we are, so long as people can always find us. Rose says hello, by the way."

Rose Friedman had fired a .30-30 round through my heart and out the back of my chest. She believed she didn't have a choice. I'd dug into things Rose couldn't bear to expose. She'd tried to murder me, and I'd failed to die. In a flash of despair, she'd joined Acceptance.

That's how Acceptance worked. It lurked everywhere. The moment you hit bottom, it offered help. It cauterized your pain.

"I hope she's happy," I said.

"It's not your fault," Boxer said. "Nothing you could have said could have helped the kind of guilt she had. She was even a challenge for us. Sadly, she still is."

I did not want to talk about Rose Friedman. Not only had I failed to die, I'd failed to pull her back from self-destruction. "I'm hoping you can help me."

"Helping the police with their inquiries?" Boxer said. "But of course!"

If Acceptance thought I was an authority figure, I wasn't going to argue. "Do you know the guy who blew his brains out? He walks around in a suit."

Boxer's face turned sad. "Terrible. That poor man."

You're just sad you missed your chance with him. "He pulled a gun on some of us today."

"He did?" Boxer said, shocked. "Are you sure?"

"I know a revolver when I see one," I said.

Eric shifted his weight and crossed his arms across his chest.

"Of course you do, Detective," Boxer said. "That's just—surprising. It wasn't that he had picked it up randomly?"

"He shot at us," I said.

Boxer frowned. She looked more worried than anyone I'd ever seen in Acceptance. "That's…disturbing. I'm asking around for you. Are you sure it was him?"

"If it wasn't," I said, "then someone else is walking around with a head carved out like a jack-o'-lantern. What about two people stuck together?"

"Stuck how?" Boxer said.

"They look like they were having sex and just..." I flapped a hand. "...merged together."

Boxer shook her head. "Never seen that one."

"They're not sane," I said.

"I imagine not," Boxer said.

"And they were cooperating with the suicide," I said. "They trapped us. And almost got us."

The worry on Boxer's face coalesced into outright concern. "That's not good. Were they hungry?"

"Nobody was starving," I said. "I know you don't like to get involved. You don't want people to think you're creepy. But I already think you're creepy. And the rules have changed. Again. You never really needed much smarts to use a handgun before, but now you don't even need a brain. If you see them anywhere, if you hear of anything about them, I need to know."

"I have..." Boxer started.

"Yes?"

"I have... This is hard to describe," she said. Her brow knitted a moment. "Please, sit." She took a step back and sank into a pew.

I kept standing. If it offended her, she'd just accept it.

A cross-breeze from some cracked window brushed Boxer's hair, then went still.

"You know we can communicate over distance," Boxer said.

"Yes."

"There's something..." Boxer let out a deep breath. "Something's leaking into it."

I'd never seen that kind of disturbed look on anyone in Acceptance. I shivered uneasily. "Tell me about that."

She shook her head. "We're—it's like a pool. A big pool and we're all swimming in it. We all support each other. We send each other love, and faith, and trust, and all the things humans need."

"Love?"

She smiled distantly. "People all need love. Even you, Kevin."

I said nothing.

"When you know someone that well," she said, "you can't help but forgive them their weaknesses. You want to help them. So yes, love.

Honesty without hypocrisy, as young Rick says." Her face grew serious. "And we know everything each other feels. *Everything*. And this… whatever this is, it isn't one of us."

"What isn't?" I said.

Boxer's lips tightened. "The fear."

Kevin knew that, sometimes, silence is the best way to get someone to talk. I'd been learning he was right about this too. I said nothing.

Boxer pushed out a chestful of air and sucked in another. "Someone, or something, is filling the pool with fear, agonizing fear. It's not there all the time, but when it hits, it's bad." Her fingers knitted together.

"How often does this happen?" I said.

"Couple times a day, maybe." Boxer seemed to notice her intertwined hands and self-consciously pulled them apart. "I can't…" She shook her head. "The last time was this morning. Maybe an hour, hour and a half before you showed up."

"About the same time we were attacked," I said. My heart beat a little more quickly. Sweat had glued a few strands of Boxer's hair to her forehead. Had the fear been *that* bad? "Do you happen to know when it's happened before? Other days, I mean?"

"We don't wear watches," Boxer said.

"Get one," I said. "Take a note when it happens. It might be coincidence."

"But maybe not. Can we…" She sat up straighter, suddenly stronger. "Yes. We can do that."

I wondered how Acceptance's connection worked. Did the creature and Suit have the same sort of mental bond? If they did, would it interfere with Acceptance? Were they all broadcasting on the same wavelength?

"Will you let me know if you see those two?" I said.

She studied my face.

I stared impassively back.

"Yes," Boxer finally said. "It's against our rules, but…yes. If it really is those poor people—we can't have that. We can't go back to what we were."

"Thank you," I said. "Jack has a radio. Let him know if one of you sees them. He can reach me right away." To call Jack's device a radio was a disservice. Frayville had had a collection of fully programmable, decentralized wireless handsets, capable of operating over several miles without any central tower service. They could carry several separate conversations at once without interfering with each other, encrypting everything to prevent eavesdropping. The only thing that would beat those radios would be the actual cellular phone network, and even then, it would be a close race.

"We will." Boxer closed her eyes. "Whatever it takes to make this stop happening, we'll do it. We can't—" She drew a shuddering breath. "We can't go back. We can't."

"Whatever's going on," I said, "it's something new. Something from…outside, probably."

Boxer's eyes snapped open. Fear, sorrow, and surprise chased their tails across her face. "You don't know," she said softly.

"Know what?" I snapped.

"The border."

"What border?"

"I can tell you, but the sheriff, of all people, really needs to see it."

"I'm a copy, not a cop. Sure as hell not the sheriff."

"Eric's not the city utilities man. And I'm not a teacher," Boxer said. Her eyes stared off in a direction I couldn't see. "And yet, here we are. Give me a moment—okay. Can you go up to the Big Boy past Legacy?"

"When?"

"Now would be good. Pendleton will meet you there. He will guide you to the researchers."

"I know where the Lightners are." Alice worked with Brandi and Steve Lightner, trying to crack Absolute's secrets out of Legacy.

"Not those researchers. The ones at the border. The biologist and the geologist."

"We have scientists?" I said. "Real, actual scientists?"

An honest smile broke Boxer's face. "You bet. Pendleton is a big guy, you can't miss him. He'll be out front of the restaurant."

"And what am I going to look at?"

Her smile evaporated. "Another world ending."

Chapter 13

I PULLED the police cruiser into the Winchester Mall parking lot on top of South Hill. The lot had begged for new pavement before the human race noticed Absolute, and nobody'd had asphalt to spare up until the day it had digested them. Someone had dragged the abandoned cars scattered around the lot into a ragged row, but a minivan and the girls' tiny white plastic electric two-seater sat in the handicapped spots near the east entrance.

Ceren must have driven today. Alice parked next to the handicapped spaces.

Other than a few scattered oaks and maples, rolling fields with distant pines and elms along the far side filled in the highlands up around the mall. Absolute hadn't restored the final corn crop, leaving the fields as furrowed black earth filling the air with the smells of dust and loam. To the north, looking over the edge of the ancient glacial ridge beneath the mall, the world fell away into the sky.

The Big Boy restaurant squatted heavily just past the mall and right before the lifeless black dirt of the first cornfields. The red brick and dark glass building looked vacant but not abandoned, as if everyone had decided to stay home today. Jack had said something about people using the place for communal meals, but I didn't see any sign of inhabitation.

Then again, Jack seemed to live and sleep at his adopted bar. Maybe the cook here was less obsessive.

There was no sign of the Pendleton person Acceptance had told us to expect.

I'd barely shut the car door behind me when Eric's utility truck pulled up. "You don't have to come along," I said as Eric climbed out.

"Not doing house-to-house alone," he said.

"Fair enough."

"B'sides, if the world's ending again, I wanna know."

"It's not an *again*," I said. "It's a *still*."

Eric's jaw clenched and he nodded. Eric was taller than me, and had these hard slabs of muscle from lifting heavy things all day long.

His every movement strained his shirt sleeves. Despite facing and escaping Boxer in the church, he still seemed jumpy.

"If we're both going," I said, "let's take my car. Following Acceptance, let's not split up." Acceptance had never threatened anyone, as far as I knew. Nobody in Acceptance had ever lied to me, as far as I knew. But I didn't know everything, and I didn't have enough trust to hand it out to everyone.

Eric rolled his left hand into a fist and tapped his key fob. The truck door locks clicked. He'd picked up a rich tan, unsurprising after all the work we'd done outside, but that wasn't what had changed. He still wore the same Carhartt industrial pants and shirts he'd worn before.

"Are you curling your hair?" I said. I thought it looked darker than usual, too, but wasn't sure.

Eric's hand jerked towards his tight black curls before he could restrain it. "I hear the ladies like that," he said, his tone telling me to mind my own business. We all have our secrets.

"They probably do." His mention of *the ladies* brought the creature back to my mind. I knew some people had sex without trouble—at least, without any weird trouble. Without any trouble that they hadn't had before Absolute. You only had to look around Jack's at dinnertime to see the slow dance of individuals negotiating to become couples and couples who'd passed that threshold.

And then there was… I needed a better name for them in my head than cow-sized spider monster. It. I needed a better name for *it*. I needed to remember where I'd seen the woman's face before.

And there was whoever had committed murder with a bathtub. Presumably the same person who had cracked Reamer's mother's skull.

It's not that I didn't want to be a police detective any more. I *couldn't* be one. Police get their authority from the community. A cop without a chief or a mayor or a council or something is just a vigilante.

But I couldn't ignore murder and assault.

The question was, were they all the same culprit? Or had three jackasses separately topped yesterday's to-do list with *Start Trouble*?

And what had Acceptance meant about the end of the world?

And, and, and, and.

At least that jackass Woodward didn't have flamethrowers.

I leaned against the cruiser, smelling sun-scorched concrete and distant trees, watching the brief gusts of wind scuttle topsoil dust across the parking lot and trying to still my thoughts. Eric kept turning his head, watching.

When the only sound is the breeze, traffic noises carry a long way. We heard the truck long before we saw it. A gasoline engine. Right after the nukes started flying, the Building the Future people had converted the official vehicles to diesel and slashed gasoline production, conserving resources for the fight against Absolute. But now someone had found gasoline, somewhere, and used it in an engine that needed tuning so badly that its roar had syncopation.

A moment later a dirty, rusted pickup truck with a battered cap emerged from behind the tree line on the other side of the lifeless field and roared into the parking lot. Eric and I shifted to watch it creak to a halt. The truck's springs groaned in relief once the driver climbed out.

"Pendleton?" I said.

"Hail," the man said.

I'd seen Pendleton around town. It would have been hard to not see him.

Pendleton stood a few inches over six feet and weighed at least three times what I did. A flotilla of chins formed and disappeared as he moved his head. He took short steps on massive legs. The bright orange-and-blue button-down shirt did nothing to conceal the massive gut overhanging his belt like a flabby mushroom. The lime-green necktie barely made it to the bottom of his ribs.

"Our stalwart defender of the law, Detective Holtzmann," Pendleton said. He waved a hand at Eric. "And Mister Hayward, the gentleman who does all the *real* work. Welcome, good peoples!"

"Acceptance said you had something to show us," I said.

Pendleton gave a tiny bow from his waist. "And so I do! Would you care for a chauffeur, or would following me be your preference?"

I didn't even look at Eric. "We'll follow."

"By all means. We're going south down Main, about two miles, beyond the last farm."

We got back into the cruiser. Pendleton drove like an elderly man afraid of losing his driver's license. We were trailing the rust bucket at about twenty miles an hour when Eric said, "You been out here yet?"

"No. Too busy searching," I said.

Eric grunted.

The road grew more cluttered as we went on, bits of metal and burned spars of wood the length of my forearm scattered randomly across both lanes. Larger chunks of metal, some clearly identifiable as parts of cars, others just melted chunks, irregularly dotted the roadside. Someone had clearly dragged these larger chunks of debris aside. We passed empty fields on either side, each marked off by towering maples and elms. When the farmers had cleared the land, they'd left slashes of old-growth forest along the property lines. The brilliant green leaves against the blue sky and black idle earth seemed primal, like the world had been drawn with only three colors. Some of those tree lines had ragged scrub all through their bases, forming thick wild hedges you'd have to walk around rather than through.

What with all the growth and the debris, we found ourselves driving down a visual tunnel. Acceptance had given me a hint, but the view still took me by surprise.

Finding yourself up against the edge of the world will do that to you.

Chapter 14

THE TREE line disappeared, revealing only charred ruins.

"Holy hell." Eric's soft whisper seemed louder than anything in front of us.

Frayville had a dozen homes burned to ash and charcoal spars, a couple store windows shattered, a whole bunch of abandoned vehicles and empty streets, and willow trees that grew melons. We had damage from neglect and weather, but the town still stood. Leaving town, we'd passed through vacant farms with idle black topsoil, into the beginning of the hardwood forest surrounding the town.

And after a quarter mile of heavy-crowned oaks and maples, we'd emerged into the aftermath of war.

Rain-soaked ash and trees burned to stumps of black charcoal filled the land all the way to the distant horizon. Nothing moved out there. No birds. No animals. No insects or planes. No sprouted weeds waving with the wind. A pitiless sun scorched the deep blue sky. A single tree trunk stood at the edge of my vision, miraculously upright, a black mast making the tumbled ruin around it even more desolate.

A forest ravaged by fire starts turning green in a couple weeks.

Grass and weeds linger in a bombed-out war zone.

But this was different. After months, this landscape was a black and gray lifeless husk.

I'd taken my foot off the accelerator without noticing, and my police cruiser slowed to an idle roll. I brought the cruiser to a halt and absently put it in park. I'm sure something in the back of my brain was worried about the cruiser coasting into a drainage ditch choked with broken burned branches and soot, but I can't remember. All I could see was death and ruin. The end of the world.

Ahead, charcoal and gritty ash covered the road, petrified by rain into tiny canyons and peaks. I smelled only faint hints of carbon, like a family's backyard grill left idle for a month. This fire had been extinguished for months.

The tree line stretched to our left and right, as straight as if Absolute had plopped a ruler down and run a razor blade along the edge. The looming elms and bushy maples, all crowned with bright green leaves, weren't even singed. To our left, the lake formed a distant green line between the black ruin and the sky.

I suddenly became aware of the fresh sweat soaking my armpits and spine and my heart trembling behind my ribs. Knowing that Absolute destroyed humanity and won its war with us was one thing. Seeing the world in ash and cinder made it real.

Even the fake seagulls wouldn't fly over this scorched landscape.

Frayville was a tiny terrarium lost in an incinerated world.

Chapter 15

"THE VISTA overwhelms one, does it not?"

I'd never even noticed Pendleton approaching. Big as he was, he couldn't compete with the immensity of the destruction before me. Everything outside Frayville, all the way to the horizon, had burned to soot and crumbled charcoal. My pulse thudded in my ears and my every muscle clenched in atavistic dread.

The fire burned out long ago, but my brain provided the stench of the smoke from Michigan's Viking funeral.

"It must have been quite the conflagration," Pendleton said. He hunkered down next to the driver's side window, somehow sitting on his raised heels despite his incredibly excessive weight. "I needed to avert my eyes upon first seeing it, and I had assistance you lack."

He's part of Acceptance. I'd known that, but having him inches away broke the trance of my reeling brain. Was he waiting to offer me that assistance? "How far does this go?" I made myself say.

Pendleton shrugged his massive shoulders, sending a ripple through his sea of chins. "Who knows?" He waved an arm at the road, covered with ash and debris. "Most of that came from the woods, but some citizens had their domiciles down there. There, on the left, you can see what remains of the power station."

A few hundred yards down the road, a sagging chain-link fence marked off a square. Jagged metal stubs and shattered shells of soot-streaked gray steel were all that remained of whatever equipment it had secured.

"I'm certain that a fraction of that metal blew as far as the thoroughfare," Pendleton said. "Frayville has always been isolated, but our next expedition will require a front-mounted plow. Or, perhaps, a tracked vehicle. Perchance, does the city own a tank, Detective?"

I slowly shook my head. "No." Had humanity burned everything at the end in its fight to contain Absolute? Or was this collateral damage? Had we—*they* put Flint and Bay City and Saginaw to the torch, and the firestorm just charged north on its own? Had it stopped at the Mackinaw Straits? Maybe the fire had burned the Upper Peninsula by coming around the long way, up through Wisconsin. How could I ever know what happened?

Enough. I almost slapped myself, but instead clamped my teeth on the inside of my cheek and ground down. The slow swell of pain helped me focus, dragging my consciousness back from the incinerated ruin. "Eric?" I said.

Eric's jaw hung open as he swiveled his head from side to side. "Yeah." His head swiveled to the right, pointing with his blunt chin. "Who's that?"

I leaned to peer around his head. A tiny electric two-seater car, just like the one I'd got for the girls but ruby red, sat parked just off the road in what had once been a gravel driveway. I glimpsed a blue awning behind it, and someone moving underneath.

"That would be the good doctors Langley and Frost," Pendleton said. His ponderous vocabulary irritated me more every time he spoke. "They're the people with whom you really want to speak."

Eric visibly brought himself back together. "They with you?"

"They're not members of Acceptance," Pendleton said. "I merely help them carry equipment out here when they need it. Science is fascinating, but I fear my mind, my thoughts, work along a different pathway."

I sucked a deep breath through my nose. "Come on, Eric."

The flimsy plastic awning stood out in the ash, a dozen yards from the tree line and the road. Stacked translucent storage boxes built a neck-high barricade between the awning and the devastation to the south. Two women sat in folding canvas chairs in the shade, staring intently at several laptop computers arranged on a folding table. Despite the warmth, both wore denim pants and heavy boots with light summery shirts. Bundled wires poured off the back of the work table and trailed across the charcoal ground towards the tree line, while another bundle ran to a head-high mast with a two-foot dish antenna pointed towards the lake.

Pendleton pointed out a rough path ground through the ash. Even though someone had raked the larger chunks to the side and people had repeatedly stomped through the chunks of burned wood and incinerated ash, despite the rains that had come and gone, at each step my sneakers sank with a crunch and raised a little puff of dust. How deep was this stuff? How much ash would be left once we burned the world?

We were ten feet away when the redheaded older woman raised her voice and said, "Be with you in a moment. Look." She pointed at the laptop screen. "It's the same ripple, from the east."

The brunette shook her head. "Yes, but we don't have the cascade signals." She took a microfiber cloth off her lap and absently swiped her forehead, smearing the ash there even more.

"We don't always get the cascade," the first woman said.

"Usually, we do—hey, what's that?"

The older woman peered back at her own laptop, and they started jabbering back and forth about tremors and signals and a whole obtuse technical vocabulary. Both interrupted the other in rising excitement, fingers stabbing back and forth.

I muttered to Pendleton, "What's going on?"

The huge man shrugged. "I fear I don't know. They've been studying the trees for a week now, but they haven't disclosed any findings."

Eric glared at them, looked at me, and tromped into the charcoal towards the tree line.

"We've got one!" the brunette shouted gleefully. "And it's right here!"

The redhead swiveled to another laptop. "On the cameras," the redhead said, typing frantically on her keyboard. "High-speed one live, high-speed two, high-speed three."

"Come on," the brunette said. "We've got you, we got you—"

The redhead's eyes narrowed as she stared at the laptop, then went wide in sudden terror. She jerked her head up from her screen. "You!" she screamed. "Get away from the tree line!"

I spun to look.

Eric stood a couple yards from the tree trunks, hands on his hips, staring up into the canopy of a hundred-year-old maple. He jerked to look back at her shout, a surprised scowl on his face.

"Get back here!" the brunette shouted.

"Christ, you'll wreck it all!" the redhead said.

"It's about to blow!" the brunette said.

Eric took a tentative step towards us.

A grumble rose through the soles of my shoes, like a laden dump truck getting closer and closer.

A yard behind Eric the ground exploded, geysering dirt and ash into the sky.

Chapter 16

ERIC, THE big lummox, staggered a second step towards us, desperately trying to keep his feet.

Dirt and dust and chunks of cinder and charcoal fountained twenty feet into the air, blowing a hazy column of ash towards the thin horsetail clouds. I crouched back and jerked my arms up, palms defensively cradling the crown of my head so that my arms protected my head. The ground vibrated through my feet.

Eric threw himself forward. His feet skidded on the burned-out cinders, plunging him face-first into the ash.

One of the women under the blue plastic awning screamed.

Something launched itself out of the new hole in the ground.

A three-foot-wide cylinder, corrugated in gray and brown, thrust up from the ruptured earth. The ground shook like a busy construction site. My eyes vibrated in their sockets.

The cylinder grew into a tapered column ten feet high, then twenty, then thirty. In the tree line behind it, the branches of the old-growth elms and maples shuddered and shook, a susurrus of leaves forming a chorus for the rhythm of the flying dirt clods hitting the ground.

The top of the column split with a crack, a baseball bat breaking on an inside fastball. Two tendrils writhed into the sky, bifurcating again and again, until their tips formed pencil branches.

Branches that spouted leaves.

The ground stilled.

My guts still quivered with echoed vibrations, but I slowly lowered my hands and stood straight. Charcoal and ash dust coated my arms, my clothes, and probably my face.

I worked my mouth. My tongue, too. The ash tasted thick and bitter.

Where the ground had exploded now stood an elm tree, utterly indistinguishable from those behind it. Its leaves still quivered with the force of the tree's rise, but in another breath they, and all the trees around, returned to breeze-stirred peace.

Eric raised his ash-smeared face from the cindered soil. White eyes blinked out of a comically charcoaled face.

"You okay?" I said, taking a step off the trampled path towards him.

Eric spit. "Yeah." He climbed to his feet, brushing uselessly at himself. Plunging into the cinders had ground ash and charcoal into his clothes, his arms, his face, while geysering dirt had coated his back.

Beside me, Pendleton dourly surveyed the wreckage of his colorful shirt. "I fear this apparel has seen its last."

"You're lucky you weren't killed!" one of the women behind me shouted.

"What did you think you were doing?" the other said.

Eric said, "Thought—" He spit black and wiped at his mouth. "Thought we were waiting for you all." He held his hands before him and cautiously worked his fingers.

"You were right in front of the camera," the redhead said. "If you blew the video, I'm gonna smack you."

The brunette peeked over her shoulder.

Eric trudged towards me, fruitlessly brushing at the ash and dirt covering him.

One side of my mouth quivered up. "Bet the ladies will really like that hair now."

Eric glared at me, his eyes brilliant against his dirt-pied face, then stepped up right next to me and rubbed his hands wildly through his dark curls, throwing clumps of dirt and debris in my face.

"Hey." I snorted, hopping back. "I have my own charms, mister."

Behind me, the redhead said, "We got the footage." She looked up to glare at Eric. "Your foot is the star of the first couple seconds, but you moved before it sprouted."

I forced out a deep breath to try to clear my jangling nerves. "So. Can we try this again? Hello. I'm Kevin Holtzmann."

"I'm Cathy Frost," the redhead said. Her voice sounded a little rough, like she was my age, but the smooth skin on her sharp features put her in her twenties. She moved with too much confidence to be that young, though. Thirties, maybe?

"Willa Langley," the brunette said. Her mouth had a perpetual twist, as if she chewed something bitter.

"You're the sheriff people are talking about," Frost said.

"I'm not the sheriff," I said. "Kevin was a detective with the Frayville police."

Sympathy or something like it flashed across Frost's face. "They're calling you the sheriff."

"And I tell them the same thing." I nodded at Eric, who was still trying to knock the worst of the filth off his skin. The gentle breeze hadn't yet erased the stink of fresh-stirred ash from the air, and his work added a new plume of gray. "This is Eric Hayward, Frayville DPW."

"What brings you out here?" Langley said.

"Acceptance sent us. She said I needed to see…" I waved a hand at the incinerated horizon. "This."

Frost tightened her lips. "So. Bad timing."

Pendleton said, "I assure you, ladies, that we had no awareness that anything so spectacular was imminent."

"We got the data," Langley said. "And even without that, we've supported the theory."

"What theory?" I said.

"The border is growing," Frost said.

I eyed the newly sprouted hundred-year-old elm. "Yeah, I'd say so."

Frost shook her head. "We hadn't caught it in action. The seismometers had picked up the vibrations, so we knew something was happening. We didn't think to mark where the trees were for a few days, though."

"That's a normal tree now?" Eric said, peering at the elm.

"Normal?" Langley said. "As normal as any of us are, yes."

Eric took a step back towards the tree line.

Frost said, "Hang on, Mister—Hayward, was it?"

Eric froze.

"This isn't done." Langley glanced at a laptop. "The readings say another one's coming."

Eric quickly tromped back next to me.

"How long has this been going on?" I said.

"How thick is the forest belt? How quickly does the belt grow? Where did it start from? Answer those and I'll tell you." Frost said. She looked at Langley. "We're in the right place, so let the cameras run." She stood, brushing her hands against her jeans. "Either of you want a bottle of water?"

Ash plastered my tongue. "Please."

Eric worked his mouth again, then spat black phlegm into the cinders behind him. "Yes, ma'am."

I stepped beneath the awning's tinted shade, grateful for finally getting out of the scorching sun. A swig of lukewarm water from a plastic bottle washed away the worst of the ashen taste. Eric took a bottle and walked a few yards into the charcoal to rinse his mouth.

"Seismometers," I said. "Isn't that what they use for earthquakes?"

"Among other things," Langley said.

"So the trees are a mini-earthquake. How fast—"

"No idea," Frost laughed. "We'd seen the vibration, but this is the first time we caught a flow in action. We'll need a lot more observation to find out. All I can say is, this is the most active part we've seen so far. Probably because it's closest to the lake." She looked thoughtful. "We should go to the other side, see how it compares."

I glanced at the distant green line of the scum-choked Lake Huron. "What does the lake got to do with it?"

"Everything," Frost said. "As far as I can tell, the lake is the source of the tree's biomass. Willa's seismometer mesh picks up subsurface activity moving from the lake to the next outbreak of trees. We've been chasing it all around the ring."

"Ring?" I said.

Frost spun a finger in the air. "The ring around Frayville."

My stomach sank, and I turned my head to survey the devastation. Ash and charcoal, stumps of burned trees and telephone poles, stretched all the way to the horizon. A brick wall crumbled low, made fragile by intense heat—all that remained of an unidentifiable building, maybe a warehouse or a home. No way to tell now. Ash coated the highway thickly enough that after a few yards, I couldn't tell where it lay. The breeze stirred intermittent dust devils.

The words didn't want to leave my mouth. "This goes all the way around?"

The animation in Frost's face and voice faded away. She looked down at the ashes swirling around her feet. "I'm afraid so."

I'd suggested to Acceptance that something from outside had made Suit and the two-bodied dreg cooperate. Acceptance had sent me here, to see there was no outside world.

Despite the June sun burning the blue sky, the breeze suddenly carried a chill.

Frayville could contain everything that lived on Earth.

Or whatever had come into Frayville…was tough enough to survive out there.

Chapter 17

I COULDN'T just stand at the edge of the devastation and quietly freak out. A dead, incinerated world might surround Frayville, but behind me were hundreds of people. Sort of people. Creatures with the memories and passions of people. Whatever they were, they needed my help.

If we truly lived in a little island of life, alone on the Earth, we couldn't afford to lose any more of us. We were as close to human as probably still existed on the Earth. I couldn't bear to see that vanish.

We'd had one murder. One assault. An attempt on my life—and worse, on Alice and Ceren.

I took a deep breath, imagining calm flowing through me with each exhalation, and narrowed my focus to block the plain of cinders. The blue plastic awning we stood beneath. Frost and Langley, biologist and geologist. Massively flamboyant Pendleton, part of Acceptance. Eric, who had my back even when it meant he bathed in cold cinders.

The barrier of trees encircling Frayville. The growing ring of brand-new old-growth trees. None of it made sense, some even less than most.

"What's making the trees grow?" I asked.

Frost looked annoyed. "The lake. The biomass is coming from the lake, and being rearranged into trees. It's the same shape-shifting Absolute's Taken used, but applied to trees."

I felt glad she hadn't said *the same shape-shifting* we *did*. The scattered flashes I remembered of my days as Absolute's puppet were enough. "No, I mean, what's controlling it?"

"We just found where the trees are growing." Langley didn't pull her eyes from her laptop. "Don't ask us where the brains are."

"Legacy," Eric said. "Gotta be Legacy."

"Probably." Frost swigged a mouthful of water from her bottle. "But that's just a guess. I have no evidence one way or another."

"Gotta be," Eric said.

Frost shrugged. "We'll figure it out. I check in with Steve and Brandi every few days, when we come to this side of the Ring."

"Vibration is increasing." Langley tapped her keyboard. "Looks about a hundred meters west. Plus or minus a whole bunch."

Frost took a seat under the awning and waved Eric and me to follow.

"Y'know," Eric said, "don't think I'm dirty enough. Where'd you say this thing was going to blow?"

"If you want a ride back in *my* cruiser, you're plenty dirty."

Pendleton said, "I would be pleased to offer you a return ticket in the back of my truck, if it means I get to see a repeat of your earlier performance. Perhaps, if you get slightly closer to the next explosion, you can achieve a moment of flight."

"Just don't stand in front of the camera," Langley said. "We already have enough footage of those boots."

"Back of the truck?" Eric said. "Ah, forget it."

A faint, subterranean vibration rose through the soles of my feet.

Frost bent over Langley's shoulder, rapt. "I'm guessing in three. Two. One."

I braced my feet and squinted west along the trees.

"Now," Frost said.

The warm breeze sifted ash.

"Now?" Frost said.

I glanced along the tree line, towards the distant green of the algae-choked lake. Was an underground sewer line really carrying slurry towards us?

On the surface, nothing moved.

"That's odd," Frost said.

To the west, dirt and cinders ruptured from the ground, far enough along the tree line that it all fell well short of us. Another shaft of wood burst upward, twisting into gray branches and leaves. In seconds, the ring of trees around Frayville had one more member that looked as though it had been there for decades.

"Does it take longer, the further away from the water the tree sprouts?" Frost said.

"Nope," Langley said, tapping her keyboard. "You don't know how to read the seismometers."

"It's not that hard," Frost said.

"It's not," Langley said. "But you can't do it."

I said, "Thank you for your time, ladies."

Frost looked up. "Any time. Listen, some of us meet up at the Big Boy for dinners. Come up some time. We could use some law around the place."

"I'll do that," I said. "I'm not the law, though."

"You're as close as it gets," Frost said. To Langley, she said, "We should probably pack up, see if we can get ahead of it."

"Permit me to offer my services as beast of burden," Pendleton said.

"You, I don't get," I said. "It's hot out here, and you're offering to Sherpa? You look like you'd rather be in a big hammock reading Shakespeare."

Pendleton chuckled like an avalanche through his huge body. "Indeed, sir! Yes, I would. But there's work to be done. And right here is one of the places where we're learning about the world." He raised his arms expansively. "I have claimed the role of a digger who helped excavate the tomb of King Tut! A place—"

Pendleton's vast face stilled. His eyes locked onto something invisible in the far distance, his attention focusing away from everything I could see.

Acceptance.

Pendleton blinked. "Excuse me, Sheriff. You're needed downtown."

The hair on the back of my neck raised. "Oh?"

"Now." Pendleton's voice had a bizarre mix of detachment and intensity, as if forcefully recalling badly memorized lines. Acceptance had trouble sending words through its members.

"Where?" I said.

"Follow—follow the—gunshots?"

Eric and I looked at each other. I was halfway to the cruiser before Eric finished cursing and started running.

Chapter 18

I LIKE to roll the cruiser through town at a leisurely fifteen miles an hour—especially now, when so many people have gotten used to walking. In the month that we'd been freed from Absolute, I'd also held off from blasting the cruiser's siren through town. But that didn't mean I had to.

The siren's cyclic bellow shattered the town's quiet while the cruiser's feral, growling engine swept up the pieces and shoved them into the trash. We hadn't found any deaf people yet, but just in case, the blue-and-red strobing from the roof made sure nobody could miss us.

Acceptance could communicate between members, using some sort of knock-off telepathy where words stumbled but feelings flowed. They'd made a point of not demonstrating that ability anywhere except the church, and had refused to tell me things that would have kept Alice and me from a lot of pain. They'd screwed me over by keeping their silence. But now Acceptance had broken its own rules by allowing Pendleton to pass along that message.

Eric, still grubby with ash and stinking of exhausted cinders, braced his feet against the floorboards and fumbled the seat belt in place around him as we rocketed through the forest belt, past Winchester Mall, and down the big hill overlooking the Sand River and Frayville.

We'd barely cleared the hump of the hill when I grabbed for the radio mic. "Jack!" I shouted. "You there? What's going on?"

Nobody answered in the first second. I almost keyed the mic again, but forced myself to concentrate as we hit the bottom of the hill and started across the bridge. I lifted my foot from the accelerator and hovered over the brake. *Downtown* might mean the end of the bridge or a mile further down.

My radio crackled. "Holtzmann?"

"Talk to me, Jack."

"Some damn fool just shot off a whole load of ammo." The bartender sounded more annoyed than afraid.

"Any idea where?"

"Hang on, I'll go out."

I flipped the siren off. In a town without traffic, without radios, without thousands of people, the siren drowned every other sound in town.

The radio crackled. "No more shots, but there's some shouting out here. South, I'd say."

Most of Frayville was south of Jack's. "Any better fix?"

We coasted off the bridge and into town, rolling between the boarded-up restaurant and the Quick-Stop. Eric's head swiveled around as he tried to look in every direction simultaneously.

Jack finally answered. "Nope."

"Let me know what you hear." I dropped the mic on the seat and punched the button to roll down the windows.

"What now?" Eric said. His eyes looked wide in his cinder-blackened face.

"We listen for shouts. I keep the engine low so we can hear, and we roll north."

"How are we going to find them?"

"I just told you. Listen."

We coasted down the five-lane road at twenty miles an hour, ears straining to sift every sound from the hot June wind blowing past and the diesel motor grumbling through my seat. I needed a dispatcher, someone to give me an address so my experienced partner and I could roll up and claim charge—or, better still, a couple junior officers who could do the legwork and call in the detective to play the heavy.

Instead, I had a dependable but inexperienced snowplow driver who looked like a vaudeville character.

Main Street had tobacconists, card shops, restaurants, and banks for ten thousand people. As far as I could tell, maybe two to three hundred of us lived here now. Someone had broken into most of the pharmacies and party stores by shattering the glass doors, but more recently people had attached plywood over the breaks and swept up the broken glass. Trees rose from square gaps in the sidewalks. Someone had cranked up music so loud that the repetitive bass line carried out to us.

But no hint of gunfire.

Far ahead, a bicyclist pedaled away.

We rolled forward with alert ears, coasting through quiet intersections. I hardly touched the gas. Better to arrive a couple minutes late than to drown out the sounds of trouble with engine noise and go past it all.

"Kevin," Eric said, pointing.

A few hundred yards down the road, the bicyclist had hopped off his bike. He jumped in the air over and over, waving his arms above his head.

I touched the gas, and we lurched forward, bearing down on the kid and his bicycle.

The bicyclist had shaved half his head, but the other half hung past his shoulders and over his eyes. I knew him—Rick. A teenage boy who wanted to be suave.

And part of Acceptance.

I hit the gas hard.

Rick pointed both arms across the road, down one of the side streets. We took that turn at speed.

Tiny homes lined the street, each an identical brick rectangle with a flat roof sloping towards the front. Each house had a concrete driveway running up to a carport attached to the west side. Most of the houses had a tree out front. From years of visiting before, I knew that every house had a dirt-floor basement, a narrow kitchen separated from a tiny living room by laminate-countered cabinets, and two cramped bedrooms flanking a shabby bathroom. Everyone who didn't live in these blocks called the neighborhood The Catboxes. Eric and I had swept this street last week, taping a strip of caution tape beside each door to mark where we'd been.

And in front of one of the houses, a dozen scattered men formed a rough semicircle, backs towards us, shifting forward and back as if they circled an angry bull. Half of them carried rifles.

I whooped the siren once.

A couple of the men jumped. One glanced my way, then twisted his head back around and danced a couple of steps backwards, shouting.

I skidded the cruiser to a halt and hear the cries.

"Go, Will!"

"You got this!"

"Get it, Will!"

Three men hopped back, rifles raised, hooting.

And revealing the tentacled horror in the middle of their circle.

Chapter 19

TAKE AWAY the pink, worm-like tentacles sprouting from its shoulders, put some muscles on the frighteningly emaciated frame, add flesh to the sharp face, and heal the bloody wounds gouging its flanks, and it might have almost been a dog. Once. Long ago. Short brown fur covered its back and the top of its head, with black at its belly and feet. Tentacles whipping through the air, the creature advanced on the man in the middle of the grassy circle.

The creature's angry barks carried an unearthly metallic screech.

Half a dozen pink worm-like tentacles had sprouted from its shoulders to lash at its victim.

The man backed against the tree looked like a big, beefy good old boy, the kind you see hanging around the gun and knife shows down in Oscoda, so proud of the weapons he'd bought but didn't know how to use. This guy had his hair in a late-twentieth-century mullet and a cocky grin. He held the gleaming black assault rifle by the plastic stock, waving the barrel end back and forth to intercept the flailing tentacles. Lines of blood streaked his exposed face and hands, and slashes in his cotton gray-and-brown camouflage outfit showed red beneath the torn fabric.

The ex-dog snarled and lunged, its back feet kicking up grass with its charge.

The man swung the rifle down, knocking barrel against the side of the creature's muzzle. "Ha! Olé!"

The creature fell back, teeth exposed through torn cheeks, growling. The tentacles moved more quickly.

The men circled on the lawn shouted encouragement. "Get him, Will!" "You got this!" "Take it down!" Nobody moved to help Will, but the gunpowder stench filling the air told me they'd already contributed their ammunition.

A chunky man lay on his back at the far side of the road, stretched along the curb. One hand gripped at his shoulder, trying to slow the blood soaking into his shirt.

Eric sat in the cruiser's passenger seat next to me, staring, his jaw hanging open.

"A hundred on Will!" a scrawny man bellowed.

A lanky man in a short-sleeved flannel shirt shouted, "*Two hundred! On the critter!*"

I grabbed the shotgun. Guns wouldn't help—even before Absolute's final attack, we'd known that firearms only annoyed the Taken. A hunter I knew had proven you couldn't kill a deer with a bullet unless you did it exactly right. These men clearly didn't understand the new rules. I hoped I could prevent them from paying too steep a price to learn how the world worked these days. And a dog was smarter than a deer, making it more dangerous.

"Eric," I said.

He didn't respond, staring at the dog.

I elbowed his shoulder. "Eric!"

He jerked and looked at me. "Yeah? Sorry."

"We can't let that thing get out," I said. "And these dumbasses can't contain it. I need your help."

"You got it."

I glanced around. "The house they're in front of? The front door is open. We checked it; it should be clear."

"Uh-huh."

"I go into the doorway, get its attention. When it chases me in, you slam the door behind it. I'll be going through the house and out the back door. That should hold it a little while, so we can figure out what's next. Once it's locked up, see if you can help that guy in the gutter."

"Got it," Eric said, fumbling for the door handle.

I kneed the cruiser's door open, cradled the shotgun in my arms, and sprinted towards the house.

I darted around the twelve or so shouting men and their six—no, seven rifles. They never looked away from the spectacle as my athletic shoes pounded over the grass as I curved towards the single-story brick house. Like most of the cheap boxes built the previous century, this one was a brick square maybe thirty feet on a side. Small windows sitting high in the walls surrounded a grungy pair of larger double-hung windows in the living room. The blue wooden door stood open in the intact frame.

As my feet touched the aluminum threshold, someone screamed behind me.

I stopped and whirled.

Eric stood maybe twenty feet away, dancing with adrenaline and impatience, eyes switching between me and the brown-pelted monster. The man attacked by the creature sagged against the thick oak tree, face even more bloody. One slash crossed his eye, and blood poured down his cheek. The exhausted man hunched forward, waving his rifle defensively, but moving it more like a fan than a club. The ex-dog, walking forward stiff-legged, snapped and barked, its tentacles lashing the air even faster.

Why hadn't I gotten a damn Taser?

I snatched a fist-sized rock from the dead earthen flowerbed beside the door and hurled it at the four-legged horror. "Hey! Fido!"

The rock struck the creature's gaunt pelvis and dropped to the ground.

The creature yipped and whirled.

I grabbed another rock and whipped it at the monster. "Here, boy!"

The monster snapped at the rock as it hit the ground a foot in front of it. It looked up from the rock and locked eyes with me before sprinting into motion.

I hopped backwards a step, turned, and ran.

The Catboxes all were laid out the same: a living room immediately inside the front door, with a counter separating that space from the cramped kitchen, and a side hall leading to the two bedrooms, the tiny bath, and the stairs down to the dirt-floored half basement. Eric and

I had searched every one of these homes for survivors only a couple weeks ago, and I'd grown heartily sick of the repetitive layout. This place wouldn't fit into that memory, though—I would have remembered the shredded couch and toppled pressed-board coffee table.

Something nagged at my memory. Something important in this place. I remembered the dark green paint on the walls and the yellow Formica countertop with the scummy little microwave and the cast-iron fry pans on the kitchen wall. The stink was new, though, a thick animal reek that clotted in my throat every time my chest heaved for air.

No time to wonder. I pounded through the living room towards the kitchen.

Something crashed into the half-open front door, slamming it back against the wall.

My shoes slipped on the kitchen's dusty blue linoleum, upper body tilting back to the edge of falling. I yanked myself forward and felt my balance return barely in time.

The ex-dog snarled. Its toenails dug deeply into the tightly woven living room carpet, coming free with tiny snaps as it charged. Strange that I could hear that over its tortured breathing.

I flung myself around the corner into the mudroom at the back door.

And ran straight into something tall and boxy. Sharp edges gouged my chest and punched my breath free from my body. I bounced back, stumbling, wheezing.

My grip weakened on the shotgun I'd carried from the cruiser, its barrel striking the edge of a kitchen cupboard, sending a shock down my arm. I tried to catch the shotgun, fumbled it into motion, and slammed the barrel harder into the counter. The shotgun dropped heavily to clatter against the linoleum.

My fingers tingled from the impact, but I barely noticed. The aches in my chest matched up perfectly with the dusty off-white shapes in front of me. I'd rammed into four massive window air conditioners, the old illegal Freon kind, stacked in the mudroom, blocking the door.

Each air conditioner must have weighed eighty pounds.

The doorknob showed clearly to the side of the stack of air conditioners, but it didn't matter. I wasn't nearly strong enough to pull the door open past that kind of weight.

Now, too late, I remembered why the house seemed familiar. When Eric and I had passed through, I'd seen these air conditioners and laughed, thinking of all the contraband we'd found in almost every house we searched. I'd wondered if the guy hoarding the air conditioners could actually get Freon.

I hadn't wondered if they would be the death of me.

The ex-dog snarled at my heels.

Changing air pressure hummed against my eardrums.

I heard a thud.

Eric had slammed the front door.

Chapter 20

THE HORRIFIC ex-dog must have slowed to savor feasting on my innards, but it still closed fast, only a yard or two away. Any moment, its razor-thin tentacles would slash my back, my face, my throat.

Coppery fear bulged in my throat. My planned exit through the mudroom, blocked by three hundred and twenty pounds of air conditioners.

The narrow window, set high in the wall of the greasy kitchen, wouldn't pass Alice. No escape that way. Nothing else. Nowhere else.

Trapped.

Toenails razored holes in the linoleum with the creature's every step. Something sliced the air by my ear.

I flung myself forward into the cramped mudroom, turning sideways to squeeze through the narrow gap between the door frame and the air conditioners.

Half a dozen tentacles clanged against the air conditioners' aluminum shells. The ex-dog growled, a metallic tang of frustration lending it sharpness it didn't need.

My back slammed against the wall-mounted shelves opposite the doorway as I scanned for any kind of weapon. Gallon jugs of laundry soap—what was I going to do, make myself too slippery to catch? A pegboard on one side held a haphazard collection of cheap, rust-spotted pliers and screwdrivers. An empty hook should have held a hammer, but someone always takes the damn hammer.

I grabbed the next best thing, swinging the broom to my front just as the ex-dog's head filled the gap into the mudroom.

The K-9 guys and their well-trained charges had always touched me with jealousy. Police dogs were incredibly loyal and so well trained that they functioned as an extension of their handler's will. The bond between officer and dog looked stronger than that between human partners. The Detroit officer who'd taken a bullet for his dog wasn't an anomaly. The bond went beyond friendship, gifting the dogs with an almost civilized presence.

This was not one of those dogs.

Yellow-stained teeth flashed between pale gums and flapping black lips. Brilliant blue eyes shone under pointed ears lined with thick black fur. The creature had no spare flesh, though brown-furred skin hung loose off the skull and the thick brown ruff hung limp from its chest. Black fur circled the eyes and haloed the ears. At the ends of the gaunt legs, bony feet ticked against the dusty linoleum. Stupidly, it actually seemed to matter that I could name the breed it had once been: Rottweiler.

Half a dozen long, thin tentacles sprouted from its shoulders and lashed through the air.

I clutched the broom's brush end and stabbed the hard wooden handle at the ex-dog's face.

The creature growled and hopped back, carefully just out of reach. Tentacles slashed the air over its shoulders, but the narrow gap between doorframe and air conditioners didn't let it bring them into play. Yet.

In another minute or two, when I didn't come out the back door, Eric would realize the plan had gone wrong. I'd come to know Eric pretty well over the last couple of weeks. Big and deliberate, he wasn't slow. But he wouldn't be quick enough. Nobody could ever be quick enough to beat one of Absolute's bastard children.

The dreg that had been Alice's father had taught me that once something devolved, its shape changed like water. They could change to meet any challenge. Given the minute or two I'd need for Eric to come help, the ex-dog would reshape itself to charge through that gap. Once through, it would tear me into extra-chunky dog food in seconds.

The dog lunged forward, shoulders slamming into the aluminum frames of the air conditioners, shacking the stack. Metal cases hummed like busted bells.

I stabbed with the broom handle.

The creature danced back easily.

The damn thing hadn't *really* been trying to get me.

It had been testing my responses.

Rotties are smart.

Damn smart.

I needed a better solution—quickly.

Always keeping my face to the dog, holding the broom pointed at the creature's body, I searched the mudroom with my eyes. A small modern furnace huddled beside the back door, the air conditioners looming over it. The tools hanging from the pegboard were more dangerous than the broom, but I didn't want to get close enough to stab it with a screwdriver. And if guns didn't stop one of us—even when we weren't maddened and transformed—I had no reason to think that a Phillips Number Three would do any better.

I coughed, the mudroom's sharp chemical smell cutting through the creature's animal funk. Acetone? Something. Maybe I could burn it.

I glanced down. Old paint cans lined the floor behind me, beneath the shelves. A couple of rectangular metal cans with colorful labels stood to the side. Paint thinner?

The second my gaze moved down for a better look, the creature lunged. I jabbed the broom, splinters from the handle digging into my palms. The handle stabbed into the dog's gaunt forehead, the wood momentarily bending with the force of its lunge, before snapping straight and flinging the dog back.

Fire, I'd need fire. Something to ignite the thinner. If it was thinner.

I didn't carry a lighter.

If I got out of here, my first stop was the party store five blocks away and the rack of lighters on display behind the cash register.

My heart hammered. Sweat soaked my back and armpits. Fire? I didn't have that kind of time!

An extension cord! Strip the female end, electrify it—no, Eric had cut the power on our first visit.

The ex-Rottie fell back a step, its eyes fixed on my face. I watched, fascinated, as the creature's shoulders shrugged slightly and settled back into place. Was it losing weight even as I watched?

I pressed back against the shelves, needing to be as far from the door as possible. I didn't want to die here. I was *not* going to be eaten by *another* alien creature. Wooden shelves pressed lines into my shoulders, my spine, my buttocks. Metal and plastic handles dug into my back, corners gouged my kidneys. Something crunched and rustled against my head.

Get it together, Holtzmann! Use your damn brain. Figure it out. Maybe I could topple the top air conditioner into the gap, then knock the second one onto it. If I could reach the tiny window in the back door, I could break it and yell for help. I couldn't crawl through, but I could summon help.

The creature sat, watching me. Fist-sized clots of blood tarred its coat, the scrawny muscles beneath twitching every few seconds. I could swear the damn thing smiled, seemed to know it had me trapped. The tentacles waved lazily, like seaweed.

I kept the broom level.

It barked, twice.

I edged towards the far corner, my back tight against the shelves. My head slid off the crinkling surface and scraped against the raw edge of the fiberboard shelf. I'd had my head pressed against a stack of heavy paper bags.

Paper bags of dog food.

Three fifty-pound bags of cheap dry dog food, stacked one atop the other on the top shelf, where the dog couldn't get at it.

I glanced at the creature—at the food—at the creature.

The ex-dog stared impassively, its gaze locked on my face.

Clutching the broom in my right hand, ready to bluntly spear the creature, I reached up with my left and crinkled the lowest bag of dog food.

The creature's rear end wiggled. Tentacles withdrew to coil neatly on its flanks. Its whines still carried the metallic undertone, but the cocked head robbed it of malice.

I grabbed the top bag in one hand. One tug, and it plunged to the floor beside me.

The ex-dog held itself utterly still from the ribs forward, but the stump of a tail wiggled madly.

Chapter 21

ERIC'S VOICE squeezed through the high window at the back of the kitchen. "Kevin! You there?"

"I'm all right!" I shouted, not taking my eyes from the spectacle on the kitchen floor or my hand off the broom. "Back door's blocked. Come in the front."

A few seconds later the front door creaked open. "Kevin?"

"Back here."

Eric tromped up beside me. "What—oh, wow."

I'd given up refilling the big dog dish, instead just tearing open the huge bag of chow and letting the ravenous Rottie devour mouthfuls as quickly as possible. He'd already eaten half the bag, scattering bits of kibble across the smeary linoleum into the tiny gaps beneath the stove and refrigerator. The Rottie attacked kibble with a single-minded focus, crunching and swallowing as quickly as he could.

But the dog's tentacles had retracted back into its shoulders. Fresh muscle swelled between the ribs, and that hollow stomach had started to inflate. Eyes closed, the dog hunted individual kernels of food with its nose and tongue. With only a couple minutes of eating, it looked less like a monster and more like a cruelly starved pet. What I had thought was a thick alien stench filling the house was only the musk of a trapped, starving animal.

The loose skin over the Rottie's face twitched and shifted, inflating as fresh tissue grew over bone.

"What's going on out there?" I said.

"They're doing first aid on the guy who got shot," Eric said.

"Shot? How—no. They got excited. Started shooting, got one of their own."

"Yep. How'd you know?"

"I saw it every hunting season."

The dog licked its lips and looked up at us.

Fresh sweat erupted on my back. I hefted the broom and took a step backwards.

The Rottie looked between Eric and me. His back end wagged

twice, the stump of a tail wiggling frantically. Toenails clicked on linoleum as he started towards us.

I took another step backwards, holding the broom in front of me.

The dog hugged the wall, staying just out of broom range, as it slipped into the hall leading to the back of the house. Seconds later, I heard the sound of lapping.

The dog might have starved, but a toilet had kept thirst away.

"You're feeding him that dry crap?" Eric said.

"It was what was here!"

I made myself relax as the dog came back into the hall, deliberately holding the broom at my side instead of as a barrier.

"You gotta get better food for him," Eric said.

"I'm not keeping him."

"Why not?" Eric held out a hand as the Rottie trotted back to the kitchen, head held high and ears perked. "Gonna be a beautiful animal when he gets some meat on him. Smart, too."

"I've got my hands full with the girls."

"Someone's gotta take him."

Kibble crunched.

"Why don't you?" I said. "Look, I have to get out front before these guys start shooting something else." I offered Eric the broom. "Can you keep an eye on the dog?"

"Don't need a stick for a good boy like him."

This isn't a dog, I wanted to say. *It's a monster.*

Eric's set jaw and suddenly hard eyes, even through the smeared ash and cinders, told me he knew my thoughts and didn't care.

"Fine. Just—" I gave up and leaned the broom against the kitchen counter. "There's more kibble in the mudroom."

I left the house with Eric murmuring to the dog. I'd never taken Eric for a dog person—at least, not the sort who confused dangerous animals with the stuffed variety. Human dregs didn't recover if you fed them, but the dog seemed to be on his way back.

And where had the dog come from, anyway? Eric and I would have noticed it when we searched this house before. Had it somehow climbed into the house and gotten trapped? Was it really a dog, or was Absolute playing with us?

Keeping one ear open for Eric's screams, I made myself step outside.

Outside, one wounded man sprawled at the foot of the big oak tree. Another lay at the far side of the street. Men in mismatched camouflage outfits stood around them, offering advice. A scrawny guy knelt by the tree, pulling bandages from a first-aid kit. After the closed-in fug that passed for air inside the house, June's muggy heat felt fresh and clean.

Every part of me ached as if I'd spent a couple hours in a spinning concrete mixer. A dull ache throbbed behind my left eye. But I needed to stop these men from turning any more animals into monsters, and that meant I had to take charge.

Walking to the closer group, I made my voice firm. "Let me guess." Faces turned to me. "You opened the door. You saw the dog. You shot it."

"It came at us!" said a chunky middle-aged guy wearing a gray urban camo shirt and green-and-black splattered shorts, a rifle slung over his shoulder.

"It was hungry." I eyed his rifle. "That rifle does about nine hundred rounds a minute, right? So your thirty-round magazine made it, what, two seconds? You're damn lucky only one of you got shot." My pulse thumped in my temples, and my breath shook. "Unless you idiots shot more than one and hid the bodies?" I knew it was too personal even as I said it, my adrenaline and frustration leaking out my mouth.

"You got no call to be talking to us like that," Camo Shorts said. "You're not a cop. You told Woodward that and everything."

I needed to cool off. I needed an experienced partner to take over for a moment so I could catch my breath. "You're one of his people? You're right. I'm not a cop. I'm just the man who kept that dog from slicing your friend to lunch meat." I looked down. "How is he?"

The prone man groaned.

The man holding a patch of gauze over the wounded man's face said, "That damn thing took Will's eye!"

"That dog had been locked in that house for days, starving. You opened the door, it ran for freedom, you filled it full of bullets. I'd call you even." Eric and I had checked that house, what, ten days ago? There was no dog. I hadn't seen a dog in Frayville since Absolute released us.

Absolute changing the rules, again.

"Even!" shouted the wounded man. "I lost an eye!"

"Eat a melon." I started toward the road crowd, raising my voice. "It'll heal."

After the mayhem in the house, the neighborhood felt still and silent. The small knots of talking men somehow gave perspective to the vast silence around us. Somewhere distant, a car growled. The warm breeze rustled leaves overhead. If I hadn't known better, this could have been a quiet Sunday morning outside tourist season, before anyone knew of Absolute, before humanity burned the Earth to ash.

But half a block further from Main Street, a dreg wobbled in the shade of a melon tree: a gaunt figure in jeans and a flannel shirt. His head looked misshapen. I didn't want to look closer to find out why.

Had these trees exploded out of the ground? The grass? Stepping off the alien grass and onto the asphalt road dissolved a thread of tension in my spine that I hadn't noticed before.

The prone man in the road looked up as I approached. "Thank you for coming so quickly, Detective." Blood soaked his shirt through the wad of gauze jammed against his shoulder. Despite his obvious agony, he sounded clear and coherent. "I will be well." He heaved in a breath. "Thanks to you."

"You can't be all right," said a flabby good old boy kneeling beside the injured man.

"I'm not." The injured man spoke around gasps of air. "It hurts like a son of a bitch. But fighting doesn't help pain. You have to accept it."

I stopped. Pendleton's message made a lot more sense. "Acceptance, I presume."

"And Otto Dow."

"Holy shit!" The flabby man simultaneously tried to get off his knees and throw himself backwards, and succeeded only in tumbling onto his spine, hitting his head on the asphalt with a thump like a drum before clawing up the tree behind him and to his feet. He stared at Otto's drying blood on his hands, then frantically rubbed his palms on his pants.

The other men took a step or two back. One glanced at Otto and scurried towards the other ring of men.

"You didn't tell them?" I said.

Otto started to shrug, then clenched his teeth and hissed. "They—they didn't ask."

Acceptance members I'd met had never introduced themselves as such. I'd noticed that underlying equilibrium every time—or had I? How many people were in Acceptance, anyway?

I found myself mentally flipping through the people I knew like mug shots. What about Alice and Ceren? No—listening to them talk for three minutes would convince anyone they were full-on teenage girls. No, they couldn't accept anything, good or bad. Eric was kind of placid, but no, he'd always been that way. Jack the bartender? Too happy. Woodward? I should be so lucky—no, that would be bad.

I made myself breathe deeply. Someone had too much cologne. Familiar cologne. "It's considered polite to introduce yourself."

"I'll remember that," Otto said. His face was pale.

"Are they coming for you?" I asked.

"Don't know," Otto said. "Can't feel them."

"Freak," someone stage-whispered behind me. I ignored it.

"So what happened?"

"We're searching houses."

"What for?"

"People," said a sinewy man just beside me. He stuffed tobacco into his unshaven cheek and spit onto the road near Otto's head.

"Resources," Otto said. "Cataloging. What's—" he grimaced "—around?"

"And people," someone said behind me.

I knew I'd smelled that cologne before. I nodded and kept facing Otto. "So did Woodward put you up to this, Danny?"

Danny stepped out from behind the other two men who just happened to have been standing between him and me. He wore jeans and a brand-new button-down shirt still sharply creased from packaging. "*Mister* Woodward asked us to get a list of people living down here, and see what kind of gear we could find. We'll need to know what we have to work with so we can get things going again." He barely came up to my chin, but carried himself straight as if trying to substitute posture for inches. Even though it must have hurt his ability to grab the medium-caliber pistol holstered at his hip, each finger still bore a gold ring. He wore a clunky walkie-talkie on his other hip.

"And making a list means you go running around armed like the Michigan Militia?"

Danny shuffled forward. "It's useful work. We're not lounging around like some of those lazy, useless people. There's too much to do, and not nearly enough time for it. And at least *we're* not running off on our own, doing whatever random hobby we feel like."

I didn't let the dig catch. "So tell me. Did Woodward have you search the houses marked with caution tape?"

"Nope," Danny said, his words radiating enough fellowship and willing cooperation to make me nauseous. "We just started here, on this street."

"Danny, you should tell the truth," Otto said. "Woodward specifically asked us to search these houses."

Danny glared at Otto.

Otto flashed a carefree grin through his obvious pain. "Detective Holtzmann's smart. He'll figure out if you lie."

"So Woodward deliberately sent you into buildings we'd already searched," I said. "*That's* why you have all the guns."

"You don't know what's in these places," said Tobacco-Chewer, launching another load. This one hit only a foot from Otto's head. Otto reflexively closed his eyes.

"Yes, we do," I said. "Eric and I searched them already."

Danny smirked. "So you left that monster in there on purpose so it could rip Will's face off?"

"I don't know how that dog got in there." I didn't *know* how it got in there, but I had a sick feeling in my gut that I could make a pretty good guess. "But I am sure it attacked you *because you shot it*. You saw a starving dog and completely lost your cool."

"That's not a dog," Danny said.

"It was a Rottie," Otto said.

Danny whirled. "Shut up, you freak."

Tobacco-Chewer spat another wad of juice. This on landed maybe six inches from Otto's curly brown hair. This time, Otto didn't blink. Tobacco-Chewer glared even harder.

"Knock that off," I said to Tobacco-Chewer. "You have a whole street to spit in. Use it." Now *that* was a sentence Kevin had never said during his whole police career.

Tobacco-Chewer's chest inflated and he turned his glare on me.

"Cool it, Kenny," Danny said.

The man deflated slightly, then deliberately turned and spat a gob of thick, brown spit onto the asphalt a yard from my feet.

I looked away from Kenny, surveying faces around me. "The point is, the only things guns do now is cause pain. Shooting one of these things will only anger it, and they don't deal well with anger."

"That just ain't true," Kenny the Tobacco Fan said. "I been hunting. Bagged me a nice deer."

"You've talked to Deckard, our local hunter, haven't you?" I said. "Then you know you've got to do it right. Panic fire, spray-and-pray—you only clip what you're shooting at and it'll get real ugly for you. Except people. People know better than to believe we can survive getting shot. When you fill us full of bullets, we die."

"Some things don't change, I guess," Kenny said, his words blurred by the spit in his mouth.

"They're our guns," said the chunky man who had been doing first aid on Otto. "You can't take them away from us. We have rights."

"I'm not taking anything away from anybody," I said. "I'm just reminding you that firearms—they don't really matter anymore. I"—*Kevin*—"I was a Detroit cop. Before. I've shot more rounds than most of you. Do you think I'd quit carrying my piece if it had any use at all?" I slapped my belt. "You want to defend yourself? Try a Taser. Maybe Mace." Mace might be good. I needed a Taser, and Mace, and a lightning thrower. "The only thing you're doing with those guns out here is shooting up houses that someone might have wanted to live in."

"You're no cop anymore," someone said. The crowd around me had grown thicker, as men drifted from Will's boring first aid to our exciting argument.

"That's right," I said. "I'm not a cop, I'm a copy. The other side of that is, you don't have any rights to protect you from the consequences of your own stupidity."

Narrow eyes stared above tight lips and clenched jaws. Their silent glares made Frayville's surrounding quiet even deeper.

A sudden knot of fear stuck in my throat. I tried to keep it from my expression as I met one set of eyes after another. Everyone here, including me, had lost our families, our future, our species. We all groped to find our way, looking to build an attachment to anyone any way we could.

Firearms were a big part of northern Michigan life. Back Before, Michigan north of Flint played home to more hunters than any other part of the country. Many people collected guns, and had made owning firearms an integral part of their lives and their identities.

I'd just kicked that in the teeth.

I was correct, firearms were useless—but reminding them of that only reminded them of what they'd lost when Absolute created them.

Fists clenched. Feet shifted. In a thousand subtle details, Danny's crew crept from angry towards violent.

Without a useful weapon, nothing could keep this crew from overwhelming me except my minuscule animal magnetism and charm. I'd survived a bullet through the heart once, so I knew I wouldn't die. Not easily.

But they didn't have to kill me to do the worst kind of damage. They could crack my skull and turn me into old lady Reamer, or something like Suit. And every time they saw my mindless body shuffling around, I would remind them just how macho they were.

Danny smiled broadly and chuckled. "Tell you what, Detective Holtzmann." He spread his hands. "We think our guns are a good idea. But if you really think they're that much trouble, why don't you talk to the boss about it? You know, the expert the government sent to be in charge?" He lifted one hand to point behind me, past the short, dark-haired man.

Lyle Woodward's huge gasoline-driven SUV idled up the street towards us, sunlight glinting off the mirrored windows.

Chapter 22

THE URGE to violence leaked out of the crowd like air from a punctured lung. My shoulders sagged slightly as part of my tension dissolved.

What had promised to be an epic beating on an isolated street crumbled into a bunch of crooked union thugs waiting for the boss to proclaim my fate. The dozen men around me softened their stances, turning their attention from my lone self in their midst to the monster SUV strutting to a stop against the curb some ten feet away, in the shade of a maple towering on the easement between the sidewalk at the road.

Lyle Woodward came across as a blowhard, trying to leverage his prior position as the Building the Future lead for Frayville to sweet-talk his way back to the top. But while Eric and I had been trying to find and help people, this particular blowhard went and assembled a private army.

When the entire population of the world is a mere two hundred people, a dozen men willing to use force is formidable.

The tiny Catbox homes along the street suddenly looked even more empty, as if any potential witnesses had drawn their shades and turned up their televisions. Bright, coppery fear tainted the back of my throat. The June sun might be slicing the residential street into circles of leafy shade and light, but we might as well have been at an isolated shipping dock at midnight, with fog obscuring the few lights.

"Good day, Kevin!" Woodward said as he slammed the car door. "What brings you out with my friends?"

"Gunshots," I said. "Lots and lots of gunshots." I held a hand out at Otto, sprawled at my feet, still pressing the blood-soaked gauze to his shoulder. "Your friends shot each other trying to kill a dog."

"Weren't a dog," said short Kenny around his wad of tobacco.

"Was so a dog," called Eric.

Eric stood outside the front door of the nearest house. His teeth and the whites of his eyes still stood out against the cinders and ash smeared on his skin and clothes. The Rottie sat beside him, brown-masked face cheerful, tongue lolling out. The skin had filled out over the bones. What had been a gaunt horror now seemed a young healthy animal.

Eric held a chain leash in one relaxed hand. "Cuddles here just needed a really good meal. She hadn't eaten in days." He started towards us. The dog hopped up with him, keeping at his heel so well that the short lead remained slack, steel rings glittering in the sun.

Woodward nodded. "So. A dog." His eyes took in Otto lying on the road, and Will prone beneath the tree holding a bloody rag to his missing eye. "Danny, we need to talk. This can't happen again. You need to watch out for your men."

Danny's lips tightened. "Yes, sir."

"You heard the gunshots and came running?" Woodward said to me.

"Something like that. They need to be more careful with their guns. Who knows how many bullets got fired off here?" I looked around. "I'd be shocked if nobody else got shot. Not to mention how much damage stray rounds did."

"Indeed." Woodward studied his crew. "This didn't go well. Shooting citizens is unacceptable. Clearly we need more suitable tools."

I felt it coming even before his gaze sharpened and sliced towards me.

"Having the suitable tools would help ensure that we have no more tragedies such as today, no more of our precious citizens being hurt. That's why I must insist you give us a flamethrower."

"For this crew?" I laughed. "Not a chance."

The men around me shifted angrily.

"Surely you see—"

I held my chin up and tone firm. "Remember what I asked you about fire discipline? These guys don't have *any*. I'm sure they're great hunters, but downtown? Something surprised them and they filled the whole block with bullets." I waved a hand at Eric coming up beside me. "All because Fido here was starving?"

"Cuddles," Eric said. "Found her collar on the counter."

"*Fine*. Cuddles. If they had a flamethrower, half the neighborhood would be going up."

Woodward nodded. "I thought the caution tape meant you had checked the houses. I don't think too much of your search if you missed the dog the first time around."

"I have no idea how he got in the house," I repeated, this time feeling even more of a fraud. I did have an idea, a pretty good idea, but I didn't know. Even when I checked my idea, I'd let Woodward figure it out on his own.

"She," Eric said. "Cuddles's a she."

"Fine!" I said. "*She* wasn't here when we searched the first time."

Woodward nodded, eyebrows raised. "As you say." He raised his voice slightly. "You didn't think of anything as elementary as taking an inventory as you searched these homes, which is why I'm having my most capable and prepared men follow after you and clean up your mess. We must know what we have to work with, so we are prepared for the next disaster."

"What makes you think you'll be dealing with it?"

Woodward looked professionally somber, his attitude conveying that he was so very sad that I couldn't grasp something as simple as Frayville's desperate need for proper leadership. "As much as I admire your willingness to help people, an organized team is always more effective than a lone cowboy waving his…authority, or lack thereof, around. We must be ready."

Suddenly, I saw his end game so bright and clear it was as if he'd flown a broom through the blue sky overhead and described it in detail using smoke signals.

Nobody knew what Absolute had planned for us, why it released us, or why it even *created* us. Or whatever came next might be a natural disaster. Or a human error that triggered an escalating nightmare. Maybe something as predictable as the Frayville water plant failing. But something would go wrong. Eventually. Inevitably.

When the next disaster hit, and it would, Woodward would be ready.

He'd move against it. With his men.

He'd demand cooperation. With a team of people already working on the problems, and with no time to argue, anyone would go along.

Let them cope with the problem and we live. Get in the way and we die.

He would stop the disaster. I saw that now. He'd stop the disaster because he was an ass, but a competent ass. The only problem was, when the disaster ended, he'd be the man in charge.

The worst part was, he was right. A posse always beats the lone cowboy.

And if a disaster didn't happen on Woodward's schedule…an unguarded water-treatment plant wouldn't be all that difficult to sabotage.

Woodward looked at me as if he could read my mind. "Clearly the houses you've searched aren't always abandoned." He sighed, the weight of the world and all its intolerable short-sighted selfish idiots pressing down on his noble shoulders. "If you insist on hoarding, there's nothing I can do to stop you. That doesn't mean we won't look around ourselves to see if you missed anything. If my men do find some horrible creature in one of these houses, how do you suggest we deal with it?"

I gritted my teeth. knowing I was going to regret this, but also knowing I had no choice. "Eric, may I have your handset?" Eric reached past Cuddles and dropped his radio into my hand. I punched a few buttons on the digital radio, changing the settings before handing the device to Woodward. "That's set to contact my handset and my cruiser. If they really find something that needs burning, they can call for backup. Call me for stupid crap and I'll take it right back."

Woodward's hand closed around the handset. My fingers didn't want to let go for what would be the last time I'd touch it. I knew *he'd* never return it. "That's enough for now."

"Sit, Cuddles," said Eric. "Good girl!"

"Danny," Woodward said, holding out the handset. "Maybe you and Timmy can discuss who should carry this."

"Sure thing," Danny said.

I glanced around. "You lot. Firearms can't help you. Leave them home." Ignoring the glares and mutters, I nodded at Woodward. "I'll leave you to your inventory, gentlemen. If you should find anyone who hasn't come out, do try to persuade them to eat."

I turned, Eric beside me, and took two steps when the burly guy who'd done first aid on Will said, "Hey, hang on. He can't take that dog."

I stopped. "Excuse me?"

Danny said, "That damn thing took Will's eye. It's dangerous."

The Rottie wagged her rear end.

"She's harmless," Eric said. "You shot her."

"A dog what's bit someone once'll do it again," someone on the far side of the group said. "Everyone knows that."

"Man who's shot a dog will do it again," Eric said.

Someone said, "Gotta put it down."

"Gimme that leash," Danny said. His smile glittered. He clearly didn't care about the dog, at all. But we'd defied him, and won. This was his chance to knock us back down.

Eric drew his chest up. "Not a chance."

I glanced at Eric, at Danny, at Woodward. The men around us stood a little taller. Hands were clenching into fists.

Dammit, were we going to fight over a dog?

Eric glared at Danny.

Cuddles edged closer to Eric. Her tail stopped wagging, and she showed Danny a tooth.

Yep. Time for a good old-fashioned beat-down of epic proportions.

Chapter 23

AS A brawling arena, the middle of the street has a lot to recommend it. My feet wouldn't slip on the asphalt. The sun, high overhead, wouldn't get in my eyes, and the surrounding trees even cast nice shade. It wasn't full of heavy or sharp pieces of stuff that could be used to brain me, like an alley or a junkyard would be. Frayville didn't have any traffic to speak of, so the beat-down wouldn't get called on account of oncoming vehicles.

The only problem with the arena was that Eric and I were in it, surrounded by a dozen angry men. The kind of men who went hunting and fishing every weekend, who worked with their hands and their backs. Tough, burly men who wouldn't think twice about hauling a load of bricks across the yard or dragging a gutted elk three miles back to the truck. They'd heave and huff about how heavy it was afterwards, but they'd never think it was too heavy.

Police have to stay in shape, but exercise muscle is different than labor muscle. And I already felt incredibly battered. Even with Eric at my side, and Cuddles at my side, any brawl would quickly turn to a beating.

Eric wasn't going to surrender the dog.

And looking at him, neither was I.

Otto lay near my feet. The stink of his blood coagulating infused the green summer breeze with a bitter coppery taint. I felt him tensing, as if preparing to scramble out of the way. These men didn't like Acceptance. I couldn't blame them—the thought of people forming a mental bond at a touch unnerved me too. Once they finished beating Eric and I, Otto would probably get a few kicks too.

Cuddles the Rottweiler, standing between Eric and me, grew rigid. Her rear end stilled, not even making a pretense of wagging. Her ears flicked from side to side.

Lyle Woodward lounged against the large SUV, carefully avoiding putting a wrinkle in his immaculate suit. I knew his type. He wouldn't *order* them to beat us, but he sure wouldn't stand in the way either. At least, not until Eric and I learned a little humility. A dozen men, each with two punches and a kick for Eric and the same for me, would inflict a whole lot of damage before Woodward called them off.

I didn't move. My pulse throbbed in the back of my throat. With each second, tension stretched my nerves further.

I wouldn't start the fight. I wished I could be certain I'd be the one to end it, though.

Beside me, Eric's knuckles popped as he rolled his beefy hand into a fist. The tiny noise felt loud in the silent suburb.

I *really* wanted to call for backup.

Kevin was the cop. And he was dead. I was just a copy. Too slow to make any difference.

"Excuse me, gentlemen?" said someone behind me.

I knew that voice, and wanted to simultaneously sag with relief and prepare to fight harder.

Heads turned.

Veronica Boxer stood a few feet back, still in the pale green pantsuit she'd worn at St Michael's Church this morning. The gemstone rings on her fingers cast sparkling rainbows in the sunlight. She carried herself like a favorite aunt.

Immediately behind her and to one side slouched teenaged Rick. His half-head of black hair hung neatly over his right ear and eye. Silver rings shone in his nose and left ear.

I didn't recognize the older gentleman in a neat linen suit, leaning on a brass-headed cane next to Rick. I didn't know the three people standing behind them. But I knew who they had to be.

"Always a pleasure to see you, Acceptance," I said.

The crystallizing anger around us broke. Men started glancing between me and Eric, between Boxer and Otto, lying bleeding on the pavement.

"Good day to you, Detective Holtzmann," Veronica said. I'd heard that tone from elementary school teachers and successful business executives. It was a good day, because she declared it so. But it could just as easily become the worst day of your life, if she decided that. With a lot of practice, that voice can sound hard as stone. Veronica's voice sounded like the steel hammer that broke that stone into gravel.

Every time I'd seen Rick before, the half-shaven teenage boy had been smiling. Not today.

All six of them looked somber and serious. Standing in a wedge with Boxer at their tip, they looked like a spearhead aimed straight to the heart of the group of men.

Right next to me, almost close enough for me to swing a fist, Danny said, "What do you want?"

Boxer turned her head slightly to face Danny, moved her lips in a way that might have generously been called a smile, and held out one hand, palm up. "Our friend Otto is hurt. We thank you for taking good care of him. But he really needs to get home and get some rest now." She tsk'd her tongue against her teeth. "Otto, Jim told you to be careful today."

"Yes," Otto said. He leveraged himself up on his good elbow, holding the arm with his wounded shoulder tight against his chest. "Jim did, indeed, ask me to be careful. But you know how it is. These things happen. It's not anybody's fault, I'll be fine."

Danny glanced between Otto and Boxer. "Hang on, he was sneaking around, trying to capture some of us normal—"

"Otto was not sneaking, young man." Boxer raised her chin, meeting Danny's eyes, then dragging them into an alley for a smaller type of beat-down. "When you asked for help, you didn't ask anyone for their qualifications, experience, or background. He volunteered. You took him, gladly. You did not ask if he knew Acceptance."

"That's how it is? That's how you want this to go?" A sneer curled Danny's mouth, exposing a cracked canine tooth on the upper left. "Fine. That's how we'll play it."

The tension in the crowd shifted. The very idea of Acceptance disturbed a lot of people. People joined the comforting mental network in moments of extreme despair, often right after they failed to commit suicide. Some people thought Acceptance was all about finishing the job razor and poison couldn't complete. That sort of outlook had to leave them twitchy. But right now, the six people in front of us formed an eerily still and severe wedge. Any group of people, no matter how intent on their purpose or how close they felt, showed a little variation. Even identical twins show identical feelings differently, with a slightly different twist of the mouth or a clenched jaw or eyebrows bent inward.

Boxer and her little group all had identical expressions.

Shivers I didn't dare show tickled my spine.

Touching someone from Acceptance wasn't enough to join them, as far as I knew. But the touch was a necessary part—again, as far as I knew. Which meant you needed tools to have a brawl with them. None of the men around us looked ready to swing a punch and come into contact with any of Acceptance.

I made my voice cheery. "You're probably just in time. Otto could use a clean shirt and a good meal, if nothing else. Food will help him heal. Did you bring a car, or does he need a ride?"

Boxer inclined her head. "Our pickup is about fifty yards back. Mister Twindle will drive it up momentarily."

I stepped to the side. "Otto shouldn't stand on his own."

The two largest men at Boxer's rear stepped forward. The good old boys around us shuffled in retreat, leaving them lots of room as they hoisted Otto in a fireman's chair.

"Come on, Eric," I said. "Time for us to go."

The twanging tension in my spine only increased as we followed Boxer's people the few yards to my police cruiser. She flashed me a quick, secret smile of gratitude as I grabbed the door to the cruiser and swung it open.

Eric urged Cuddles into his side of the cruiser and climbed in after.

"Before you go," called Woodward. He'd edged his way up to the front of his men, still looking relaxed and in charge, moving forward whenever Acceptance moved back. "Let me know if you need any help finding the fiend who attacked that old lady last night. I have a feeling you're going to need all the help you can get. Really. People are counting on you, you know."

Crap. I'd almost completely forgotten about that brutal attack, what with seeing the edge of the world, my girls and I getting attacked, dealing with demon dogs and dimwits. I had no idea where to start finding Nat Reamer's attacker. "That's what I do these days. Find people who do wrong and stop it from happening anymore."

"It is what you do, isn't it. And on that ominous note—number one? People are coming together, wondering who will be number two. We're getting organized. You can be part of that." Woodward's smile cranked wider a rehearsed degree at a time. "Or you can get dragged into it."

Nat Reamer's attacker might be the disaster Woodward waited for.

"My name's Holtzmann. Use it."

"No," Woodward said. "I don't think so. As you reminded me last night, that name doesn't belong to you. Do have a good day now."

Chapter 24

I BACKED into the driveway of another anonymous Catbox house to turn the cruiser around towards Main Street, leaving it in idle while Boxer and the Acceptance Muscle Squad moved with synchronized precision. They gathered Otto and loaded him into the bed of a gleaming blue pickup truck with a dented side fender. Once their truck hummed into gear, I pulled out, leaving Woodward surrounded by a knot of his own vehemently arguing muscle men.

In the passenger seat, with the Rottie half on his lap and half in the footwell, Eric exhaled so hard a few of Cuddles' longer ruff hairs moved. Or maybe they just moved on their own? Sweat had broken through the ash and cinders covering Eric's face. One filthy hand gripped the huge dog's chain collar, the other gently stroking her shoulder.

Cuddles' head swiveled back and forth between the road and Eric's face. We barely made the turn onto Main Street when she lunged to her paws, almost taking Eric's hand off, and shoved her blocky head out the passenger window.

"Hey!" I waved my hand to ward off the ferociously wagging rear end and tail nub smacking the air near my face.

Eric's hand came up to the dog's rump, resting on the flat of her hips by the tail nub. "Cool it, Cuddles."

If anything, Cuddles' rear wiggled even faster.

"Eric!" I stomped the brake, locking the wheels into a squealing stop in the middle of the empty Main Street. "Backseat."

"Come on, Cuddles." The Rottie seemed just as gleeful in the rear seat, her head filling the view in my side mirror, her tongue trailing into the wind.

Eric returned to his seat and belted himself in.

I sat still, my hand on the gearshift. *Relax. Breathe. Will the hammering heart to slow.*

Eric looked at me, studied my face a moment. "That almost went ugly."

He didn't mean Cuddles.

"Yeah." I let out a deep breath, trying to clear my head. "We gotta do something about Woodward." *And everything else. Everything is top priority, so nothing ever gets prioritized until it explodes.*

Eric nodded. One hand reached into the back to scratch Cuddles' flank. Cuddles' rump flailed faster.

"Okay," I said. "How about this. Let's swing by your place, let you wash and change clothes. You need another radio, so we hit the locker at the station. Take you back up to get your truck."

"Need dog food."

"Damn right you do. You don't feed this dog, I'll shoot you myself."

Eric nodded. "Let's go." As I chunked the cruiser into gear, easing us along Main Street at an easy fifteen miles an hour, just as I liked, Eric coughed.

I flicked a quick glance his way.

Eric looked…embarrassed?

"Gotta ask you something," Eric said.

"Sure."

"Kids say you got shot."

A memory of smothering darkness flickered through me. "Yeah. I did."

"How bad?"

I chewed my lower lip. Alice and Ceren had seen me take the first shot. They'd seen the bullet punch through my sternum and pop out the back of my chest. They'd seen Rose Friedman jam a hot steel rifle barrel into my mouth. I could still feel the barrel's front sight knocking against the back of my teeth.

I hadn't told them what it was like. I hadn't told anyone anything. Just remembering it sent black tendrils of unease through my soul.

"What with those guys," Eric said. "What almost happened. Might be important."

"No, I get it." I steeled myself. "Through the heart."

Eric nodded, not looking at me. "Shoulda killed you."

"Instantly. The shooter knew what she was doing."

"Don't want to poke," Eric said. "But after that—"

"I get it. You might need to know." I glanced in the rearview mirror, but only saw a giant lolling tongue trailing dog spit. "You might really need to know it." The passenger side mirror showed only vacant asphalt and abandoned businesses. Two people walked away from us, far too distant to overhear. "It's like this. I went down hard, but I had a few seconds to think. A few seconds of life. And I decided I was alive. That I wasn't going to die. That I was one of the—"

My mouth wouldn't form the word *Taken*. I made myself breathe through a mouth dry and sticky without saliva.

"I decided…I decided that if I was made out of the same stuff as—as Absolute's Taken, that I didn't have to die. Not from a bullet. So I didn't. I didn't die and my chest healed."

Eric nodded, mouth working as if he was chewing over my words. "Hurt?"

"What do you think? It hurt like a sonofabitch!"

Cuddles pulled herself back into the car and cocked her head at me.

I hadn't meant to raise my voice like that. Deliberately, I unclamped my hands from the leather-wrapped steering wheel. "Sorry. Not your fault."

"'S okay."

"You get hungry after. Really hungry. You need energy to—"

"Change."

"Yeah," I said quietly.

I turned onto Eric's street.

"It's not for sure," I said. "Guns can kill." Jesse's face, pale and shocked as blood poured from the gaping gunshot wounds in her gut. Teresa's screams of rage as Jesse crumbled. "Your body probably lives. But if you decide you're dead, the body that gets up off the ground is a dreg, not you."

"Thinkin' the best plan," Eric said, "is don't get shot."

"Always a good plan. Go with that."

I pulled the cruiser to a stop in front of Eric's tiny brick house.

"Wanna come in?" Eric asked.

I glanced in the rearview mirror. What if Eric took Cuddles in, and Cuddles went bad? If the dog transformed to a monster, best I be nearby with the flamethrower. "You've got room for either me or the dog. I'll hang here. I have to think some things through."

Eric studied his filthy hands. "Might be a few."

"I've got a lot to think about. Go on."

Eric climbed out of the car and started around to let Cuddles out. The dog saw him coming and squirmed right out the window, rolling to the ground in an undignified heap.

"Lots of dog food," I said. "Big crates of it."

Eric patted his thigh. "Cuddles!"

The dog followed him into the minuscule cottage. Any pretense of my good mood trotted right along after them.

Damn Eric for bringing up things I never wanted to think about. Not ever. *Teresa. Jesse.*

I'd shot people before. When I—when *Kevin*—was a Detroit cop, I'd shot half a dozen people. Killed two. I'd only drawn that Springfield XD in self-defense, but once drawn, I damn sure defended myself. I'd fought against seeing the headshrinkers every single time. Only after months of therapy could I even admit that I'd needed that help.

Killing people tears the soul.

Frayville didn't have a headshrinker. Absolute had apparently decided that bringing everyone back from the dead wouldn't cause anyone any sort of mental troubles. Or it didn't understand people. Or it did and just didn't give a damn.

That was the least of its crimes. Someday, I would find a way to burn that alien bastard out of the world.

I had murdered Jesse. She and Teresa had tried to suck Alice and me into a group mind of "decent" people. Whatever *decent* meant. When they failed to seduce me into joining them, they decided to take us by force. I'd tried to slow them down with the shotgun.

Four or five shells, and Jesse had kept coming. The next one put her down. I think she decided she was dead.

Her body lived. Teresa had used it as a puppet and sent it shambling after me. It hadn't turned out well. I'd returned the next day to look for Jesse's body, and found only a smear of dried blood on the asphalt.

One day I'd turn a corner and see Jesse the Dreg. I shivered at the thought.

Nope. We didn't need a headshrinker.

I shook my head to try and clear it. Absolute. Jesse. Teresa was out there, somewhere. Probably inside the circle of life surrounding our little unburned island. Or maybe she'd filled a backpack and set out for the horizon. The world couldn't have totally burned. Not completely. Could it?

I rolled my neck and rubbed my eyes. The afternoon sun warmed the car even as the tree-scented breeze carried my sweat away. I'd parked so I sat in the shade, but the leather seat would grow uncomfortably warm even so. I tasted old bile.

A dead person in a bathtub. Electrocuted. Murdered.

Nat Reamer, attacked in her home. Skull crushed.

Suit and the—the poor double-headed bastards, whatever I wanted to call them.

And the girls. Alice seemed okay, sunk into decrypting Legacy, but something had upset Ceren even if she wouldn't show it.

I sat, and ruminated, turning the complex weave of problems over in my mind like raw crystals, studying each facet for a way to slice things into more manageable shapes. I didn't have any clues, but that didn't matter. Police don't get clues. We make our own clues by talking to everyone and scrutinizing every detail over and over until we see something new. An anonymous body? An unknown assailant? That took old-school policing: get out on the street and knock on doors.

Relaxing behind the wheel, eyes half-closed, listening to the breeze in the trees and the distant gurgle of the sludgy surf, plans slowly gelled. Not great plans. Certainly not complete ones. But I'd fill in the details as I discovered more.

The quiet gave me time I desperately needed. Time for my heartbeat to slow and my aching muscles to rest. Time for my body to start repairing the day's stresses.

The warmth on my leg brought me out of my thoughts. Enough time had passed that the sun had shifted, casting a narrow slice of heat through the car window and onto my thigh. The dashboard clock said that Eric had been an hour.

Alarm crept through me. He'd been filthy, yes. But how long could a shower last? How big of a water heater did that little cottage have?

I hadn't heard anything from the dog, either.

Maybe the Rottweiler wasn't as harmless as Eric thought.

I launched myself out of the cruiser, barely bothering to slam the door behind me as I trotted up the patio square front walk to Eric's house. The place had been a cottage a generation ago, and somehow hadn't been knocked down. It couldn't be more than six hundred square feet, with tight shingles and narrow windows, almost overshadowed by the furnace's massive propane tank on the side.

The door was open a few inches. "Eric!" I shouted.

"Don't come in!" Eric sounded panicked.

"What's the matter?"

Cuddles barked as Eric said, "I—I'm tied up today. Rest of the day. You go on."

Had Cuddles become a monster? I put my hand on the door. "You need your truck."

"Be fine." Hysteria tinged his voice.

Eric had worked for the DPW. I'd talked to him after he'd found wrecked cars with the remains of the passengers still inside. Eric worked on cleaning the storm sewers in the spring, when all sorts of vileness saved up over the winter washed down the drains. He'd helped deliver a baby once, when a run to salt the roads during a terrible blizzard had gone bizarrely wrong. The man had never sounded so completely distressed.

One of the things you learn as a cop is that some of the people who most need your help most want you to leave. The sick insist they don't need a hospital. The lost demand to be let to find their own way. Just as if they'd murdered someone.

I pushed on the door. Before it could swing open, something knocked it back towards me. I stuffed my foot into the gap before the door could slam shut and used my shoulder to shove it open so I could bull my way inside.

The dimness made Eric's home seem even tinier on the inside. I blinked, trying to adjust my sight after the brilliant sunshine. An overstuffed, leprous green velour chair big enough to accommodate Eric's big frame sat in one corner, where it got a commanding view of the wall-mounted screen. A rough table next to it. Kitchenette in the other corner. The whole place smelled, even tasted, of an old wooden building with a little too much bachelor.

And Eric, on his knees behind the door. He wore clean clothes, and his cinder-free skin reflected a little light in the gloom. Cuddles stood next to him, tail low, her head on his shoulder.

Eric had his arms around the dog, face turned towards the floor.

He was shaking.

Cuddles whined.

Horror stabbed my guts, and for a heartbeat I didn't dare move. What had happened? We were made of alien stuff—*anything* could be wrong. Nightmarish images of flowing flesh poured through my brain.

"Eric?"

"Get out." He spoke without hope.

I licked my lips. "Whatever it is, man, I got your back. You know that."

Eric shook his head slowly.

"If you need some time, that's okay. I'll wait."

"Wait?" Eric suddenly hissed. "Been waiting my whole life." He lunged to his feet and glared at me. In the dim light leaking through the narrow curtained windows, I suddenly realized exactly how big Eric stood. He hadn't grown, but fear and rage gave him a whole new stature.

I blinked. Water plastered Eric's hair to his head, but his skin had a weird, dark cast. "Did—did that ash—did it not wash out?"

"It's not ash," Eric said. His hands knotted into fists. "It's me. I'm *black*."

"It's a stain? That's not—"

"It's not a fucking stain, Holtzmann!" Eric roared. "I'm *black*. I've *always* been black!"

Chapter 25

IF SOMEBODY forced me to do so, I might have guessed Eric had some Italian or Greek in his background, enough to give his skin a healthy tint. His cramped cottage even seemed like an old European house, with too much mismatched furniture packed tightly in the tiny space and the musty smell of a home that had stood against the damp for centuries. As my eyes acclimated to the gloomy interior, I made out more detail: the framed, exquisitely detailed oil painting on the wall over the couch, one fry pan and a single soup pot on the kitchenette counter next to the miniature microwave, cheap canned spaghetti on a shelf, the faint gleam of a stainless steel fixture over a single-bowl sink.

Nothing moved: not me, not Cuddles the Rottweiler, not Eric.

Eric himself stood tall and straight, eyes focused on me, teeth bared between a snarl and a grimace. The white teeth shining between his lips drove the change home to me.

Even in this gloom, Eric's skin gleamed a rich, dark chocolate brown, a thousand shades darker than it had been.

Surprise whirled my thoughts. "It's okay," I said. "We'll figure this out."

"What's to figure?" Eric growled. "'m black. Always been, only I could pass. Now everybody's gonna know."

I kept my hands open and my stance relaxed, putting lie to my heart knocking against my ribs and the pulse throbbing in my throat. I knew our bodies could change—the dregs showed that. It had happened to me, when I'd almost burned to death. But I hadn't seen a change like this.

Skin color is ordinary. We all have one. But the tone of our skin, the texture, carries so much weight, in every culture. If I'd been Eric, I would have freaked out too.

But I'd been a police officer. I knew how to deal with freaked-out people.

"It's not you," I said. "Absolute is screwing with you." I knew I was talking too fast, but couldn't seem to slow myself. "You *know* it's Absolute. But it doesn't matter, none of this matters, nothing is going to change, I'll still have your back, just like I did before."

"Like you did before, when you thought I was white," Eric spat.

"I worked in Detroit," I said. "Good men come in every color. So do assholes."

"Been lying to you all," he said. His face had an unhealthy pallor, with fresh sweat sprouting on his forehead. His shoulders shook with fear.

"No," I said. "You are who you are. You're still the man who watched out for Alice and Ceren when they came around to Jack's that first night. Remember?"

Eric didn't nod his head. Other than a slight tremor moving through his body every couple seconds, he stood motionless. Light glinted from the tear running down his face.

"So you've been passing," I said. "So what?"

Eric quivered for a moment, then took two steps and flung himself into the corner chair. The chair creaked under his bulk.

Cuddles slowly walked over and quietly slid her chin onto his knee.

"Mom watched me," he said softly, staring into a dark corner, his hand automatically finding just the right spot behind Cuddles' ear. "Every minute. If I even talked like her, or like my grandma, she'd throw me over her knee and beat me blue. Was always so sore, had to learn to sleep on my stomach. My dad, he said I had to pass. Said he loved my mom, but I couldn't be like her, had to be white, like him. If anyone knew, they'd throw me out. Never get a good school, a good job. Mom died, Dad burned all her pictures and everything, moved us up here."

"Man," I said, raising one hand to rub my forehead. "That's really messed up. Who would do that to their kid?"

Eric shook his head. "Nah. He was right. Black man got nothing. Long as nobody knows, I'm good."

"You're still good," I said. I fought to slow my voice, to keep from babbling, but the words elbowed each other to escape my mouth. "Nobody's going to put you down, nobody up here."

"They'll treat me different. Fought for the job, y'know?" Eric idly scratched Cuddles' head between her ears without taking his eyes from that empty back corner. "Fought to get it. Fought to be the best damn man in the department. Took every shit shift they had. They weren't going to catch me out for nothing."

"And that's why you're here. Because you worked. Not because of your skin color."

"They knew I was black, they wouldn't'a hired me."

Protests wanted to bubble up out of me, but I made myself stay quiet. We both needed to think.

And besides, he might be right.

Dammit, he probably *was* right. Frayville didn't have Detroit's grotesque racial problems, but I—*Kevin*—had broken up too many bar fights in this little town to say otherwise.

Cuddles shifted her head further up Eric's thigh. Her tail nub thrashed.

I wanted to babble. Drown my fear and worry in words. Instead, I carefully composed myself before speaking. "When did this happen?"

"Been getting darker for days." Eric stared into the shadowed corner behind the tall chest of drawers in the back of the house. "Kept telling myself it was just the sun. Tanning."

Eric paused.

I clamped my tongue between my teeth to hold myself silent.

"The ash," he said. "Planted my face in the ash. Walked around with you like one of those old minstrel shows. Sometime then."

"You didn't feel anything?"

Eric shook his head, still staring into space.

I knew we could change. But regrowing my heart, or healing wounds, was a wholly different thing from changing skin color. As far as anyone knew, skin tone meant nothing to Absolute—but a lot of human beings thought it meant everything. Why this specific change?

"Way I see it," I said, "you've got to decide." I kept my voice deliberately slow. "You've been a good man, long as I've known you. That didn't stop you from getting the all-expense paid trip to Hell just like the rest of us, but you got back up and made things better. Helped people."

"Even you." Eric stared at Cuddles' head. "You known me for years, but even you. You're losing your shit."

"Because you changed!" I said, louder than I intended. I took a deep breath and slowed my voice down. "Yeah, I'm freaked out. I'd be just as freaked if you turned lime green."

"Green," Eric said. "Right."

"Absolute is screwing with you. You going to let it stop you? Or are you going to keep saving this town?"

Eric snorted. "Ain't saving nothing."

Cuddles whined.

"What we have in Frayville—that is it. Everything we've got, it's right in here." I raised my hand in a vague half-circle. "Out there? It's burned. Gone. Maybe there's another town out there, somewhere—but maybe those government bastards set something up to torch the whole country. The whole world. You're the one shutting down the houses so they don't burn, or flood, or who knows what. You're making these houses last, so we have more to work with."

Eric still scratched behind Cuddles' ears, but seemed more thoughtful.

"Yeah, I'm with you, but I'm looking for people. People are easy. If I tried to shut down these houses, it'd take me all day to do one."

Eric studied the far wall, or something beyond it.

His hand behind Cuddles' ear stilled.

I fought to hold my silence. Give the man time to think.

For a breath, stillness.

Eric's hand scratched Cuddles' ear again. "Looking for people, sure but mostly old rock albums."

"Only if they're easy to find."

"Anyone have CDs that old, they'll be packed up in the basement along with the rest of Grandpa's gear."

My breathing eased. If Eric could give me grief, he'd be okay. And some things are too big to swallow all in one go. "Hey, I have classic tastes."

"Classic, like 'should be in museum'." He leaned forward to scritch Cuddles' shoulder. "An' this dog ain't gonna feed herself."

"If you stay sitting here long enough, she might munch on you."

Eric nodded, grabbed the arms of his chair, and heaved to his feet. "Right. The station?"

The tension in my ribs receded—barely—and I breathed more easily. "Sure. Open a window before we go, air this place out. You're gonna need some dog shampoo, too. A gallon of the stuff should get you going."

"Painted shut."

I wanted to ask Eric why he stayed in this dank little place when we had empty homes all around us, but he'd already exposed too much of his heart. Any more prodding and his brave façade might completely shatter. He'd worked too hard to assemble it, and I wasn't going to knock it down. "Fair enough. Radio, then drop you at your truck."

We'd get Eric on his way, and I could start digging into the murder. And worse than murder.

Chapter 26

THE VACANT, linoleum-tiled halls of the Frayville police station echoed with the dozen years I'd tromped up and down them. Eric had pulled the main breaker on our first visit two weeks ago, making the only illumination the dim amber emergency lights every few yards mingled with sunlight reflected through the one-way glass of the windows. I'd hoped that would soften some of the memories, but the change in lighting only emphasized different aspects of the abandoned precinct. I'd missed the pocks in the walls last time, but in this light they clearly stood out as scattered bullet holes. Experienced officers had resorted to panic fire. It hadn't helped. A broken fluorescent light dangled wires and ballast from a shattered fixture. The last time through, I'd looked behind the reception desk only to see rusty, long-dried blood soaking the duty officer's tall padded stool and spilling down to pool on the tile. This time I walked past without looking, but the muggy June heat gave the old blood a special rancid strength that rammed up my nostrils into my brain.

Cuddles whined and hugged Eric's flank, almost bumping him aside. "Easy, girl," Eric said, reaching down to scratch the back of her head. I'd made a point of not staring at Eric on the drive to the station. His new chocolate-brown hue made him squirm, and I didn't want to add to his discomfort.

We passed a long stretch of charred wall where someone had played a flamethrower over the non-flammable cinderblock, melting the fiberglass ceiling tiles to expose the concrete vault overhead. A few scattered, misshapen bones lay strewn on the flame-mottled tile right before the basement door.

Our flashlights picked slices out of the dank stairwell as we lumbered down. As we descended, the increasingly clammy air hugged my face like a wet cloth. Without air conditioning, mold and mildew had already set in. Perhaps we should have propped the stairwell door open, given the place a chance to air out before Michigan weather rotted out the whole building. The ring of keys rattled in my hand, reflecting shards of light through the stairwell as I fumbled for the right key. We'd locked this door. Without power to run the elevator, this stairwell was the only way into the basement cells or the secure storage. Keeping that door locked was the best way I knew to prevent the kinds of mayhem that show up in future textbooks under "What Not To Do."

I'd just closed my finger around the big silver key when Eric said, "Look."

The disk of illumination from his flashlight showed the round circle where the doorknob had been. Someone had brutally knocked the knob off the door, then attacked the lock innards.

I turned my flash to the floor, twisted metal and broken screws scattered in the light.

Putting the key ring back in my pocket, I hooked the round doorknob hole with one finger. The door pulled easily open.

I suddenly felt like I'd swallowed a brick that not only weighed down my guts but left a trail of sandy, pebbly debris on its way through my bowels. The basement of the police station had a few cells and a couple of storerooms. The evidence locker.

And the weapons locker.

I'd put a really good lock on the weapons locker.

"Come on," I said, walking quickly through the broken door.

The weapons locker was at the back of the basement, the door visible by the single, tiny green light on the electronic coded lock. The lock had a battery backup good for a year, but I'd added a heavy-duty long-tined padlock to the manual deadbolt.

The padlock lay on the floor, one tine sawed through. Someone had beaten out the deadbolt with more force than finesse.

The weight in my guts turned sour.

The electronics controlled separate deadbolts that sank into the floor and ceiling. Cutting through them would take hours, even with a power saw and really good blades.

Maybe they'd given up before the door surrendered.

I touched the doorknob.

The door swung towards me, without even a groan of protest.

Until Absolute appeared, Frayville hadn't had a weapons locker like this. No police station did. Even those cities where they'd over-militarized every officer to the point of carrying fully automatic rifles on duty didn't have racks of flamethrowers or tanks of flammable gel. Absolute's appearance had sent a torrent of specialty armaments to every police department, fire station, and National Guard base in the United States. My flashlight picked out crates of incendiary shotgun shells lining the back wall. The room smelled of gunpowder tainted with grease and oil.

Eric swept his flashlight around the room. "Looks okay."

"They didn't break in for no reason," I said. "Grab a radio—no, two. Two radios. Let me check everything." While Eric got two boxed handsets out of the cage, I prowled the aisles.

They could have taken shotguns. That wouldn't have been bad—although, if they wanted a shotgun, Jerry's Gun Shop would have been a lot easier. They could have wanted the medical supplies, or the hand grenades.

I found a discarded plastic shroud and a scattered twist ties on the floor in front of the flamethrower rack. "Crap."

"What?" Eric said.

"They took a flamethrower." My light scanned the shelf. Had they only taken one? How many had been here before? Why hadn't I thought to take an inventory? The weapons locker had a log book, but on that last night, nobody had bothered to sign anything out—the few officers awake had obviously grabbed and dashed. "Maybe three, four tanks of fuel. Looks like they took a manual too."

Each fuel tank gave about twenty seconds of flame. A minute or ninety seconds of fire doesn't seem like much, but when you see that river of stinking heat pour out, tiny droplets of gel igniting everything they touch, you realize that it's not a minute of fire. It's sixty one-second blasts of toxic death. A quick punch with a flamethrower will set almost any building ablaze, and that gel won't stop burning until it's exhausted. One second of spray will kill anyone. By then, anything short of brick or stone will be burning on its own.

"Woodward," Eric said.

I shook my head. "If Woodward's guys'd had a flamethrower, they would have used it. Half the town would be on fire." The clammy cool of the basement chilled the sweat coming off my back. Out of habit, I put my hand to my chin to rub it thoughtfully, only to recoil when I touched the painful, permanent blister there. "We'll have to stop by First Baptist. Let the guys know we have a stray."

"Okay." Eric's flashlight played up and down the racked weapons. "Hate to say it, but Woodward's got a point."

"Maybe. But don't ever let him hear you say that."

Eric snorted. "Waited till we was down here to say it." The light stabbed a flamethrower. "We oughta have someone else who knows how to work these. You need a backup."

"Sure do," I said. "You want one?"

Eric snorted. "Hell, no."

"That's the problem. Anyone I would trust with one is too smart to want one." I gritted my teeth and studied the fuel tanks. I had three in the cruiser. Did I need a fourth? What if the intruder came back and took the rest?

I couldn't carry the whole weapons locker in my back pocket. My back and legs ached even more at the thought of lugging the gear I'd chosen up those stairs. I grabbed a boxed Taser and balanced it atop the pile. "Come on. Help me get a new padlock on the door and we'll get going."

"Like that'll help," Eric said, hefting the two shoebox-sized handset kits.

"It won't stop someone who really wants in. But I want them to work for it." I picked a spare padlock, still in its clamshell packaging, off the supply shelf. "Just because the place can be robbed doesn't mean that the Frayville All-Night Armory and Coffee Shop is open to the public."

Another crime, another investigation.

But unlike the attacks, I had the sinking feeling that we'd have no trouble finding out who had taken the flamethrower. Or what they planned to do with it.

Chapter 27

FRAYVILLE'S FIRE station loomed between the police station and city hall, a wonderful central location right across the big park from Paul Fournier Elementary. From there, a fire truck could reach anywhere in town within minutes of a call.

Too bad all the phones were down.

Frayville's surviving fireman and his apprentice had moved to the First Baptist Church which, although lacking firehouse amenities like a big garage or the traditional pole, did have a tall steeple and a belfry large enough for a comfortable lookout. Fred Pearson and his apprentice, Harry whatever-his-name-was, took turns keeping watch over Frayville.

I pulled the cruiser into the church lot and rolled to the edge of the steps, right next to the gleaming yellow, small rig. Frayville had a larger response vehicle, but with only two firefighters, the smaller rig made more sense.

I'd worked with Fred and Harry more than once. We'd had five house fires since Absolute released us. I'd set four of them myself, to kill the inimical dreg within. Rose Friedman had started one with a Molotov cocktail, because I was inside. Despite all that, I hadn't been to the church since they made it a fire station.

You haven't ever been here. Kevin was at the church lots of times.

I pushed the thought away. "You coming in?" I said.

Eric studied his hands. Something in my brain insisted that his chocolate skin looked false, as if he'd rubbed shoe polish all over himself. But the palms of his hands were pale pink. I suspected the soles of his feet were as well. Just as if he'd been born with that skin shade.

"It's okay," I said.

"I know," Eric said. "Don't feel much like explaining it, though."

"Fair enough. Who knows," I said, climbing out of the car, "tomorrow morning we might *all* wake up bright green."

"Don't have that much luck."

The flimsy plastic weight of the Taser at my belt seemed to somehow unbalance me. It weighed much less than a proper firearm, but enough to constantly remind me of its presence. I told myself I'd get used to it.

The church's doors stood propped open, letting the muggy breeze pour through. The vestibule gleamed with bright white high-gloss paint. A dusty hanging board with slots for slide-in numbers announced that today's hymns were numbers 409, 112, and 62. Beyond the glass wall separating the vestibule from the church sat rows of uncomfortably hard wooden pews, facing a carpeted shallow stage with a modest podium backed by a simple polished wood cross looming from the back wall.

Acceptance had chosen to permanently station someone at Saint Michael's.

The fire crew used First Baptist.

Frayville had a couple more churches. I wondered who had moved into them.

"Hello!" I called.

A muffled voice answered from a side hall. I took a few steps that way before Harry stumbled out of the pastor's office, running his fingers through his hair. Harry still had adolescent gawkiness, with oversized ears and hands, a head that threatened to bobble on his too-thin neck. He struggled with a yawn. "Kevin," he said sleepily.

"Sorry to wake you," I said.

"No trouble," he said, putting a hand before his mouth to hide his yawn.

"You did last night?"

"Half of it." He glanced at the simple white circular clock on the wall. "Guess I needed another nap."

"It's tiring," I said, "but we're all glad you're doing it."

Harry waved a hand. "I keep saying that we should just follow you around, but Fred says we might have a second firebug. What's up? You about to burn down another building?"

"I'm not. But someone is."

Harry's eyebrows perked up. "Really?"

I nodded. "Someone stole a flamethrower last night."

Harry's face collapsed. "Huh? Which kind?"

"Gel, not propane. Grabbed a few cans of fuel, too."

"How much fuel?"

"Enough to burn down most the town."

"Shit. That's why you didn't radio."

I shrugged. "Seemed a better idea to come tell you." I didn't need to tell them I'd given my radio to Woodward. I'd set Woodward's handset so that it could only contact mine, and locked the configuration with my passcode, but I'd learned years ago that bad news is best delivered in person.

Harry stood straighter. "Like we aren't screwed enough."

"I'm looking for it, but—"

"The easiest way to find it is to wait for the fire."

"Right. I'm still looking."

"I'll let the boss know."

"Thanks. He's upstairs?"

"He's supposed to be."

"Next fire you see, radio me right away. On the way, if you can."

Harry's thin eyebrows came together. "What if we see someone with the flamethrower?"

"You stay more than sixty feet from him, that's what you do." That sounded great, but what was *I* going to do? The Department's contingency plan for a person with a stolen flamethrower relied heavily on calling a sniper up from Flint. "I'll figure it out." Maybe I could get a hunting rifle, put a bullet in a gel tank. Have one large explosion instead of sixty small ones.

A heavy door slammed open just a few feet behind Harry, making us both jump. "Fire!" shouted heavyset Fred Pearson as he barreled into the hall. "Fire—Harry, there you are. Kevin? Pardon us."

Harry was already sprinting towards the front door, all traces of sleep gone. Fred followed, a little more heavily.

I fell in beside Fred. "Where is it?"

"It's not you for once," Fred said, his words bouncing out of his mouth every time we leaped down a step. "Olinger, third block east of Main."

I stumbled. "What?"

"Olinger," Fred shouted as he climbed into the fire truck, "three blocks east."

My mouth went dry.

Right by Ceren's home.

Chapter 28

THE BRIGHT yellow fire truck roared down the empty Main Street, lights and sirens flashing.

I tailgated, fuming with impatience but unwilling to try to swoop the heavy cruiser around the even heavier fire truck. If we'd had half a mile of straightaway, the cruiser could have eaten the road, but on this short stretch I'd only cut off the truck and slow it down.

The fire was on Ceren's street, on her block. Not necessarily our home.

If Ceren's home was on fire, the fire truck needed to beat us there. They didn't need me at all.

Unless Ceren and Alice had come home early.

If her home really was the one on fire.

That truck was too damn slow.

I clenched the steering wheel, grinding my teeth, as the fire truck pulled into the far lane to make a broad swinging turn onto Olinger Street. A black column of smoke rose from the north side of the road, the side Ceren's house was on.

Kipuka Blues

"Might not be you," Eric shouted over the siren.

The air pouring through the windows increasingly stank of burning plastic and metal and treated wood. "Who else? We shut the rest of the block down, remember?"

A shroud of flame haloed Ceren's sprawling ranch house. Heat and smoke burst from the windows. The afternoon sunlight washed out most of the flame's yellows and reds, but the foundry-level heat distorted vision for a good ten feet around the building, forging a barrier of hot air all the way to the street.

The fire truck came to a stop on the opposite side of the street, another forty feet down. Fred and Harry leaped out, pulling on their fire gear and seizing hoses. Fred ran for the hydrant with a huge wrench in his hand.

They weren't in time. They were never in time. Too slow to save the house. Too slow to save, not Ceren's home but suddenly *our* home. We were too slow, we had nothing left to save.

I stumbled out of the car and stared at the conflagration. Heat baked my face, my arms, my exposed legs. My chest felt as hollow as the standing walls, and each breath brought in the stink of flaming chemicals and wood.

Had Alice and Ceren been inside? Had they made it out? I'd seen house fires like this before, the blackened, brittle bones left behind. I didn't see the puttermobile, but if Alice drove she'd have parked inside the garage and I'd never know for sure until the fire burned out and I could check, could go into the ruins—

Eric yanked my shoulder. "Kevin!"

I shook to knock him off, unable to tear my sight from the black smoke pouring into the sky and the overwhelming taste of hot cinders and the dry heat blasting across the road.

"Gotta check out back," Eric said. "Kids might be down the street. Gotta look."

I drew a shaky breath and coughed.

I'd lost Julie and Sheila. The thought of losing Ceren and Alice drove railroad spikes of terror into my chest.

But Eric was right.

"Going east," Eric said. "You go west. Meet in back."

I jerked a nod.

Eric and Cuddles stampeded away.

Alice's unused home stood beside Ceren's, separated by a driveway and about ten feet of lawn. Even with the gouts of flame I had plenty of room to dash between the houses, the intense heat bubbling the swelling siding on Alice's home and fanning the blades of grass into glowing embers. The air shimmered and flickered with heat.

Cursing, I bolted around the far side of Alice's house, scraped through a narrow gap in the prickly hedge, and dashed around Alice's detached garage into Ceren's backyard.

In the back of the house, torrents of flame clawed through the burst-out windows from the family room and bathroom. A chunk of the gently sloped roof exploded in a shower of glowing pine and molten asphalt shingle, releasing a column of flame to scratch at the sky. The fire roared louder, like a subway train released from the tunnel into the station. I paused for a breath and sucked in a chestful of invisible smoke instead, triggering a bout of coughing as I staggered across the lawn.

No Ceren.

No Alice.

A few older oaks towered over the unfenced yard, their leaves nearest the house already rolling into shriveled husks and falling to the ground. The greasy stench saturated my senses.

Eric tromped towards me from around the other neighboring house, eyes scanning back and forth, Cuddles staying low on his flank. He saw me and shook his head.

I stared at the house, desperately hoping it had been unoccupied. Were the girls still up at Legacy? If they were, how had the fire started?

The sound of water exploding into steam burst from the front of the house. A hazy cloud rose from the gap I'd rejected, as Harry and Fred fought to save the homes on either side.

Eric grabbed my shoulder again. Had he been saying something? "Look!" He yanked me partway around.

Suit stood at the corner of the house directly behind ours, the gap where his left eye and that whole chunk of his skull had been showing the yellow brick wall behind him. His dark blue suit hadn't gotten any cleaner since I'd shoved him out of my way this morning. His empty right eye socket stared at me, his body gently swaying before smoothly turning towards the billowing steam roaring up beside the house.

One of his filthy hands dropped the five-gallon gas can.

The other, a butane fireplace lighter.

A gray ring surrounded my vision.

I tasted panic, like aluminum and dirt, chewed-up nickels spilling into my maw.

My brain kicked into overdrive, dragging my body behind.

I screamed and dashed straight at Suit.

Chapter 29

IF SOMEONE burns down your house, and you're a cop, you can't beat them to a bloody ruin. You just can't. That's too personal. It'll end your career. My partner should have jumped on me right then, pinning me to the ground, keeping me from criminally assaulting the perp until he would need years to regain the use of his arms and legs.

I'm not a cop anymore. We didn't have a police department. My brawny partner was a power and light worker with a mad-on the size of the world.

The girls—*my* girls—might be dead inside the holocaust.

Eric and I charged straight at Suit.

The heat from the inferno that had been my home, our home, if only for a few weeks, pushed at my back. The smell of burning wood faded, replaced by scorching copper anger and the harsh rattle of hot air in my parched throat.

Suit stood against the back of the house behind us, arms limp at his side, face partially obscured by a bushy willow tree, feet planted in a neglected, moss-filled flower bed ringed with rocks the size of pickle jars. Even through the dangling fronds, I clearly saw the monstrous break in his skull, large enough to have taken an eye, his brain, and the whole crown of his head. Somehow, the other eye still twitched in its socket. His gore-soaked blue pin-striped suit stood out against the yellow brick wall.

I was pretty sure I hadn't known Suit before Absolute, had no idea why he'd attacked me. His hollow head didn't have enough brain to form a grudge, to eat, or to stand upright—or to breathe.

Today, I would forcibly remind his body that dead things lie down and rot.

Suit's one eye focused on me. He stood immobile for a second while my feet tore up the thick green lawn between us. His right hand fumbled for his jacket pocket.

Assaulting me was one thing. Even when I'd served as a patrol officer and detective in Detroit for years, none of the thugs and criminals I'd tangled with had credibly threatened my family. Suit had ambushed the girls and me this morning, and jumped straight to burning down our home. Even the worst thugs I'd dealt with hadn't escalated things that quickly.

I had no idea what Suit planned for a sequel and I didn't care.

He wouldn't get the chance.

Suit's hand closed on something in his pocket. He'd just started to pull it out when my shoulder blasted straight into him.

We crashed into the smooth yellow brick of the house's back wall. Suit's breath exploded out of him, adding the stench of old fruit and decaying teeth to the stink of the rotten blood and decaying brains drenching his suit. Something cracked inside one of us. I hoped it was him, but didn't care enough to check.

I yanked Suit off the wall, pulling him back a step so I could slam my palm into his chin, knocking his hollow head back against the wall.

The crack of skull on brick would send a person's brain ricocheting off the inside of their temple, buying me another moment to plant a knee in the perp's groin. Suit's loose joints rocked as if he were a rag doll barely kept upright, but he didn't fall.

His hand fell out of his pocket. A handgun, a little automatic, tumbled to our feet and bounced across the wet moss hugging the ground.

I only thought I'd been angry before. Now, blank, blind fury engulfed me, setting my pulse hammering in my throat and wrists, making each breath somehow sharp and bitter.

We'd lost too much. *I'd* lost too much. Absolute had ripped everything away, and when I'd started to reassemble some kind of life, Suit torched it. If Alice and Ceren had been in the house when it burned, if he'd killed them—brain or not, Suit would learn to scream again.

Suit's mouth didn't open. His filthy, bloodstained face didn't have any expression. But he raised his hands against the wall as if surrendering.

"Kevin!" Eric screamed.

Cuddles barked, low, angry threats.

My world didn't have room for Eric, or the house fire, or anything beyond the blood rage scorching my soul. Suit wasn't merely a dreg that'd burned down my home. He was the burnt world outside Frayville. He was all the pain I'd endured, all the pain Kevin hadn't survived.

In my heart, for that moment, Suit was Absolute.

I threw an uppercut right into Suit's solar plexus. Suit's breath wheezed out of him again.

A predatory grin split my face. I shifted my weight back to ready more punches to Suit's chest.

The Beast With Two Backs rammed me like a tractor-trailer rig.

I slammed sideways into the bed of moss, bouncing my forehead against an exposed oak root. The horribly joined couple stomped straight across me like a tractor-trailer over a squirrel. A hoof-like hand tromped my cheek, smashing the other side of my head into the pillowy green moss, a foot kicked my ribs, and one of the trailing feet stomped my gut, punching air out of me and the nausea right in.

Gulping air, I rolled to my side, fumbling my hand beneath me, and tried to push myself upright. The foot to my gut had knocked the unthinking rage out of me, replacing it with an equally mindless need for air.

I couldn't come apart now. Merely beating Suit into a bloodier mess wouldn't solve anything. I had to understand, to use my brain, even though everything in me screamed out in righteous fury.

And to do that, I had to get to my feet.

Before Two Backs slowed and turned back to trample me again.

I got my head up in time to see Eric take a swing at Two Backs with an aluminum lawn chair as it charged past him. It bounced off the woman's exposed spine, sending them stumbling and eliciting a metallic shriek of rage, but not seeming to do any real damage.

Here in the sunlight, the malformed pair seemed even less real. The woman moved on hands and feet, her hips twisting to the sides so she could crab-walk more easily on her elongated arms. Her head was yanked so far back that her spine should have snapped, but the eyes shone with a rabid hatred reflected in her every step. Her mouth snarled, irregular sharp teeth glistening with saliva.

The man hung beneath her, his hips and gut fused into hers, his swaying back brushing the top of the grass. One hand clutched at empty air above her head. The other clutched her to him, his olive skin fused into her pale white flesh, the two colors diffusing into each another where they met, those fingers sunk impossibly deep into her spine. He still reminded me of an egg sac trailing beneath a monstrous gravid spider.

His head was close to the woman's neck, but wrenched sideways so he could watch where they went. His mouth gaped just as wide, his teeth just as sharp, his eyes just as tormented and insane.

The man's legs came up after them, knees up, trying to push the whole nightmare forward. Somehow, filthy ragged socks remained on his feet, the bottoms torn out but shredded elastic flopping around his ankles.

Cuddles hopped towards Two Backs' flank, snapping at the trailing knee.

She danced back with fresh blood on her fangs.

Two Backs clawed at Eric with the upright arm as they tried to slow and turn.

Eric hopped backwards, just out of reach, waving the aluminum-framed lawn chair. The seat's multicolored woven plastic straps glittered like a matador's cape.

I got my feet beneath me just as Suit regained his balance. The lone vacant eye turned to me.

I shifted my weight and kicked Suit square in the groin, hard enough to lift him off the ground. Suit didn't shout, but the air huffed out of him satisfyingly. I'd heard that a major nerve runs straight from the genitals to the diaphragm that helps us breathe. While Suit was made out of alien cells, the way he doubled over and struggled for air made me confident that Absolute had left that little detail in place.

"Eric!" I shouted.

Keeping the lawn chair raised between Two Backs and himself, Eric glanced over his shoulder at me.

"Flamethrower!" I shouted.

Two Backs had stopped itself, and lurched sideways, trying to aim itself back at Eric and me.

Eric glanced at Two Backs, and Suit, then at me.

Suit still stood bent at the waist, arms limp, hands brushing the ground, trying to pull a breath into his lungs.

I kicked Suit in the chest, hard.

Something inside it cracked.

Suit staggered.

I bent over myself and seized a fist-sized rock from the edging of the flowerbed. "Go!" I shouted. "Flamethrower!"

Eric glared at me, then turned his attention back to Two Backs. The monster had started a curving charge back towards Eric. Cuddles stood at Eric's side, straight-legged, head low.

I flung the rock. It soared past Eric to thud into the ground in front of Two Backs, bouncing off the grass to disappear under the woman's tromping hands.

The creature stumbled. The female head swung between Eric and me. I'd shot her this morning at the mansion, but the shoulder had no sign of the bullet wound—not even a scar. If I could take a rifle round through the heart and come back, she could handle a lousy revolver shell in the pecs.

I grabbed another rock. "It's me you want!" I shouted. "Come on!" My fingers slipped on the dirty rock, but I tightened my grip and let fly.

Two Backs' male head snarled as the rock hit a few inches from his head and bounced away.

"Come on!"

Two Backs charged me.

Suit was starting to straighten. I grabbed his shoulder and the waist of his coat and spun him around me, planting him between Two Backs and me.

"Go!" I shouted. "I got this!"

Two Backs crashed into Suit.

I jumped aside, barely escaping their tangle, my feet dancing for balance.

Suit fell to the ground, bouncing.

Two Backs trampled right over it.

I drew my Taser, flipped the cover open, and squeezed the trigger.

Twin lines shot out of the tiny plastic weapon, plunging right into the woman's midriff.

My Taser crackled and hummed.

Two Backs' legs lost all their coordination, instantly tangling together. The woman's back arched, jaw wide, teeth spread in agony. Both mouths erupted in an eerie metallic shriek.

Two Backs took another faltering step, breaking free of Suit.

I squeezed the Taser trigger again, sending another charge through the lines.

Two Backs painstakingly raised one hoof-like hand. The man's face shuddered and convulsed. The woman's head arched backwards, flecks of foam spraying from the side of her mouth.

The hoof-foot came down.

One last pull of the trigger sent the last of the Taser's charge down the lines.

Two Backs collapsed.

Eric glared, then bolted back towards the car.

Cuddles didn't even look at me, but took off right after Eric.

Leaving me with the monsters.

Chapter 30

A SCREAMING tornado of fire gouged the endless sky above Ceren's home, *our* home, polluting the rich blue with cinders and ash. The air stank of burning plastic and insulation, added to the rancid, rotten blood soaking Suit's abused blue pinstripe and Two Backs' vinegar-with-spoiled-lunch-meat reek.

My temple throbbed where I'd cracked it against an exposed oak root. My whole body ached with fading adrenaline, anger burning the last of the temporary strength to sustain that battle mania for just a little longer. My calves and thighs and abs promised to cramp, soon. My sight kept catching on irrelevant details: scattered mismatched and weathered aluminum lawn furniture; a child's plastic tricycle tangled in an abandoned garden hose; red embers drifting from the sprawling oak canopy.

If the canopy caught, nothing would stop the flames. We'd lose half the town.

Not my problem. Harry and Fred would deal with the fire.

My job was to keep the two dregs down long enough for Eric to come back with the flamethrower. Long enough to kill them.

Kipuka Blues

Two Backs lay on its side, mismatched limbs flailing at the grass as its misbegotten body fought to recover from the Taser charge. Suit sprawled on its back behind Two Backs, limbs every which way like a dropped marionette. Suit's abandoned handgun, the second one it had tried to use on me in less than a day, caught my eye, cushioned on the moss some twenty feet away. I didn't even try to reach it. I'd shot Two Backs earlier that day, and it had healed so fast it didn't even have a bruise.

The discharged Taser fell from my hand and bounced on the soft lawn. How long would that full charge last? Would Two Backs get up again? Or Suit, after the trampling it took?

I crouched knees-down, keeping my back straight and my eyes on the dregs, and fumbled in the flowerbed. My hand closed on a chunk of stone the size of a loaf of bread—too big. The next one, a granite grapefruit, came up easily and fit comfortably in my left hand.

Unlike the others, I didn't throw this one, but instead took it with me a few steps away from the neighbor's home. Two Backs didn't seem crazy enough to let me steer it into ramming the house's yellow brick. Instead, I positioned myself so Suit again blocked the straight path between Two Backs and myself.

My breath came hard, as if rubber bands squeezed my chest. My heart shuddered between my lungs, beating far too hard. I'd been in fights before—had I gotten that badly out of shape? No—worry later. Fight now. I moved my weight onto the balls of my feet and rolled my shoulder to loosen those aching muscles.

Maybe I should move forward. Use the rock. Turn Two Backs into One Head, and then No Heads.

No, losing the head didn't necessarily stop a dreg. Just look at Suit. It still struggled, uncoordinated, trying to get itself to its feet, waving like an upended turtle.

Two Backs stopped flailing. Its limbs fell limp to the ground.

I let out a pained wheeze. Maybe the Taser had done it.

Two Backs methodically swung the free male arm to set the hand flat against the ground. Muscles clenched, and the creature heaved itself onto its belly.

Suit stopped struggling and lay flat.

Two Backs growled. Both jaws tightened, lips spread, the irregular fangs grinding against each other, so askew the mouths couldn't possibly close.

I hefted the rock, studying Two Backs, waiting. I could throw rocks all day and still not stop the creature. My idea might work, but it would need speed and accuracy.

If I screwed up, one of those misshapen mouths might chomp my hand off at the wrist.

I still didn't understand all the new rules. Maybe I could regrow a hand, but I didn't want to have to try. Patching a tiny hole through my heart had taken everything I had in me. I focused on my breath, trying to get more oxygen to all my muscles and help them relax.

Anger still shrieked in the back of my brain, but I forced it back. Put it in harness.

My anger would serve me, I told myself.

Not command me.

Two Backs rose to its four feet and both hands. All four eyes narrowed at me.

Suit lay still, arms and legs flat against the ground.

I realized what was about to happen exactly as Two Backs charged, trampling right over Suit and towards me. A moment ago its movement seemed erratic, but somehow after its fall it had developed a smooth stride, the rear feet swinging perfectly with the forward feet and hands.

My breath caught for a heartbeat. My nerves felt jagged and overcharged. I made myself bend my knees, ready to move, rock held in one hand. I needed to relax, despite the steel tension running through my muscles. Relaxation meant speed, and I needed speed. I had to be fast enough, this time.

Two Backs' charge ate the distance between us. Both mouths opened. The male let out a horrific screech that sounded like an angry man with a circular saw. The woman's head focused on me, eyes narrowing.

Ten feet.

Five.

A split second before Two Backs would slam into me, I lunged to the side, feet barely clearing the creature's bowlegged front arms. My trailing hand clutched the rock, trying to swing it into Two Backs.

The rock struck something, hard, while I still had one foot in the air.

Eric wasn't the only one who could play matador.

The impact knocked my hand back, wrenching my shoulder, sending me spinning and dancing across the grass, the world twirling, my feet racing to get beneath me, arms waving to try to hold my balance. The rock flew from my fingers as I waved my arms. Two desperate steps, barely ahead of my own weight, then my foot came down solidly and I caught myself just before I staggered into the brick wall.

I spun to put my back to the friendly brick and scanned the yard.

I quickly found Two Backs crumpled face-first in the lawn, its trailing body pushed up against it. Blood gushed from the male head, right above the eyes. The female head rolled loosely, stunned.

In a flash, I saw Two Backs for its true self. It wasn't a monster. It was two people. Two people who had shared the greatest intimacy with each other, and had it go horribly wrong. I had an involuntary memory of my hand sticking to Teresa's stomach, a moment where I could feel my own hand through her skin.

Two Backs could have been me. Half me.

What would happen to two people connected so intimately that each felt what the other felt? If Acceptance could pass feelings across miles, what had happened when these people's brains plugged into one another? Nothing good.

No wonder Two Backs was insane.

But did that give it reason to keep trying to kill me?

My body craved air, pulling it in, not wanting to take enough of a break to exhale. I deliberately pushed the old air, trying to breathe slowly and deeply. If I hyperventilated now, I'd die. I got another, slower breath, feeling my heart respond in kind by slowing its woodpecker pulse a fraction.

Two Backs didn't move.

Suit followed, well, suit.

I didn't know why they attacked me. But when Eric got back with the flamethrower, I planned to light them both. I was going to treat these three as the monsters they looked, rather than the people they'd been. The thought pulled at my heart like a lead weight.

We needed a better solution.

But that was the future. These three would be crisped as soon as I had the flamethrower.

Ceren's house still blazed. A curtain of steam floated from the inferno as Harry and Fred pumped water into the exposed flames and across the neighboring houses. The entire roof and upper floor had collapsed into the basement, leaving the surrounding walls standing in flickering shrouds of flame. While I panted, the rear wall groaned and collapsed inwards, the fire roaring even louder. Even across two sprawling backyards, a fresh wash of heat roasted the sweat from my skin.

I hoped desperately that Alice and Ceren weren't home, that I'd drive up to Winchester Mall to find them utterly ignorant of the conflagration. I hoped to have to tell Ceren that Two Backs and Suit had destroyed her home.

I hoped that Eric would get back with the flamethrower before Two Backs got itself together. I wasn't sure I had the strength of body or will to pick up that rock again and get close enough to use it one more time. I didn't see anyone moving around the house, although I heard Fred shouting instructions over the wind tunnel roar of the burning house.

Suit sat up.

Normally, Suit moved with the slow deliberation of a secret drinker feigning sobriety. Now, even that normality evaporated. This time, Suit put his hand on the ground and rolled to his feet with easy dexterity. His one eye focused on my face and his fists came up. He had no brain. Forget how could he move at all, how could he move that well?

Suit sprinted towards me.

No—not towards me. Off to my side.

Towards the handgun he'd dropped, now lying on the mossy ground near the corner of the house at my back.

I swore and dashed towards the gun. *Faster. Run faster.*

Suit had also lost his clumsiness, transforming into a silent, swift sprinter.

I'd survived being shot once. A semi-automatic like that might have thirteen, twenty rounds in the magazine. If Suit had the brainpower to aim and fire, at this distance he could put maybe half of those in me.

I dashed for the gun as quickly as I could, demanding speed from my screaming muscles, Suit closing in just as fast.

Too slow. Again. Always too slow. He was going to beat me.

I ran harder, focused only on eating distance.

Suit slowed, already bending to snatch the handgun off the grass.

I threw myself forward, face-first, arms outstretched, cutting Suit off with my falling body.

My left hand closed on the semi-automatic's barrel as my face slammed into the ground. Moss and mold and dirt crashed into my mouth.

Suit tripped across my back, his knees thudding into my spine a beat before his hollow head smacked the brick wall.

Air exploded from me, spraying spit, moss, and dirt from my mouth. I thrashed, struggling to drag myself forward and out from under Suit's dead weight.

Suit collapsed, falling towards my feet.

I squirmed forward, ripping my legs out from under him and scrambling to my feet, narrowly avoiding an aluminum-frame folding lawn chair with a faded mesh seat and back. The handgun was an old Hekler & Koch, a .38 semi-automatic, plastic grip, no front sight. It felt light—the twenty-round magazine probably only had a few rounds.

Pivoting to face Suit, I raised the weapon. "Don't move!"

I knew the gun couldn't stop him. If he kept bringing a firearm, he must think it would work. How was he thinking with that empty cavity in his shattered eggshell skull?

Suit knelt in the dirt, leaning against the smooth yellow brick house, head turned so his one remaining eye stared at me.

The eyebrow bent down.

Was Suit *glaring* at me? Half his skull blown away like an empty eggshell, and he glared at me?

"What is your problem?" I shouted.

Suit remained silent.

"Look—if you understand me, you better show it. Otherwise, you're a dangerous animal that needs to be put down."

Suit knelt, watching me. The lone eye still glared, but his jaw hung slack. One knee rested in the moss, the other foot planted in the dirt.

"If you're still in there, raise your hands. Don't make me burn you."

Suit shifted his weight.

My hands shook, making the automatic wobble. I clamped down to stabilize it. My heart pounded so hard I thought my pulse might shake the weapon free. "Put your hands up."

Without moving his arms, Suit slowly rose from his crouch.

"I said don't move!" Where was Eric with that flamethrower? I felt like he'd left an hour ago, but my brain insisted I'd only been alone with the two dregs for maybe twenty seconds.

Suit took a step towards me.

I squeezed the trigger.

The automatic rocked back in my hands, the sound of the shot bursting above the roaring fire behind us.

A blossom of fresh red blood swelled from the left side of Suit's chest, directly over his heart, freshening the weeks-old dried gore there. Suit staggered back, arms spread.

I'd healed my gunshot wound with my mind. I'd decided that I could heal, and compelled my body to pull itself together. Maybe Suit didn't have enough brain remaining to pull off the same trick.

Just to be sure, though, I pulled the trigger again.

The pistol clicked on an empty chamber.

One round? What kind of brainless idiot carries an automatic with one round?

Oh. Right.

Chapter 31

I DROPPED the pistol and raised my hands defensively. My overstrained biceps protested the effort. Even at this distance, the pyre of Ceren's home washed heat across my bruised cheek.

Suit stood still, eyes still fixed on me despite the fresh blood welling from his chest.

Two Backs' middle legs stirred. The female head groaned.

I had to keep them occupied for another minute or two. Until Eric got back with the flamethrower.

Suit took a step towards me.

"Oh, come on!" I said.

I *needed* that flamethrower.

No—wait. Maybe I didn't.

I seized the top of the aluminum lawn chair I'd almost tripped over a second before, hoisting it above my head.

Suit shambled towards me, one step, two steps, raising its arms.

I strode at Suit and swung the lawn chair down onto his hollow head.

The front legs were a single square of aluminum, and the back legs a separate square. One leg cracked against Suit's shoulder, making him stumble, so I shoved the lawn chair to the side to squeeze it over him, trapping his arms against his body. The bar that had previously run along the ground now pinned his back.

Suit's eye still glared at me.

His hands flapped at his sides, trying to swing up but trapped by the flimsy aluminum square.

I glared back at him. "Last chance." I pushed the lawn chair, making him take a step back.

Suit rocked from side to side, wrenching the lawn chair.

I grabbed tighter. "No, you're not getting out this way."

Painstakingly, Suit's right hand slid up onto his belly.

I rocked the lawn chair myself, making him struggle for balance. "No, no crawling out." I pushed him back, making him take another step. "I don't need the flamethrower. All I need is the fire. And thanks to you—I have all the fire I need."

Step by step, one small shove at a time, I shoved and yanked Suit towards the imploding ruins of Ceren's home. The air grew hotter and drier, each breath sucking the moisture from my nose and tongue. A column of ash and steam and smoke billowed into the sky, growing with each step until it filled half my world. Suit struggled feebly, but my constant erratic flexing of the lawn chair didn't give his slow motions any chance of escape. I bent my knees, trying to shield my prickling skin from the worst of the fire. Each breath I took stabbed heat into my chest, and the flame became a physical pressure that pushed me away like a headwind.

But if I was hurting, Suit had to be in worse shape.

Finally, at the edge of the patio, maybe fifteen feet from the edge of the house, I couldn't stand it anymore. I couldn't possibly take another breath of that incendiary air. I shoved the lawn chair, sending Suit stumbling towards the inferno, and dashed back towards the prone Two Backs.

Eric found me gulping air on my knees a few yards from Two Backs. My face, my arms, my legs, my chin, every scrap of exposed skin felt covered in sparks from the heat. My heart had begun to slow, and I wondered how bad the burns were.

"You okay?" Eric plunked the flamethrower down beside me.

I sucked air. The fire's reek of chemically-treated wood and burning plastic had a new tone, a gut-clamping taint of burning meat. "Yeah."

Two Backs lay sprawled across the grass a few yards away.

I put my hand on the flamethrower tank and used it to push myself to my feet.

I didn't want to burn Two Backs. They weren't monsters. Not really. Just two people who hadn't understood the rules and had paid with their minds. All they left behind was a violently insane body fueled by a massive appetite. Despite its origins, Two Backs had to be destroyed. If they'd attacked me, they'd attack anyone. Maybe they already had.

With grudging haste, I pulled on the heavy leather gloves clipped to the flamethrower chassis and the tank straps onto my back. I unclipped the nozzle while I trudged up to Two Backs, reflexively checking the air mixture valve.

No—not the Beast With Two Backs. A snarky name is one thing when it's trying to kill you, but they had been people. Human beings. Copies of human beings.

Corrupt alien vessels to hold sacred human souls.

Souls that had accidentally destroyed themselves.

And if I couldn't save them, I could at least respect them as I burned their empty shells.

The man's head lay sideways, still. The nasty crack I'd given him on his forehead had stopped bleeding, a scab already starting to form. The woman's torso was arched as far away from the male's chest as it could be, but her hips and gut remained melded with the man's. Her head lolled back as if her neck was a spring.

I flipped the safety. "I'm sorry."

The woman's eyes flickered up in their sockets, then back down. She tried to focus her gaze at me.

She spoke. Her thin voice trembled with exhaustion and effort, the misshapen mouth choked with random fangs further distorting an already changed voice.

"Help…ee…Evin."

Chapter 32

THE FLAMETHROWER nozzle wobbled in my hands. That couldn't have—no. Not possible.

Making myself ignore the misshapen couple for another moment, I carefully flipped the weapon's safety on and cranked the main valve shut. I clipped the nozzle onto the backpack, then knelt on the spongy grass beside them.

Without the screeching fury, the woman's face looked haggard and pale. Irregular fangs still lined her misshapen mouth, distorting her jawline, but her short-cropped hair and eyes looked familiar. I studied her distorted form, molten and mingled with the man's body, and searched for anything recognizable.

"Kevin," Eric said behind me.

Cuddles whined.

The woman tried to lick her lips. Her tongue wasn't long enough to get through the misaligned fangs jammed into her jaw. The razor points sliced bright red lines in her tongue before she quit trying. "Elp…" Her misshapen jaw wouldn't let her bring her lips together, distorting her words.

"I'm here," I said. The burning house, the neighborhood, everything seemed very distant. Eric stood beside me, face slack in amazement, but he might as well have been on the moon. Nothing seemed real except the woman's voice. "Who are you? What happened?"

"Ecky."

"Ecky?" My brain churned trying to attach the sound to a name, mentally subtracting the fangs and shrinking her mouth. Vicky? I'd known a Vicky in Detroit, but—no. Maybe the Vicky at the Pilot stop out on I-75? No, that Vicky had much darker hair. Maybe—

Something came together in my brain. I concentrated on the woman's face, trying to see past the fangs and the distorted jawline, mentally pulling the planes of her face back in line. Suddenly I saw the shadow of another person inside this face. "Becky? Becky Ferndale?"

She nodded.

I'd met Becky with her friend Mick the first day I'd left Kevin's home, after Absolute freed us. They'd wanted chicken for dinner, and had learned the hard way that if you behead a chicken, both the head and the body get really, really angry. I remembered a severed chicken head scuttling towards me across a stained concrete floor, using its wattles as feet, somehow screeching without lungs.

Horrified sympathy brought me to a knee beside her. I stripped off my gloves. "Becky. Oh my God, what happened? How?"

"He wouldn't stop fighting," Becky said. Her chin shook and the fangs distorted her words, but the more I listened the better I understood her broken words. "Then danger got us."

My training took over. *Understand one part at a time.* "Who wouldn't stop fighting?"

Becky raised a hand well on its way to becoming a padded hoof and jabbed the unconscious man in his exposed chest. "Him. Paul."

"When?"

Becky shrugged. "Who knows? Picked him up. I wanted a night, and we—" Her eyes closed. "I could've got out. Pulled away. I know I could." She quivered. "He fought everything. Felt him fighting. All the time."

I'd almost slept with Teresa. No, not almost—the only reason we hadn't finished was the Molotov through the window had cut things short. When I'd tried to pull away, my hand stuck to her bare stomach. That truncated encounter had led to my own terrifying transformation, one I felt almost certain I'd recovered from.

I wasn't sure how I'd recovered.

But I remembered feeling myself through Teresa's skin. What if that fire hadn't cut things short? Would we have wound up like Becky, except with me on top? What if our nervous systems had connected even further, and I'd felt everything she felt? How deeply was Paul attached to Becky? Nauseated horror knotted my guts and my throat clenched.

A loud pop behind us broke the fire's crackling roar. A fresh wave of stench from something plastic incinerating washed over us from the burning house.

I shoved my sympathy down. "Why are you attacking me?"

Becky shook her head. "Danger. Sent us to burn your house. Danger made us."

"What danger?"

"It's a *name*," Becky said, hissing in frustration and anger. "Danger, he found us. Touched us. He's got us. Like—like Acceptance, but—"

Becky's voice caught. She fought a sob, and lost.

"He's afraid. He's always afraid. But now…" She made herself draw a shaky breath. "He's pissed. Danger wants—dead. All three of you, dead."

A momentary thrill fluttered through me. Someone wanted me dead? Given a name, even a stupid one, I could find him. And if Danger was angry at me, that meant I knew him. "Do you know why?"

"This morning, you three dead. Two, three, four."

Her words sent electricity through me.

Becky tried to lick her lips again. "He's mad now, though. So mad."

I glanced up at Eric. "He's called Danger?"

Eric shrugged. His eyes were wide and white in his dark face.

Becky shook her head. "No. Calls himself. Only heard him." A tear tracked down her muddy cheek. "Help us. Get us—apart."

"I'll help any way I can." I couldn't say anything else. "Fight him, Becky. Fight this Danger asshole. How can I find him?"

Paul groaned.

Becky bent her head back and screamed. "No, you bastard!" She swung her hand clumsily, clouting the side of Paul's head.

Paul's eyes fluttered at the impact. "Uhh…"

"Becky!" I shouted. "How do I find Danger?"

Becky's mouth opened wide.

I shuffled back, needing to get a couple feet between me and that mouthful of razors.

Becky rolled down, mouth open, poised to bite off Paul's face. She stopped short as if yanked on a leash, her forehead jerking back. She screamed again, this time with a grating metallic tone beneath the cry.

Cuddles barked in alarm.

As Paul awoke, she was reverting into Two Backs. "Becky! Where do I find Danger!"

Becky's eyes rolled up into her skull. "Red! Van!" Her voice rose, every syllable lengthening and growing louder. The last word was a scream. "Biiiig."

Everything that made Becky *Becky* and not merely a body disappeared from her face. She squeezed her eyes closed.

Paul's head shook. His half-open eyes squeezed shut.

When all four eyes opened again, it was the Beast With Two Backs that looked out at me again.

I rolled to my feet and danced back, bare hands fumbling for the flamethrower valves. Main valve. Safety. A click, and the tiny blue flame at the end of the nozzle came alive. Eric shuffled to stand just beside me.

Two Backs watched me as it shifted itself upright.

"Fight it, Becky!" I snarled. "You have this. You can beat this. You too, Paul! You are separate people! Nobody can stop that!"

Two Backs rolled to their six feet, still staring at me.

My hand tightened on the trigger. "You move at me, and I *will* burn you." My breath came fast and hard. Fear and dread formed a knot the size of a fist in the back of my throat.

With all four eyes, Two Backs studied me. The eyes moved together, flicking from my face to the flamethrower to Eric in perfect synchronization.

"I mean it. You touch me or mine again, and I will burn you to ash." Could Danger hear through Two Backs' ears? Did I want him to know I knew? "And if Alice and Ceren—" My voice caught. "If you have hurt them, Absolute itself can't stop me coming for you."

Two Backs took a clumsy step backwards. Then another. Both heads turned to the right, and it made a tight circle and began loping across the backyards, away from the burning ruins of Ceren's—our—home.

I took a step after it.

"What are you doing?" Eric said.

"Follow," I said quietly. "Becky's in there. Maybe she can lead us to this Danger character."

Two Backs trotted into the gap between the yellow brick house and the plank Cape Cod beside it. I pulled my hand from the flamethrower trigger and lumbered after it with Eric. The heavy flamethrower tank thudded uncomfortably against my back, making me stagger, and I fumbled to tighten the shoulder straps without slowing.

We got between the houses to see Two Backs standing in the middle of Elm Street, both heads steadily fixed on us.

It had two more dregs for company.

Only a few feet in front of the yellow house stood a dreg I hadn't seen before. The left side of her head was folded in on itself at the temple, as if by a brutal impact. Old blood covered the side of her face, matted her red hair, and soaked her flimsy royal-blue silk teddy. Her feet were bare in the grass. In one hand she held a yard of steel pipe with brown stains on the end.

My gaze flickered to the other side and almost moved past the creature standing in front of the Cape Cod house. From the vaguely human shape, I thought it had been a man. Or a woman. All that remained were innumerable multicolored worms, writhing around one another. Thousands of two-inch tendrils waved all over the creature, moving in perfect rippling synchronization like a sea anemone that had learned to walk. The chest swelled and shrank, not with breath, but with the soft tide of worms shifting from one part of the body to another, rising to the head, sinking to the hips, seething from side to side.

Bile surged to the back of my throat, and I clamped down to stop the vomit.

"Shit," Eric whispered.

My head swiveled from one to another. Two Backs stared at me. The woman with the crushed skull stared just as intently. Did her eyes move in synchronization with Two Backs'? I couldn't look at both of them closely enough to tell.

I didn't want to burn Two Backs. Or the woman. They were…not innocent, but not responsible.

Wormface, though… My hand itched to swing the flamethrower nozzle at that worm-covered monstrosity and hold the trigger down. Never mind that the blast would take the house beside him too.

But I couldn't burn all three before one or two of the others got to us. I was too slow, again and still and always.

Wormface slowly raised an arm, pointing back towards the flames of Ceren's house.

"Don't want us following," Eric said.

"Were the girls in the house?" I shouted at Two Backs.

The distorted faces only watched me.

Right at that moment, if I'd known Alice and Ceren were in the house, I would have gleefully accepted my own death if it meant burning them down with me.

But if they were alive, if Danger meant to keep after them, then I had to stay alive to protect them.

I swallowed my trembling anger and somehow kept my finger from clenching the flamethrower trigger.

Churning tendrils at the end of Wormface's arm drooped and raised, mocking a shooing motion.

"The girls are out of this!" I shouted. "You have a problem with me? Keep it between us. If they're hurt, I will burn this town to the ground to get you."

Wormface's hand didn't so much turn as flow upward. Worms squirmed repulsively into a mockery of a fist.

Two entwined worms rose from the fist.

A middle finger.

Teeth gritted, I stepped back into Ceren's backyard and out of their sight.

Letting them walk away.

Chapter 33

WE CAME around from the backyard and saw Fred and Harry fighting the bonfire that had been Ceren's home, our home, but now seemed only a cinderblock-lined pit of smoldering wreckage. Everything felt wobbly around me, the heat and stinking flames and frustrated fury filling my head with cotton and smoke.

I heaved the flamethrower to the back of the police cruiser, not bothering to strap it in place, and swung the driver's door open.

Eric said "What you doing?"

"Mall," I said. "Alice. Ceren."

"Not like that," he said.

"What d'ya want, me to change clothes?" I waved a hand at the inferno. "Maybe a fucking shower? I gotta go!" My head felt like something beat at the temples, from the inside.

"Pop the trunk," Eric said.

"What the hell!" I plopped myself into the driver's seat. My thumb missed the trunk button, but I mashed it on the second try.

Eric bent into the trunk as I fumbled for the ignition button.

The button must have been slippery or something. I couldn't quite hit it.

"Here," Eric said, twisting the cap off a liter bottle of water as he handed it to me. "Drink, we go."

I snatched the bottle, spilling a few drops on my dirty hand. "Whatever."

The fluid exploded in my mouth. My stomach almost convulsed in shock, and the world wobbled around me.

Suddenly the stiff seat felt plush under me. My calves and thighs ached, my spine burned, my shoulders felt as if I'd been carrying buckets of molten lead. I sucked at the water like a starving baby who'd just discovered their first bottle. My head whirled, the throbbing surging louder before receding.

Dragging Suit to the inferno had given me nice first-degree burns across my face and the exposed parts of my arms and legs. I shouldn't have worn shorts today.

But if I'd worn long pants and fireproof clothes, I probably would have gotten close enough to the fire to scorch my lungs. You can't breathe burn ointment.

When I drained the first bottle of water, Eric handed me a second.

He'd been right. A fight, running into the fire…I was too parched to drive.

Halfway through the second bottle, I paused to heave air in and out.

"Better?" Eric said.

Salt stung my eyes as I nodded. I *needed* to ignore my body, ignore every sensible precaution, just grab the wheel and slam the pedal to the floor and race up the hill to Winchester Mall, see if Alice and Ceren were safe. Shock, worry, and the aftermath of adrenaline trembled my every muscle.

I took half a minute to strap the flamethrower in properly. By the time I finished, Eric had Cuddles in the back and himself strapped into the passenger seat.

"Let's go."

I tried not to think about Two Backs and the other dregs as we drove through the ghostly downtown. Ghost town? Frayville was a town of ghosts. We were the kind of you could kick and burn and beat and drown just to get a couple of sick jollies. I passed a few people idly peering into the broken doors of abandoned shops or lugging overflowing bags of supplies back toward their claimed homes.

All ghosts.

Or maybe hermit crabs, trying to shuffle into the shells of someone else's lives.

My foot itched to press the accelerator to the ground and race up the hill to Winchester Mall, but I kept the speedometer at an even thirty. I didn't want random people following my example and drag racing up and down Main Street. The girls were either already dead, or safely up in Winchester trying to unlock Legacy's alien knowledge. I burned to know which, but running over jaywalkers to soothe my own distress two minutes sooner wouldn't help anyone.

The cruiser rumbled over the concrete surface of the big four-lane Sand River Bridge towards South Hill when Eric said, "Anything you need me to do today?"

I pulled in a deep breath against the tension of my diaphragm. "Things are starting to get rough. The bathtub murder, Reamer's mother, now this—I have to figure them out. Maybe…talk to Jack. It might be best if people stay in groups until I find this Danger. Warn them about dregs working together."

Eric nodded. "This goes bad, you radio me. If he's hurt your girls…"

Fear and anger knotted my gut. "Thanks. When it goes down, you'll know."

Eric swung down the sun visor and studied his darkened face into the small mirror. "You offered before," he said, peering at his reflection. "Flamethrower."

"Yeah?"

"I want one." He angrily slapped the visor back up. "Coulda burned Suit. Coulda burned the worm guy. We coulda taken them all. Don't want a flamethrower, but I think I got to have it."

I nodded, part pleased and part frustrated. Pleased because Eric was a good man. Frustrated that we even needed to think about handing out flamethrowers. "Best man to get a weapon is the one who doesn't want it. Let me get the girls settled—" *Please*, let me get the girls settled! I deliberately relaxed my jaw and my abruptly clenched fists. "Tomorrow morning, okay? Meet up at Legacy first thing? I'll want to see the girls safely up there." Exploring a dimly understood alien machine now qualified as safer than hanging around town.

"Be there."

I pulled into Winchester Mall's decrepit parking lot and saw the girls' little white puttermobile.

A weight fell away from my soul. My heart soared.

The tiny electric cart sat askew in the middle of two handicapped spaces, right where Ceren liked.

Eric heard my sigh of relief and snorted. "One less problem."

"Less?" I said. I pulled the cruiser to a stop beneath a scrawny maple tree struggling for life in a choked island of dirt. Relief thickened my voice. "Now I have to tell them." I took the spare radio from the seat between us and clipped it to my belt, opposite my own radio.

"Heh." Eric climbed out and patted his thigh. Cuddles squirmed through the cruiser's back window again and scooted to his side.

"Hey!" I said. "She's going to scratch the paint. You keep saying she's a lady, open the door for her."

Eric laughed. It wasn't funny, but after today he would have blown a hernia laughing at a fart.

"Take it easy," I said, closing my own door.

"You too." Eric reached down and scratched Cuddles' head. She promptly sat, tail wiggling in the asphalt.

I turned towards the mall entrance.

"Kevin?"

I paused, looking over my shoulder. "Yeah?"

Eric nodded. "Thanks."

"You too." I studied his deep brown face. The change of color had surprised me, but already it looked almost…not "normal". Right, maybe? As if it had been there all along, but I hadn't noticed. "Anyone gives you shit, well, tomorrow you learn to use a flamethrower. Make it look like an accident."

Chapter 34

WINCHESTER MALL swallowed me in cool, dry air. Dirt-crusted, frosted skylights blocked the June warmth and cast just enough light to silhouette the wooden bench and the hexagonal information pavilion just inside the smoked glass doors. The air conditioning hadn't been run for months, yet the air had the loamy tang of a greenhouse. My burned skin prickled and my sweat instantly cooled.

Maybe Legacy sucked the heat out of the air.

Silence pressed in on my ears.

The weight of the extra radio on my belt tugged at my pants, dragging them to slip past the band of my underwear, but I hooked a thumb under the belt and hoisted them back up rather than stopping to tighten anything.

I walked quickly down the curved hall. Someone had methodically unlocked the roll-down chain gates at each storefront but hadn't rolled them all the way up, leaving the bottom of each gate dangling a few inches above the waxy tile. Even without the main lights switched on, the mall gave the impression it was about to open. That little change made the place feel alive.

The only time these stores would open was when someone had a desperate need for rhinestone earrings or summer wear. Or posters of boy bands with extinct boys.

The puttermobile told me that the girls were here. I forced myself not to run, deliberately keeping a steady, cool pace. Running in would alarm them.

I can walk awfully quickly.

The mall's central plaza had once been a hexagonal open space, with a terraced floor dropping down to a floor full of chairs, planters, tables, food stands. The Legacy crew had hauled most of the free-standing furniture out of the terrace into barricades blockading the display windows of the anchor stores. Concrete planters that had once imprisoned trees now held bare dirt, and wooden benches bolted to the floor held either plastic storage crates or cushions. Broad branches of the mall sprawled out from the plaza. Since my last visit here, they'd brought in a huge fuzzy couch to put at the far side of the room, next to a shadowed opening in the bubbles.

The north hall, that had once led to the pet supply shop and the big sandwich shop, overflowed with giant bubbles of green foam. Beachball-sized spheres had oozed out of the hall, colors ranging from teal to viridian, all with an opalescent sheen. Spills of smaller bubbles ran in irregular rivulets across the main hall, some along the walls, a few stretching across the ceiling like a foam leak. One stubborn strand tailed up the silent escalators to the mezzanine. A rich greenhouse smell saturated the room.

I already knew that the bubbles were Legacy. But looking at them dumped the word straight into my brain again, sending a shiver down my spine. A scrap of chilly alien knowledge Absolute nailed into my brain before letting me go.

A half dozen tables covered with complex computer gear sat at the edge of the bubbles, all interconnected with network and power cables. A thick power cord ran off towards one of the food kiosks. Another bundle of mismatched cables ran towards a low bulge of green foam, where they plugged in.

Legacy, the alien library Absolute had left for us, had USB and network ports. And other, less pleasant ways to access it.

Sitting cross-legged in an office chair much too big for her, her tongue sticking out the corner of her mouth, Alice peered at a computer screen the size of my—*Kevin's*—monster invite-the-neighbors-and-the-precinct television.

The knot of fear in my chest melted, freeing my breath for the first time since Fred announced the fire.

Alice's hands lay still on the keyboard in her lap. She typed furiously for half a second, then became still.

I made my shoulders relax. Tension creaked away from my back.

"Officer Friendly!"

I suddenly realized other people were in the room.

"Brandi," I said. Brandi towered at least six foot eight and wore pink streaks in her black hair. Kevin had seen her around Frayville before, but never had talked to her. She didn't like me—I'd chased her buddy Reamer through here, intent on smacking answers out of him. But she liked Alice, so she had some taste.

Alice looked up. "Kevin!" She blinked. "What happened to you?"

"Trouble. Where's Ceren?"

"Off with Steve," Alice said.

"We blow a circuit breaker every time Steve fires up the Beast," Brandi said.

I looked around. "You have a beast?"

"The big computer they found," Alice said.

"Did Alice tell you she found frames?" Brandi said.

"She mentioned it last night," I said. "It sounded impressive."

"It was." Brandi smiled at Alice. "Steve and I saw those patterns for weeks and never put them together. We found a machine with a petabyte of RAM down at the credit union, so we can start to analyze them, but we need more electricity to keep it running."

I looked up at the dim light filtering through the dirty skylights. "Is there even enough solar here?"

"Of course. The whole roof has panels, and we've turned off the main lights and the AC."

"Kevin," Alice said, her voice shaking a little. "What happened to you?"

"I'm okay," I said. "Once Ceren gets back, we'll talk."

Brandi plucked a radio handset off a table. "Steve?"

The radio buzzed and clicked. Ceren's distorted voice said, "He's got his hands full."

"You're who I want. Officer Friendly is here to see you and Alice."

After a short pause, Ceren said, "On my way."

Brandi put the radio down. "Two minutes."

"Thanks," I said. Ceren's voice eased the last of the tension from my shoulders, leaving behind aches and strains. I needed some ibuprofen and a hot shower, and my clothes needed burying.

"You smell like a chemical plant," Brandi said. "The sooner you stop stinking up the place, the better."

I didn't just stink of the fire. Dried blood on my shirt, the bright pink of burned skin, and the dirt ground into my knees and hands advertised today's fight.

"Are you okay?" Alice set her keyboard on the table and hopped out of her chair.

"I'll be fine."

A door banged in the distance, and footsteps pounded towards us. Ceren materialized out of the gloom of the western hall. Her hair was still bright electric blue, but today she wore it tied back in a stumpy ponytail. She wore jeans and a silkscreen T-shirt from the last Mesh tour—still on the mom rock kick, it seemed. Her heavy boots didn't slow down her trot. "Kevin!"

"Something happened," Alice said to Ceren.

Ceren stopped a few feet from me. "You look like hell. Hell, you smell like hell. What's going on?"

"I should." My gaze bounced between stocky Ceren and elfin Alice. "Suit came back. And the Be—the two-person dreg."

"What happened?" asked Alice.

"I'm sorry, Ceren." I tightened my lips. "They burned down your house."

Ceren's eyes got wide. Her breath stopped.

Tough as she was, I figured Ceren would cry, even just a little.

She slapped me.

Chapter 35

HER OPEN-PALMED slap to the side of my face knocked me stumbling back.

"Damn it!" Ceren shouted. "How could you?"

My foot caught on a thick black power cable, and I toppled against an equipment-laden table. Something sharp stabbed my scalp, then the floor lunged up and slugged me.

I lay for a moment, stunned. I'd escaped the fight with Suit and Two Backs without taking a serious blow, but Ceren's slap set my jaw throbbing, eyes watering, and unleashed the taste of fresh blood in the back of my mouth. The skylights bloomed in double vision, two fuzzy views drunkenly circling each other. The back of my skull ached where I'd slammed it against the tile floor. The whole courtyard of the mall, with the monstrous green bubbles of Legacy tumbling into it, all felt very far away. I knew Ceren was strong, but I'd gotten weaker punches from weightlifters.

Brandi loomed over me, even more out of focus. "Hey, you okay?" She would have loomed over me even if she wasn't so tall.

I blinked and gasped for air. My vision snapped back together, revealing Brandi's sharply angled face twisted in concern. "Yeah." The side of my head burned.

"You're bleeding. Stay there."

The room swam back into view. I lay next to the equipment tables, surrounded by electronic gear, computers, and office chairs. Legacy's bubbles loomed in the background. The air tasted of loamy greenhouses.

Ceren stood a couple yards back, sobbing. Alice tried to hug her, but Ceren shook her off.

I levered my elbow up under me. The motion didn't make my head hurt any worse, so I rolled to my knees and slowly rose to my feet. "I am sorry, Ceren."

Ceren looked shrunken, tears spilling out of her. One hand clutched the bottom edge of her T-shirt, pulling it into a knot.

Alice tried to put her arms around Ceren again. This time, Ceren let her.

Brandi brought me a gauze bandage. "I said stay down." Her voice lacked its usual heat. "Put this on your head, you're getting blood on my nice clean floor." She went to Ceren. "Honey, that's awful."

I pressed the bandage to my scalp and found fresh blood.

Ceren drew a shaky breath and glared at me. "What happened?"

"Eric and I were working," I said softly. "We followed the fire truck, and it was your house. Suit was there, and Two Backs."

Alice gave a little laugh. "Two Backs. That's good."

"What?" said Ceren.

When your face has burns, a blush hurts. "Uh, the two people melted into one."

Brandi stared at me. "You mean they were doing it, and got stuck?"

"More than stuck." A drop of blood from my scalp wound rolled past my ear. "They grew together. They're violent. They and Suit came after us in a house this morning. Then they showed up at Ceren's house."

Alice kept her arms around Ceren's shoulders, but turned to look at me. "Did they set it? Or did they show up to see it?"

"Suit had a gas can and a lighter. And Two Backs said they were sent."

"They can talk?" Alice said.

"Sometimes." I put a hand to my jaw, trying to work it despite the pulsing muscles. I'd have one more nasty bruise to go with all the others I'd collected today. "The woman's head on Two Backs told me that someone named Danger is somehow making them attack us."

Ceren's breath caught. "Who is he?"

"I don't know." I looked at Brandi. "You hear of anyone calling themselves Danger?"

Brandi shook her head. "If I do, you'll be the second to know." She held the radio to her mouth. "Steve, when you can take a break, come up here."

I said, "When I knocked out the male head, the woman—Becky Ferndale—said that Danger made them do it. He had some kind of control over them."

"So we find those fuckers," Ceren said. "We find them and burn them."

"Suit is gone," I said.

"Good," Ceren snarled.

"But Danger already replaced Suit. There's a woman with a TBI, and someone who—who's really changed. I'm guessing he's controlling people that can't think well."

"TBI?" said Alice.

"Why?" Ceren clenched her fists. "Why is he coming after you? What did you do?"

I tried to shake my head, but my brain sloshed uneasily inside my skull. "Traumatic brain injury, Alice. And Ceren, I have no idea. But the bad part is, he's not coming after me. Not just me."

Alice's eyes got wide.

"Becky told me that Danger wants all three of us dead."

"What the hell!" Ceren said, shaking out of Alice's hug.

"We need to be careful."

"We need a place to stay," Alice said.

"That's easy," Brandi said. "You two can stay here, with Steve and I."

Her words felt like a knife slipping between my ribs. "That's not a good idea," I said without thinking.

"Why not?" Brandi said.

"Danger probably knows Alice comes up here. We need a place he doesn't know about, a place he doesn't know we've been." That sounded good enough, I hoped.

Brandi grimaced, then turned to the girls. "You're welcome here. Both of you."

Alice glanced between Ceren and me. "Thanks, but Kevin's probably right."

Ceren just glared at me.

I took a deep breath. "Ceren—I understand if you don't want to stay with me. It's your choice." Speaking each word made my chest pound harder. I'd fought to bond with the girls, to try to build our own little family. "But you at least need a place where Danger doesn't know to look for you."

Ceren deliberately relaxed her fists. One hand smoothed the clenched knot at the bottom of her T-shirt. "Yeah," she said. "We'll find a place for us." Her eyes met mine. "At least until we find out why this happened."

I could only nod.

"We don't know why," Alice said, putting a hand on Ceren's bicep. "It could be something any of us did."

"I know!" Ceren said. "I…know."

"I'll find Danger," I said.

"It's okay," Alice said. "It's only a house."

Ceren twitched, her hands coming up as if to shove Alice. Instead, she stepped back. "It's not okay! That was everything I had! My parents' stuff! Pictures! Videos!" Her voice trailed off. "All…my…family…" Her shoulders shook, and she started to bawl.

Alice appeared at her side, hugging her. I took half a step forward, uncertain, wanting to reach out to her. Brandi caught my eye and shook her head, then waved me over to a bench on the other side of the sunken floor. "Here, sit down for a minute. Quit with the bleeding."

My muscles ached as I sank onto the wooden slats. "Thanks."

"Sure." Brandi watched the girls clutch each other. "You really care for them."

"Of course I do." I kept my eyes on Ceren. Tears spilled down her red face. "Alice was one of my daughter's friends. She slept over at… at Kevin's house a couple times."

"Let me see your head," Brandi said. "Steve and I are lucky. We didn't have kids. We have work that needs doing. It stops—a lot of other things. No, hold still. You need another bandage. Really, someone should shave this side of your head, but I think it's clotting okay."

"You were a field medic too?"

"First aid. Girl Scouts." Brandi tsk'd as she seated a second layer of bandage against my head. "Hold that. It's not deep, just messy. You'll be fine. Careful with the shampoo."

"Thanks." If I could grow a new heart, I could grow that skin shut.

"You take care of those girls, okay? They do like you. And they need some kind of family."

I took a deep breath. "We all do." Sudden jealousy tore through my chest. Maybe Brandi wasn't the original Brandi, and her husband, Steve, not the real Steve. But their copies had each other. They weren't alone.

I didn't have my wife or daughter, even as copies. Kevin had murdered them both rather than let a psychopath with Absolute's full powers torturously copy them. I'd grieved for Julie and Sheila. I'd grieve for them every day I lived.

But that didn't mean I could condemn others who still had their loved ones.

Even if a snake of envy writhed in my guts.

Brandi stepped back to admire her handiwork and smiled, with more than pleasure at a job well done.

"What?" I asked.

"Just thinking," Brandi said, "Do you want to spell out to Ceren what 'the beast with two backs' means? Or shall I?"

Chapter 36

ALICE TAILED the cruiser through Frayville's back streets, the puttermobile easily keeping up with my sedate pace. Rather than go over the bridge, where everybody could see, we took the side road down into the wooded Sand River valley, crossed the creaky little two-lane bridge by the dilapidated railroad tracks, and up onto the old crackerbox homes on the south side of town. I finally pulled to a stop in the graveled driveway of a blue clapboard two-story with a spacious attached garage.

Ceren was out of the puttermobile before I had my door closed. "Why here? This place sucked. *Nobody* liked it."

Alice came up behind Ceren. "It wasn't very good."

I hadn't thought it was all that bad. "A couple reasons," I said. "One, nobody knows we looked at it. Two, the garage is big enough for all the cars. We pull in, close the door, and nobody will know we're here. Once this is sorted out, we'll pick a better place."

"If they're playing with fire," Alice said hesitantly, "I'd rather they burn down a place we don't like."

Ceren twitched, but nodded.

"You okay?" I said.

"Yeah." She pushed past me. "Lemme get the garage door."

I wanted to go after her, but she wasn't ready to talk. For days now she'd felt upset but hadn't been ready to talk. The fire had understandably made things worse.

I hadn't, and doubted I ever would, but I *could* go to Kevin's house. I could get photos and watch videos of birthday parties and sit on Julie's bed. I couldn't bear to walk into Kevin's home, but I had the option. Wearing Kevin's wedding ring weighted my heart enough on its own, but I couldn't bear to take it off, either.

If Suit and Two Backs had burned down Kevin's home, the dreg gang wouldn't have been able to turn me back. I would have burned however many I could have before they took me down.

The garage door rattled up. The police cruiser filled the left side, while the puttermobile looked like a child's toy in the right.

I helped the girls carry a few bags of clothes from the mall into the house's spartan living room. This summer home had utilitarian paint and secondhand furniture, but the closets had clean sheets, the fridge still worked, and the wood-slat horizontal blinds kept the house's secrets from the street.

"What now?" Alice asked as I dumped the last mall bags on the scarred cherrywood table.

"Now, I figure things out." I unclipped the spare radio from my belt. "This is programmed to go straight to my radio. You see anything weird, you call. A dreg shows up, you run. Got it?"

"Two Backs shows up, I'm going to run him over," Ceren said.

"Not in that car you're not," I said. "They could probably tip it over."

"We need a truck," Ceren said. "A big one."

I said, "Right now, you two lay low."

"We can't just hide," Ceren said.

Alice looked around nervously. "Are you sure this place is safe?"

"Nobody knew we were coming, but I'll check for dregs." If Two Backs or Wormface had hidden here before we arrived, I'd have to keep the girls with me. "I have to go talk to someone, try to get some more information. I'll be back in a bit and drive us all to Jack's for dinner."

Ceren crossed her arms. "Fine."

That was one angry, hurt girl. I couldn't blame her—if anything, I should feel grateful she decided to come with me. If Ceren had stayed with Brandi or struck out on her own, I didn't know what Alice would have done.

I'd wanted a family. The thought that this one might not work squeezed my heart so hard I had trouble breathing.

"First," I said, "I smell like a dead cow. Maybe I can figure out how Danger is controlling those dregs in the shower."

Alice cocked her head. Her eyebrows came together. "You mean you don't know?" Her voice still sounded like she was asking a question, but I'd never heard that implied *are you an idiot?* from Alice before.

I stopped. "What?"

"Seriously," Alice said. Her confidence evaporated. "I thought—no, never mind."

"Don't do that, Alice," I said.

"What?"

I sighed. "Alice, you're younger than me. But you've got brains. This is not the time to be modest. If you've figured it out, I really need to know."

Alice looked at me, then at Ceren.

Ceren still looked angry, but her lips had a small pucker of puzzlement.

Alice said, "I thought it was obvious."

"To you," I said.

"Controlling the dregs is probably the easiest thing in the world," Alice said.

I turned my hands palms-up and shook my head, baffled.

Alice said, "You know, like, Acceptance. They didn't plan to connect, it just happened. And there's, there's…" She swallowed. Her face turned paler. "You know. Teresa. Jesse. You know."

"So people can connect that way," I said.

Alice shook her head slowly. "So what if you try connecting to something without a brain?"

Chapter 37

BY THE time I got out of the shower and into the clean jeans and polo shirt I'd scavenged from the mall, I had parts of a plan.

Becky claimed that someone named Danger forced her and Paul to attack us. Danger probably drove Suit, and the worm guy, and the woman with the cracked skull. I didn't know anything about him except that he had a big red van.

And that Danger wanted Alice, Ceren, and I dead.

Becky had counted us as *two, three, four*.

You'd only count us that way if you already had counted number one.

Danger and his dregs might—*might*—be behind the attack on Nat Reamer. He might have left the number behind. A warning? A signature? A boast?

Nat Reamer lived in the lower half of a sagging two-story brick building a block off Main Street, behind the chain pharmacy. Ian Reamer's glittering new truck sat far up in the driveway, with a smaller, older sedan snugged up behind it, its bumper hanging a few inches into the sidewalk. I parked the cruiser at the curb and hiked up the poured concrete steps to rap on the doorframe. The inner wooden door stood open, the screen door snugly closed.

The man who answered had the unlined face, bright teeth, and neat hair of a twenty-something upper-class businessperson, and the red eyes and loose expression of someone working double factory shifts. "Hello?"

"Kevin Holtzmann. I'm looking for Ian Reamer."

"Come on in," he said, gesturing with his free hand as he pushed the screen open. "Ian!"

Ian's mother sprawled in a ratty leather recliner in the living room, wearing an old blue housedress and a thin blanket on her lap. Next to her, a younger woman staring blankly at the ceiling lay on a beige corduroy couch with patches worn to smooth translucence. The place smelled of damp plaster and decades of home cooking. The television hung on the wall displayed an old *Law & Order* episode frozen in brilliant color. Reamer was just turning from the television, a remote control in his hand. "Holtzmann."

"Reamer." I looked around. "How are you?"

"Holding things together." Faint webs of capillaries tinted his eyes.

"You look like you need a nap." I glanced over at the other man, leaning against a doorframe like it was a comfortable bed. "Both of you."

Reamer worked his jaw and swallowed. "It's a lot of work. Caring for people."

My brain flashed back to Julie as a newborn, back to my own father as the cancer ate him. "Yeah. It is." I glanced at Nat. "Any change?"

Reamer shook his head.

I took a deep breath. "I need to see where it happened."

Reamer nodded. "Sure."

The young man held out his hand for the remote. "I got this."

Reamer led me to the tiny kitchen in the back of the flat. If he raised the leaves of the small, scarred laminate table, four people would barely fit to eat dinner in here. The fridge rattled and buzzed, and a herd of silent appliances threatened to stampede off the overflowing Formica counter.

"I mopped the floor," Reamer said quietly. "Had to."

I frowned, but I couldn't have expected him to leave his mother's blood drying on the floor until I could get over here to investigate. Instead I said, "How is she doing?"

Reamer shook his head. "About the same. I found her old Blu-Ray collection; the murders seem to calm her down. But she wakes up and wants to know where I am." His voice didn't shake, but buried anger burned in his eyes and the corners of his lips.

"Was anything missing?"

"Nah. She was just..." Reamer spread his hands. "Lying out here." He pointed. "The back door there was open. And there's the fridge, I left that alone."

Five bold but wobbly black strokes at shoulder height made a misshapen *#1* on the well-used, age-stained white fridge.

"Okay." The screen door swung easily at my touch. While the frame was as weathered as the rest of the house, the scars in the wood had the discoloring of age. "Did she keep the doors locked?"

"I kept telling her to."

So: no. "Are any of the houses around here occupied?"

"I think the one behind us, to the left, is."

I stepped out the back door onto a patio barely large enough for two folding chairs and a strip of lawn. An ivy-draped wooden fence too tall to see over caged me in with the one-car garage and a propane grill. The home shaded the yard from the late afternoon sun, and the thick green ivy growing over the brick and the fence made the space feel almost cool.

"Who's the couple?" I asked.

"I knew Jerry back in high school." Reamer set his jaw. "We…went different ways after."

He did something legal. You stole cars and peddled drugs. "What about her?"

Reamer shook his head. "Janet's his wife. She couldn't take it, OD'd on pain pills last week. Hasn't woken up since. I was helping Jerry fix up a place where he could take care of her."

I flinched.

The alien matter we were made of resisted injury. My head had stopped bleeding, and by tomorrow wouldn't even be sore. I'd willed my heart to heal. But willpower comes from the brain, and brains are fragile.

Reamer's mom. The woman with the crushed skull. Now Janet.

If you wait long enough, everybody hits their head.

Was that our future?

Had Absolute resurrected us only so we could become dregs?

Helpless anger surged up my spine into my skull, making my heart pound more quickly.

I thought I'd seen the worst that Absolute could do to us, understood the violations it built into our bodies. But: no. Every time I learned something new, I found some new horror it had inflicted on us. We were sentenced to life, without parole.

The alien would pay for every single atrocity. One day.

I made myself focus on the tiny backyard, on Reamer's thin, aggrieved face, on the ivy, on anything except the impotent rage.

"Jerry and I have kind of thrown in together," Reamer said. "We're going to take over the upper floor for the two of us. That way, someone can always be downstairs that way, or at least nearby. We'll take turns on night duty."

Reamer had been one of Frayville's worst criminals. Still, he seemed to be trying to be better, and I wanted to encourage that.

I made myself nod. "You're doing good."

Reamer shrugged. "What else can we fucking do?"

"Was anything out of place?" I asked. "Did you pick anything up?"

"No."

I studied the lawn foot by foot. "You're sure?"

"Yeah. All I did was I mopped the place up. Why?"

My gaze met Reamer's. "Where's the weapon?"

His eyebrows rose, and lips drifted apart in thought. "I didn't find anything like that."

"And nothing is missing?"

"Let me check." I followed Reamer back into the kitchen, where he carefully opened cupboards and ran his fingers along the crowded counter. "I don't see anything wrong."

"What about the number one?"

"What about it?"

"Do you have a big black marker?"

Reamer frowned and slid open one drawer after another. "Pens, pencils—here's one." He pulled out an elderly black marker and popped the cap. "No, it's dry." Reamer replaced the cap and stuffed it back in the drawer. "No marker."

"So," I said. "The perp brought his weapon, and something to sign his work with. That means premeditation. Did your mom have anything valuable?"

Reamer shrugged again. "Some jewelry. You could get better up at the Winchester, or down at O'Dell's."

"Did she have any enemies?"

Reamer snorted. "Not any more. I mean, she used to raise a ruckus down at City Council meetings, but no." His gaze grew distant. "She outlived them all."

"Huh."

"What do you think?"

"None of the usual reasons make sense." I lifted my hands. "It's not robbery—go to an empty house or the mall or the store, take what you want. How old was your mom?"

Reamer stiffened, standing up straight. "She *is* eighty-nine."

"Is, of course. Sorry. You said, it's not like she's been running around raising trouble. Have *you* had any arguments lately? Anyone have it in for you?"

"Other than you?" Reamer waved a hand as if brushing his words away. "No. Spent a couple weeks finding out what we had in the way of gas and parts, making sure the fuel we have wouldn't evaporate, but nobody else seemed to care."

"Right. Do you mind if I look through the place?"

"Go on."

No matter what her son had become, the younger Nat Reamer thought long term. A quick glance showed me she'd purchased fine furniture decades ago, apparently with the expectation that it would last the rest of her life. Turns out she lived a lot longer than she expected. Every chair and mattress felt as thin and worn as she did, but tidy and cared for. The tiny master bedroom had a hand-knitted blanket on the double bed and photographs on the walls. Nat and her husband with two children, a boy and a younger daughter. Long-gone aunts and uncles and ancestors, some of the photos so ancient they must have been taken by an old-fashioned camera on light-sensitive paper, twentieth-century style. In the second cramped bedroom I found a cardboard carton stuffed with mechanic's coveralls and a couple pairs of rubber-soled boots next to a narrow bed with an intricately woven spread. The alcohol tang of creams, ointments, and remedies cut through the mildew smell of decaying plaster.

Ten minutes later I caught up with Reamer in the living room, trying to persuade his mom to eat a spoonful of chopped canned spaghetti. She wasn't interested in helping. Nat stared straight ahead, seeing nothing, not even opening her mouth wider. Once he worked the spoon through her slack lips and scraped it off on the back of her teeth, she chewed absently. Bright orange sauce trailed out the corners of her mouth and down the towel lying over the front of her housedress. Jerry sat at Janet's feet, one hand folded loosely over her ankle. On the television, fake investigators murmured quietly about fictional murders.

"Thanks," I said.

Ian looked away from his mom. "You learn anything?"

"Some. Nothing that makes sense yet. Before I go, though—do you know anyone called Danger?"

Reamer shook his head. "Can't say that I do. How come?"

I chewed the inside of my cheek. How much to say? I didn't want Reamer finding Danger and going all vigilante. "The name came up with some other attacks."

"I can ask around." Reamer looked back to his mother. "I don't get out much right now, though."

"I understand. How about you, sir?"

Jerry shook his head, still staring absently into space.

Proper procedure demanded I take Jerry's attention and ask him again. Looking at him sitting vacantly on the couch cradling his comatose wife's ankle, I couldn't bring myself to do it.

"I'll let you know," I said.

"Thanks," Reamer said.

As I walked down the steps and back to the car, I couldn't help thinking I needed to find the right perspective. The attack on Nat Reamer made no sense. None. She didn't hurt anyone. And numbering people? The only way that made sense was if someone wanted to scare people.

I wanted to blame Woodward, but this wasn't his style. Woodward wouldn't play master bootlegger and order hits on people. If he staged a disaster, it would be spectacular and obvious.

Nat's attacker believed cracking an old lady's skull made perfect sense.

Chapter 38

MOST OF the night's dinner crowd arrived at Jack's a little early, tight knots of people grabbing the best tables, and the remainder the best they could find. Woodward held his court in the large booth with the red vinyl seats in the back corner. I watched out of the corner of my eye. Woodward deliberately ignored us when Alice, Ceren, and I walked past and claimed a wobbly wooden table meant for two beneath one of the less obnoxious neon beer signs.

Ceren casually reached back and snagged an unused chair from the next table over.

"Just so I understand," I said.

Ceren sighed as only a teenager can sigh, loud, long, and smelling of the indescribable frustration of having to put up with idiot adults.

"I'm not a complete tool," I said. "The place will work out okay?"

"I never said that first part," Ceren said. "But yeah. It'll be okay. For now."

"It's not bad," Alice said. Her voice sounded a little distant, but that was understandable. She couldn't keep her eyes off the small plate filled with three petite, white-frosted cupcakes with chocolate sprinkles. Jack had not only kept his word, he'd thrown in extras for Ceren and me.

"They'd all laugh at us for picking Old Town," Ceren said, jerking her chin and aiming a death glare at the people over my shoulder.

"Don't tell anyone where it is," I said. "That's the point right now."

Ceren nodded. Her cheeks flushed for a moment with either anger or embarrassment, and she tore off a chunk of bread with her teeth to hide the color.

You wouldn't expect a place like Jack's, all pale, varnished wood and beer-sign neon, to smell of rosemary and thyme. He'd been grilling at the big propane rig parked in the back alley, and passed out savory venison chops and canned mixed vegetables. He'd also chunked up willow melons in a big bowl. Maybe seeing what it did for Nat made an impression on him. More bread—one of these days I'd have to figure out how the man baked bread at a grill. Maybe he snuck over to one of the houses on the other side of the alley and used the oven there, but I'd never seen it. The crowd felt restless, or maybe I was only noticing the ragged glances and quiet voices and people looking from table to table because I felt threadbare myself.

Today I'd faced Suit and Two Backs twice. I'd gotten up close and personal with a burning house—no, *our* house, burning. I'd dealt with an enraged Rottie named Cuddles and persuaded her to put her tentacles back. I'd argued with Acceptance, tried to pull Eric out of his own nightmare, and met Cathy Frost and Langley, Langley...what was her first name? Damn it, I needed to start writing things down in my notebook again.

You'd think the end of the world would mean the end of paperwork. You'd be wrong.

The venison became tasteless in my mouth. I made myself swallow, wishing I didn't have to keep talking. Here, now, the girls were close enough to adults. In the colonial days, when the younger children hit thirteen or fourteen, they'd get married and head west to claim new land. Alice and Ceren, all of us, were the new pioneers. "Something we should talk about."

"What now?" Ceren said.

"Eric and I went up past the Winchester today," I said. "Down towards the freeway?"

"You're checking houses out in farm country now?" Alice said.

"No, it was—unrelated." I attacked the chop with the dull, serrated knife. "You go a few miles out of town and it's…"

I set my knife and fork on the edge of my plate with a sigh, reached up and scrubbed at the sandy grit in my eyes. "It's all gone."

"Gone?"

"It looks like everything outside Frayville burned."

"Wow," Ceren said.

"I talked to a couple of scientists who are studying the edge," I said. Taking a bite would keep me from talking for a moment, but the topic stole the savor even from Jack's delicately seasoned venison. "It's all burned up. They say it goes all the way around the town, and all the way to the horizon."

"We're like a kipuka?" Alice said.

"A what?" I asked. Ceren looked, puzzled, at her.

"It's when a volcano blows, and sends lava everywhere." Alice said. Her hands wobbled across the table to mimic a river. "You get a chunk of land that's too high, like a hill or a rock, and the lava flows around it. You get trees and grass in the middle of the lava field? It's called a kipuka. Once the lava cools, it looks like an oasis on the moon."

I shook my head. "I don't know why we need the Internet back when we have you. Yeah, that's pretty much where we are."

"How far does it go?" Ceren said. She seemed more fascinated than distressed, thankfully.

"As far as I could see. The scientists I met out there, they said it goes to the horizon. At least."

"Huh," Alice said.

"I'm sure there's something out past it," I said quickly. "I mean, maybe the state forest burned, but if we could get onto the freeway, or out on I-75, we could get down to something."

"Maybe it didn't," Ceren said. Her eyes gleamed. "Maybe we're it."

I nodded. Of course Ceren leapt to the worst possible option, so she could get ready to fight it. "That's possible."

"Wow." Alice studied at the venison stabbed on her fork and put it back down.

"I wanted you to hear it from me," I said.

"We'll have to go look," Ceren said.

"Give it a couple days," I said. "Let me figure out what's going on first, and I'll take you."

"Why?" Ceren said.

"Look," I said. "For all I know, Danger is gunning for you two first. Don't give him extra chances. Besides, the edge is dangerous."

"It's not still burning, is it?" Alice said.

"No." I rubbed my forehead. "The forest, it's growing. Every few minutes, a hundred-year maple pops out of the ground."

Ceren's brow furrowed.

"You know those time-lapse films that show flowers opening?" I said. "The trees explode, go from zero to full grown in about two seconds. One almost got Eric. He's lucky he wasn't killed." His unexpected change might make him feel otherwise. I raised my head to scan the room, but Eric wasn't here. Maybe he'd decided to open a can of bachelor chow instead. I'd have to make sure he was okay. Maybe I'd drag him in the next day.

The copper cowbell hung over the door rang. Eric stood in the doorway. In the white-and-neon light, silhouetted against the day's brightness, he didn't look merely brown, but tar black. Cuddles stood at his side, tail end wagging maniacally and floppy ears perked.

Eric had his chin up, jaw set, and shoulders back. He stepped into the bar with his weight on the balls of his feet, hands half-curled. I really hoped there wouldn't be any sudden loud noises in the next few seconds or Eric might detonate. I watched the fight or flight reflex jittering up and down his body, and desperately wished I could help him.

Alice followed my gaze. "Who's—wait, is that Eric?"

"He needs a friend right now," I muttered. "Hey! Eric! Come on over. Ceren, can you grab him a chair?"

Kipuka Blues

Voices around the door suddenly went quiet as people noticed Eric. Then someone said, "Holy shit, it's a dog!"

The bar fell silent, then dissolved into chaos. "Where?" "How?" People in the back stood up to see, sliding out of the coveted booths to peer between heads. Behind the bar, Jack raised himself to his toes to peer at Cuddles and Eric.

A woman sitting near the door rose to her feet. "Oh my God, can... Can I pet him?"

Eric said, "Her." He reached down to scratch Cuddles' neck. Cuddles promptly sat, tongue lolling out, head cocked.

"Well, that broke the ice," I said.

"Oh wow," Alice said, shrill with delight. "Wow. A dog!"

Ceren stared at Eric, transfixed. "What happened?"

"Woodward has a gang of hooligans looting houses," I said. "They found the dog and shot it. Eric rescued it."

"We got a dog?" Alice popped to her feet. "I have *got* to see him."

"No," Ceren said with a flash of anger, teeth gritted. "I mean, his skin."

I lowered my voice. "He turned black when the tree exploded. Turns out his mom was black. He's been pretending to not be black his whole life. Absolute picked something that would screw with his head. He's freaking out about it, so don't make it a big deal."

Ceren shook her head.

"I know we're getting the dirty end of the stick right now, but don't give him grief on this," I said.

"You don't understand," Ceren said, staring at Eric.

"What's to understand?"

Ceren spun to glare at me and hissed, "My hair is blue."

"So?" I'd had no idea what color her hair really was until I'd seen hanging photographs of Ceren's parents with their charming brunette child.

She shook her head, sparks of anger spitting from her eyes. "It's not dye." With the back of her outstretched, shaking fingers, she pushed a few shoulder-length electric blue strands in front of her face. "My hair grew out this color. On its own. My hair. Is. Blue."

Chapter 39

THE CROWD in Jack's went as nuts over Cuddles as if a Hollywood blockbuster movie star had unexpectedly walked into the bar to pass out cigars and first class upgrades. A few people still sat working at their dinners, but even they kept an eye on the churning crowd surrounding Eric and the massive black-and-brown Rottie. This mob would test if the dog really was as good-tempered as she seemed.

Dogs had helped humanity claw civilization out of nature. They'd been our partners and friends for hundreds of thousands of years. I assumed that Absolute had taken dogs, and squirrels, and birds, and all the other animals like a xenocidal Noah—but as far as anyone knew he'd only resurrected humans, whitetail deer, a few pigs, and chickens. Cuddles' sudden reappearance exposed yet another gap in our artificial lives, filling another emotional chasm we hadn't had space to feel.

Absolute hadn't resurrected anyone younger than thirteen years old. Or any dogs.

But suddenly, there was a dog. What came next? Would someone find a baby?

Cuddles' sudden existence lanced the protective callouses we'd used to cover our hopes, to shield us from the things we missed so desperately, and exposed them all to the merciless sun.

But at the moment, Ceren's distressed anger offered its own strange hope. I knew that glare, the lurid fury burning behind her eyes.

Her hair had turned that unnatural blue on its own, and it terrified her. When Ceren gets scared, she attacks. I was surprised she still had any hair at all, hadn't shaved herself bald to prove it couldn't scare her.

The crowd's excited babble gave us a bubble of privacy. I leaned closer. "When did this happen?"

"About a week after you moved in," she spat.

My brain churned. "When did you notice?"

"*About a week after you moved in.*"

"I mean, how. How did you notice?"

Ceren's voice shook. "I went to redo it, and the old, faded blue washed out. But so did the brown."

"And you saw this."

She nodded.

My brain churned. "I think that's it," I said slowly.

"What?" Ceren snapped.

I leaned closer to Ceren, trying to keep my voice as quiet as possible while still letting her hear me. "Eric's hidden being black his whole life. I guess it's weighed on him, but I never knew. Nobody knew—that was the point."

"Who cares if he's black?" Ceren said. "I thought he was part Latino or Mexican or something."

"Some people care a lot."

"That crap really happens?"

"How many black people have you seen up here?"

"Before or after?"

"I haven't seen *any* after, so before."

"Some. What does that have to do with anything?"

"Because they weren't welcome. The people here—not everyone, but a lot—liked not seeing any skin darker than a good summer tan."

Ceren leaned back. "We had black kids in school, they were fine."

"But there's always one or two jerks," I said. "And it only takes one asshole to ruin your day."

Ceren drew a deep breath.

"And you. You wanted your hair blue. You did a *lot* of work with dyes and bleach and all that chemical crap to get it, to keep it that color." Ceren opened her mouth, but I plowed over her. "When I got shot, when I put my heart back together, it was my mind that did it. I told my body to grow back, and it did."

Ceren's eyes widened. "So you're saying…Absolute didn't *do* this to me, *I* did this to me?" She asked the question, but I knew she'd just let her mouth run while her mind raced ahead. The anger faded from her eyes, replaced by the frightening, obsessive intelligence of a teenager who thinks she's discovered a new way to game the system.

I nodded at the excited hubbub. "Just like Eric did it to Eric."

"He wanted his skin to change?"

"No! But he thought about it. It weighed on him. He's felt like he was living a lie." I worked my jaw, thinking. "And then he saw his face covered in black ash. That must have driven him nuts, and he didn't dare say a word. It's all self-image—how he sees himself, how you see yourself, it's becoming real."

Her mouth worked. "So—you think it's not Absolute fucking with me? Not more than normal, anyway?"

I shrugged. "I've heard you gripe about that dye. And you know, the whole point of swearing is that when you *need* bad language to tell people just how pissed you are, you have it. Like right then."

Ceren snorted. "Could it be more than hair and skin? But why—" She quieted, but her eyes turned upward as she thought.

"Has anything else changed?"

"No." But she looked away.

I nodded. *So yes, but you don't want to talk about it.* "Okay. Look, be careful, all right? Don't go thinking you need extra arms or anything. I'd hate to see you turn off your heart, or make your head fall off. Let's talk about this tonight at the house, when it's a little quieter. We're both smart, and Alice is smarter than both of us. We'll figure this out."

Ceren nodded. "Okay." She glanced at the crowd that had swallowed Eric, Cuddles, and Alice alike, then attacked her venison with fresh interest. I followed her example.

A few moments later, Eric shouted "Hey! People! Quiet down a minute!" The hubbub subsided, and Eric continued "You all're upsetting Cuddles. Give a lady some room, okay? She'll be here *all* night, and—ask the sheriff if you don't believe me—you wouldn't like her when she's angry."

The last bite of chop caught in my throat. The crowd's cheerful laughter swallowed my cough, and I scrabbled for a drink of water. Ceren looked at me curiously, but I shook my head. "Not here."

At the back of the room, the stone-still faces, mouths set in tight frowns, told me Woodward's little court hadn't found Eric amusing at all. They sat with heads together, peering angrily and enviously at the diffusing cluster of people surrounding my friend and his dog. *One of you could have been the star*, I thought. *That'll teach you to shoot wild. No, it wouldn't teach them, but maybe it'd make them pause before using a rifle like a fire hose.* But tonight of all nights, Eric needed a distraction. Cuddles' presence was far more intriguing than Eric's skin.

Ceren nodded. "Gonna check with my crew."

I pounded my chest to clear my throat. "Sure."

"Over here," Jack shouted from far end of the scarred, gleaming pine bar, waving a red-and-white knob of thighbone and gristle over his head. "Got something for our guest of honor." The crowd cheerfully parted, and Eric found himself with the corner stool. I couldn't see Cuddles through the tables and chairs, but then her head rose to gleefully snatch the bone from Jack's outstretched hand.

"Listen," Ceren said, leaning close. "Don't—don't tell anyone, okay?"

I nodded. "If that's what you want. Eric's having a rough time, though. He thinks it's Absolute."

She grimaced. "Yeah, him you can tell. He's okay. Just—" She glanced around uneasily.

"I get it," I said. "Why don't you and I talk to Eric? That way you can tell him exactly what you want. Once the rush is over. We'll say hi to the dog while we're there. Nobody'll notice."

"Sure." She flashed half a smile and scuttled off to join the couple of teenagers who'd taken over the darts corner.

I finished the last shards of my meal. Jack had found something buttery for the vegetables, and he'd salted them, but you can't do much to help industrial-size cans of veg mix. I ate them anyway.

Alice plopped herself into her chair. "Wow. A dog. I couldn't get even close."

"I'm not surprised." I set my fork down on my empty plate. "You know, I have the inside scoop. Cuddles and I, we go way back. Tomorrow morning I'll introduce you."

"That would be great!" Alice gazed longingly at Eric eating supper on the far side of the bar.

"You crack anything else on Legacy today?" I asked.

"I did a couple chunks of Python to start breaking apart the frames," Alice said while shoveling food into her mouth. "Once Steve gets the Beast running for more than thirty seconds and SkyBSD on it, we'll start crunching data. Maybe tomorrow morning."

My mouth went dry. "You mean we'll be able to talk to Legacy? Tomorrow?"

Alice shook her head and began slicing her venison into chunks almost too small to stab with her fork. "Not a chance. That's when we can start figuring out what's inside the frames. Who knows how many layers it's encapsulated, and then we've got whatever the upper protocol is, and—it's huge. We're going to be at this for months." She stabbed a sliver of meat with her fork. "Years. But it's a start?"

My chest loosened. I wanted answers—why had Absolute attacked us? What made it think it should devour the world? Why create us? "You know what you're doing," I said.

"Not even close," she said. "But it beats the Booth of Befuddlement."

Absolute hadn't only put dozens of different kinds of digital connectors on Legacy. In a private nook inside the bubbles, you'd find two vaguely human handprints impressed into the green foam. Put your hands there, ask a question, and Legacy would pour a chilly, alien answer directly into your brain, leaving you disoriented and nauseated and probably more confused than before.

I hadn't tried the Booth. Others had already asked my questions and gotten vaguely ominous answers.

How long would we live?
Forever and ever, world without end.
What is Immanence?
Imminent.

"You've been up there a while," I said. "You think you can really get into Legacy with computers?"

"One problem at a time," Alice said. "But I'm pretty sure Absolute thinks we can. Why else would he have given it all those connectors?"

Eric had only a couple people near him now, all looking down at the floor. I couldn't see Cuddles, but I could imagine her joyously attacking the meaty bone with a chorus of cracks and snaps. People stayed for a moment or two, admiring the Rottweiler and chatting with Eric, then moved on to give others a chance.

I felt sure that a pre-Absolute crowd would have been more trouble. Had Absolute changed people so that we got along better? Or had he chosen to resurrect people with common ideas of how to behave?

Maybe, on the other side of the ring of ash surrounding Frayville, other people Absolute freed were rioting and destroying what humanity hadn't already burned. Our little kipuka might be the safest place in the world.

Or maybe nobody was out there. Frayville really might be alone. How would people take that?

I shook away the morbid thoughts. Worrying about the entire world was a little out of my jurisdiction. Even if I had a jurisdiction. Which I didn't. Right here in this little town I had murder by bathtub barbeque, an assault on harmless Nat Reamer, and Danger's dregs. Maybe I was right about Eric and Ceren changing themselves, but that was a tiny answer to only one of many, many questions.

Alice finished her meal while I pondered options, then scuttled off with Ceren before she headed back to the house. I started asking people around me if they'd ever heard of someone called Danger. Nobody had, but most offered to tell me if they come across it.

I'd just headed towards my third table when Ceren squeezed through the tables back to me. "Hey," she said quietly.

"What's up?"

"You asked us to tell you if anyone was missing."

Chapter 40

THE KIDS who claimed the back corner of Jack's bar, near the bedraggled dart board, ranged from thirteen to about seventeen and wore everything from ragged cutoff jeans and T-shirts to expensive club wear. I'd seen most of them there each night, talking and laughing and artlessly flirting, and constantly resisted the need to ask them where their parents were. Same place everybody else not there was, and I couldn't adopt all eight of them.

But a few nights ago, there had been nine.

Now they looked worried as Ceren led me back. Eyebrows were pulled low, and their youthful voices held uncomfortable intensity instead of their usual boisterousness. I caught slices of conversation.

"—three nights ago—"

"—pharmacy—"

"—running, like—"

"Guys," Ceren said. "This is Kevin. He used to be a cop, but he's mostly okay anyway."

Faces turned to me. A kid barely old enough to have a driver's license tried to adopt a tough expression, but his youth and worry ruined the effort.

I kept my expression professionally calm. "Ceren says you all have a problem. Someone's gone missing. Will you tell me about it?"

A young lady wearing too much bright makeup and a ridiculously tight green shirt said, "Keith Gifford. He hasn't been around since dinner a few nights ago."

"He was supposed to meet me down at the gravel pit four days ago," said a boy in cutoff jean shorts and a death metal T-shirt, sitting with his chair leaned back against the dark wooden wall paneling. "I figured he got a better offer."

"What's your name?" I said. "And what was going on at the gravel pit?" I asked.

"Larry. We were shooting targets."

I wanted to shout at the kid to leave the firearms alone, but at least they'd chosen a decent place for it. The Frayville gun range was about fifteen miles out of town, and probably covered in cinders and ash. "What kind of better offer?"

Larry looked at a brunette girl in a blue blouse on the other side of the table. She flushed bright red and looked at the table.

"Ah, that kind. Did *you* see Keith after that dinner?"

The girl shook her head, face beyond red and verging on purple.

"So the last time any of you saw him was at dinner five nights ago? Or was something going on after?"

The kids nodded with a chorus of "yeah."

"Where does Keith live?"

"He took over one of those big mansions on Lagrange," Alice said. "A couple blocks from the beach."

"Because every kid needs their own mansion," I said.

A couple kids shifted uneasily, looking at the walls.

"Hey, doesn't bother me any," I said. "I'm not the one who'll have to keep that place clean."

"Lay off," Larry said. "Bill and Jettie are going to throw the big parties."

The girl in the tight blouse said, "Hey, if you trash my place, I'll just move."

"Well, there's Bill's then," said a young man in a button-down red shirt and wide black tie.

"Yeah, your place was cool," said the girl in blue.

They'd rather talk about anything except their missing friend. We're still that human. "Where does Keith spend his time?"

"We hang at his place a lot," Larry said. "He hooked up an old non-stream game console to one of those freaking big-ass screens."

"We're working on an old car," said the kid in the wide tie. "Trying to get a classic running."

"Something old enough to not have a speed governor?" I said.

Wide Tie started to stammer a reply.

I waved a hand to cut him off. "I'd be doing that too if I didn't have to do things like find missing people. What's your name?"

"Mack."

"So, Mack. You were probably up at Coleman's a lot, getting parts. Anywhere else?"

"Hardware store," Mack muttered.

"Does Keith have anyone?" I said. "Parent? Relatives? Friends?"

"No," said Larry. "Just us. We're tight, though."

"Maybe he just decided to…light out," said a husky blond boy at the back of the table. "See the world."

"No, you just hope he'll light out," said the girl in green.

"Why do you say that?" I asked the blond kid.

He looked at the table. "No reason."

"Keith and Bill don't get along," said the boy in the wide tie. "At all."

"Well, Bill *is* a total dork," Ceren said.

"What makes you think he left?" I said.

The kid shrugged. "Dunno. I just think he might've, is all."

Suspicion gnawed at the back of my mind like a rat chewing into a bag of dog food.

"What kind of *not get along* are we talking here?"

The kid shrugged again, looking at the table.

"Keith calls him names," Alice said.

"He's just teasing," Ceren said. "He calls everyone names."

"Keith pushes Bill around," Alice said. "That's not teasing."

"Keith pushes everyone around," the girl in green said. "He's a jerk."

Bill still looked at the table, not meeting anyone's eye.

I said, "Bill—he pushed you around more than most, though, didn't he?"

Bill didn't say anything.

"Hey, Bill," said Mack. "What's going on?"

"Where is this big house you moved into?" I said, dreading that I already knew the answer.

"Down on the beach," the girl in green said. "It's this place done all in black and white. How come?"

Bill's shoulders clenched and his jaw tightened.

Images of a luxurious bathtub, filled with the stretched remains of an electrocuted person, flashed through my mind. That and the smell. I knew it was a dead body as soon as I'd stepped into that bright white entryway with the black-and-white marble floor. I'd searched over white shag carpet and between white walls, seeing dull black plastic picture frames and gleaming black wood trim on the furniture.

"Bill." I made my voice deliberately soft and sympathetic. "Can you and I step outside to talk for a minute? Just you and me?"

"He just… He showed up," Bill said, staring at the table.

Oh, shit.

The other kids stared at Bill.

"First thing he does when I open the door is shove me. Calls me a dork. Broke my glasses." Bill's quiet voice carried through this little knot of stillness in the crowded bar. Alice's eyes were big, with tears trembling on the lower lids. Ceren scowled.

"Bill, man," Mack said, voice shaking. "What did you do?"

"He wouldn't stop!" Bill stood, turning red. "Told me to stop pissing him off! Told me to do what I'm told or he'd make me! And he wouldn't stop! I had to fight back!"

"What about the bathtub?" I said.

"I had to!" Bill shouted. He looked back down at the table, then up at his friends, his eyes wide and filled with fear and anger. "I've asked Legacy—we're here *forever*. Forever! And he wouldn't stop!" He waved his hands at the kids around him. "You guys, you told me to blow him off, but there's nobody else to help, so I had to *make* him stop!"

I'd referred any number of kids to anti-bullying programs, but Absolute had eaten those along with everything else. A bully doesn't need to be bigger or stronger—they just need to be willing to do what the victim won't. My heart went out to Bill even as I struggled to come up with what to do with him. "Calm down, Bill. We need to talk about this, you and me."

"Why?" he said. "We're in this forever. And it's each of us for ourselves, isn't it?"

"Let's get out of here and talk," I said.

Bill shook his head, sending the scraggly shock of blond hair spinning. "Oh, no," he said. "You're not a cop anymore, and we don't have cops, we don't have laws, we don't have anything, just us and what we can do, what we can take, and I'm taking it, and nothing's gonna stop me anymore." Bill paused, his breath ragged, as if the words breaking free after so long hidden had exhausted him.

His voice dropped to a breathy whisper. "Nothing *can* hurt me. Not now. Not ever again. And I will burn anyone who comes near me."

I held up my hands. "You're right, Bill. I'm not a cop. Really, I just want to talk."

Bill lunged to the side, pushing Tight Blouse's chair forward as he charged.

I shoved Alice out of the way and moved to block his path. "Hang on Bill, please, let's—"

Bill launched himself at me.

I bent my knees and held my hands up, braced to swing my arms around Bill and steer his momentum straight into the wall. It's an old trick, one I'd done hundreds of times over the decades.

Bill hit me like a loaded dump truck.

I'd been body-slammed by retired NFL linebackers and angry weightlifters. Bill did more damage to me than either of them. One moment I was ready to catch him in passing, the next I bounced off his chest and flew across a wooden table. Plates and cups and cutlery stabbed my back, and people shouted in angry surprise. Metal clattered, glass shattered, and plastic plates rattled to the floor.

I rolled over the table, crashing into a couple of shouting diners.

Untangling myself from the people I'd hit took too long. By the time I followed Bill out the back door, Frayville's first post-extinction murderer had vanished into the abandoned town.

Chapter 41

WHEN I staggered into the alley, my left knee throbbing painfully from knocking into the table, I found no sign of Bill. The empty rows of hollow homes behind Jack's offered too much cover. No way could I catch him. I paused, one hand on the warm metal of the emergency exit, feeling fresh pain wash through me.

That shouldn't have been possible.

Bill had struck me like a rhinoceros. Even if I could run him down with a limp, if I caught him, he'd crush me.

Nothing can *hurt me. Not now. Not ever again.*

If Eric's self-image had changed his skin and Ceren's her hair, what would happen to a young man who'd decided to stand up for himself? A boy who'd faced his bully and won? A boy who equated winning with strength? Someone sick of being hurt?

I waited a moment, caught my breath, shook my head, and gimped back into the bar.

Most of the evening diners were looking at the door as I walked in. A few were helping the people I'd accidentally plowed into when Bill bounced me out of his way. Eric sat by the emergency exit, one hand on a forgotten bottle of Budweiser and one eyebrow raised, looking at me. Cuddles had stood to all four feet, her head low and eyes fixed on the doorway, seemingly echoing Eric's concern.

Inquisitive faces turned to me. I held the doorframe with one hand, taking the weight off my pulsing knee, and caught my breath. What was I supposed to say?

"It's okay, folks. Nothing to see here."

A chubby man in jeans and a polo shirt stomped up towards me, indignant anger written on his familiar face. "What the hell were you doing, Holtzmann? You kicked Kenny in the head."

Where had I seen him before? Who was Kenny? "Is he okay?"

"You made him swallow his tobacco."

The face clicked. I'd seen him earlier today, wearing urban camo and carrying a shotgun. One of Woodward's thugs.

I'd flown into the crowd of Woodward's men who'd overflowed from the big man's booth.

"He's in the bathroom puking his guts out," the man said.

"That's pretty rough," I said. "Didn't mean to upset you like that. I was trying to talk sensibly with one of the young men, but he didn't like that idea. He ran me over and then out the door."

"You had no right to be grabbing him anyway." The chubby man glared up into my face. "You're no different than me."

I felt flushed, adrenaline spiking tension in my muscles. I tried to stand still, but just couldn't manage it, not after the day I'd had. I stepped closer, but didn't grab the moron by his stupid polo shirt and start shaking. "You know what? You are *absolutely* right." I spat each word like a poison dart. "The next time I find a killer, I'll just give him your address. You can take care of the problem right from home. How does that sound?"

"Killer?" the man sneered. "Yeah, right."

Not popping the man in his piggy face took as much willpower as forcing my heart to heal. Instead, I concentrated on one deep breath. Then another, trying to think. If Woodward's thugs knew we really did have a murderer running around, they'd probably posse up and set out after Bill.

I unclenched my fists. "I apologize for interrupting your dinner. I'd offer to buy you a beer, but it's free while it lasts."

The man snorted and turned back to his buddies.

At the booth next to their table, Woodward silently studied me, his face expressionless.

"It's okay, Cuddles," Eric said, dragging my attention away from the wannabe Big Man of Frayville.

The Rottie looked up at Eric, peered out the door behind me, then sighed and plopped her rump on the floor. One paw dragged the bone away from the brass rail to where she could chomp it properly.

"Well," I said to Eric, "at least we cleared out Cuddles' admirers."

Alice slipped past the crew setting the scattered table to rights. "Are you all right?"

"Fine, Alice."

Ceren followed a second later, bulling through gaps Alice had ghosted past. "I can't believe it. Bill's such a dweeb."

I nodded. "Looks that way. I need to talk with him away from everyone, though."

"What's up with this Bill?" Eric said.

I tried to smile, but it felt tight and small. "Mister Crispy, in the bathtub, with the toaster."

Eric grimaced.

Ceren leaned back. "*Bill*? He really did that? I mean—he's a wuss."

"Not anymore," I said. "You girls see him, don't go near him. He knocked me over that table without trying."

Jack came down to our end of the bar. "You look like you could use a beer."

"Yeah, thanks." I took the proffered can of Stroh's and popped the tab. *Four cans left.* I made myself savor the first chilled, strawy mouthful before letting it wash down my throat. "Catching him wouldn't have done any good, though."

"Why not?" Alice said.

I held the can close to my chest, making myself wait for another drink. "There's no judge, no jury. Say he tells me exactly what he did and how he did it. What am I going to do?"

"It can't be open season on people," Ceren said.

"Oh?" I raised my eyebrows at her. "Who's going to do anything?"

"Someone has to," Alice said.

"Who?" I said. "I'm not trying to be sarcastic, Alice. I mean it. You say someone has to, but there isn't really anyone to do anything. Jack feeds us. The people around us, they do the work they think needs doing. There's you and me, Ceren, Eric. The Lightners up at Legacy. That's it. Couple others, I'm sure. That's it." I raised the can to my lips, savoring the slowly warming beer.

"And Cuddles," Eric said. "Don't forget Cuddles."

Hearing her name, she wagged her stump of a tail once. Cuddles' massive head remained focused on the bone, however. She'd cracked it lengthwise, and her thick tongue lapped for the marrow within.

I swallowed another mouthful. "By the way—Alice, Ceren, this is Cuddles. Cuddles, these are my girls."

"You've got that backwards," Ceren said. "You're our Kevin."

"Fair enough." I raised a hand. "They're in charge of the house, I just do the heavy lifting and pay the mortgage."

"Where you crashing?" Eric said.

"We found a place," I said.

Eric lowered his voice. "Keeping it quiet?"

"Seems best."

"It's not a great place anyway," Alice said.

Ceren glowered. When the anger at losing her home broke, she'd be a wreck. I hoped I could help her when that happened.

I drank a mouthful of beer and set it on the bar. "Hey, Jack, when you get a moment, question for you."

Jack gave Rose Friedman another can of Blue Ribbon and toddled towards us. "Yeah, Sheriff?"

I sighed.

Jack smiled.

I kept my voice loud enough for people near us to hear. "Do you know anyone who calls himself—or herself—'Danger?'"

Jack shook his head. "Can't say that I do."

"If you find anyone who uses that name, I'm looking for him. Looking *real* hard. Let me know, okay?"

"Sure," Jack said. "Sooner or later, everyone comes here."

"Thanks."

The couple sitting behind Eric had heard me, and a few of the nearby tables. Inside a few hours, everyone in Frayville would know that I was looking for Danger. Even if nobody knew that name it might draw him out, rattle him, push him into making a mistake.

Alice reached for Cuddles' head.

"Don't pet her right now," Eric said to Alice. "Not while she's working on a bone."

The girls spent a few minutes admiring Cuddles from a short distance while I pondered. The crowd started to thin around us, early diners leaving to make room for later ones.

Behind me, Woodward said, "Mister Holtzmann."

Kevin's trained policeman responses transformed my jump into a twitch. "You like walking up behind people, don't you."

"Only when they keep their back to me."

"I'm not turning my back on you." I kept my back to him. "I'm spending time with my friend. My girls."

"Jake tells me that troubled young man killed someone."

I looked over my shoulder. "My investigation is ongoing."

Woodward raised his eyebrows. "The young people tell me that he confessed."

I did not want Woodward in this mess. "People say a lot of things they don't mean. Including confessions."

"Indeed. But this certainly merits investigation. And investigating means bringing in the young man."

"He'll turn up."

"Of course he will. I'll have my men watch out for young Bill."

"You don't need to worry about him."

"Come now," Woodward said. "It's my civic duty."

"And it's my problem."

"Of course it is." His patronizing smile begged for a good hard right hook, with a swift introduction to my knee. "I have one of your fancy radios, remember? If we should happen to find him, rest assured, I will let you know immediately. I'll let you get back to your little party now."

Woodward headed back to his corner, unharmed by my fuming glare.

If Woodward's gang found Bill, they'd clean out a holding cell for the kid. A guard. Woodward would arrange a trial. He'd set up a jury. Maybe even find a judge. He'd claim the problem. And suddenly he'd be in charge. Oh, he'd call himself mayor or something, but I didn't want him—or anyone like him—ruling our little kipuka.

"Kevin," Ceren said.

"Yeah?" I said, my brain tied up with damned Woodward. He *was* right. He was an asshole, but he was right. We needed to do something with Bill. We needed leaders. I didn't want to set myself up as an alternative to Woodward—but did I have a choice? It's no good saying "not this" if you don't have an alternative idea.

"I'm thinking," Ceren said quietly.

The front door banged open.

For the second night in a row, Ian Reamer charged into Jack's. He glanced from side to side, distraught. On his second pass, he saw me, and plowed through the irritated bar crowd.

I opened my mouth to ask what was going on, but I wasn't fast enough.

"Someone took Mom. And Janet."

Chapter 42

ONE OF the advantages of having a partner detective is that you have someone to grouse to. I couldn't even drink a beer without finding a murderer or having a lapsed drug pusher scream for help. I set the half-finished Stroh's on the bar, told the girls to stay with Eric, and followed Ian Reamer's truck screeching through the empty streets back to his mom's flat.

The two-story home still looked soft, the brick walls starting to sag and curve around dissolving mortar, but someone had punched the ragged wire screen out of the front storm door, presumably so they could reach through and flip the flimsy latch. I followed Reamer through the front hall. The worn living room had been tidy a couple hours ago, but someone had just used it for a demolition derby. The couch had been shoved to the middle of the room. The old recliner had been knocked aside and the end tables toppled, strewing old incandescent lamps and tiny glass knickknacks everywhere. The room's stink of old meals and older plaster had picked up a layer of sweat and stale, coppery blood.

Jerry dashed out of the kitchen doorway, hands fluttering. Fresh dried blood ran from his nose, and fresh bruises bloomed beneath the skin of his face. "Did you see them?"

Reamer shook his head. "No, nowhere."

"Dammit!" Jerry threw his hands up. "Dammit, dammit, dammit!"

"What happened?" I said.

"They took them!" Jerry shouted.

"I went to the market," Reamer said. "When I came back, Jerry was out front running around, the place was trashed, Mom and Janet were gone. I told Jerry to stay here and went for you."

It took us a few minutes and a shot of Scotch to get Jerry to stop flailing. He choked on the drink, but I finally got him to perch on the edge of a hard wooden chair. He shook and his eyes bulged, but he eventually he told me what happened.

"This blond chick walked in," Jerry said. "Naked. I mean, she had this blue silk negligible on, but it didn't cover anything, y'know?" His hands curled into fists. "She had all this dried blood all over her, and her head—I mean, I don't know how she was even standing. I just stared, then this—*monster*—came in after her."

My guts tightened. I knew what he was going to say, but couldn't suggest anything. It wasn't evidence unless he said it. "What kind of monster?"

"Two people, but all mashed up and twisted, y'know? Like, they'd been going at it too much."

Two Backs. Or, Becky Ferndale and Paul.

"She grabbed me." Jerry's red face bulged with passion, making his new bruises more noticeable. His tight eyes opened only enough to let tears flow. "I mean, I wasn't expecting anything. I should've fought, but she just grabbed me and threw me on the floor, then that monster was jumping up and down on me. I think I've got broken ribs."

"You'll be a lot better tomorrow," I said. If self-image could blacken Eric's skin and turn Ceren's hair blue, maybe Jerry could heal himself overnight.

"Not without Janet I won't!" Jerry shrieked, clawed hands grabbing my shoulders.

"We'll find her," I said. "But I need your help to do that. What happened next?"

Jerry exhaled. It seemed like his body deflated as the air whooshed out. "They knocked the wind out of me. I just lay there a moment, trying to get my brain together, you know? Then they dropped the damn couch on me."

I leaned back.

"It's a sleeper." Jerry shook his head. "I couldn't move, y'know? I could hardly breathe."

"I get it." Imprisonment by furniture. That was a new one.

"Then the monster. The guy's head drops down right next to me, right in my face." Jerry shuddered. "Those teeth—I thought it was going to bite my face off."

"What then?" I kept my voice calm and soothing. Jerry only needed some encouragement to tell me everything.

"It looks at me, then it talks."

I blinked in surprise. Two Backs had shrieked at me, but never spoke. Becky had talked only while Paul was unconscious. "What did it say?"

Jerry shook his head. "Both of them together—both heads. They sounded like an old sci-fi movie, all distorted and stuff."

"What did *they* say?"

Jerry looked at me, tears flowing down bruised cheeks. "He takes one. We take two."

Chapter 43

I COULDN'T get much more useful information out of the increasingly frazzled and distraught Jerry. I told him and Reamer I'd search for Nat Reamer, Janet, the girl in the "negligible," and Two Backs, then picked up Alice and Ceren at Jack's. By the time we got to our temporary home, the horizon split the June sun, the day's stored heat radiating from the ground overpowering the cooler air. Exhaustion gnawed at my every nerve.

He takes one. We take two. The words churned the ice in my guts. I'd killed Suit, shoving him into the burning remnants of Ceren's home. And Danger had replaced Suit with Ian Reamer's mother and Jerry's wife.

I should have gone out to search for Nat and Janet, for the dregs, for Danger, for Bill, for Acceptance or Absolute, for anything that might assemble today's madness into a coherent whole. Instead, I plopped down on the living room couch to think for a moment, my sweaty legs and back sticking to the cool vinyl, listening to the warm breeze rattle the stiffened fabric of the vertical blinds. The world blinked away.

I woke in clammy, unfamiliar darkness to find someone had tucked a thin sheet around me. I pulled it around me like a cloak, staggered to the bedroom I'd claimed, and fell onto the bed and into unconsciousness until the dawn sieved through the blinds.

The bed was too cold. Too big. I ached for Sheila's warm body beside mine, not even her words, merely her presence. I wanted to go out to the kitchen and see Julie hunched over a cereal bowl, hair sleep-messed and one eye unwillingly cracked open.

But that wouldn't ever happen again—Kevin had saved them.

Saved them from being like me.

At moments like this, I wished he hadn't.

A couple minutes standing in the shower, letting lukewarm water batter my sore neck and shoulders, helped me feel alive again. I'd soaped half of myself before realizing that my skin didn't hurt.

The first-degree burns from shoving Suit into the fire? Gone.

My fingers tentatively probed my scalp. Yesterday's bloody wound? I couldn't even find the spot where it had been.

I knew I could heal. I'd used my will to regrow my heart. But now I'd recovered while I slept.

No, that wasn't exactly new. When I'd been splashed with burning diesel the day before that heart shot, I'd healed. But those wounds had been horrific. The bruises and contusions I'd accumulated while searching houses hadn't healed overnight.

Had they healed more quickly, though?

Staring into the bathroom mirror, I studied my reflection. Kevin would recognize this face, from the sagging darkness beneath the eyes to the two overlapping teeth in my lower jaw. In the last ten years or so, my forehead had advanced along the sides of my head, isolating what had been a widow's peak into a widow's peninsula. I even had Kevin's oversized pores at the base of my nose. My muscles ached with yesterday's struggles. My feet hurt.

I felt every one of my forty-five years. *Kevin's* forty-five years. Absolute had created me only months ago.

Just how far would self-image take me?

I stared into the mirror. "I'm not sore. Those aching muscles, they don't hurt."

My back burned as I straightened, putting lie to my words.

I grabbed clothes from the bagful scrounged from Winchester Mall yesterday. The shirt hung a little loose over my gut, and the pants needed a tighter belt than I thought they should.

Healing my heart had left me ravenous. Had healing yesterday's scalds chewed an inch or two off my flabby abs? Or were these scrounged clothes just cut differently?

I'd put on weight the last few weeks, what with eating Jack's cooking every night. Kevin had struggled to maintain fighting weight his whole life, and I didn't have the energy to pick that battle up right now.

My stomach growled with modest morning appetite.

The refrigerator stank with black rot, but I found a can of beef stew

Kipuka Blues

in the cupboard, warmed it over the gas stove, and ate it directly from the pot. By the time Ceren and Alice tromped down the stairs, both wearing jeans and T-shirts, I was putting the washed pot and spoon in the drying rack.

Alice looked worried. Ceren's red eyes and freshly scrubbed cheeks showed she'd been crying. Losing her home must have hit her hard last night—she still wore the Mesh tour T-shirt she'd worn yesterday. It was damp, as if she'd washed it out last night rather than dive into the new clothes we'd looted. She wouldn't welcome me drawing attention to any of this, though.

"Morning, girls."

Ceren grunted, stomped to the coffeemaker and hit the button.

"How you doing?" Alice said. She wore the radio I'd given them on her belt.

I nodded, feeling the ache. *My neck doesn't hurt*, I told myself. "Better for a twelve-hour nap, thanks."

Ceren plopped into a wooden kitchen chair, propping her head on one hand and draping the other across the rectangular laminated kitchen table. She never spoke much at breakfast, but this was a bit much even for her. I ached to tell her that things would improve, but I had no reassurances this morning. And they both deserved better than empty lies.

"Good." Alice rummaged in the can cupboard. "We've got... How can anyone not have oatmeal?"

"There's chili," Ceren grunted.

"For breakfast?" Alice said. "Ick."

"I had stew." The artificial taste lingered on my tongue, and a strand of processed beef seemed to be caught between two molars, but the carbs and fat made a warm, soothing bundle in my stomach. *We didn't get toothbrushes. Crap.* I rolled my shoulders, trying to work the morning aches out.

Self-image. What would happen if I convinced myself I was twenty years old again? Did I even want that? "What are your plans today?"

"Coffee," Ceren's thumb idly swept back and forth across the ridged metal trim around the edge of the tabletop. "Brain after."

At least Ceren didn't seem angry with me. At this particular moment.

"I'm going back up to Legacy." Alice grabbed a can of beef chow mein from the cupboard, made a face, and stuffed it back. "Brandi said she had the code to parse Legacy frames almost ready. We should be able to figure out the next layer of encapsulation."

I nodded. "Okay. Ceren, you mind going with her again?"

Ceren grunted. I took that as an affirmative.

"I'm going to follow you into the mall," I said. "Steve and Brandi should know some of what's going on." I didn't want to leave the girls alone while Danger's dregs hunted all three of us, but I couldn't tell them that tidbit amidst everything else.

"There's a bulk food store in there, isn't there?" Alice said.

"I think so." Most people didn't want to spend time near Legacy when so many places were easier to pillage.

"Fine." She grabbed a can of ravioli. "I'll get some stuff today."

"I have a lot of questions to answer today," I said. "If you need me, though, if anything happens, you use that radio and call. Okay?"

Alice cranked the opener around the ravioli can. "Sure."

Ceren rose from her chair and deftly swapped a mug into place beneath the coffeemaker, letting new coffee dribble in while she filled the mug from the carafe, then swung the carafe back into place before taking a sip and sighing. She slumped back into her chair, took another sip, and said, "What's going on?"

I sucked on my cheeks for a second, thinking. I had shielded my daughter, Julie, from the ugly parts of police work, and wouldn't have even considered telling her or Sheila anything about the vileness I coped with each day. Frayville had been infinitely better than Detroit, but even a small town had a bottomless well of human pettiness that could seed violence and hatred and blood without warning.

We lived in a different world, though. While Alice and Ceren planned to spend the day at the mall, they couldn't even count on mall security for protection.

"This person, Danger," I said. "He's collecting dregs. He can control them. Set them after people. Then, someone stole a flamethrower from the police station. Third, it seems your friend Bill killed the boy bullying him."

Ceren shook her head slowly and took another sip. The mere presence of the coffee steam swirling around her face revitalized her.

"Keith wasn't a bully."

"Bullies don't think they're bullies," I said softly. "The question is, how does the victim feel? Bill felt trapped, and there wasn't anybody to help him."

What were we going to do with him? We couldn't let a killer walk around free, and yet our little community didn't have the structure to imprison him, or execute him, or even let him off with a warning. People called me the sheriff, but that was a job I didn't want and certainly didn't have the authority for to fill the position.

"He should learn to take a joke," Ceren grumbled.

"Joking is fine between friends," I said. "But you have to be friends first. Sounds like Keith pushed him around, aggressively told Bill that he's weak, over and over. And Bill couldn't stop it."

Ceren grunted and sipped her coffee.

Sitting around a strange table, listening to Alice babble and Ceren grunt, still felt weird. I ached for the mornings I'd had with Sheila and Julie. Sheila took the chore of making breakfast and made delightful eggs and pancakes. She didn't just make oatmeal—she'd make oatmeal flavored with orange and anise.

In contrast, my dinners were edible. Mostly.

But the three of us would always sit and eat and laugh about the day to come, in that familiar but slowly expanding chemistry of a growing family. Julie had hit the age where she didn't want anything to do with Sheila and I in public, but she still talked with us in private, mostly willingly.

But that was Kevin's memory. Not mine.

I wasn't Kevin. *That* was what I needed to remember.

Any future I had, with Alice and Ceren or just in this crippled community we called home, depended on accepting what I was.

I wasn't a cop anymore. Nobody was. And I'd never been one, even though I had someone else's memories of working the job.

I forced myself to think about something else. Say I seized the mantle of authority. I came in and played sheriff. *Should* we do anything to Bill, then? Could we do anything to Bill? He'd discovered a clumsy new strength, maybe as a result of killing Keith. I pushed back from the table and hunted through the cupboard for a mug without success, until Ceren poked my arm and nodded to the right.

I filled a mug of coffee and pondered. I felt sympathy for the kid, but sympathy might not play into things at all. If Bill's strength wasn't a one-time thing, if he went out-of-control berserk, we might have no choice but to burn him in self-defense.

Ceren's coffee made road tar seem tasty. I managed half the mug before setting it down. "If you're ready, let's find out what fresh mayhem today has for us."

Chapter 44

AFTER A quick radio consultation with Eric, I followed the girls' puttermobile along the meandering macadam road running through the Sand River valley and up the dusty two-lane dirt road to the top of the hill and Winchester Mall. We avoided the big four-lane bridge and Main Street. I didn't know if Danger was watching Main Street for the police cruiser, but I couldn't be sure he didn't. Steve and Brandi Lightner were already working, so I left Alice and Ceren with them and went back to the parking lot to wait for Eric.

Eric pulled in maybe five minutes after me. When he stepped out of his truck, I marveled at his softly burnished black skin gleaming in the morning sunlight. It was different, but striking, and it already looked natural. No, it looked *good* on him.

I cursed under my breath. With Reamer's news and Bill, I'd totally forgotten Eric's troubling transformation.

I told myself Eric's change of skin tone didn't matter to me. But it did.

I couldn't figure out if it was the way his body changed that bothered me, or the blackness.

And whichever it was, both bothered him a lot more.

I walked around my car to meet him, hands outstretched. "Morning, Eric."

Eric nodded. "Hey."

Cuddles strutted at Eric's flank, head raised, looking around eagerly.

"Man, I hate to say this," I said, tightening my lips. "I owe you an apology."

Eric looked puzzled.

"I figured something out last night, and wanted to talk with you about it. Before we start the flamethrower class, can we go in and talk with Ceren?"

Eric's eyebrows rose. "Talked with her last night, when you were out looking at Reamer. Told me about her hair."

I relaxed. "Glad to hear it. I totally spaced on that."

Eric shrugged. "If *you'd* told me, might've slugged you. Can't go hitting a teenage girl, though."

"Yeah," I said. "Ceren would hit you back."

Eric smiled with half his mouth. "Rep can take it. Badass now, you know? Like old Sam Jackson, but with attitude." He sighed. "Hate to admit it, but the kid makes sense. Self-image. Dammit."

"Yeah. If we all turn into what we think we are…"

I gently fingered my chin. Kevin had jammed a hot gun barrel under his chin in a failed attempt to blow his brains out. I had the blister. It hadn't healed in weeks—if anything, it felt more and more tender. Was that my self-image, too?

After an uncomfortable pause, Eric said, "Right. Flamethrower?"

We spent half an hour going over my police-issue flamethrower. Eric practiced pulling the nozzle, setting valves, and replacing the nozzle until I felt confident he could do it almost automatically. We scorched a few plumes into the decaying asphalt, lips pulled back and eyes narrowed against the torrent of flame's incredible heat. Cuddles hung twenty feet behind Eric, occasionally barking, the sound deep and loud enough to be heard over the crackle of frying air.

Once Eric had the basic operation down, I took him around to the windowless wall of bricks along the back of the mall and had him spray a burst at an angle against the mall's non-flammable rear so he could see the stinking river of heat and light deflect and diffuse away from the impact. "You see how that fire spread out, right? Whatever you do, don't fire straight at a wall. Or in an enclosed space. And never, ever fire upwind. Not unless you want to burn off your own face."

"Got it."

"And don't put the nozzle right up against anything. You'll blow up."

"Right."

"Aim at the base of what you're trying to hit. Don't burn someone in the head. Burn their legs or their abdomen, the fire will go up quick enough. Fire *anywhere* occupies enough of their attention, believe me!"

We walked back around to the front of the mall, near our cars. While the mall had looked abandoned, the flamethrower burns across the asphalt changed its feel from simple vacancy to a threatening absence of people. Suddenly, the parking lot evoked old violence. I felt small and fragile, revolted by all the blood and ash of the last day.

"You might as well take that flamethrower," I said before I could change my mind.

"What about you?"

"I'll go by the station later and get one."

Eric frowned. "Don't go alone." He unbuckled the tank from around his midsection and easily slipped the heavy weapon off his shoulders. With Bill's transformation, I was glad to have Eric's strength at my side. "You gonna need me today?"

I studied the decrepit parking lot, shaking my head at the trees beyond the open fields surrounding Winchester Mall. Even with the steady June breeze, the air still stank of combusted flamethrower gel. Scrawny trees grew in small dirt islands, choked by the lake of surrounding asphalt. I thought there had been a tree in the island closest to the mall entrance, but now it held only churned-up dirt. Why would someone dig up a tree? "Don't think so. There's too much chaos right now. I need to get a handle on some of it. I'm not up for house-checking today."

"No problem." Eric thumped the flamethrower tank into the back of his truck. Links of stout steel chain clicked across the tank as he locked it securely into place. "You be careful. You're taking on everyone's problems."

"They're not everyone's problems." I stopped. "That is, they're problems that affect everyone. Jack's love life is his own headache."

Eric snorted. "Not what I meant, you know it."

I shook my head. "Who else is doing it?"

"That shit will wear you down."

"What am I supposed to do?" I snapped. "Just—walk away? Pretend this isn't happening? Wait for Bill to kill someone else, or the flamethrower thief to burn half the town, or Woodward to declare himself king? One of the houses we haven't checked to release a dreg, a really dangerous one?"

"Easy," Eric said.

"No, really. I'm up for ideas."

Eric held out his hands, palms towards me, and took a deep breath. "You're right. It's important stuff. Just don't let it get to you. That's all."

I deflated. "Yeah. Sorry, it's a bit much."

"What I said. Don't lose it."

I looked around. "Anyone who hasn't lost it, has lost it."

"You right there."

Cuddles nosed at Eric's hanging hand.

"Got an idea," Eric said. "Gonna work on a project today, if you don't need me."

"Go ahead. Keep your radio on." I grinned. "If you hear a scream that trails off, and then static, come find me."

"Huh. Hear that, gonna find me a hole and pull it shut after me."

"Probably wisest."

I watched Eric drive off, Cuddles' massive head hanging from the open passenger window, tongue flapping in the breeze, then went towards the mall to say good-bye to Alice and Ceren.

When I opened the main door, the sound of distant crashes washed over me.

Then a scream.

A metallic, inhuman screech.

I dashed towards the chaos, already knowing I was too slow, too late.

Chapter 45

GUNSHOTS, CONTROLLED and coordinated, one after another.

I bolted towards the mall's hexagonal center court, fear roiling my stomach and sweat rolling down my face. I'd brought Alice and Ceren here for safety—had Danger sent his dregs after them?

Brandi and Steve had brought big translucent plastic tubs of equipment into the mall's courtyard, stacking it on folding tables and empty benches bolted to the mall's tile floor. Now those bins lay everywhere, tops unsnapped, spilling parts and tiny screws and cables in tangled sprawls. Toppled tables spilled desktop computers to the floor, their metal and plastic cases dangling free from the chassis underneath. Leaning stacks of lumber and metal plumbing pipes had scattered like straws across the floor. In the dim light seeping through the dirty skylights, the mall's central court looked like the aftermath of a riot.

My eyes didn't understand the creature looming over Ceren. And my brain didn't want to accept what my eyes reported, couldn't put the pieces together into a comprehensible form.

Bile surged in the back of my throat.

This wasn't a dreg.

Whatever it was didn't look even vaguely human. Or even like anything evolved on Earth.

Alien in the purest sense of the word.

The disk-shaped blue-and-black body, about the size of a card table, swayed atop three bright yellow tentacle-legs, each as thick as my thigh. Two skeletal, articulated limbs with too many joints rose like cranes from one edge of the disk, snatching and discarding pieces of computer equipment from a crowded work table. Dozens of yard-long tentacles as thick as my pinky lashed out from the edge of the disk and danced across the table, blindly probing abandoned computer cards and hard drives and connectors.

An almost-human torso, Indian brown and complete with dark round nipples, rose from one edge of the disk-shaped body, its apparent normality made more awful by the single cantilevered arm extending from what should have been a shoulder. Tendrils oozed out from the end, slithering around the aluminum framework of the oversized computer dominating the table.

A perfect sphere of gleaming black and meaty red perched loosely atop the trunk, covered with innumerable eyes. A few eyes looked human, green and brown irises next to faceted insectile orbs and oval crystals familiar only from nightmares.

Plus other bits. Ridges of horn and skin. Flaps of skin that sagged open and pulled taut without any rhythm. So many different types of wrong flesh obscenely jumbled, I couldn't absorb it all.

The tentacles slicing the air and probing the table didn't seem random. Every motion had a purpose. A whiplike tentacle that sliced the air one second might join three others to snatch a printed circuit board half a second later.

I—*Kevin*—had seen creatures that moved like this, somehow managing a dozen limbs simultaneously.

Kevin had seen them on classified footage recovered from networked cameras. Many times. Meat puppets, abandoning their disguises and swarming the humans around them.

This was a primal piece of the alien that had devoured the human race, laid waste to the planet, and forced me to kill my wife and daughter.

Absolute.

Rage alone wouldn't kill Absolute, and I didn't have a flamethrower. Or even a gun.

But Ceren sprawled on the ceramic tile floor, her legs beneath the monstrous body, torso angled away from me, either unconscious or dead.

Unchained fury flared in my bones.

Absolute ate the entire world.

I would *not* allow it a second chance at Ceren.

Even if I had to burn the mall to slag and ash.

I glanced around. Toppled tables, overturned chairs, spilled boxes of computer cards, spools of power and network cable spilled into tangled loops, dumped plates of canned corned beef hash—*there*.

With three steps I snatched a six-foot length of iron pipe off the floor, just thick enough to fit comfortably in one hand. It was heavier than I thought. I needed both hands to wrench it up into the air like a wobbly flagpole.

I doubted I could kill even this little part of the monster. Even if I did, it wouldn't truly touch the alien that had exterminated life on Earth. More like cutting off its fingernails would have been to a human.

That didn't matter. None of that mattered. The only thing I cared about was Ceren, dangerously enclosed by the thing's tentacular feet. It seemed interested only in the oversized computer on the table. She might be safe, right now. That chance wasn't good enough.

Another bark of gunfire.

Black ichor splashed from the creature's trunk. The goo oozed the length of a hand down the torso, then seamlessly osmosed back into it.

I followed the bullet's trajectory back to its origin near the abandoned food stand. Crumpled on the ground, Steve looked upward at nothing.

Six-foot-eight Brandi stood with one foot on either side of Steve's torso, an automatic pistol with one of those ridiculously extended magazines in her hands. The pink-streaked black hair didn't seem so ridiculous now—Brandi looked like an ancient warrior painted to terrify her enemies.

Alice stood behind Brandi, hands clamped over her mouth to choke a scream, eyes bulging in horror.

Brandi's gun barked. The bullet slammed into one of the insectile eyes, smashing it into a spray of blue-and-black ichor.

The creature didn't even stumble.

Half a second later, a replacement eye oozed out of the head like a time-lapse pimple.

Other tentacles slithered across the old-fashioned mechanical keyboard, producing a clatter. White text on a black background poured across one of the monitors, moving far more quickly than anyone could read.

Between Absolute's tentacle-feet, Ceren stirred.

She's alive.

Even more adrenaline ignited along my nervous system.

Kevin had often wondered what he'd do when faced with Absolute. Would he run screaming? Or stand his ground and die?

I took five long steps across the debris-cluttered floor, tottering to keep the weighty pipe balanced overhead. "You!" I shouted. "Get away from her!"

Absolute kept sorting through the computer pieces on the table. I thought I saw one eye blink several times.

I swung my arms forward, my body leaning back, and sent the pipe crashing down on the ball of eyes.

The orb crunched and squelched. Eyes slammed shut, each oozing a few drops of something. Tears? Ichor? I didn't have time to guess.

The pipe bounced off the alien, back into the air. I added to its momentum until it reached the top of its rebound, then grunted and heaved the pipe back downward.

I cracked the pipe across Absolute's disk-shaped back. The sound of breaking cartilage both soothed and fed the anger blazing in my soul. "I said, get off of her!"

Some of the flailing tentacles smacked against the pipe.

I heaved it up before Absolute could grab it.

Ceren shifted. One hand creaked to her head and rubbed her scalp. Brandi fired.

A bullet splashed into the torso.

The noise snapped Ceren alert. Her hands and feet scrabbled for traction, and she scooted a desperate yard backwards until her head slammed against the black wrought iron legs of a bench beside the pylon of the store directory. Her mouth flapped, eyes wide with animal terror.

I swung the pipe like a baseball bat, trying to both knock Absolute away from Ceren and keep myself out of Brandi's field of fire. "I said, get away from her!"

Ceren's legs kicked but she couldn't scoot any further, trapped at the intersection of the bench and the flat tower of the mall directory. Her face turned bright red, and she grabbed the bench leg as though she meant to hide behind it.

The pipe crashed into Absolute's torso just as another bullet hit his ball of eyes. Absolute actually shifted an inch in response to two simultaneous impacts.

Ceren's scream sounded both angry and afraid.

I pulled the iron pipe back for another blow. This time I'd put my whole body behind the strike. It would take me into tentacle range.

I'd take that risk if it gave Ceren room to escape.

Absolute stopped flailing its tentacles at the keyboard, instead plunging them into the computer's exposed guts.

I stepped in with the pipe, again swinging it like a baseball bat, turning my body with the blow, trying to focus every scrap of power and weight I could summon in that couple inches of metal at the far end.

The torso crunched, folding in around the end of the pipe.

This time, Absolute's tentacles instantly whipped around my bludgeon and stayed. I clamped down my grip, elbows locked, grimly determined to hold the pipe at my waist and pull it free.

My shoulders groaned with upward pressure from the pipe.

My feet left the ground. I dangled from the pipe, watching as Absolute raised it.

I balanced on my hands for a moment, the pipe even with my waist, until the pipe shifted and I lost my balance, plunging down. My feet smacked the floor, the impact echoing up my frame and clanging my teeth. The force of the fall stunned my hands and crumpled my elbows, letting Absolute wrench the pipe free of my grip.

Somewhere, metal screeched and popped.

My head spun and I tasted bright copper at the back of my throat. I wobbled on my feet, taking half a step sideways to clutch at my balance, adrenaline making my heart hammer in my throat.

Absolute swung the pipe back and forth over my head.

Brandi's gun barked twice, quickly.

I danced back two steps, hurriedly snatched a length of two-by-four from the floor, and hopped forward. My two-by was shorter than the pipe, and not nearly as heavy. A blow from the pipe would wreck me, though, and I'd rather the lumber took the first hit.

I couldn't see Ceren from this angle. "Ceren!" I shouted. "Go over the bench!"

I had to get around Absolute. Cross Brandi's field of fire. Put myself between it and Ceren.

Absolute's torso and legs remained perfectly still. The pipe hovered in midair, held aloft by two thin tentacles. Its other tentacles and both of its overly jointed arms worked furiously inside the computer, while the overhead cantilever used its own tentacles to pin the machine's chassis in place.

I glimpsed a small bit of metal shooting by my head, too slow to be a bullet but fast enough to hurt, and involuntarily ducked.

From behind the bench, metal snapped.

I raised my two-by like a baseball bat.

Then Ceren lunged up into view, bent at the waist, head facing Absolute, a yard of black metal in her tight grip. Teeth bared, she slashed the pole against Absolute's closest leg.

Absolute wobbled.

Ceren struck again on the backswing.

Ignoring the pipe looming over me, I raised my club and charged.

Ceren raised the black metal bar for a swing.

We both struck simultaneously, her on the leg, me on the torso.

"Dammit!" Brandi shouted. "Get out of the way!"

Brandi's gun snarled.

Ichor flew from an alien insect eye.

A handful of thin tentacles slapped my face like wet, slimy worms, not leaving welts but making me gag in revulsion as they fondled my cheeks, my nose, my lips, leaving a trail of ooze that stank of things that should be inside a body. Then they wrapped around the two-by-four and jerked it from my hands.

I staggered back, trying to quell my nausea at Absolute's touch.

Metal clattered hollowly on the floor, and I heard Brandi fitting another magazine into her pistol.

The tentacles stopped moving.

Absolute froze in place for a single beat of my frantic heart. The unmoving eyes seemed to be studying me, Ceren, Brandi and Steve, the whole of the Winchester Mall atrium, even Legacy.

Ceren raised her bludgeon for another strike.

The legs blurred.

Absolute launched itself back towards the entrance I'd come in, using the three legs to spin the disk-shaped body, almost like a rolling coin.

I didn't even stop to breathe, but bolted after it, my boots crushing bits of scattered computer hardware before hammering the clean tile beyond.

Absolute changed its form as it ran, its flesh pulsing and oozing, becoming longer and thinner, its gait changing from the three-legged roll to a trot. It didn't slow down to change form, or when it crashed through the mall doors out into the world.

I sprinted onto the cracked asphalt of the parking lot.

Motion to my right grabbed my attention in time for me to see Absolute leap atop the parking lot's closest island of dirt, the barren one that I'd remembered having a tree the day before. Flesh flowed and shimmered like mercury as most of the alien body sank into the soil.

The bizarre cantilevered arm didn't vanish. It flowed straight up, reforming into a starving, scraggly tree like all the others in the lot.

Heart still pounding, I dashed to the island. No longer churned up, the dirt looked as if it had been hard packed the day forever ago when the tree had been planted.

I felt a scream begin to tear its way out of my body and clamped it down. Moving deliberately despite the furious tremors rippling up and down my spine, I wrapped my hands around the tiny tree trunk and pulled. This wasn't a tree. It was a fake, more fake than most.

I pulled until my shoulders and calves cramped, until battle exhaustion smothered me. Unable to stand, I collapsed to my knees and glared at the tree.

"Fuck."

Chapter 46

I FORCED myself to walk back inside Winchester Mall, hair soaked in sweat, shirt glued to my skin, and dirt scraped into my knees.

Absolute. I'd had it. Had a piece of it and let it get away.

Never mind that I couldn't possibly have stopped the alien with a club, or that this was only a tiny piece of it. That it hadn't even condescended to notice me trying to murder it.

Seeing the alien had resurrected my rage. Absolute had taken the Earth. It had overcome every defense the human race had raised against it. It had ignored everything from handguns up to thermonuclear bombs on land and plutonium in the ocean. It had exterminated us, and created us, and left us to discover the rules of our new existence. The hard way.

I ached to catch Absolute. To burn it down. To find its home and tear every scrap of knowledge out of it before executing it for something beyond genocide. Absolute hadn't merely wiped out the human race—it'd killed every creature that had ever lived on the Earth. It'd wiped out a billion years of genetic history.

The extinction of the dinosaurs was nothing next to what Absolute had done.

As I stalked back up the hall between lines of closed shops, my fingernails dug into the palms of my hands and my vision thudded with my pulse. I tried to slow my breathing, but my shaking body demanded more air.

I had reason for my fury. Everyone did. I'd sworn to destroy Absolute, to learn what I needed to burn it to the ground—and I would.

But right now, I had Ceren and Alice to worry about. Plus Steve and Brandi. Well, Steve, at least. Brandi had taken care of herself.

By the time I returned to the ruin of the mall's central plaza, my chest had stopped aching and my pulse had slowed to a gallop. Alice stood with Ceren next to the bench Ceren had sheltered alongside, holding her friend's shoulders.

Ceren shrugged Alice away. "I'm telling you, I'm fine. Geez."

Brandi knelt beside Steve, holding his hand. "Come on, baby. Wake up."

"You two all right?" I said to Alice and Ceren.

Alice nodded. Her face was white, her chin clamped tight.

"I'm not all right, I'm fucking pissed." Ceren's twisted black iron club shook in one hand. "As hell."

I glanced at Steve, still sprawled next to the abandoned food stand, surrounded by a minefield of jagged shards of broken plastic cables and bent metal, Brandi kneeling over him. Brandi still clutched her automatic in one hand, finger over the guard but the barrel waving towards the back of the mall. Her empty hand fluttered over Steve's face and chest. "Wake up!"

"Steve needs us," I said as quietly as I could manage. "Pissed is fine, but—later. Treat for shock now. Can you grab something for under his feet, a blanket?"

Ceren gritted her teeth. "Yeah."

Alice looked relieved. "Sure?"

"Go," I said, and carefully wove through the wreckage of overturned tables and scattered electronics towards Brandi and Steve.

Steve was a bulky man, verging on plump. Ex-military police, he knew how to carry himself in a fight—at least, a fight against someone with two arms or fewer. Now he lay sprawled limp, legs every which way, one arm over his head, the other hand clutched in Brandi's shaky grip.

I knelt on Steve's opposite side. "What happened?"

"That monster walked in." Brandi's voice shook. I didn't look at her face—she wouldn't want me to see the tears. "Steve was working over at the Beast, the big computer we got for cracking Legacy's signals." She forced a deep breath. "It shoved him aside, not a word. Steve got up and punched it."

"He tried to punch *that?*"

"It didn't look like that!" Brandi said, her voice quavering the longer she spoke. "It looked human when it walked in. A big fat bastard. Steve shouted and punched it in the back of the head, and it changed. It knocked him all the way back here and it changed."

I nodded.

Steve wasn't bleeding. His face seemed relaxed, almost composed, but paler than usual. If he'd been thrown twenty feet, though, he might have injuries we couldn't see. What would we do if he had a broken spine? Feed him melon?

I needed to keep desperate Brandi from accidentally hurting Steve further, though. "Brandi. Brandi!"

Her face jerked to mine.

I ignored the streaks of tears. "Do you have a first aid kit handy?"

She shook her head. "Never needed it."

"Upstairs. The janitor's closet. You know where that is?" I'd noticed it the day I'd first met Brandi and Steve.

Her head jerked a single nod.

"Big first aid kit there. On the wall. On the right as you go in. Go grab it."

She glanced back at Steve.

"You want to help Steve? Or you want to stay here and cry? Grab it! Go!"

Brandi recoiled with a furious glare, then climbed to her feet and dashed up the dead escalator.

By the time Brandi returned, Alice and Ceren had brought a short plastic box to prop under Steve's feet and a blanket from the bedding store. Brandi dropped the tackle box first aid kit near Steve's head, dangerously close to my foot. "Here."

The first whiff of smelling salts made Steve cough and convulse. I whipped the canister back as his head thrashed. "Easy, Steve, easy. Stay still."

Steve's hands planted on the tile on each side of his hips and he raised his head. "Where? What?" His feet shifted to a more natural position, and I relaxed. His back wasn't broken—or, if it had been broken, he'd healed it before he woke up.

"Hang on," I said. "Alice, Ceren, prop his feet up. You took a nasty knock. Stay there a moment. Let me check you out."

"You're not a doctor," Steve said.

"I had first aid training every year since I was eight," I said, taking his arm and putting my index and middle fingers over his wrist. His heart beat quickly but regularly. "Boy Scouts, then police. Let me look into your eyes." The pupils were the same size, and dilated when I held my hand to cast a shadow over them.

"Far as I can tell," I said, "you'll be fine. But rest for five minutes. Keep your feet up; you probably have a touch of shock."

"I'm fine," Steve said.

"Stay right there!" Brandi snapped. "You got knocked out."

"Are you cold?" I said.

Ceren hefted her thick plaid quilt.

"Christ, no," Steve said. "I'd melt under that thing."

"Then stay right there," Brandi said. "Or I'll nail that comforter to the floor with you under it."

Steve lifted his hands and spread his fingers in mock surrender. "Yes, dear."

Suddenly I missed Sheila terribly. "*Ten* minutes," I said, my voice thick. "Don't let him fall asleep."

Brandi knelt beside Steve again. "You idiot."

I took a step back to give them some space. The closest place to sit was the bench Ceren had hidden beside. I jerked my head at Alice and Ceren. "Come on."

The aftermath of the fight and the chase had left my back and legs burning. My shoulders ached with tension. I knew Steve and Brandi had water somewhere around here, but for the moment I only wanted to sit and straighten my mind and body.

Muscles creaked and joints popped as I dropped onto one end of the bench. "Have a—"

The wooden bench seat rocked beneath me, the back corner sagging alarmingly with my weight. My arms flapped at empty air as a wooden slat cracked.

I scrambled to my feet before the bench completely broke. "What?"

Puzzlement brought some color back to Alice's face. "It broke it?"

Ceren flushed bright red and looked back at Steve, lying on the tile fifteen feet away, with Brandi sitting cross-legged beside him.

I peered around the edge of the bench, where the wrought iron frame met the tall sign of the mall directory and the work tables that had hemmed Ceren in.

The left rear leg of the bench was missing.

Mostly.

The cheap welds where the leg had met the arm rail and the seat frame had snapped.

The leg had been secured to the floor with heavy bolts through two metal flanges. The bolts and flanges remained. The flanges were twisted and distorted, as if someone had yanked on the leg with incredible strength until the metal had ripped.

I glanced at the other rear leg.

The leg was bent.

Like someone had put their feet against it, for traction.

Involuntarily I looked up at Ceren.

My adopted daughter still resolutely stared at Brandi and Steve. Feeling the pressure of my gaze, though, she turned. Fresh fury filled her face, the black wrought-iron leg in a white-knuckled grip.

Chapter 47

THE SHOPPING mall atrium and the scattered broken debris from the fight faded from view. For a second, I only saw Ceren. She wore mid-thigh denim shorts and her old, faded Mesh concert tour T-shirt with a fresh tear in the shoulder. Her teeth were clenched, and a blink showed a sheen of angry tears hovering over her eyes. White knuckles rimmed in red clenched the wrought iron bench leg she'd wrenched off of the bench and out of the ground.

Beside her, Alice sensed the abrupt tension. She glanced between Ceren and me curiously.

"It's okay," I said quietly.

Ceren's hand shook, then she flung the metal bar at the floor. It hit hard enough to crack a ceramic tile, bounced six feet into the air, and thudded down amidst a table full of small tools, scattering everything across the table and floor in a chorus of clatters. "It is not all right!" she shouted. "Everything breaks when I touch it. I'm getting bigger and bigger, every day, like I'm a fucking monster, and it just won't—my clothes don't fit, I hurt everywhere, and it just won't—isn't—"

Ceren's face—bright red already—seemed about to implode when she stopped screaming long enough to suck in another breath.

"You're no monster," I said. "Being a monster is something you do, not something you are. And you try to do the right thing."

Alice said, "What's wrong?"

"I'm—I'm—" Ceren shook her head, then stalked over to the iron bar she'd flung away a moment ago.

I couldn't help tensing. A teenage girl is the most emotionally volatile creature on Earth. A little detail like not being human wouldn't change that.

But Ceren only grabbed the bar from the table, whirled, and raised it in one fist.

And squeezed.

The bar quivered in her grip.

Then hot black iron oozed like clay between Ceren's clenched fingers.

Alice's mouth dropped open. "Wow."

Ceren stomped back towards me, holding the bar out in front of her like a leper's bell. "I'm a freak."

"You're strong," I said. My heart, barely slowed from the fight with Absolute, hammered anew. Forcing iron like that made it heat up, but Ceren didn't seem to notice. I tried not to let my worry show in my face.

"That's not strong!" Ceren shouted. "That's fucking *wrong!*"

"You're still my best friend," Alice said.

"You're still my girl," I said. "In every way that matters. Both of you. This is just more Absolute weirdness."

Ceren trembled, unaccustomed tears glinting in her eyes. "It's just—it's wrong."

"That depends," I said carefully. "Are you going to leap tall buildings in a single bound? Or are you going to knock over banks?"

"You're still you," Alice said.

"Oh?" Ceren said. "You say that, when you just keep getting thinner?"

Alice turned even more red. "That's just dieting."

"You're not dieting," Ceren said. "You had a can of *ravioli* for breakfast. You're just too damn thin. Like Kevin's getting fatter."

"I am not getting fatter," I said. My gut tugged at the buttons of my shirt, but I sucked it in. Hadn't that shirt felt loose this morning? "I mean, I am, but I've always—"

"We are fucked!" Ceren shouted.

"Ceren, honey," Brandi said. She'd risen to her feet and stood behind Ceren.

Ceren jumped. "Don't *honey* me! I'm not a baby! I'm like the Hulk or something. Get near me and I'll break you!"

My mind churned. Soothing a child is a parent's hardest job. And I hadn't raised Ceren, I'd only accepted responsibility for her. I'd known her only a month, and the techniques I'd used for my Julie didn't get any traction with Ceren.

"It's pretty freaky," I said. "I'd be scared too."

Alice's calm demeanor dissolved into tears trickling down her cheeks. "Every time I think we're getting used to this, something happens and we're lost again. I can't take this. I am tired of being so *afraid* all the time."

Ceren whirled to face Alice, hefting the bar. "Anything messes with us, I will break them into bitty pieces."

I let out the breath I hadn't known I was holding. If Ceren could react to Alice's fear by offering to protect her, she'd be okay. Eventually.

I spread my arms. "We can do this. Whatever this is. We will figure it out."

From behind Ceren, Brandi said, "I'm getting taller."

Alice blinked. Ceren turned to look at Brandi.

What with the fight, I hadn't taken more than a heartbeat to look at Brandi. She wore a shapeless T-shirt, denim jeans that came halfway down her calves, and strap sandals over bare feet.

Brandi tugged at a side seam of her jeans. "These aren't capris." Her voice stayed firm, daring us to challenge her. "My legs have gotten longer. The shirt, it's from the men's big and tall store on the second floor."

"What is *happening* to us?" Alice said.

"It's like Ceren's hair," I said. "And Eric."

I patted my stomach through my shirt. My shirts had been a little tighter than usual, but I'd marked that up to Jack's bountiful cooking. Long hours sitting in a police cruiser didn't mesh well with a healthy diet. I'd hoped that searching buildings with Eric would help take some of that off, but—

"I've fought this spare tire around my middle my whole life," I said quietly. "I was a chubby kid. I grew up and exercised the weight away but I know it's there, always."

I got tired of staring at my shoes, so looked up to see Brandi, standing in the same place, her shoulders slumped, her knees bent, looking a smidge shorter. "Brandi. Do you wish you were short?"

"I'm good with being tall," she said.

I licked my lips. "And you—see yourself as really tall? Like when you dream, you're tall in your dreams?"

"I am tall everywhere. *Really* tall."

"Ceren," I said. "You're brave. You're tough. I don't know any teenager who stands up for others like you do for Alice. And damn few adults."

Ceren's face wrinkled with embarrassment, but I plunged on. "And you know the world is dangerous. You know you have to be tough and strong to meet it. The dregs, they've changed. Why can't we change like we think we need to?"

"You think I'm doing this to myself?" Ceren said.

"I think you think about protecting Alice and your friends," I said. "Maybe your body is picking up on that. You changed your hair color. Why not your muscles?"

"But—" Ceren grabbed an end of the iron bar with her free hand, then peeled the other hand out of the grooves she'd squeezed into it. Freed from her clench, the iron looked thin as a toothpick. As she let go, it sagged and bent under its own weight. "This isn't—I mean, this is just…wrong."

The bent bar clanged to the ground.

"So make it right," I said. "I mean, why did you even try to pull a leg off the bench?"

"I was desperate," Ceren said. "I needed something to protect me and Alice."

Alice sidled closer to Ceren and tucked her hand around Ceren's bicep. "That dreg was horrible."

"Forget horrible!" Ceren snapped, reaching up to touch the tear in her shirt. "That thing ripped Mom's shirt! The last thing of hers I'll ever have."

Ceren was wearing her mother's shirts? That explained the old bands.

Alice tried to give her a hug, but Ceren stepped back. "Don't. I'm sick of crying. Those dregs burned my fucking house, they came here, they tried to kill us."

"That wasn't a dreg," I said.

Ceren glared at me. "Of course it was a dreg. There's nothing else it could have been."

"How are you feeling, Steve?" I said.

Steve sat up behind Brandi and crossed his legs. "I've felt weirdly fat myself, these last few weeks."

"What was it!" Ceren shouted.

"I don't *think* it was a dreg. I think it was Absolute."

"Bullshit," Brandi said.

I said, "Steve can tell us for sure. Steve, can you check the computer it was ripping apart? What did it do? It grabbed something. What did it take?"

Brandi moved to help Steve. He feebly protested, but let his wife help him to his feet. I went to grab an intact swivel chair for him. The chair had wheels, but I had to carry it across the debris-strewn floor to the big computer. Ceren and Alice had already cleared floor space for the chair by the time I reached the table.

Steve tried to sit, then bent over to lower the chair's height before settling in. "Well, love, that thing didn't break your chair." He peered into the computer's exposed boards. "This'll take me a few minutes. Go—do something. Let me work."

Brandi glanced around. "Anyone see the broom?"

Alice and Ceren glanced at each other.

I said, "If we have to wait, we can help pick up."

"We need a dumpster," Ceren said.

I looked around at the scattered debris. "This is all the manufactured stuff we're going to have for… a while. Don't throw the broken stuff away. Put it in a box or something."

Inside ten minutes, we had cleared the floor and made a start on restacking plastic storage bins of spilled cables and computer parts.

Ceren was helping me get one of the big screens back on a righted folding table when Steve swiveled away from the computer. "This is a weird one."

"What is it?" Brandi said.

Ceren and I balanced the video screen on the table before I said, "Oh?"

Steve was shaking his head. "This computer is full of disks. We have almost an exabyte in a raid-z5 of thirty drives for captured data, plus a mirrored pool for the operating system and applications. All that mayhem, and it took one hard drive."

I needed a heartbeat to excavate the actual fact out of the technobabble. "Was it important?" I said. "What did it steal?"

Eyebrow furrowed, Steve said, "It's a one in sixteen chance. It took a copy of Alice's frame capture software and Brandi's new analysis tools."

Chapter 48

"YOU THINK Absolute stole our software?" Brandi said. "Absolute owns the whole damn world. Why would he be here?"

I pulled in a deep, clammy breath through my nose. "You've been with Legacy most of your time, haven't you?"

"So?"

Ceren said, "Aw, shit."

"Exactly," I said.

"What?" Alice said, head flicking between the three of us.

"Go a few miles south of here, and you hit the edge," I said. "We're—the whole town—we're surrounded with burned-out ash. Everything burned but Frayville. All the way to the horizon, there's no sign of anything but ashes and dust."

My words turned Brandi's face even paler. "But the lake. That mess is alive."

"You can't burn the lake," I said. "If Absolute is here…"

Ceren said, "Maybe there's no place else to be."

"It couldn't burn the whole world!" Alice said.

"Absolute wanted to take the world," I said. "If it's actually all burned…we're the ones who did it."

I could easily imagine the scene. Countless old movies had given me variations on it. The North American command base buried under Cheyenne Mountain. A room lit only by computer screens. A huge wall displaying a map of North America, cities as neat dots on green land. Red seeping in from every coast, oozing out of the Mississippi River, down from of Hudson Bay. Grim faces watching Absolute's final attack. Tense voices: *We've lost contact with the UK. With Japan, with Moscow.*

Another voice: *New York City has fallen. Detroit. Podunk, Iowa.*

And the command after each loss: *Detonate. Detonate. Detonate.*

With each command, a chunk of the map turning black.

Similar scenes in Russia. Japan. Egypt.

Everywhere.

The human race had spent almost three years preparing for Absolute's last invasion. Each county stocked dozens or hundreds of incendiary devices. The only places that might have been spared would have been lifeless deserts, places with too little material to catch fire. Like the desolate badlands where Kevin had fled with Sheila and Julie.

I'd even found the paper doomsday manual, the North American Cauterization Plan. In the Morpeths' home, where Bill had killed Keith. Inevitable human logic: burn out the parts Absolute seized, in the hope of stopping the alien's advance.

If humanity couldn't have the Earth, then no one could.

Somehow, Frayville had been spared the final conflagration. Equipment failure? Or had those grim warriors tried to blow Frayville, only to learn that Absolute was in their command center? Had tentacles ravaged Cheyenne? Or had Absolute raised some sort of defense around us?

"I don't buy it," Brandi said. "There have to be other people out there."

"I can't prove it," I said. My gut insisted that Absolute was in here with us. "But if someone in Frayville can do what *that* did, then we are *way* behind the curve."

"Whatever." Brandi shook her head. "What would Absolute want with my software, anyway? And Alice's?"

"I have no idea," I said. "But I can almost guarantee we're not going to like the answer."

I spent a few minutes helping Brandi, Ceren, and Alice move a couple broken tables and chairs to a pile next to a planter filled with barren dirt in the middle of the unused back hall. The simple task gave my brain time to clear. Ceren seemed calmer and Alice more thoughtful. Steve tried to help, but Brandi badgered him into sorting some of the debris into "usable" and "busted" piles. He didn't argue too much—Absolute throwing him halfway across the atrium had probably given Steve a nice collection of bruises.

Would Steve heal quickly, like I had last night? Or did I heal more quickly than others? Had anyone else in Frayville been shot through the heart and lived? I'd have to find out how Steve felt tomorrow morning. Would he be bruised and aching, or bounce back?

Once we had the large debris cleared from the atrium, leaving scattered cables and components over the gray tile, I clapped my hands off on the sides of my shorts. "Well, it's been fun, but I'd better get going. I have people to see this morning."

Alice looked worried. "Be careful."

"I'm always careful," I said.

Ceren snorted and grabbed a plastic bin. "You have the weirdest definition of careful."

Steve looked up from the computer he was working on. "If you find that hard drive, let me know. It's a couple inches square, a connector on one end. I wrote the number two on it in big black letters."

"I thought you still had a copy," I said.

"I do." Steve turned back to the computer, a minuscule screwdriver absurdly clenched between three fingertips. "I want to know who took it."

Brandi said, "We all do." Did her nod have a little more respect than before? "See you."

"I'll walk you out," Alice said.

I studied Ceren for a moment. She sat on her heels, gathering scraps of broken computer cards and dropping them into a plastic storage bin meant for paperwork. Her touch seemed consciously delicate, but the festering cyst of emotions that had grown in her for the last week seemed lanced, if not healed. We'd have to talk more, but not right now. Not in front of everyone. And maybe now she could talk to Alice about what had happened. "Sure. Let's go."

Alice said nothing until we got close to the mall exit. I had reached for the door handle when she said, "Kevin?"

I stopped, turning back to her.

Alice flung herself at me. Her arms clasped around my back as she buried her face in my chest. "I'm really glad you were here."

I gave her a quick hug back. "I'm glad I was, too."

She hung on longer, an unhappy fourteen-year-old aching for reassurance. I patted her back a moment. "It's okay. It wanted the computer. It got what it wanted and it left." She didn't need to know that Absolute had dissolved into the dirt, taking the hard drive with it. The scraggly tree—that stubborn, impossibly rooted scraggly tree—had been its arm.

Maybe I'd get Eric to bring the backhoe. Dig up that tree. See how deep the roots went.

I squeezed Alice again, then let her go. "Hey, Alice. Really. You're okay."

Alice reluctantly released me and took a half step back. "Kevin? You remember when you found me with Teresa? In the apartment?"

"Sure I do." Alice had gone missing. Jesse and Teresa were some of the very first people I'd met after leaving my home for the first time. Jesse had told me that Teresa was missing. We'd gone to Teresa's apartment to look for both of them, and found them.

Teresa had been trying to suck Alice into the mental connection she and Jesse shared. Before we'd escaped, they'd both tried the same with me. Forming their connection required intense emotion, which is why they'd tried seducing me.

I still remembered Jesse's lips scorching mine. Their perfect, electric touch returned to me sometimes. Usually in the middle of the night. When I felt most alone.

"If it hadn't been for you," I said, "they would have had eaten my mind."

Alice licked her lips and looked up at me, her eyes wide, lips parted. "When they came after you—when they were kissing you—does it really feel that incredible?"

Chapter 49

THE CANNED stew I'd eaten for breakfast staged a rebellion in my guts. My knees almost buckled from the surprise. Being asked about a sexual assault on me, which Alice had been an inadvertent part of, hadn't been what I thought I'd be doing when I woke up this morning. But something had put it on my karmic to-do list, right after "fight off a chunk of Absolute" and "help my other adopted daughter chill out enough to stop pulling steel apart like taffy."

Alice was fourteen years old. She was my Julie's friend.

No parent wants to talk about sex with their kids. Sheila and I had each talked with Julie every four months since she was ten. It never got any easier, but I got accustomed to it. Sheila had put recurring reminders on our calendars, staggered two months apart. Sex was a part of life. It was everywhere, and kids had to be prepared to deal with it.

Kevin's chief of police, Tom Pink, told me that he looked forward to those talks with his sons. He enjoyed embarrassing the hell out of his kids.

But Alice wasn't my daughter.

When I'd found Alice and Teresa in Teresa's apartment, Alice had been sitting blankly at the back of Teresa's living room. She hadn't responded to anything I said. Teresa had been trying to force her mind onto Alice's. Alice had fought. Eventually Alice had found enough of herself to club Teresa across the head with a table lamp, giving us a chance to escape.

When Teresa and Jesse had thrown themselves at me, I'd thought Alice was as good as unconscious.

From the sound of her voice now, I was wrong. Alice had felt everything.

She was young enough to be my daughter.

And I'd tried to be a father to her.

The hug she'd given me took on new shades of meaning. I'm happy to hug a kid for reassurance. Alice had pressed herself tightly against me. Had she been fighting shock from facing Absolute? Or had that clench been more—adult?

A shard of my surprise and revulsion must have shown on my face. Alice took an alarmed step back, fresh fear on her face, then set her jaw. The summer sunlight, dimmed by the dirty skylights over the mall entrance, made her look even more determined.

No, she couldn't be thinking that. And if she was, I'd shut her down.

She could be thinking of anyone.

But if I walked away right now, she might get horribly hurt.

Or destroyed.

I held myself still, trying to pitch my voice as both neutral and inviting. "You felt that, huh?"

The blush used Alice's cheeks as a staging area and launched assaults on her forehead and down her neck. "I couldn't not. I wasn't trying to—I mean, I already felt everything Teresa did, even stuff she didn't know how to feel anymore, like the inside of her bones and skin and stuff, and Jesse was coming close enough that I could feel her too, sort of, aching knees where the kneecap kind of rubbed against the other bones and her back itched, but it wasn't nearly as much as Teresa, and then they grabbed you and it was, like…"

She took a deep breath, held it for a beat, and then looked me in the eye. "It was like you exploded."

I shouldn't have been surprised. During the attack, I'd felt Jesse and Teresa in much the same way. I arranged my lips in a small, embarrassed smile. "I thought you were unconscious. Stunned. Or something."

Alice's thin frame shivered slightly, her eyes looking backwards in time. "I wasn't trying to be awake. It was Teresa. It was like she sat on my brain, you know? When she put her attention on you, it let me get my breath, start to think. If she'd been paying me more attention, I couldn't have snuck up on her."

"I don't blame you," I said quickly. "I'm just surprised. Surprised it happened, and surprised you didn't bring it up before now."

I remembered all of Kevin's excruciating discussions with Julie. I'd done my best with her. But all that human advice meant nothing now.

"Look." I turned my glance a few degrees off Alice's bright face, staring sightlessly at the gleaming steel chains of a roll-down gate hanging a few inches open before a men's dress shoe store. "Did your mom or dad talk to you about these things?" I knew Alice's mom had died a few years ago, but maybe she'd had at least one talk with her daughter.

"I had those lectures at school," Alice said. "And my Aunt Bell, she had a talk with me last year."

"Right. *Those* lectures." *And your womanizing dad said nothing.* I rubbed my face with one hand. "So, um. Look. Sex is… There's a… It's a mystery. We don't know much. The diseases. Did Absolute resurrect, you know, herpes and AIDS?" Why was the mall getting so hot all of a sudden? "Did everyone who had those diseases get cured when they came back? Or did he not bring people back who had them?"

Alice nodded.

"And pregnancy—well. Who knows?" A drop of sweat formed at the base of my neck and started tickling a path down my spine. "Thing is, I don't want you to be the one to find out the hard way. Not right now."

"Gross, Kevin. I'm not thinking about—I just… No. I'm…I'm just—wondering."

No, you're thinking about it. You're fourteen and full of hormones and you got a taste of something that felt pretty incredible and you want another bite, you want the whole thing. I tried to slow my thoughts. Yes, Alice was thirty years younger than me. But it wasn't her fault that she'd been exposed to something she wasn't ready for. It wasn't my fault that that exposure had come from me, that she'd felt what I felt.

Teresa's abuse of Alice had angles I hadn't even imagined. I needed her to understand what had happened. Even for these days, it hadn't been normal. Or good.

"That was an attack," I made myself say. "An assault. The two of them sexually assaulted me—yes, it felt good. Sex can feel pretty good. But that was too much. They fed their own feelings into me, so I don't even know if what I felt came from me or from them. And I couldn't stop it even though I wanted to stop. It was like a feedback loop. Truth is, I don't know how sex works now."

Alice's crimson face stayed focused right at me. She'd decided to ask, and wasn't going to look away. "It wasn't just them."

My heart had pounded while I faced Absolute, but that was a pale imitation of the fast, thready pulse pounding in my body now.

"Alice. Did someone—" When I'd been a police officer, I'd had to ask this question at least once a week, if not once a day. But now that it was my Alice, I found the once-routine question literally unspeakable. "Has someone…taken liberties with you?"

"No!" Alice said. "God, no, nothing like that. I mean, there's always jerks? But I get away from them."

"Good."

"No, it was—" Alice gulped. "When we were getting away from them. In the apartment. You grabbed my hand. You felt like… I mean…" Her words trailed off.

I remembered that moment. Alice had clubbed Teresa with a table lamp. The shock of pain had broken the entrancement long enough for me to knee Jesse off of me. Despite beaning Teresa, Alice still looked vacant, so I'd grabbed her hand and pulled her into a run.

In that moment, I felt everything Alice felt. She'd been raised to behave. To conform. She'd known at a fundamental level that she'd be just fine if she followed the rules. And then Teresa had tried to eat her soul, leaving her burning with humiliation. And from somewhere deep inside her, she'd felt a sudden upwelling of anger.

At that moment, I'd been intoxicated with the desire Teresa and Jessa had forced into me. The attack had scrambled my perceptions, giving everything a surreal sheen.

I'd released Alice's hand almost immediately.

But apparently I hadn't been quick enough. In that instant of contact, her swelling rage found its way to me, while my lustful delirium squirreled into her.

I made myself turn back to her and look directly into her face.

"I won't lie to you, sex can be great. It can also be terrible. And to make it worse, I don't even know how sex works now. What I do know, though, is it can go wrong. Very wrong. Look at Two Backs."

Alice flinched.

"And Teresa tried once before, the night before she kidnapped you. I had no idea it was a trap. The only reason she failed to suck me into them was because Rose Friedman threw a Molotov of burning gasoline on us."

Alice's flinch looked frozen.

I gritted my teeth. I didn't want to say this. I had to say it. She needed to know and there would never be a better time. Or a worse one. "And that's how your dad got the way he was."

Alice trembled.

"It was sex. Teresa tried to, well, pull him into their connection. Like she did with us. It didn't work with him. Only something else happened."

The attempt had left Alice's father, Doug, horrifically transformed, his very brain destroyed.

Doug had been the first dreg I burned. I still remembered the stink of flamethrower gel, then the terrifying sound of crackling, flaming flesh.

"And you're…" I rubbed my face again, looking at the floor, breaking eye contact with Alice's embarrassment before I realized what I was doing. I breathed deeply and deliberately looked back at her. "You're at that age. The age where kids start to experiment. Or maybe you've already, you know, kissed a boy."

Alice's mouth opened.

"Or a girl," I said quickly. "You don't have to tell me, that's your business. I mean, I'm here for you if you want to talk about it. I'm always willing to listen."

No, you're wussing out. It's easier to say you'll listen than to answer the question.

You wanted a family? Wish granted. Now be a father.

I hated it when the little voice was right.

"What I can tell you is I'm not so much as even kissing a woman until I have a better idea of what made Two Backs what she—they are. And I'd really appreciate it if you'd do the same."

Alice closed her eyes. We'd talked about her father, but only the happy memories. I didn't want her to remember him as he was, not at the end, or how he'd become like that.

Or how I killed him.

I'd had no choice.

I'd burn him again.

"Your dad…" I said. "At the end, whatever happened to make him what he was—I tried to save him. Tried to help him. Because he was your dad. I didn't want to—"

"I know," Alice said. "You had to. I mean, you told me. Ceren told me too."

Ceren had been with me when I burned Doug. And on this topic at least, her friend's testimony meant more to Alice than mine ever could.

Alice took stood still for a few seconds, her eyelids almost closed. She nodded and looked up at me. "When you figure it out—about sex, I mean," she finally said. "Will you tell me?"

I tried to swallow, but my mouth was dry. "I will."

"Promise?"

I had to pull in a deep breath before I could say, "I promise."

She closed her eyes and nodded. "Thanks."

Yet another conversation I wouldn't look forward to having.

I heaved in a deep breath. "You okay?"

"Yeah. I'm sorry."

"Don't be." I made myself smile. "I'm glad you felt like you could ask me. It's not a comfortable conversation."

"I did an Internet search this morning, you know? And nothing came up."

I chuckled at the tiny joke, even while wondering how many times my Julie had done an Internet search rather than asking Sheila or me. Melancholy slowed my pulse.

After a moment of silence I said, "If you're good, I need to get going. There's a lot of trouble today."

"Yeah." Alice gave a smile. I couldn't fool myself that it was easy for her to do. "See you at dinner?"

"I wouldn't miss it for anything. Jack's doing leftovers tonight."

Alice stood in the open door of the mall entrance while I walked across the cracked asphalt to my cruiser. The summer sun and clear blue sky had transformed the police cruiser's interior into a steamy swamp, rich with the old sweat and bleach of years in service of the extinct human race, but at least the sun hadn't directly hit the black vinyl of the driver's seat. I turned and waved at Alice, then made a point to loop the cruiser past the doors and wave again before pulling out onto the road.

First, a stop at the police station. Get myself a new flamethrower. A few spare radios, since I seemed to be handing them out to almost everyone.

I had a teenage boy who'd committed murder. Someone who called himself Danger, who had set the dregs against Alice and Ceren and myself. A dreg begging for my help, but I might have to burn her instead. Woodward setting himself up as a feudal warlord. A stolen flamethrower. Two brain-injured people, vanished.

And now, I had to figure out how sex worked before Alice got herself into a whole new type of trouble.

Plus we needed a place to live, Eric had turned black, and we might be the only living things in North America, or maybe the world.

That little list included only the trouble I knew about. How many more people had gone missing? How many more people had dregs after them? Was my little family uniquely targeted, or was this part of something bigger?

I needed help.

I needed eyes.

I needed a weapon.

Fortunately, I could get them all in the same place.

The help wouldn't be happy about being drafted.

But Acceptance had screwed up.

And to save my little town, I would use it against them.

I was going to enjoy this.

Chapter 50

THE THICK stone walls of Saint Michael's Church kept the place cool even under the noon sun. Ceiling fans dangling from the high, arched ceiling turned barely enough to keep the air from complete stillness. Narrow slots at the top of the glorious stained glass windows let the hot air escape. I stopped for a minute in the vestibule, letting the sudden shift of temperature cool my blood.

This had to be the hottest June in years.

You think nuclear winter was bad? Wait 'til you get ash summer on top of it!

I shoved the memory away. I'd ponder the weather when I had time. And I couldn't afford distractions while facing Acceptance.

"Kevin!" called Boxer from the office chair near the pulpit. "Welcome! Come on in, take a load off. I have a fan up here, it helps."

The church still smelled faintly of incense. Nobody had lit any in weeks, but the aroma had sunk into the building's bones. My shoe treads squeaked against the thick, gleaming planks of the floor with my every step between the pews.

"How's Otto?" I said, keeping my voice light.

"He's at home resting. Thank you for coming to his aid." Boxer looked like she should be in college, but she'd been an elementary school teacher before Absolute murdered us all. Today's rings were smaller than yesterday's, each a scintillating round dot that shattered the light coming through the stained glass. Had she worn the rings before Absolute, or had she gone shopping at the mall after?

"That's what I do," I said. "Run around and help random people."

She smiled. "You're a good man, Kevin."

"Someone has to be."

Boxer shook her head. "No," she said with a sad smile. "They don't."

"Do you know something I don't?"

"Too many things."

"That's what I'm here about."

"Please, have a seat."

I hesitated. You get a psychological advantage by looming over someone, yes. But Boxer was relaxed in the rolling office chair, leaning back a few degrees, hair ruffling in the breeze of the box fan spinning a few yards behind her. Boxer, even Acceptance, wasn't Woodward or his cronies.

And more importantly, *I* wasn't Woodward. I didn't *have* to play those games.

Especially not when I had the big stick already.

I sat on the first pew, putting one elbow over the back and one knee on the seat so I could face Boxer more comfortably.

"What's going on?" Boxer said.

"Everything. You know Woodward's building a private army."

"An army?" Boxer smiled. "You're terribly dramatic. He has a group of men who've volunteered to help him. Someone does need to think about the future."

"There's dregs teaming up. They're gunning for Alice and Ceren and me. Maybe more people than that, but definitely starting with the three of us. I'm pretty sure they attacked Nat Reamer. Split her skull. She's a dreg now."

Boxer looked sober. "That's terrible."

"You heard that I'm looking for someone called Danger? He's controlling those dregs. He's acting through them. They're his puppets."

"You're certain of this?"

"I got it from one of the dregs. The Bea—the one that's two people. If you knock one head out, the other one gets free. She told me."

"That's horrible." Boxer grimaced, but the twisted mouth faded almost instantly. The people in Acceptance accepted everything. Even the horrors. They constantly reassured each other. Boxer's revulsion had echoed out to the other members, and they'd responded with reassurance and comfort and, of course, acceptance.

"Someone's stolen a flamethrower. We have a young man running around who's killed someone. He's scared enough to be dangerous."

Boxer shook her head.

"I'm trying to track all of these things down. And they're all ahead of me. Every one of them is ahead of me. I can't keep up. And one of these problems is going to get more people killed."

"That really is terrible."

"So I'm here to ask you a question."

"You know we—Acceptance—won't intervene," Boxer said. "We're already alien enough. People are scared of us—no, they're terrified. We accept that. But if we start to act together, if we arrange matters to our liking, then we become even stranger. And people won't stand for that. That's when they'll get the torches and pitchforks."

"My question isn't like that," I spoke calmly and deliberately, letting Boxer hear that I meant no harm to any of them. "I'm not asking for you to break your rules. Hell, I even think I understand why you have that rule."

Boxer raised her chin and her eyebrows in surprise. "Really? If you're not asking for us to do something to help you, what are you asking for?"

"I want your answer to a question. It's really a somewhat common question. It's this: What kind of world do you want to live in?"

Boxer's head tilted, her eyebrows drawing together over her nose.

"Take your time." I leaned back, stretching both legs out in front of me and folding my hands behind my head. Blood choked off by the hard edge of the pew rushed back into my leg. "People have wrestled with that question for centuries."

"I don't see what you're getting at," Boxer said. "*We* don't understand what you're getting at."

"It's like this." I lowered my hands and drew my legs back under me. "We might be the only island of life left in North America. Maybe on Earth. And we are under attack from within. We have limited resources, and a flamethrower running around loose. We don't even have a society yet—the closest thing we have to a community is Jack's dinners. And Woodward's army. We have dregs organizing into another army. And then there's you. Right now, you're aloof. Each of your members is off doing their own thing.

"About the only thing you've ever been clear about—any of you have been clear about—is that you protect each other." I sat up straight and leaned towards Boxer. "From which I can draw only two conclusions. When a member of Acceptance is in trouble, you'll use your abilities to help that person. But when our little community is in trouble, Acceptance could not give a shit."

"We care very much!" Boxer's flash of outrage subsided almost instantly.

"Individually, maybe. I have no doubt that some of you are doing important work, just like Jack and Eric. But I need to track down Danger, whoever—or whatever—he is. I need to find this missing flamethrower. And I need to find Bill before he kills someone else. This is all happening today. Now. You people could easily keep your eyes and ears open for any of these things—and you will. But you won't tell me. You'll guide me around by the nose, but you won't say."

I let the anger roiling in my gut leak out to heat up my voice.

"Thanks to your silence, Jesse and Teresa damn near ate me alive. Alice—you know Alice? One of my girls? Fourteen years old, and it's a young fourteen. Turns out she was sexually assaulted—*inside her own head*. You know how badly that's going to mess her up? And she's going to have to live with that forever, and we all have to live with her, with that damage, forever. But let one of you get shot in the shoulder, something you know perfectly well we can recover from, and you press the magic Acceptance-signal and bring out the whole brigade. And don't you *dare* tell me that the little show when you picked up Otto wasn't meant to impress everyone, because it damn well was. You *choreographed* it."

I turned the tap of anger down, easing my voice. "You've made your feelings *quite* clear." I brought my voice back down. "The rest of us can *burn*. And Acceptance completely does not give a single, solitary shit."

Boxer sat rigid. Her breathing continued unchanged.

I didn't take my gaze from her eyes.

Kipuka Blues

"We are doing work that benefits the community," Boxer said.

"You hang around the edges. What was Otto doing, helping Woodward's good old boys? We have threats we don't even understand. That we don't even know to look for." I crossed my arms and stared into Boxer's eyes. "We have the disadvantages of, of—of whatever we are. You have, you *are* the advantage. And if we're going to survive, we—the people living here in Frayville—*we* need every advantage."

Boxer looked at me for a long breath.

"Mister Holtzmann," Boxer finally said. "We do not see it that way. But I understand how you do. What is it you would have from us?"

I overrode the blood pounding in my throat, trying to keep my tone calm and reasonable. "I want to know who Danger is, and where he is. He's driving a big red van. I want to know where Bill is. Bill Gifford. One of the kids, he's a little older than Ceren. Husky, blond hair. I want to know where Woodward's deployed his goon squad. And I want you to keep your eyes out for this flamethrower."

"I can't make this decision on my own, you know," she said. Boxer sat so perfectly still that even the multicolored star field reflections from her myriad rings didn't move. "And your request is far too complex for us to discuss on conference call. We will have to meet in person. All of us."

"More people are going to die," I said. "How long is this going to take?"

"I've summoned everyone," Boxer said. "They're on their way."

"Good." I leaned back again. "I'll wait."

"We conduct our deliberations in private," Boxer said. Her body relaxed. "Our discussions would only…worry you. But I will let you know as soon as we have reached a decision."

I could believe that all of Acceptance in one spot would disturb me. How would they behave? All moving in synchronization? Would they even speak?

"All right." I pulled myself to my feet, unclipped the radio from my belt, and set it on the pew. "When you have a decision, call. This is set to go to my radio and mine alone. If you decide to stay out, I'll need it back. There's only so many to go around."

"Very well." Boxer said. "For what it is worth, *I* would like to aid you. You may consider me your advocate."

"In that case—I need to talk to the research team. Langley and Frost. Pendleton was helping them. How about telling me where to look."

Boxer looked absent for a moment. "They're...out Pine Board—no, Pinewood Road. To the...left."

I nodded. "Thank you."

"And if we decide against you, I will return your radio."

I snorted. "I never doubted that, actually. How long is this going to take?"

Boxer shrugged. "They are all coming here. We will talk until it is settled. We have water, but no food. I understand the urgency."

"Thank you."

There didn't seem to be anything else to say. I took a few steps backwards, then turned my back on Boxer and walked out. I wasn't any better off than when I walked into the church, but I had hope of assistance.

And telling Boxer *exactly* what I thought felt damn good.

Probably the best feeling I'd get all day.

Chapter 51

PINEWOOD BARELY qualifies as a dirt road. It runs along a barren stretch of northern shore too rocky for a beach and too chaotic to build on, weaving between tilted slabs of pale gray slate and green-speckled granite dredged up by glaciers ten thousand years ago. Before Absolute, it had been home to outcast seagulls and the most stubborn weeds. Now, the only life was the tree line a couple dozen yards inland, with the looming, bright green presence of the alien Lake Huron behind it.

I'd only just turned onto Pinewood when I saw Pendleton's dilapidated truck coming towards me at a good clip. We both had to slow down and hug our edge of the road to pass each other, and still his driver's side mirror would have clipped mine if it hadn't been a foot higher.

The massive Pendleton raised a hand in greeting. He shouted a word as my open windows passed his, but I couldn't make out his words over the wind of our passing and the unnatural mossy breeze off the algae-filled lake.

I didn't really know Lake Huron was full of algae. I hadn't gone to the waterline and taken a good long look. I didn't want to. It might not be algae. It might be something worse, something I hadn't even imagined. We had enough problems. It was green, it reeked of moss and leaves and decades of fallen leaves, I'd call it algae.

Before Absolute, the forest to my west had been mostly pines planted by the Civil Conservation Corps a century before, an attempt to recover from the voracious logging of the 19th century. Those yellow-barked trees had run in neat lines, like proud soldiers lined up for inspection before marching into battle for ecology and employment.

That forest was gone, replaced with a tangle of ancient oaks and maples that looked as if they'd stood untouched for centuries. I tried not to think about the change; it was easier to pretend that I was in a strange new place, driving along an unfamiliar shore, instead of trying to assimilate the ongoing changes to the town I loved.

After a few miles, the old-growth forest suddenly surrendered to burned-out cinders and spars of fire-devoured tree trunks. The lake wind whirled cyclones of ash across broken rock and pits of still, treacly mud left from last week's rain. The haze of moss suddenly mingled with the reek of cinders and ash.

Nothing but the crumbly, dusty remnants of exhausted fires, all the way to the northern horizon.

And a little ruby-red electric two-seater car, parked on what had been the road some five yards further in, with a stubby rental trailer behind it.

I didn't see Frost or Langley anywhere, but the slabs of rock limited my visibility. I parked the cruiser in the middle of the road just outside the forest and climbed a plateau as high as my ribcage to get a better view. Two figures crouched over something in the ash, maybe a quarter mile inland. Half a mile? The total lack of landmarks in the cinders made gauging distance difficult. I grimaced, spat in the ash, and started walking.

Hiking through the trackless ash felt like a forced death march across the moon. The gray ash reflected the brilliant sunlight, while the black cinders soaked in the heat and radiated it back up at me.

Charcoal crumbs and filthy, sticky black ashes burrowed between my black socks and my leather shoes, sliding down to dig at the soles of my feet. Each step raised soot or squelched into a slurry of rain-drenched cinders. What should have been a few minutes walk became a quarter-hour trudge that left me with sweat-slick clothes and a mouth tasting of long-dead fire.

Both women wore ash-stained khakis and broad straw hats from the tourist shops to keep the sun off. They knelt over a black plastic box the size of a milk crate, stuffed with electronics and circuit boards. Behind them sat a four-by-eight solar panel, propped on a fire-rotted stump so that it faced vaguely south. Two tall backpacks sat on the bottom of their frames, leaning against each other to keep out of the ash.

"Sheriff!" said Frost.

Langley nodded at me, wiping her forehead with a forearm. "Holtzmann."

"Hi," I panted. The ground was baking hot. No wonder Frayville was roasting, if everything around it was soaking up the heat! "What are you doing…" I made myself take a deep breath. "…out here?"

"Collection point," Langley said. Her mouth never lost its sardonic twist. "Local seismographs relay data here. We're setting them up everywhere so we can extrapolate the rate of expansion."

"How fast the trees are growing?" I said.

"And where," Frost said.

I had no idea what we'd do with the information. "Cool. Let me know what you figure out."

"It'll be in all the best peer-reviewed journals," Frost said.

Langley snorted.

"Or when you figure out this weather," I wheezed.

"Don't tell me our local police officer came all the way out here to inspect our project," Frost said.

"I'm not a cop," I said. "That was Kevin."

Frost winced, and I read the sympathy in her eyes. "What can we do for you?"

My mouth ached. That stupid short march had left me drained and dehydrated, and I'd left my water in the car. "You're hooked up into a whole different group of people than my usual crowd. Have you had any trouble with the dregs?"

"Dregs?" Frost said.

That word hadn't spread that far. "The brain-damaged people. They ones who should be dead, but aren't."

"Oh, the shells. No, they're pretty harmless."

Shells felt like a kinder word than *dregs*. I'd have to see if I could make it more popular. "Any thefts? People going missing?"

Frost pursed her lips and shook her head. "What's going on?"

"We've had a rash of trouble downtown. I'm trying to see if it's just us, or if it's everywhere."

"We're all pretty quiet," Frost said. "As far as I've heard."

I gnawed my lower lip. "I'd really like to talk to everyone. There's about twelve of you that meet for dinner each night?"

"Yep," Frost said.

"Fourteen," Langley said.

"I have to ask around at dinner tonight down at Jack's. There might be a pattern to this, but people wouldn't think to tell me. Can you ask your group? We eat at six, usually. I can run up later, if you folks will be around."

"I can do that," Frost said. "Anything to help the police."

"Like Kevin said," Langley said, looking up from the electronics crammed into the plastic box. "He's not the police."

"It wouldn't matter if I was," I said. "People didn't tell us anything they thought we didn't need to know."

"People like to handle their own problems," Frost said.

"Until they can't," I said.

Frost and I looked at each other for a moment. Blowing ash had caught in her short red hair, and in wiping sweat off her forehead she'd smeared muddy soot over her eyes.

"Are we good?" Frost said over her shoulder.

"The equipment checks," Langley said. "I'm calibrating the reception."

Frost looked back at me. "Anything else?"

The heat radiating up from the char field baked my skin. My tongue felt like dry wool. I had no idea how Langley and Frost had stayed out here long enough to set up their equipment. "No, that's it. It's trips like this that make me miss cell phones."

Frost gave more of a smile than the comment rated. "I'm going to take some stuff back to the car. Give me a hand?"

I did not want to carry anything in this heat. "Sure."

Frost reached into the unzipped top of her backpack and hauled out a plastic gallon jug of water. "Here, this'll help."

"You're a lifesaver." The water was warm and stale, with the limestone taste of Frayville's wells, and hit my throat like balm.

"Took me by surprise the first time, too," Frost said, accepting the jug back from me. "I'd brought this little liter bottle from the gas station for the whole day. I lasted about half an hour."

"Eighteen minutes," Langley said.

"You were just glad I gave you an excuse to go back," Frost said.

"You wussed out first," Langley said, looking into her box. "That's what matters."

Frost gave me a cardboard box half-full of metal stakes and thin collapsing antennas. She heaved her backpack up.

My chivalry reflex kicked in. "Hey, let me carry that for you."

"The straps are all adjusted for me," Frost said, shrugging her shoulders into the pack. "I'd spend the next week trying to fix it."

"Fair enough." I balanced the box on my shoulder and we set out.

Walking through the irregular ash field made conversation impossible. Flat stretches of charcoal concealed shallow ditches. Ridges of cinders slipped underfoot. A dry patch might be a crust over inches of slurry. Even following our own trail demanded focus.

I set the box down behind their trailer and pulled two bottles of water from the trunk of my cruiser. The first I tossed to Frost, who caught it neatly out of mid-air. I cracked the seal on the second and drained it in one long draught. Fighting fires, tromping through old fires, searching stuffy houses baked by the sun—if this kept up, I'd have to schedule hydration breaks every two hours.

"Thanks."

I shrugged. "You were going my way."

Frost slipped out of her backpack and eased it to the ground. "Listen, Kevin do you— It is Kevin, right? Your name?"

I nodded.

"You know what I did for a living, Kevin?"

"You're a scientist." I grabbed another bottle of water and offered it to Frost. She shook her head. I nodded and twisted the cap open before sucking down half the bottle.

"I'm a biologist. Post-doc. Before Absolute, I studied gene transmission between species. For the last three years, like every other biologist, I studied the Taken. I got the updates from NORAD, from NATO, even translations from the Chinese. I know everything the human race knows about Absolute."

Heat, dehydration, my argument with Acceptance—all forgotten. My heart surged with fresh energy. "Do you know how to kill Absolute?"

Frost laughed. "You don't mess around, do you?" She shook her head. "Just go straight to the trillion-dollar question." She took a breath. "Fire. Electricity. Destruction of biomass. If I'd had the magic bullet, we wouldn't be here right now."

"Of course." I looked back at the tangled brand-new old-growth forest, hoping my embarrassment didn't show too much.

"No worries. You probably haven't talked to a scientist about Absolute, have you? You just got what they had on television?"

"We sat through Building the Future training programs every week."

Frost nodded. Her tiny, fine-featured face suddenly looked solemn. "I told you to set some context for the next bit."

I looked back at her. With that background, anything she could tell me about Absolute would be useful.

Frost took a deep breath. "You told me how you're not a police officer. That you're not who you remember being. And you're really hung up on that. It's giving you trouble."

"Fact of life," I said, my face flushing a little more from how easily she read me than from the heat. "The sooner we all get used to it, the better off we'll be." I brought the bottle to my lips, trying to hide behind the clear plastic, and began drinking down the rest of the bottle.

"I hear a lot of that," Frost said. "Speaking as a biologist, though, it's very, very clear. You are wrong. Everything we know about the Taken indicates that you are, unquestionably, the real Kevin Holtzmann."

Chapter 52

I COUGHED water into my nose, panicked, sneezed, and completely lost my breathing rhythm.

Nothing next to the chaos in my mind.

The desolate plain of cinder-covered stones seemed to reel away. Behind me, the viscous emerald surge of Lake Huron rolled out its unsettling, too-slow susurrus.

Frost's words repeated in my ears. The phrase *You are the real Kevin Holtzmann* absolutely refused to sink into my brain. They were the wrong shape. I knew the individual words, but they refused to assemble into coherent meaning.

My entire identity started and ended with me being a copy. I'd used that knowledge, that perspective, to cope with the end of the world, the deliberate extinction of the human race, my own alien existence.

Frost's quiet, factual tone made her seem quite confident that dynamiting my world had been the right thing to do.

Suddenly dizzy, I dropped the empty water bottle on the soot-covered road and reached for the police cruiser's trunk ledge. Heat blasted off the sun-scorched metal, and I flinched away. I shuffled my feet, trying to keep my balance, but the world still rocked. "Say that—No. Don't say that again. What are you talking about?"

Frost focused on me, my face. Her gaze felt soft, considerate. "I'm talking about the actual biological mechanism of how Absolute claimed people."

Memories roared through me. Standing in a Utah desert, the ground roasted to the texture of stone by centuries of heat. Staring at the Taken copy of Jared Collins, serial rapist and murderer, as he threatened Sheila and Julie. Desert plants, stretching and twining into an inescapable cage around us.

Sheila's head coming apart with Kevin's first two bullets. Another bullet in the back of Julie's head, at the bottom of her skull. Blood and bone and brain scattering through the air.

Hot gunmetal burning my chin.

Squeezing the trigger.

The trigger not moving.

Absolute's copy of Collins, laughing as countless alien thorns punched through my skin. Fronds crawled up my nose, in my ears, my mouth.

One last breath.

That final attempt to scream.

The cold, sharp slices that ended Kevin.

That created me.

I blinked and the feel of alien thorns vanished, replaced by the heat of the sun hammering down on me. "No. You're wrong. I remember it. I remember—Kevin *died*."

Frost's next words tumbled quickly, as if she knew she only had seconds to get out the most words, the most convincing words, before it was too late. Before my brain couldn't absorb anything else.

"Absolute can arrange biomass any way that it desires. It can grow new limbs, new bodies, sure. But that takes a lot of energy and work. When Absolute claimed existing biomass, when it made the Taken, it didn't disassemble and rebuild them. It's more like an infection. Absolute added new genetic programming, rearranged some parts, moved some pieces. I won't lie to you, it was a *lot* of changes, but tiny. Billions of tiny changes. Looked at all together, Absolute added less mass than a kidney transplant to each of the Taken. Would a kidney transplant change who you are?"

I heard her words, but my mind refused to accept them. Absolute ate and copied people. That's what it did. That's what all the training docs said. That's what it did. If I wasn't a copy, how had I wound up in my home town, surrounded by impassable, trackless charcoal?

Frost gave me a soft smile, totally oblivious that she'd kicked over and strewn the few pieces I'd assembled of my jigsaw puzzle life. "Don't you get it? You don't have to be all freaked out because you're a copy. You're not. You *are* Kevin Holtzmann."

I'd had to accept Kevin's memories to cope with Teresa and Jesse. I'd claimed Kevin's losses as my own, even though I wasn't Kevin. I'd built my whole short life around them. I'd decided to be a good person, a worthwhile person, even if I wasn't human.

If I wasn't a copy created by Absolute—

If I was the real Kevin Holtzmann, then Julie and Sheila—

—hot metal machine pistol slamming into my hand—
Julie
"No," I said.
Frost leaned back in surprise. "I'm afraid it quite—"
"It isn't!" I shouted.

Frost took a step backwards, eyes wide in fear beneath the hat's shade, hands raised protectively.

"Kevin Holtzmann is dead!" I shouted. "He tried, he died! He didn't make it. I am a *copy*! I'm not real, I can't be real!"

"Okay," Frost said, taking another step back. "Whatever you say, officer."

"I am not an officer!" I screamed.

Everything felt simultaneously too far away and too close. My throat swelled. My chest felt too tight to breathe. My hands, my head, everything shook.

Everything hurt.

Sheila— Julie—

"*I am not Kevin Holtzmann!*" I screamed at the blue sky.

The whole world throbbed with my heart.

The gun bucking in Kevin's hand.

Sheila's head dissolving.

Barrel at the back of Julie's head.

The gun bucking again.

The gun in Kevin's hand.

My hand?

I didn't save them.

I killed my wife and daughter.

I almost knocked Frost over throwing myself into the police cruiser, started it, slammed it into gear. The spinning wheels sprayed dust and soot through the three-point turn. My vision shuddered gray with my heartbeat.

Finally pointed back towards town, I stomped the accelerator.

Chapter 53

MY BLOOD burned, aflame but too turgid to move. My breath, ragged chokes, squeezed through the swamp of horror drenching me.

The narrow dirt road, weaving between slate slabs. I continually adjusted the steering wheel, slick in my grip. Speedometer touching seventy, ninety. Wheels sliding and spinning in soot.

Slate ahead. Road weaves. Stomp the brake.

Skid in a shower of cinders.

Throat so tight it hurt.

I am not Kevin.

If I *was* Kevin, that meant that *I* had murdered—

I stomped the accelerator. Diesel roared in response.

Too soon, the dirt road widened into the asphalt of Lakeshore Drive. I took the transition at speed, bouncing the whole cruiser, a moment soaring beyond gravity, beyond the pain. The cruiser crashed to the ground, jolting the wheel in my hand.

What the hell does a stupid human goddamn biologist know about Absolute, anyway?

Absolute was alien. Unknowable.

The cruiser's tires bit hard road and caught. The sudden acceleration pushed me back in my seat.

Eighty.

Ninety.

One-ten.

Rectangular sign. Lettering too small at this speed. A big number: 25.

One-twenty-five, one-thirty.

Engine a roaring Tyrannosaurus.

Wind bellowing through open windows.

Sprawling homes on plantations of grass flashed past me.

Lake dissolving into undifferentiated green.

Alien lake. Like Absolute.

We don't know.

Frost has no clue.

Sheila.
Julie.
Gun in my—in Kevin's—hand. Barking death.
Kevin's hand. Not mine.
Frost knows nothing. NOTHING.
My eyes watered. My breath shuddered in my chest.
One-forty.
Engine's roar. Not louder than my scream.
Houses suddenly shrinking into strobes of bright clown colors. Rental district.
Hold the accelerator pedal down.
Road curved. Clench the wheel.
Fingers slip—grab tighter.
Last turnoff coming up. Then the pier. The bay.
Eyes watering—no.
It's wind, not tears. Blink it away.
A big reflective yellow-and-black arrow, pointing right.
Big yellow signs.
FISHING PIER
ALL TRAFFIC KEEP RIGHT
DEAD END
The accelerator was already on the floor.
One-fifty and pegged.
Julie.
I stood on the accelerator.
Through the parking lot.
The cruiser bouncing over a short curb.
Transfixed within the car by my rigid legs and arms.
Booths. Tourist traps, empty of bait.
No more tourists.
Ever.
Kipuka. Island of life in a sea of lava.
Nothing else.
Nobody but Absolute.
Forever.
Pier.
The cruiser's radiator struck the thick steel chain strung between

two posts at the beginning of the pier. The whole cruiser vibrated with the sudden high-pitched snap, sending its echo through my skull. My gaping jaw slammed together on my tongue, adding the bright copper taste of blood to the mixture.

Snapping steel wasn't enough to clear my brain.

But it shattered the horrified scream inside my head.

The pier stabbed a few hundred yards into the shallow Lake Huron inlet at the mouth of the Sand River. The cruiser rocketed towards the end, tires eating concrete, the narrow tongue of pier shrinking against the burgeoning green water. Flimsy chains hung between concrete stanchions on either side.

If I drove off the pier, if I shattered my body and brain, I'd abandon everyone.

I'd tell Alice and Ceren to destroy themselves.

Tell Eric he was an outcast.

Even Steve and Brandi. Jack. Even Reamer.

I yanked my foot off the accelerator and stomped on the brake.

Tires squealed and screeched. My weight dumped forward, held against the seat only by my locked elbows. The anti-lock kicked in even as the steering wheel bucked in my sweating palms.

The pier started to skew around me. I eased the wheel a few vital degrees, trying to straighten. Turn too sharp, and the cruiser's two tons of steel would snap through the guard chains on either side. I'd avoid flying off the end of the pier only by sliding off the side.

The whole cruiser shook and shuddered. I couldn't even glance at the speedometer.

My blood, once aflame, now froze.

I stood on the brake, calves and thighs cramped with the force, back pinned against the back of the seat, an inch of air between my butt and the bottom cushion. Rigid bars seemed to have replaced my shoulders and elbows; my hands felt welded into place around the steering wheel's fake leather.

The end of the pier drew closer.

I was not going to drive off the end of this pier.

Whoever I was, I was not going to kill myself.

If I wasn't Kevin, then I wasn't guilty.

If I was Kevin, then death was too good for me.

A bright, fresh guilt stabbed through me. And what about Alice? Ceren? I'd made them promises. Eric. Jack. Brandi and Steve. Reamer and his housemate, what's-his-name.

Even Acceptance.

Becky and Paul. Far as I knew, I was the only one who really understood that Becky and Paul were still two people trapped together.

I shrieked.

The green lake filled more and more of my vision.

Tree-lined far shore, impossibly distant.

So much slower than I had been going but still far too fast, the end of the concrete pier sliding closer.

Rubber on concrete, louder than my own scream.

The end of pier skidded closer. Yards—

—feet—

and disappeared beneath the hood.

The guard chain snapped like dry straw.

The windshield cracked.

My scream ran out of breath.

The cruiser plunged off the end of the pier and into the alien green muck of the bay.

Chapter 54

THE WORLD turned green.

My brain shifted into overdrive, and the whole world slowed down.

My heart felt like a slow bass drum throbbing against my ribs as the cruiser soared off the end of the pier and into the transformed lake.

Lake Huron smelled wrong: moss and deep pine forest. It moved wrong: waves too tall but too slow, a turgid roiling that made my bowels churn exactly the same way, a slimy, oozing surf that lapped, sluglike, at the shore. Yesterday, standing on the road looking at it made my hands unconsciously ball into fists. I'd refused to approach the shoreline any closer than thirty feet or so.

And now it surged leprously beneath me, swelling to become the whole of my world.

I tried to suck in a breath, but my body felt as slow as the world around me.

The cruiser's engine roared, the drive wheels spinning free.

Wind roaring through the open windows.

Straight-armed against the wheel, spine wedged against the seat back, I couldn't help but imagine the impact impaling me on the steering column. The cruiser's massive bulk dragging me to the bottom. Trapping me there. It wouldn't kill me. Nothing could kill me. But what would happen when I ran out of air, when that alien green lake oozed down my throat, filling my sinuses, my stomach—

The cruiser plunged not quite nose-down. More like one of those insane hills in San Francisco, where it looks like you're driving straight into the ground.

An eternal quarter-second later, the cruiser's front grill touched water.

The water sagged at the impact.

No splash.

No spray.

The lake's surface bent around the cruiser's nose like a cheap mattress hit with a falling bowling ball. The water around the car bent back, rubbery, absorbing the impact—until it split.

The lake tore like freshly spooned gelatin.

The cruiser's nose plunged into the rupture.

My weight surged onto my hands and feet, the shock of sudden deceleration shrieking in my knees and elbows. No sudden rush of impact, more like I'd slammed into a stack of thick foam padding at thirty miles an hour. A thunderous glooping noise filled my ears, punctuated with the shriek of bending metal and my own hummingbird heartbeat.

The cruiser skewed and slid.

Green glops spattered against the cracked windscreen.

The cruiser's undercarriage slapped against the lake, knocking my crown against the roof.

The sound of water sizzling on hot metal.

Everything shook.

Wobbled.

Quivered.

Then lay still.

My back hurt, the spine compressed when I'd knocked my head into the ceiling. The crown of my head sparked, my teeth aching from clanging together. My chest burned, the empty lungs burning for air even as my paralyzed diaphragm knotted.

Green, gluey lake oozed down the windscreen, globs blocking out everything except different shades of sunlight.

The cruiser lay at an angle, nose and driver's side angled down by thirty degrees or so. Beyond the passenger side window, blue sky. Loathsome green syrup wobbled at the edge of my window.

I'd braced myself, but the impact had knocked me bonelessly free. I lay at the intersection of driver's door and the front seat, my chest resting against the hard ring of the steering wheel, my knees crammed beneath me.

My breath broke free. I sucked in great chestfuls of rich, piney air.

Viscous green sludge bulged and swelled at the edge of the passenger window, held intact by its own surface tension.

Another breath, and the swell burst.

Green scum began trickling down my door.

The sight rattled my shaken brain into motion. I grabbed the overhead bar and the steering wheel, wrenching myself sideways from the horrible sludge oozing into my space.

I had to get out of the car, back onto the dock, before the lake swallowed the cruiser.

And me.

The surface tension broken, the gelatinous ooze slid more quickly. What started as a trickle down the door turned into a tiny current.

I had seconds to get out the passenger door.

I braced myself on the accelerator and the seat back once more, this time using the tension to hoist one painfully aching leg up over the transmission hump. My head swam. A tight knot of terror filled my throat. I breathed deliberately, trying to keep enough air going in and out to hold panic at bay.

If I panicked, I'd go into the water.

One leg up. My free hand scrabbled for a grip, finally settling for digging sweatily into the hard foam of the passenger headrest. I shifted my weight, trying to swing up.

The police cruiser lurched with the motion.

A horrible sucking sound filled the cabin.

Green ooze poured over the window, a torrent sluicing into the driver's foot well.

I desperately tightened my legs, trying to keep the knee hooked over the transmission hump, my hand clenched to the headrest, pushing myself up towards the passenger window and freedom.

Maybe, just maybe, I could swim through this sewage.

If it sucked me down with the car, though, I'd never get free.

And *never* might be a very long time.

Scrabbling for a grip, my lower hand slapped straight into the goo at the edge of the door beneath me.

A million shouting voices filled my head.

Chapter 55

COLD GREEN ichor oozed around my hand. It seemed full of infinite, tiny mouths sucking at my skin. The layer of ooze between my hand and the metal edge of the driver's side window made the metal and plastic unspeakably greasy and filthy.

The slime turned my stomach.

But worse, the touch filled my head with impossible, unfamiliar voices, all at once.

You don't need ice cream.

I love you.

Critical hit, roll for damage.

    Screaming. Laughing. Crying. Dozing.

Blue sky laced with amber fire.

Where are my clothes?

Help me.

A gut-stab of hunger, somehow driving up my arm and into my own gut.

Cold, so cold.

Where is everyone?

Oh my God, it's beautiful!

The voices triggered a convulsive spasm, knotting me around my gut—

—but ripping my hand away from the ooze.

The voices instantly stopped, leaving me gasping and sweating. Bile burned in the back of my throat.

I still had a knee over the car's transmission hump, but I'd lost my grip on the passenger side headrest. Fortunately, my head caught on the edge of the driver's side headrest, painfully cranking my neck, or I would have slipped right down into the slime.

For a moment, all I could do was gasp for breath.

Whatever the lake was, it wasn't water.

I unthinkingly went to wipe sweat from my forehead, and stopped with my hand in front of my face.

I'd plunged this hand into the slime.

But my hand was bone-dry.

Not a trace of green.

Not only that—it was *clean*. The smear of soot I'd picked up on the plain of cinders: gone.

My fingernails gleamed pristine white, everything beneath them purged.

My wedding ring gleamed like new.

The cruiser shuddered and shifted, the passenger side turning even more skyward.

The trickle of green through my window turned into a torrent.

Atavistic fear slammed me into motion. I scrabbled up the cruiser's interior like a monkey climbing its tree when it hears the hyenas, my feet somehow finding places to stand on their own, my hands grabbing and clawing and heaving until I had my head out the passenger side window, then my shoulders, my gut, my hips on the window frame.

A heartbeat later, my hands and knees rested on the police cruiser's quivering, lurching flank.

The pitiless sun burned out of a sky scoured blue. The cruiser wobbled on its side, half-submerged in the slowly roiling lake. The sandy shore gleamed white and gray, its safety impossibly far away.

Perhaps twenty feet behind the cruiser's trunk, the concrete Frayville Pier loomed a couple yards above the water.

My gaze seized on the end of the pier, next to the broken safety chain dangling into the lake.

Iron rungs.

A maintenance ladder, set into the concrete.
All I had to do was cross twenty feet of lake.
Without touching it.
The quivering car lurched another half foot down.
And I had to do it *now*.
I raised myself to a crouch, took a step.
The car shuddered.
The lake gave a horrific slurping sound.
That did it. I got myself into a stoop and bolted towards the trunk, the pier.
My shoes clanged on the cruiser's metal body, pounding dents with each step.
The cruiser's nose jerked a little more downward.
The trunk, only a couple feet out of the lake.
The pier, impossibly distant.
I planted my last step right over the taillight, letting my toes go barely over the edge, and put everything into a desperate, driving leap.
For a heartbeat I sailed through the air, arms outstretched.
The pier came closer.
I flung my hands out.
Dropping too fast.
My feet, running on air like a cartoon character racing off a cliff.
The lake, rising beneath me.
Too fast.
I wasn't going to make it.
If those voices swallowed me, I'd never escape.

Chapter 56

PANIC AND instinct had me clawing at the air.
If willpower alone could drag me to the pier, it would have.
Instead, a foot crashed down on the lake—
I bounced off.
My next foot came down.
I was stumbling, staggering, right across the surface of the lake, my feet moving barely fast enough to keep me from face-planting in the horrific green sludge.

My hand had come away clean.

It was like cornstarch! Stick your hand slow into a mix of cornstarch and water, it comes away gooey. Slap it quick—run across it—and you bounce right off.

My instincts told me to stop. Catch my balance.

Instead, I propelled myself faster across the uneasily, turgidly slow, shallow waves of Lake Huron, arms outstretched for the pier and the life-saving ladder.

The lake shuddered beneath me, turning hard at every step and immediately softening.

A foot stuck for a heart-wrenching blink—I'd stepped too slow.

Keep moving or be eaten.

I tried to time my steps to my jackhammer pulse, one stumbling, overdone step at a time.

One final surge, and my hands closed on a rusty iron rung anchored deep within the concrete of the Frayville Pier.

Sobbing with relief, I clawed my way up the pier.

Behind me, I heard a massive sucking sound.

I didn't look until my hands touched the pier's cement deck, until I hoisted myself up and clawed myself to safety, my cheek pressed firmly into the sun-scorched pebbled walkway, arms outstretched, fingers digging for safety, air heaving in and out of my lungs.

Eventually my heart slowed enough that I could think, my lungs stopped their desperate heaving for oxygen. I pulled myself to my hands and knees, still feeling the hot concrete burn on my exposed face, arms, and legs. Every muscle tender, throat parched, I hoisted myself to my feet.

The cruiser was gone.

Lake Huron surged with unnatural slowness, its innumerable voices undisturbed.

Out here, on this pier, the lake full of voices and moss might be the whole world.

I leaned against a waist-high pylon for a minute, trying to slow my racing heart and catch my breath. My thoughts drifted around each other, needing a slow minute to reassemble into coherence.

At least now, Frost's words had lost their appalling grip on me.

You are the real Kevin Holtzmann.

Ridiculous.

I had dozens of problems. People needed me. But as long as Frost's statement burned in the front of my brain—as long as there was the faintest *possibility* that they were true—I couldn't focus on anything else.

And as my tattered brain reassembled itself, I thought I could prove it.

Chapter 57

KEVIN HAD died in Utah.

I woke up in Frayville, Michigan, near the tip of eastern shore of the Lower Peninsula.

Surrounded by burned-out cinders from horizon to horizon, Frayville had no usable roads to the outside world.

The question then became: How did I get here?

I had suspicions. I couldn't backtrack my own path, but maybe I could backtrack Cuddles the Rottie's story. She'd somehow gotten into a locked house. My gut told me her tale might, just *might*, resemble my own.

I hoofed it up the concrete pier, away from the all-smothering lake, and into the residential streets along the beach. A garden hose slaked my thirst and let me splash coolness over the sweat drying on my face. Two blocks in I saw a tiny azure electric two-seater car plugged into a solar-shingled house. Security on these high-tech cars relied on the cellular network and the Internet, which had evaporated months ago. I easily reset the car's ignition lock and buzzed through downtown at a whopping twenty miles an hour, half its top speed.

There's a reason we call these plastic carts "puttermobiles."

The Catboxes felt completely different from yesterday. Sunlight slapped the road and bounced away, making me squint. After Lakeshore and the cinders, though, the block's scent of trees and grass and growing plants felt soothing. I drank in the peaceful feeling, spreading it on the burning, itching mess inside my skull, behind my eyes. Even the ramshackle siding, peeling paint, and slumping carports caressed my eyes like a glass of cool water on a scorching July day. Given the choice of a whole town full of empty homes to live in, almost all of which were nicer than anything down this street, nobody would choose to live in these shabby, cutout boxes. Except for the couple of people who had barricaded themselves in their homes and refused to come out, we'd found the whole street vacant.

My brain felt blissfully empty. After Frost's declarations, after Suit and Two Backs, after losing another home and a string of assorted atrocities and abuses, after discovering Lake Huron was even worse than I imagined, I desperately needed a few moments without my own company.

Innumerable thoughts and worries clamored for attention.

I ignored them.

The house where we'd found Cuddles was easy to identify. Bullet holes—a whole lot of bullet holes—ripped through the vinyl siding, interrupted only by shattered windows. The yellow tape Eric and I had stretched across the door now hung to one side. Walking softly, trying to ease my pained joints back into looseness, I strolled up the front walk. Eric hadn't locked the door, and it swung open at my touch.

Three empty dog food bags lay in the middle of the living room floor, each torn open lengthwise. Not a scrap of kibble remained on the grungy kitchen linoleum. I followed the familiar floor plan to the end of the hall, where a narrow doorway opened onto a descending flight of rickety wooden stairs. With each step down, the air grew cooler and clammier.

All of the Catboxes had unheated basements floored with tan clay pummeled flat by decades of feet. This particular basement also sported ancient, humidity-warped wooden shelves along all the walls. Tidy cardboard and plastic boxes bore handwritten labels, barely legible under the single soft LED light: CHRISTMAS. 4TH. HALLOWEEN. SCHOOL. KIDS WINTER. PETE SUMMER. An assortment of children's board games filled one of the lowest sections of shelving, near a flimsy plastic patio table surrounded by injection-molded chairs. Naked Romex, retrofitted low-voltage wiring, strands of network and phone cable, and antique PVC water pipes snaked through the low rafters. The whole scene was vaguely familiar from when Eric and I searched for survivors and disconnected the power last week.

I slowly circled the basement, taking deep breaths of cool air to calm the tension jittering up and down my spine.

In the far corner of the basement I found the hole. It was more of a crater, big enough to bury a wheelbarrow in. The clay slumped in a ragged ring around the crater, the hard-packed top layer broken apart as if by struck by a sledge. The walls of the crater looked almost slick, the smoothly polished sides going all the way down to the crumbles of clay filling the bottom.

Eric and I had searched this house. We didn't find anyone. And we would have noticed a Rottweiler.

Then Woodward's people had come in. They'd found Cuddles, starving.

In all our searching of the houses, with everyone I'd spoken to, I hadn't seen a single dog.

But this house had had one.

And the dog had belonged here once. Before Absolute. Otherwise, why the massive collar and the doomsday stockpile of dog food?

So how had Eric and I missed Cuddles the first time through?

We hadn't.

On the outskirts of Frayville, I'd watched fully grown trees emerge from soot and ash in seconds.

Eric and I didn't find Cuddles because Cuddles hadn't been here to be found.

If I dug far enough down, would I strike an underground river of sludge from Lake Huron?

Cuddles didn't just appear here. She hadn't weaseled her way into her locked home and been trapped. She'd been *grown* here.

Just like the unnatural trees, aging from zero to a century in seconds.

And if dogs, why not human beings?

No, *copies* of human beings?

Thoughts spilled back through me in a torrent. I closed my eyes, tried to calm my racing brain, tried to remember. My first memory free of Absolute. Falling to the living room floor. My clothes...what color had they been? I hadn't seen the color because...

Because they'd been filthy. Stiff with dirt and dried mud.

Had I found the outfit? Or had I been created in those clothes, and puppet-walked to my house?

Had I hatched from the soil right in Kevin's herb garden?

I suspected the latter.

I prayed for the latter.

Something in the back of my head screamed for attention.

I ignored it, staring at the hole. Not moving. Not talking. Barely breathing. The sight of the smooth-walled pit was a balm to my soul.

My dirt-filled clothing… I'd been raised from the Earth, not carried here by car.

I was a copy.

Just like Cuddles.

Maybe some people were still themselves, but *I* wasn't.

My thoughts still felt full of splintered steel, ready to stab the unwary, but my breathing settled down.

That's when I caught the glint of my ring on my left hand.

Kevin's wedding ring.

My heart plunged.

If I had hatched from the dirt…how had the ring gotten here?

Chapter 58

I STUMBLED into the comforting coolness of Jack's bar.

The neon was off, but the extra track of lights was on over the bar, casting dazzling reflections off the heavily varnished wood. Jack was on the wrong side of the bar, a heavy butcher knife in his hand, slicing melons into a self-sealing bin large enough to hold a roast turkey.

Jack glanced at me, nodded in greeting, and resumed slicing.

I stood in the doorway, full of an aching heavy hollowness.

Copy? Maybe.

But: real?

Maybe.

When I didn't move, Jack looked back up. "Kevin? Ye' okay?"

I made myself step towards the bar. "Vodka. Unless you have harder."

Jack hurriedly wiped his hands with a stained towel and scuttled around the bar. "All we got is Black Goose."

"Fine." I didn't know vodka from anything, except that it was the quickest path to losing every damn you'd ever given. I took the proffered shot glass and half fifth.

The stuff tasted like malted sewage with a side of high voltage—Jack had warned me for good reason. But it burned as it went down, and the comforting lump of fire in my gut promised oblivion if I fed it just a little more.

Jack studied me, concerned. "Ain't never seen you like this."

I poured another tumbler. "Get used to it."

"You want to talk?"

I shook my head. The second shot tasted just as bad as the first—apparently Black Goose doesn't kill taste buds fast enough.

"Never mind me, then. I gotta get on with dinner." He circled around to his makeshift cutting station.

I waited a whole minute before the third shot. Two minutes before the fourth. Warmth began to spread along my limbs, but didn't touch the burned-out cinder at my core.

I'd kept busy to hold the existential angst at arm's length. Searching houses for people was worthwhile work. Finding Keith Gifford's body in the bathtub had been like a fishhook in my soul, pulling me forward, letting me ignore all the questions and darkness and pain.

But Frost's words had ripped the fishhook free, taking a bunch of meat with it.

Sheila. Julie.

I needed to think. Figure something out. But rationality circled just outside my reach, beyond the swirling passions and confusion.

If Kevin (or *I?*) hadn't killed them, they'd be here. With me.

If they'd surrendered to Absolute, they'd be here. With me.

The only thing Kevin had needed to do was not tell the copy of Collins that came after us to go to hell, and I would be with my family. I wouldn't be stuck with Alice and Ceren. We would have taken them in, of course—those girls needed a family. But they would have joined something that worked, not some middle-aged lame-ass so-called cop who had always relied on his wife for the critical parts of staying human enough to raise a daughter.

My daughter?

Maybe I should find new parents for Alice and Ceren.

Someone who could handle a family.

Someone who could handle just being alive.

The next shot didn't taste so bad. Fifth? Sixth?

Maybe the next one would taste good.

Rose Friedman always said that she couldn't get drunk. *Maybe I could give her lessons. Competitions. "Race you to the bottom!"*

Nothing else to do.

I'd bullied Boxer into at least thinking about taking sides. Right now, two blocks south of Jack's, Acceptance and all its—people? Bodies? Fingers? Whatever they were. I'd have to take the two-minute walk. Tell them not to bother.

I wasn't a cop. Nobody stood behind me.

I answered to nobody.

Nobody would write me up for drinking on the job.

No, I needed to focus. Get a grip on myself.

It came down to this: I remembered dying.

I remembered Jared Collins's innumerable thorns piercing my skin, tearing into every opening in my body, carving new ones.

Kevin had gone away.

I had spotty memories after that. Yellow lines flickering on asphalt—I'd driven. Some alien imperative propelling me forward.

Then me, waking up in Kevin's living room.

What was Frost's science—her merely human science—against that?

If human science understood Absolute, humanity would have won the war.

Overhead, something thumped against the roof.

I glanced up.

A distant power tool whined.

"That's Eric," Jack said, squeezing the lid over the melon container. "He's setting up toys on the roof. Drilled some holes down here earlier. Told him, if he makes my ceiling leak, I'll cut him off *so* fast."

Eric had said he had a project. Good. He'd need something to keep him busy now that I'd found my true vocation. I poured another shot, slopping a little onto the bar.

Over the next however long it was, I drained most of the bottle. The pain in my soul didn't go away, but the vodka's burn covered it up like foundation over a woman's battered face. People came in. Voices gathered behind me. I lurked in my private gloom.

Distantly, I heard someone say that they were bored.

I had a tiny urge to take them to the lake and push them in.

Time passed, measured in a series of shot glasses. I wished I'd thought to use a different shot glass for every drink. How would I brag to Rose Friedman about how drunk I'd been without counting them out? I—

"Holtzmann!"

Someone grabbed my shoulder. I started.

A short, gristly man stood right behind me. His eyes held anger and frustration. "Don't you ignore me!"

My clouded brain churned slowly. I'd seen him before. Had he called my name earlier? Maybe.

Kenny. That was his name. One of Woodward's gang.

I drained my shot. "What. Do you want."

"I said, 'Have you seen Dan?' Danny Gervais?"

I shook my head. "Nope."

"He's been missing all afternoon."

I shrugged.

"Don't you dare blow me off, Holtzmann." Kenny raised his chin.

Jack's hand appeared between us. "Hold on, Ken, can't you tell when a man is down? Holtzmann's been busting his ass for all of us since he first walked in here. And he ain't asked for a damn thing."

"And I haven't seen him," I said. Maybe I had, passing through town today. I just didn't care. "Add him to the list of missing people."

Ken scowled and opened his mouth.

"That's enough!" Jack said. "You want to pick a fight, you do it outside my place or make your own dinner. That goes for the rest of your crew, too."

Kenny sneered at me, then slouched back to his buddies at the tables Woodward and his cronies had claimed.

Jack studied me with worried eyes. "You okay?"

"As good as I'm gonna get." I'd downed almost half a fifth of vodka, but my words didn't slur and my vision remained sharp. I hadn't drunk this much in fifteen, twenty years, but even in my twenties that much hard liquor should have softened everything both inside and outside my head. Alcohol tingled in my fingers and toes, and everything seemed a little slower, but I lacked the comfortable haze I craved desperately.

Damn it.

Rose was right.

I looked around, found the bar about half full. Tight knots of people had claimed tables, talking with heads close together. A pair of middle-aged men sat in a corner, clasping hands across the stickily varnished table, not looking away from each other as they whispered. Another couple, a young man and a younger woman, sat at right angles at a table in the middle, legs brushing against each other as they talked.

"Kevin," Eric said.

Eric was standing behind the bar. How long had he been there?

"What?"

"You don't look right."

"'m fine."

"What's going on?"

I shook my head. Now the world had punctured my bubble of despair, the shadow of drunkenness I'd managed to achieve had faded even further. I poured myself another shot. Eric opened his mouth to say something, but I cut him off with "What're you doing?"

"Multiband radio." He tapped a silver plastic device the size and shape of an old-fashioned boombox with half a dozen dials and a tiny screen. "Put a mast on the roof."

I left the shot on the bar, my interest piqued despite myself. "You're a ham?"

"Dad made me learn how to wire these up, Morse, the whole deal."

"Dot-dot-dot dash-dash-dash. Boy Scouts." My index finger circled the rim of the shot glass. "Does it work?"

"About to find out." He touched a dial. The screen lit, and the radio released a tinny chorus of static. "Not tuned to anything. Let's see."

"Eric!" Jack shouted. "Get that dog out from behind mah bar! I work back there!"

"Cuddles!" Eric said. "Out by Kevin. Now!"

The big Rottie slunk out from the gap in the bar, head lowered. It trudged over to my stool, looked up miserably, and sank to its belly beside me with a sigh.

Eric had watched the whole thing, leaning over the bar. "Drama much, Cuddles? Good girl. Stay." He turned back to the radio. "Automatic scanner." He touched a couple of buttons, and the numbers on the screen began to climb.

"Walking freqs now," Eric said, putting an elbow on the bar opposite me. "It'll take a few minutes, but if anyone's transmitting, we'll hear it."

"How far?" I said.

Eric shrugged. "Depends. Bad day, hundred miles. Good day, Dad got Antarctica. Nukes played hell with the Heaviside Layer, though. Hard to say."

Ignoring the full shot glass, I watched the numbers climb as the little radio checked every channel it knew of. I didn't know anything about radios, but I knew that the numbers represented frequencies.

And I knew what it meant when the counter flipped back to zero and started over.

Eric shook his head. "Be better overnight."

As far as I was concerned, though, the radio had already given me the answer I expected. Nobody was transmitting anywhere in the world.

One lone kipuka.

Us. And only us.

I drained the shot glass.

Chapter 59

I'D CHOKED down another few shots in my futile quest for drunkenness when reality again smashed through the faint comforting haze around my brain.

"Kevin?" I needed a second to recognize Alice's voice.

"What the hell are you doing?" Ceren said.

I lowered the shot glass from my mouth and plonked it back down on Jack's polished wood bar. "Alice." My tongue should have stumbled, but it wouldn't. "Ceren. Glad you're okay."

And I was, sort of. I felt completely gutted, but seeing them safe sparked a tiny, almost infinitesimal flicker of pleasure.

They really needed—*deserved*—a better parent. Any of the random people holding hands in here, even the couple who'd surrendered all pretense of dignity to blatantly neck in the corner, would do better than me.

Someone who could be trusted to not murder his loved ones.

That wasn't me. I'm a copy.

Frost's words still wouldn't leave my thoughts, though.

The alcohol hadn't made me drunk, but it had finally executed my sense of taste and scoured away my sense of smell.

Ceren leaned back, nose wrinkling. "Whoa, man. Kevin. What the hell?"

Alice frowned. "How much have you been drinking?"

"Don't worry about it." I set the shot glass back on the bar.

"You're not our dad," Alice said firmly. "You're our roommate. Remember? You don't get to dictate stuff to us. We have the right to know what's happening. So what's going on?"

Roommate? I'd agreed to that, sort of. They weren't moving in with me, we'd all moved in together. Roommates or not, I *was* still the adult.

"Fine," I said. "Let's find a table." What was I going to tell them? That maybe I'd murdered Sheila and Julie, to keep them from being like us?

"One with a breeze," Alice said, waving a hand in front of her nose.

I hadn't drunk *that* much. The fifth still had one, maybe two shots left in it. And my brain still felt like I'd had two or three beers. Kevin's—*my?*—usual weekend treat.

Ceren moved ahead to stake out our usual table at the back wall and stole a third chair for it. Alice flanked me while I weaved through the tight crowd. She stayed close, her hands hovering an inch away from my right elbow, obviously expecting me to topple over my own feet and pass out any second. My feet were damnably secure on the wood plank floor.

Rose Friedman was right. Absolute took intoxication from us.

No, that couldn't be right. I'd seen a few of Woodward's guys get hammered on more than one night.

Ceren straightened her leg and shoved my chair out from under the table. I pulled it in as I sat. Before they could ask me if I was all right, again, I said, "How did today go?"

"We got the mess cleaned up," Alice said. "Steve has the mirror repaired, and we're actually analyzing packets and storing data now."

"That sounds good." It did. I had no idea what it meant, but it sounded good.

"So spill," Ceren said. "What's going on?"

I shook my head. "Later."

"No," Alice said. She didn't even have a hint of her usual questioning tone. "Not later. Now."

"Not here," I whispered. I tried to glare and put some weight behind my words, but I had trouble even meeting Alice's eyes.

Ceren studied my face. "After dinner, then."

Alice pursed her lips. "Weren't we going to the movies after dinner?"

"That's tomorrow," Ceren said. "Tonight it was roller skating."

"Oh, right. Right after your boxing team tryouts."

Ceren mimed cracking her knuckles. "Oh, I'll give them something to try."

"Aren't you out of warnings?"

"I am *not* out of warnings. I am out of *suspensions*. Big difference."

"Good thing Kevin has our back. Don't you?"

I couldn't hold off a shallow smile. "Of course. I'll fix it with the Chief. No problem. Just don't bite anything off."

They were good kids, dammit.

Alice and Ceren had both been orphaned once already. Abandoning them to someone else's care now wouldn't just be orphaning them. It would be throwing them away. And I couldn't do that.

No matter how much better they deserved.

I surrendered to the girls' cheerful banter. The alcoholic softness faded, leaving me with the warmth in my extremities but sharp vision and an unpalatably clear brain. Alice tried to draw me out while Ceren fetched Jack's newest rice-and-stew concoction, bread, and three slices of willow melon.

On my belt, my police radio chirped and buzzed.

I felt somewhat amazed that I hadn't lost the radio in the lake. "Just a second."

Alice looked puzzled; Ceren, annoyed.

I raised the radio and pushed the button. "Holtzmann."

"Veronica Boxer here," came a tinny voice in my ear. "Could you come by Saint Michael's?"

Acceptance had made its decision.

Maybe they would help us.

Maybe they'd leave us to burn.

Chapter 60

I LOOKED at Alice, sucking the last of Jack's pork-and-rice leftover stew off her spoon. Ceren still had half her bowl left, and held half a fresh-baked roll to soak up the broth. Both looked curiously at me.

Saint Michael's was two blocks away. I could walk there in a couple minutes. Talk to Acceptance, and be back in half an hour.

I wasn't hungry. At all. My stomach rejected the thought of food on top of all that vodka.

Leaving my mostly untouched stew would be something of a relief.

Alice and Ceren couldn't hear Boxer's side of the conversation, not with the radio pressed to my ear. I could tell them anything.

I licked my lips. "I'll be by right after dinner," I said.

Boxer didn't sound surprised. "We will be here."

"Thanks," I said, and returned the radio to my belt.

"What was that?" Ceren said.

"Maybe trouble," I said. "Maybe help."

"You're not going to run off?" Alice said.

"Dinner is important," I said. "It happens to police officers too often. Something comes up, you run to take care of it, pretty soon, you don't have a family. This..." I looked each of my girls in the eye and sighed. "This has been a really—*shitty* day. Whatever trouble Acceptance has, it'll wait while we eat."

Alice glanced at Ceren. "Speaking of trouble..."

Ceren tilted her head warningly.

"What is it?" I said.

Ceren glanced at Alice, then at me. "Fine," she said, rolling her eyes.

Alice bent low. "Mack told me that Bill's somewhere around here. He's staying in one of the places right by Main Street. He's, like, close enough to hit if you throw a rock."

I nodded. Jack's stew didn't look appetizing, but I needed food. I filled my spoon. "Good." The stew had a nice gentle flavor, but Jack must be out of peppers.

"Good?" Ceren said. "That's all?"

I swallowed. "I don't want to hurt the kid."

"You're not going to charge after him?" Ceren demanded.

"What good would it do?" I put the spoon back in the stew. "I need to talk to him. We need to figure out what to do with him. But I get why he did it, I really do." I lifted a spoonful. "I don't think he's a serial killer. He's afraid. Sooner or later, he'll come out." The second spoonful went down no easier than the first.

Ceren huffed.

"Told you," Alice said.

"I think he can be a good guy," I said.

"He wants to be a hero," Alice said. "He really does. It's just…"

"I know," I said. Bill wanted to be a hero, but ended up a murderer. "Do you know where, exactly?"

"Mack wouldn't tell us," Ceren said.

I nodded. "We'll sort it out."

I ate in silence for a moment, trying to cram actual nutrition into me.

"Who's that?" Ceren finally said, looking at the door.

I glanced up. Doctor Langley stood just inside the door, a young woman taking point for the whole gaggle of unfamiliar people crowding behind her: a chubby woman with a brilliant smile, an overmuscled teenage boy, a gawky geezer with ridiculously long-stemmed wire-rim glasses perched on the very end of his nose.

A glimpse of Frost's withdrawn face in the middle of the horde made me wince in embarrassment. By telling me what she thought she knew, Frost had wrecked everything that I had built inside my own head.

But she'd acted without malice. She'd thought it was better that I know.

Frost had trusted me to handle it.

I'd failed that trust. She'd wanted to help me, that was all. Instead, her words toppled the house of cards I'd built to support my life here. I'd scared the crap out of her in response.

Even though I'd terrified her, she'd gathered her clan, and come down here not merely after dinner, but to have dinner with us.

I still wasn't sure where my life stood, but I owed Frost an apology. A sincere apology, the type that came with a bottle of really good wine and a heap of groveling.

I doubted that would let me face her without feeling that humiliation, not for a long time.

But if I could feel embarrassed, I would recover. Eventually. Somehow.

Around us, a few other people focused curious stares at the newcomers. I understood the fear, although my own fear felt burned out. Who were the newcomers? What did they want? Would they be the ones to shatter our community?

Or had Absolute come to devour us again?

"Missus Langley!" Eric hopped off his barstool. "Welcome."

"Eric!" Jack called from behind the bar, raising his voice over the murmur of the crowd. "I do the introducin' around here."

Eric reached his hand out for Langley. "Good to see you. Jack, Doc Langley. Science doc, not people doc. Now you can introduce her. That there's Doc Frost. More science. Jack's the best cook in town. Do your own dishes, he'll feed you."

Eric's words broke the tension. People nodded and smiled at the newcomers. Jack waved them over to the bar. "C'mon in. I'll put on the chili. We've got plenty."

Eric glanced over the seated crowd at me. His eyes showed his concern.

I grimaced. Eric wasn't the glad-handing type, but he wanted Langley's group to feel welcome. If I'd been myself, I would have joined Frost and Langley at the door and broken the ice. I hadn't done my quiet introduction, so he'd stepped in the only way he knew how.

Another person taking on the jobs I should have been doing. Another person having to do more than they were comfortable with because I needed to feel sorry for myself. Because I had to let my confusion overwhelm me. I shook my head, hints of anger beginning to overwhelm the doubt. What right did I have to slack off, just because I'd found reason to question everything?

I knew I was a copy. I knew it at a deep, gut level, burned into my bones.

I needed to pull my brain together. Get my emotional legs back and start thinking again, instead of just animal drifting.

But I had no idea how.

Then Alice poked my arm. "Kevin," she hissed. She stared at the back door, blue eyes intent.

Just inside the propped-open back door stood a wildly disarrayed woman, maybe thirty or so, wearing sweatpants soaked in mud up to the knees and a pristine red T-shirt. Her brunette hair was tangled and knotted.

Her jaw hung open. The eyes didn't move.

Stunned? Just talked herself out of a house? No, she looked vaguely familiar.

The radio at my belt chirruped.

Kenny, the short obnoxious man who'd tried to interrupt my drinking earlier, rose to offer the woman a solicitous hand. Well, that was sorted then.

Wearily I took up the radio before it could chirp again. "Holtzmann."

Veronica Boxer's voice was high and breathless. "It's back."

"What is?"

"The fear. Worse than before." The words tumbled out as fast as she could speak. "It's angry, too. And it's—"

The woman snatched Kenny's shoulders and yanked herself up to him.

Kenny's sharp shout dissolved into a gurgle.

She shoved Kenny back. Blood covered the lower part of her face.

Kenny staggered away, hands clutching at his ravaged throat, feebly fumbling to plug the sudden red geyser of opened arteries.

I knew that woman.

Her name was Janet. In any sane world she would have been dead, her mind scoured by the drugs she'd overdosed on.

In this world, her body lived after her mind died.

She'd vanished with Nat Reamer.

Another shape appeared in the door behind Janet. Another woman, wearing a bloodstained, royal blue silk teddy, with half her head caved in.

Kenny fell to the floor in front of the bar, still clasping his throat. His feet kicked, twitched, then grew still.

His hands thumped to the floor, his entire body limp and motionless.

Silk Teddy hefted a yard of rusty iron pipe over her head in one hand. Slowly she opened her mouth. Her slow and stretched voice sounded disused, hoarse, as if she had woken from a year-long coma only minutes before. Even so, we all understood what she said.

"Die…"

Chapter 61

SUDDEN VIOLENCE splits people into three groups: those who run towards trouble, those who run from it, and those who scream for help.

Stuff a whole bunch of folks into a bar. Add an overladen buffet table and every chair you can scrounge. Sprinkle in a couple of monsters at the back door, who then announce their intent to kill everyone in the room.

The monstrous mathematics add up to an immobile mass of people screaming, running to, and running from, so tightly packed together no one can move.

Seeing the empty dreg of Janet transform Kenny from an obnoxious lickspittle to a bloody, ravaged corpse did what crying and drinking and Eric and Jack and Alice and Ceren hadn't managed. The engine of my soul roared to life. Every sensation my stunned brain had blocked out crashed into me. The dense crowd of people. Jack's aromatic cooking, overwhelmed with the sudden stenches of fear and blood. The shocked screams and shouts as people elbowed and screamed and clawed each other to get in, out, or away.

All the metaphysical angst evaporated.

Act now. Or die.

I threw my arms over Alice and Ceren and yanked them towards the ground.

Alice fell immediately, smacking her hands and knees on the wooden floor with a soft cry. Tugging Ceren was like pulling on a hundred-year maple, and just as effective.

Kenny's blood saturated Janet's red T-shirt and sweats, sticking the cloth to her skinny frame. She stood perfectly still for a breath, eyes not moving. Then she jerked into motion, treading in the pool of Kenny's blood to snatch at a teenage boy, the kid who liked wide ties—Mack, that was his name.

Mack recoiled, slapping wildly at Janet's fingers, and lurched backwards.

"Down!" I shouted at Ceren.

Ceren stared blankly at me, then twitched to life and dropped down to her knees beside me.

A gunshot cut through the noise.

I jumped back up just in time to see Janet whirl and tumble, unbalanced, into the paneled wall. The impact knocked a neon beer sign off its nail, sending it to the floor with a brittle crash, but somehow she kept her feet.

One of Woodward's men, a big old boy with a gray beard and a paunch that hid his belt, stood only a few feet from Janet and Silk Teddy. He held a handgun the size of a rocket launcher in textbook firing position, both hands on the grip and feet firmly placed. He pulled the trigger again.

Blood exploded from Silk Teddy's chest. She toppled backwards.

I shouted "Everybody out the front!" I barely heard my own voice over the screaming, though.

Janet rolled to put her back to the wall. Her blank eyes didn't move in their sockets.

The wide-tie kid scrabbled away from her, joining the clot of people fighting to squeeze out the front door.

Janet pulled herself upright off the wall. Already drenched with Kenny's blood, her shirt showed no sign of a gunshot. Too much blood for me to see a new wound.

I grabbed Alice's shoulder. Her eyes were wide, her mouth hanging open in an O of shock. "Out the front!" I shouted. The crowd had started to ooze out the front door, giving us an arm's length of free space around our little table, so I gave her a gentle shove.

Ceren rose to her feet and took two steps towards Janet and Silk Teddy, her hands raised in clumsy fists. Her eyes scanned back and forth, looking for a way through.

I snagged her bicep, but my tug didn't shift her at all. I hadn't realized just how strong she'd become until my grip slipped free. "Ceren!" I shouted. "Get Alice out!"

Ceren swung to glare at me. I saw the debate behind her eyes, but with a frustrated snarl she wheeled and caught Alice around the shoulders.

Another gunshot.

I looked up in time to see Janet's throat disintegrate into a spray of blood.

Silk Teddy had gotten to her feet. Fresh blood soaked her blue silk negligee right over the sternum, but no more blood flowed from the closing wound.

The crowd was thinning as people tumbled out the front door. The screams didn't stop, though, and the stinks of fear-sweat and blood had only gotten worse, filling my nose and throat until I wanted to gag. I had my own sudden sweat, my own blood throbbing in my throat and temples.

Woodward waved his guys towards Janet and Silk Teddy. They pulled more handguns: tiny automatics, ludicrously oversized .50-cal cannons, a pretentious little semi-auto with mother-of-pearl trim.

Fire enough bullets, and some would ricochet into the crowd.

"Hold it!" I shouted. "Guns won't stop them!"

One of Woodward's guys pulled out a little plastic thing with a transparent clip. I'd seen them in the movies and in training videos—illegal to own privately, but that never stopped anyone who wanted one badly enough. The little weapon fired up to nine hundred flechette rounds a minute with enough power to rip through steel, and the clip had hundreds of rounds.

A bullet couldn't stop dregs.

But maybe, I wondered…maybe a whole bunch of bullets? All at the same time?

But the bar was still crowded. Ricochets would hurt someone.

Another gunshot cracked over the shouts. The people who'd started towards Janet and Silk Teddy had seen the guns and reversed their course, helping push people out the door. The screaming inside had faded to shouts.

Alice and Ceren were at the back of the crowd shoving for the door. I stepped close behind them, arms spread, trying to shield them with my body. The girls knew bullets weren't lethal—they'd seen me shrug one off. But that didn't mean I wanted either of them to go through the pain of being shot.

Someone screamed again.

It sounded somehow…wrong.

A gunshot. A glance showed me Woodward's men fanning out into a quarter-circle around Janet and Silk Teddy, while the big guy kept the dregs distracted with intermittent well-placed shots.

Another scream. It didn't echo right—

—because it came from outside the front door.

The front door we were almost out.

"Ready!" Woodward shouted.

A pincer movement? Stampede everyone out the front door, where they're more exposed?

It was out the door, towards the screams, or ricochets.

"Aim!"

Outside at least we'd have room to move and a chance to flee. And I wouldn't have been shocked if one of Woodward's thugs snatched the opportunity and put a couple rounds in my back.

I tried to push the girls faster, glimpsing open sky over the heads of the people in the doorway.

Another scream from outside.

Right beside me shuffled Jack, glancing over his shoulder and shaking his head.

"Fire!" Woodward screamed.

The barrage of gunfire filled the room. I couldn't help clapping my hands over my ears and crouching against the earthquake of sound.

At the front door the clog broke free, allowing the few people remaining in the bar to drain into the street.

I had an elbow on Ceren's back, giving her a pointless final push through the door, then burst through behind her, blinking against the sudden sunlight.

The fusillade immediately grew quieter, throttled by the narrow door. People fled in all directions, dashing across and down Main Street. Some shouted over the gunfire, others hugged the wall. I saw Eric with his back to a telephone pole, both hands urging people past him. Cuddles stood at his side, head swiveling in all directions, teeth bared. People surged past the big willow on the corner.

I needed a second to sort through, dreading what I knew I'd find.

Two Backs lumbered down the middle of the road, chasing a twenty-something couple. Most people could outrun Two Backs, at least in a sprint, but the chubby man moved too slowly and the woman tugged at his hands to urge him on. Two Backs' free hand waved in the air and both voices screeched simultaneously.

I spun the other way, intending to take the girls and flee, but a boy with a smashed face stood maybe fifteen feet away. I'd seen that kind of injury before—high-speed steering wheel impact, without a seat belt or air bag. Now his own dried blood soaked his T-shirt and jeans. Expressionless eyes bulged out from the sickeningly concave face, and his misaligned jaw hung impossibly far left but somehow still opened and closed in the gasps of a beached fish.

His left hand swung an oversized steel pipe wrench. His feet remained anchored to the grass, though, only clubbing anyone who came within his reach.

Across the street stood the man made of worms. He stood impossibly still, face turned toward the door of the bar even as people scurried past him.

Two Backs, inches from trampling the couple, skidded to a halt and spun around.

I glimpsed other bloody figures through the thinning crowd. Three? Four?

Beside me, Alice shuddered. Jack glanced left and right, intent, teeth bared. His tongue thrust into the gap where he'd lost the two front teeth.

Ceren curled her lips into a sneer and her hands into fists.

The dregs didn't look around. Their every eye seemed focused on the door, on the tiny knot of people standing right outside the door: Jack, me, Ceren, and Alice.

At some invisible signal, each monstrously-changed human charged straight at us.

Chapter 62

I TRIED counting, but couldn't concentrate long enough. Ten dregs? Maybe twelve?

Two Backs galumphed awkwardly down Main Street on Becky's hands and feet, Paul's trailing feet scrabbling to push them along. The boy with the smashed face staggered towards us, arms outstretched. Those bulging, misaligned goldfish eyes probably confused him more than they helped. The eyeless man made of writhing worms, paradoxically, seemed the most dexterous as he trotted across the street towards us.

And coming around the willow tree on the fairway between sidewalk and road, Nat Reamer, her worn-out nightgown soaked with sweat and sticking to her gaunt frame.

Behind these leaders, more broken shells of human beings.

The sidewalk in front of Jack's bar, with the late afternoon sun burning in the pitiless blue sky, should have felt safe. The bar served as a haven and a gathering place for what remained of humanity. We had a bright green fairway between the sidewalk and the curb, with an old willow tree to cast a halo of comfortable shade only a few yards away, right at the side street. A warm breeze carried the smells of trees and grass and a distant barbeque, incongruous against the abandoned storefronts and irrelevant businesses lining the street. The June day felt more like August, with the scorching sunlight and cloying humidity, but Frayville had endured August for decades.

If it weren't for the heavy melons burdening the willow tree and the people screaming in panic as they streamed away around corners and down the road, it'd look normal.

Danger, whoever he was, had decided to move openly.

I hoped he'd brought everything this time. If we could break through this ring of broken people with empty eyes, we could escape. If Danger had reinforcements behind them, though, we'd certainly die. Most of the dregs didn't move quickly, but they didn't stop. Ever.

My flamethrower was at the bottom of Lake Huron.

I'd parked my hijacked puttermobile half a block south. I'd felt like walking a little. A whole herd of dregs stood between here and there.

Beside me, Alice kept looking blankly at the chaotic scene. She's a great kid, but confrontation isn't her thing. Ceren, though, set her feet and looked ready to fight. Jack fumbled at his belt, under hidden under whatever Hawaiian shirt he wore, and pulled out a tiny hand Taser. He nodded at me.

Behind us, Jack's still thundered with gunfire as Woodward's men punched holes into Janet and Silk Teddy. How much ammunition had they brought?

The dregs couldn't move that fast, but I didn't think we'd be able to escape this many at once.

I knew I couldn't fight if I had to simultaneously defend the girls.

"Alice! Ceren!" I shouted a couple times before they heard me above the screaming.

Alice jerked towards me.

I pointed at the willow. "They can't climb trees! Go! Up!"

Alice latched a hand onto Ceren's arm. The bigger girl started, glared at me, and followed Alice.

The boy with the smashed head veered to intercept them.

I dashed forward, throwing myself against the boy, outstretched hands against his chest.

The impact knocked him staggering backwards, arms slowly windmilling in a feeble attempt to keep his balance.

Alice hopped to grab the lowest branch of the tree. Ceren grabbed her legs and shoved. "Go!"

Beside me, Jack's Taser popped.

Nat Reamer starfished on her feet, head tilted back, eyes bulging until they almost launched from their sockets. The Taser's thin wires ran straight into the spot where her gaunt neck met her hollow chest. Her feet shuffled and jittered, and she toppled backwards.

Jack dropped the Taser and raised his scrawny arms. His tightly rolled fists told me he had a few punch-outs somewhere in his past. We were going to need them.

Behind us, the barrage from Woodward's thugs thinned to individual gunshots.

Alice grabbed another branch and hoisted herself up out of reach.

The worm-bodied man burst into a trot, hands pumping as he charged towards us. His legs didn't seem to move quickly enough for as fast as he ran. I had the impression that each churning pink worm that made up his form didn't have a fixed position, that he ran by shifting individual worms from back to front, as if he didn't run as much as flock.

But the smashed-face kid was on his feet again, shuffling towards us.

One last gunshot, and Jack's bar fell silent.

I braced myself for Smashface's impact, planning to swing him around into the ground.

Ceren slammed into Smashface, driving him like a linebacker. Her face was red, her teeth clenched, hands clutching Smashface's ratty T-shirt as she shoved him sideways.

The dreg flailed, pummeling Ceren's back, but Ceren had her head tucked so tightly in that he couldn't land a solid blow on her head.

Smashface hit the cinderblock front of Jack's bar with a bone-creaking crash, hard enough to make me almost wince. Something snapped—a bone?

Ceren stepped back and clumsily kicked Smashface in the groin.

Using only an arm, she'd pulled an iron leg off a bench.

Her leg was thicker, more massively muscled than that arm.

Smashface lifted a foot into the air. His jaw dropped open and his misplaced eyes somehow bulged even further.

"Ceren!" I shouted. "Get up the tree!"

Ceren turned to me. "Not a chance." Not even breathing heavily, she glanced around. "Watch your own back."

Strength isn't everything. I've had fistfights with people a lot stronger than me, and won most of them. But I couldn't argue right now—Wormface was almost on us, Two Backs waddling right behind him, and a dozen more shambling on their heels.

Jack took two steps forward and swung a giant looping John Wayne punch at Wormface's head. Wormface didn't even try to get out of the way, just stood there and let Jack's haymaker crush into the side of his skull.

Jack's fist sunk up to his wrist inside Wormface's skull.

Jack screamed.

The last time I'd heard a scream like that, it had been a dumbass teenager who'd stuffed his hand into a wood chipper on a dare. This wasn't a scream of fear or terror. This was a scream of agony and existential horror, a bone-deep understanding that the screamer's life had just been changed forever.

Jack staggered back.

His hand was gone.

The red-and-black stump seared and smoked as he waved his arm in front of his face, carrying the sickening stench of burned flesh. Two tiny spurs of bone protruded from the severed wrist.

Worms for a face, acid for a body.

He grabbed each side of Jack's head with hands made of tiny tentacles.

The hands writhed around Jack's skull, stretching, reaching, drilling deeply into Jack's head.

Sizzling smoke filled the air.

Jack convulsed on his feet, suspended upright by acidic tendrils perforating his skull.

My gut knotted.

We might have been able to punch our way to the car.

But we couldn't stand against that acid touch.

I glanced up to see Alice propped in a fork of the tree some fifteen feet above the ground, jaw set as tightly as her hands held the branches, cheeks bulging to restrain vomit.

"Back inside!" I shouted.

Ceren turned immediately and ran right beside me, hurtling back into the bar.

The last thing I saw before slamming shut the heavy metal door was Jack's headless body, haloed in the hazy steam of his own dissolved skull and brain, tumbling to the ground.

Chapter 63

I SAGGED against the inside of the cool metal door, my sweat chilling as it glued my shirt to my back. My breath shuddered in my chest.

With a single punch, Jack had lost his hand and then his life.

How the hell had something like Wormface happened? Wormface wasn't a dreg. He hadn't lost his brain and devolved, but taken his body in a new, horrible direction.

The rules, changing again.

Or we just didn't understand them.

Ceren stood next to me, somehow holding herself mostly still despite what we'd just seen. Her hands twitched, though, and her gaze bounced around the bar.

Tumbled tables and overturned chairs now filled Jack's bar. The big buffet table along the side still stood, the huge vats of rice and stew still steamed, piles of fresh-baked rolls and six plastic serving bowls of sliced melon.

Jack had cooked for everyone.

He'd done what he could to care for us.

He had brought people together.

Made us a community.

That little table held the last meal ever prepared for us.

All of it wasted.

The aromas of rice and stew clashed with the bitter haze of gunfire smoke and the rising, nauseating stink of blood.

Woodward's men still stood in a quarter-circle around the back door. A couple of them gave each other high-fives. Another repeatedly hoisted his tiny little automatic over his head. Every one of them shouted and whooped and hollered.

I fumbled for the deadbolt knob and flipped it, locking the front door behind us. "They got Jack!" I shouted against their cheers.

One of the good old boys faced me, eyebrows twisted in curiosity.

"Jack's dead," I shouted again.

A couple more heads turned.

Something hit the door behind me. I kept my back braced against it. Surely Wormface would need a few minutes to burn through steel? "Hey!" I shouted.

The men fell silent, annoyed at me interrupting their celebration.

"Jack's dead," I said in a more normal voice. "The worm guy, he's full of acid."

"We'll just deal with him, too," Woodward said.

"You said guns didn't work!" shouted a man with a heavy white bandage over one eye and medicated slashes over his cheeks. I hardly recognized the person Cuddles had almost killed—Will, that was his name. "We got them, we'll get this one!"

"How much ammo have you got?" I said. "Every dreg in town is out there."

Almost instantly, all twelve men deflated and glanced nervously at each other. I could almost smell evaporating testosterone.

"You used it all," I snarled. "Of course you did."

"It worked," Woodward said.

I grabbed Ceren's arm. "Come on. Out the back, around front, half a block south, I have a puttermobile. Sort of sky blue."

"Puttermobile?" Ceren said. "What happened to the cruiser?"

"Like I said," I snapped, "it's been a *really* shitty day. You think you can run that far, fast?"

"I can do anything," Ceren snapped, standing a little straighter.

"Then let's go."

But first we had to go over Janet and Teddy's corpses.

I'd never seen anything like this before, not even as a police officer down in Detroit after a bloody gang fight. Woodward's men had filled—no, saturated—the two women with bullets. Their clothes were chewed into bloody rags almost indistinguishable from their devastated flesh. Bullets ranging from big softnose .45s to tiny flechettes had broken bone and shattered meat, cutting through the dregs until they were unrecognizable. I'd seen hamburger that looked more whole than these—

Than these people. Than these women.

Janet, wife of Jerry.

And a woman who had died in a blue silk teddy, barely more than a girl herself. I'd called her Silk Teddy—but she had a real name, a name she'd answered to. And someone who loved it when she wore that teddy.

I wished I could spare Ceren the sight.

"Come on," I said to Ceren. To the men I said, "You all want to help? See if you can trap the dregs that aren't made of acid. Gang up on them, three or four to one. Tie them up or something."

I'd wanted to help Becky, and Paul.

I'd wanted to rescue Nat Reamer.

Instead, I was going to go to the puttermobile. I was going to find Eric's truck, or hit the police station. I was going to grab a flamethrower. And I was going to burn every dreg down to sticky ash and spurs of bone.

I stepped over Janet's shattered bloody bones.

That's when Kenny sat up, screamed, and snatched for my legs.

Chapter 64

DEAD BEYOND any doubt, body stretched out on the floor of Jack's bar in a widening pool of his own sticky, stinky blood, Kenny sat up. His arms, drenched in his own heart's blood, swung in a wide clumsy arc to grab at my knees.

I danced away from his hands, my feet slipping on the blood-saturated wood floor of Jack's bar, sending me tumbling into one of the guys in Woodward's little army, a big old boy with a beard like the nest of a slovenly bird.

Ceren screamed and grabbed a bulky wooden chair, lifting it above her head as if it weighed nothing.

Woodward's guys jerked back, shouting obscenities. The guy I'd tumbled into yanked my shoulder, holding me upright for that second I needed to get my feet under me.

Woodward shouted wordlessly, hands flailing in surprise as he retreated into a table and fell back.

Kenny leaned to the side to lever himself up. Janet's shattered head moved with him, somehow attached to Kenny's gut.

No, not attached.

Embedded. Melded.

Kenny stood, wobbling horribly thanks to the extra weight of Janet dangling from his abdomen.

Horrified, I found myself standing still, watching. I remembered the videos of Absolute attacks in South America, Australia, and South Africa. Grainy, choppy security footage didn't carry a fraction of the revulsion brought on by seeing such a change in reality.

Kenny staggered a step forward. Somehow, Kenny's movement triggered spasms inside Janet's flesh. Muscles contracted and shifted around shattered bone. A bloody hand with two remaining fingers thrashed grotesquely at the end of a devastated arm.

The spasms traveled down Janet's body, to where her foot touched Silk Teddy's hand.

Teddy's body spasmed, flailing in wild, uncontrolled movements. It looked as though someone had hooked a battery to broken, bloody muscle and pulverized bone.

The guy with one eye screamed, voicing the horror we all felt.

Then Ceren stepped into my field of view, stopped next to Kenny, and swung the heavy chair she held in her hands. Swung it hard, with a scream of her own.

Straight into Kenny's head.

Wood and bone shattered.

Kenny fell back into a barstool, skull broken like a watermelon struck by a sledgehammer. Clear fluid and gray brains spattered across the bar and the mirror, adding another revolting reek to the blood and smoke and ash already filling my nose. I glimpsed an open can of Pabst Blue Ribbon on the bar, right through the space where his nose should have been.

All three bodies twitched and clenched.

Then as one, sagged.

Ceren dropped the chair. Two of the pine legs had cracked.

I held my gorge down by force of will, mind churning furiously. What had happened there? Had the broken remnants of Kenny's mind attached his body to Janet and Teddy somehow? Or had Janet been the brain behind everything, with Danger somewhere behind it? Or maybe Teddy?

Something pounded on the front door. Metal groaned. The whole frame quivered.

"Good, Ceren!" I shouted. Some of Woodward's army looked affronted that a little teenage girl—okay, a hefty teenage girl—had taken Kenny's dreg down so easily, but most nodded or smiled appreciatively. A couple guys gave her the appraising look that told me they might pick a fight with her, teenage girl or no, just to prove they were stronger. A high-school-aged boy clearly debated asking her out.

No time for any of that.

Half-formed ideas drove me to the front of the room, where I snatched a serving bowl of sliced melon from the buffet table.

Was that a hissing noise?

Smoke rose around the front door.

The door was metal. Presumably acid-proof.

But the doorframe was wood. Organic.

Vulnerable.

"Come on, Ceren," I shouted, carrying the bowl in one arm. "Out, around front, left to the puttermobile. Light blue."

At least if Wormface was attacking the door, he wasn't dissolving the tree where Alice perched.

The mélange of broken flesh that was Kenny and Janet and Teddy began to twitch anew as Ceren and I bolted out the back door into the alley.

The second I got a breath that didn't stink of confined blood and gore, I made myself snatch a piece of melon from the bowl and stuffed it into my mouth, thinking furiously.

Brandi's self-image had made her taller.

Eric's had made him black.

Ceren's had turned her hair electric blue, and then made her strong enough to tear metal.

Kipuka Blues

Frost's words had thrown my whole psyche into disarray. Was I Kevin Holtzmann? Was I a copy? Was I formed out of his flesh, or had I claimed his bloody clothes and wedding ring from his corpse? My origins, my past, those vital questions of my existence—none of that mattered right now.

People I loved had died. People I cared about were about to follow.

Not again. Not ever again. To stop that, I'd claimed the place between death and those I cared for. They would not die unless I died first.

I cannot be broken. I stand to protect those who cannot protect themselves. I protect them from pain, from death, so they can live their lives. The man between. That's my role. My place.

The melon tasted of apricots and apples, maybe peaches as well, with a faint underlying taste of rich pork. It was juicy and soft, dissolving in my mouth without much chewing, so I stuffed another slice down my gullet before we got to the back corner where the alley met the side street.

We got onto the side street before I choked out, "Hold on! Ceren!"

Ceren drew herself to a halt. "What?"

"A second." You can't eat while sprinting. I grabbed two more slices of melon and swallowed them in large gulps, then two more.

The melon was food. From what I'd seen, high-nutrition food, brimming with energy.

Energy to live up to my own self-image, I hoped.

No, I couldn't hope. I had to *know* it. Know it strongly enough to make myself into what I had to be.

From the front of the building, someone shrieked. A dreg?

No, that sounded like—Alice, up in her tree?

I dropped the bowl. That would have to be enough.

I am the defender, I told myself. *Ceren can rip a steel leg off a bench. I can will myself back to life. I will do anything to protect those I love. Danger might control them, give them purpose…but* nothing *is as strong as my will, my need.*

I powered past Ceren, picking up speed and turning towards Main Street.

The people crowded into Jack's had vanished, fleeing for safety. I didn't blame them.

A knot of dregs shuffled around the front door. After seeing Janet and Teddy, the rest of them didn't look so broken, merely dented, with their stained clothes and twisted limbs. Between their limbs I glimpsed Wormface, hugging the front door of Jack's.

Jack's decapitated body lay behind them, sprawled limply on the ground.

Alice perched in the willow tree at the crossroads, holding tightly to upper branches.

But she wasn't alone up there.

Nat Reamer mechanically raised an arm.

Her hand closed on the next branch up.

And pulled herself higher.

Nat looked healthier than most of the other dregs, even as gaunt as she was. The breeze flapped the ancient translucent nightgown around her. She moved carefully, placing each hand and foot with more concentration than I thought a dreg could possess.

Another moment, maybe two, and she'd be high enough to snap a bony hand around Alice's ankle.

Chapter 65

I SLAMMED to a stop, one arm stretched out to intercept Ceren.

"Ceren," I said as quietly as I could. "Back that way. Sky blue puttermobile. Find Eric's truck, it won't be far. There's a flamethrower in the back. If Eric's there, bring him too, but bring that flamethrower."

Ceren glanced between me and Alice, then put her head down and charged for my car like a bull rhino. Her feet ate distance in great loping strides.

I turned—ignoring Wormface trying to use its acid to burn through Jack's door like it had burned through Jack's skull, ignoring the other dregs standing nearby—and lunged for the tree.

Alice, *my* Alice, trapped at the top of the tree, a deranged Nat Reamer climbing closer with every second. These brain-damaged monstrosities would not touch my girls.

I sprinted towards Nat, scooping to snatch up the two-foot pipe wrench Smashface had dropped earlier, the weighty, rusty handle fitting coolly into my palm.

Alice stomped on Nat Reamer's reaching hand, pinning it to the branch beneath and grinding it with her heel. Nat didn't react, only reached up with her other hand for Alice's ankle. Alice yanked her foot out of the way and squeezed herself a little higher up the willow. Branches around her creaked, groaned, and sagged with her weight.

Alice didn't weigh much, but the soft wood of willows can't hold much.

I got to the willow, heaving in barely enough air to keep my muscles from cramping. Over me in the trailing willow leaves, Nat moved slowly and carefully, with an idiot deliberation.

I reached up with the pipe wrench and swung it in a great, looping arc that connected with her scrawny shin.

Nat yanked that leg out of range without making a sound. She didn't even gasp in pain.

I dragged the massive wrench back around to swing it again. The weight of the screw jaw at the end made the wrench an ungainly bludgeon.

Nat pulled herself up another branch.

The next blow hit just below her uninjured foot, smacking into the willow trunk with a crack that vibrated up my arm into my shoulder. Gray mossy bark shattered, exposing moist, pale wood.

Nat looked down at me with vacant, pale gray eyes.

Then slowly, as if with deliberate concentration, one side of her mouth twitched upwards.

Then the other.

Through her brain damage, despite the pain I'd inflicted on her, Nat smiled at me. Not a healthy smile, either. It looked as if she had never smiled before, and smiled now only because she'd found the instructions in a manual and decided to give it a try.

"That's it," I said, still unable to properly catch my breath. I needed to be on the ground to use the flamethrower Ceren was bringing, but that could happen later. If I had to chase them into the tree to rescue Alice, I would. Because I needed nothing in the world at that moment than to wipe that smirk off Nat's face.

Alice decided to do the job for me. Her stomping heel smashed Nat right in the temple.

Nat reeled back, one arm wheeling free and cracking against a branch, making that whole bough shudder. She kept her grip with the other hand, even though her bad foot slipped from the branch supporting it.

Alice's own branch groaned from the stress of her violent moves.

I swung the pipe wrench, putting as much speed and force behind it as I could manage.

The steel head bit deeply into Nat's foot and plowed on, smashing the ankle bones against the tree trunk. A sickening snap of bone made my guts twitch in simultaneous satisfaction and nausea.

The branch Alice sat on creaked anew.

Alice froze.

Wood snapped.

Her branch jerked nearly a foot down all in one motion.

Alice grabbed at other boughs to pull herself off the weakened branch. Slender, curving leaves and heavy melons wobbled all around her as she pivoted to a new perch, a few inches higher. She couldn't weigh a hundred pounds, but even so, her new supports quavered with her every breath.

Nat yanked herself back up, pulling herself with her hands and unbroken ankle.

I crouched to jump up and grab the lowest branch of the tree, pulling myself after her.

Something slammed into my side. I tumbled down and plunged face-first into the lawn, breath exploding out of me even as my open mouth bit into enough grassy black loam to cover my tongue.

Overhead, Alice screamed.

A kick in the ribs and a stomp on my spine knocked me into the willow trunk. I tried to unbend enough to use the trunk as a lever back to my feet, but something hit my temple and I collapsed onto the ground. A gray haze ringed my vision.

Two Backs.

The conglomerate creature had changed further. Paul's torso no longer seemed quite so pendulous beneath Becky's extended limbs. His rear legs had realigned a few vital degrees, letting his feet contribute to pushing them forward.

The ragged remains of socks still decorated Paul's ankles, dissolving into threads where his steps had worn the cotton away.

Two Backs somehow whirled on Becky's legs, pivoting in place. The view from the front wasn't any better. Becky's torso bent even further back, and somehow extended, making her resemble a freakish centaur. Paul's free arm had rejointed itself at the shoulder, giving them a single grasping appendage sticking out the front. His other arm, the one that had previously held him to Becky's naked form, had sunk further into her body until it showed only as a bony ridge, mostly visible by the band of his olive skin against her pale white tones.

Becky's front hands now looked like a cross between horse's hooves and wolf paws, with thick horny sheaths around stubby digits.

Their combined stink curdled my stomach.

Both mouths opened in synchronized shrieks of rage, exposing gums choked with painful-looking, overlapping razor teeth.

I dizzily rolled to the side, one hand fumbling for the tree trunk. A fading halo of gray still circled my vision. Experience told me it would fade in twenty, maybe thirty seconds.

If I had that long.

On my other side, Smashface stepped into view, the acid-filled Wormface beside him. I glimpsed more figures on my other side.

Two Backs danced forward and reared up like a horse, lifting Becky's hands—*hooves* into the air over my head.

Between the circling hooves, I saw Nat Reamer's hand clamp around Alice's ankle.

Alice screamed.

Hooves crashed down at my face.

Chapter 66

TWO BACKS' hooves came down on my head like—like—no, there's *nothing* like half a ton of horrifically mutated lovers. I dizzily threw myself forward, twisting under their appalling merged torsos, landing on my back in the grass right beneath it.

Two Backs' front legs slammed into the ground where I'd been sprawled, tearing turf.

I kicked with my legs to push myself out from underneath their bulk—but I was too slow.

Two Backs relaxed its legs and dropped right on top of me.

Their whole weight crushed into my ribs and gut, squeezing my lungs flat. Sandwiched between Paul's hard, bony back and the ground, the soft grassy dirt beneath me felt as unyielding as rock on my back and the side of my head.

In my narrow slice of vision, the circle of dregs around us stepped closer in one synchronized motion.

I kicked up and down, my legs thrashing like an angry toddler throwing a tantrum.

And the stench! Rancid sweat, vinegar, shit, and somehow, Two Backs still stank of sex.

I tried to lever my arms up to elbow myself some room, but they were pinned completely flat.

My lungs burned for the air my chest wasn't strong enough to draw in.

The hammering of my own pulse filled my head, while the weird double-thump of Two Backs' heartbeats pounded softly through my ear, pressed hard against their belly.

Two Backs' weight shifted. For a glorious fraction of a second I snatched half a breath.

Then its bulk sank down again, harder than before.

Its front legs filled my vision. Two Backs had stopped holding up its own weight, sprawling entirely on me instead.

I tried to kick my legs for traction.

They felt very far away. I couldn't tell if they responded or not.

Something inside my chest cracked—a rib?

Another crack.

My swelling heartbeat filled my senses.

A line of pain stabbed my right—arm? Hand? Something out there.

I felt myself fading. The gray on the fringe of my vision turning black, spreading.

Two Backs screamed and jerked.

In the dark, I tried to twist.

Couldn't move.

Two Backs jerked again. It scrabbled above me, torqueing my ribs back and forth, making me reflexively thrash to escape even though I didn't have room to twitch or the strength to find my own legs.

Two Backs vanished.

My lungs reflexively sucked in great buckets of air, the pain of my expanding, crushed ribs lost in the pleasure of breathing again. The world opened up around me. I breathed out and in again, noticing the stabbing in the side of my chest, right under my left armpit, but not caring. The blue June sky and the green of the trailing leaves of the willow seemed to inflate into view, and my ribs ached and burned with every breath.

I couldn't move—the oxygen hadn't yet hit my limbs, my brain, anything. Lying on my back, I concentrated on breathing in and out, knowing it would have to be enough.

But in the tree over my head, I had a great view of Nat and Alice. Nat had one bony hand around Alice's ankle. Alice kicked with her free foot, trying to break Nat's grip. The tree wobbled and swayed, the branches supporting them threatening to shatter every moment.

I didn't understand. How did I get free?

My right wrist screamed from a dozen deep pains as the oxygen restored communications between my brain and the rest of my body. A line of jagged, jabbed cuts formed a semicircle on my arm, and blood coursed down my hand.

One of the heads had bitten me, with those horrid fangs.

If the teeth could fit together better, they might have bitten the hand clean off.

I tried to grab the ground. To seize traction, to push myself upwards, to grab Nat and haul her to the ground.

Instead, I twitched feebly, still unable to move with any coordination.

You ate! I screamed in my brain. *That melon, full of energy. You said you're a defender. Now get up and defend!*

I heaved another breath, my body still not responding, and watched with furious impotence as Nat heaved herself higher, closer to my adopted daughter.

Loud noises. Gunshots?

Someone shouted.

Terror distorted Alice's face.

Then that terror melted into anger.

One moment Alice's eyes were wide and white, jaw hanging open in a silent scream. Then her teeth clamped together and her eyes narrowed.

Nat clambered up another branch, getting her head even with Alice's knees.

Alice bent over and clamped a hand to each side of Nat's head, right over the temples.

Nat froze.

Alice froze with her.

They seemed to stare into each other's' eyes.

Get up, Holtzmann, you lazy selfish bastard!

With another breath, I managed to flail to my side, and then up on one knee, wobbling weakly, but upright.

A little yellow electric puttermobile sat on Main Street, half a dozen yards south, driven by a teenage boy with a thatch of yellow hair, husky enough that when he leaned out the driver's side window, he seemed to overflow the car.

Bill. The kid who'd murdered Keith Gifford in the bathtub.

Alice had said he was nearby. He must have heard the screams, the shouts, the gunfire.

The kid aimed a little short-barrel squirrel rifle at one of the dregs off to my left.

He must have shot Two Backs. Given me a chance.

He pulled the trigger again. I heard a high-pitched pop.

Wormface staggered, bent over like he'd been punched in the gut. Tendrils flailed around him in a nightmare halo.

But Two Backs, Smashface, and the others staggering dregs were only a few implacable, inexorable steps from him.

Damn fool kid.

If he hadn't shown up, hadn't put a few rounds into Two Backs, I'd be dead.

But still, damn fool kid.

I sucked another lungful of air and fought to my feet, struggling against the dizziness in my temples and the anoxic haze in my fingers and toes and eyes. I clamped my teeth shut, willing the vomit back down into my throat. I swallowed and stayed upright.

Alice and Nat still stared into each other's eyes. Alice's face showed a rictus of obsession and anger, teeth clenched behind snarling lips.

Bill yanked his rifle back into the car. He'd ridden to my rescue, now he was going to get out of here—good. Alice said he wanted to be a hero. This was his chance to run like one.

Wormface rose unsteadily to his feet. The bullet must have struck some kind of solid core buried beneath those innumerable writhing tentacles.

I crouched to leap for Nat's ankles and yank her out of the tree.

Bill didn't drive away, though. As Smashface came up to the puttermobile's driver's side window, Bill wrestled with something inside the car. Hoses flapped behind the windscreen, and Bill straightened up into view holding a narrow, gleaming metal nozzle.

He had said, *I will burn anyone who comes near me.*

Bill had stolen the flamethrower.

The kid jabbed the flamethrower's flickering maw straight into Smashface's gut, only a pull of a finger away from igniting the dreg, the car, and himself.

Chapter 67

"BILL!" I screamed in horror. "No!"

If Bill pulled the trigger on that flamethrower jammed against Smashface's ribs, the dreg would burn. The backblast would cover the electric puttermobile, probably fill it. A confined, intense blaze would rupture the flamethrower's fuel tank. Bill, the dregs around the car, the buildings along Main Street all would be splashed with high-pressure burning gel, and ignite a conflagration far beyond anything our two-man fire department and their single truck could handle.

Not that Alice and I would care. We'd die in the first blast. Not right away—but we'd get enough gel to burn us away.

Eventually.

I had to get Smashface away from that flamethrower before Bill squeezed the trigger, despite my broken ribs and the blood flowing freely from my chomped arm.

I wasn't fast enough for this.

I sucked in a breath, and took the world's motion inside with me.

Smashface's arms had been moving towards Bill. They hung still.

Bill's rage-twisted face, distorted by the puttermobile's windshield, seemed cast in bronze.

The wind had stopped.

Wormface's flowing tendrils: immobile.

I charged towards Bill's car and the cluster of dregs around it.

Wormface began turning slowly towards me. He seemed to be moving in pantomime. The tentacles of his body no longer churned, but hesitantly shifted against each other like a stop-motion movie monster.

I veered around the questing tentacles of his hands, locked my vision on Smashface, and *moved*.

The world didn't slow down.

I accelerated.

My heartbeat felt like I was jogging, but with the slow-motion world around me, how fast was it really going? Two hundred beats a minute? Three hundred? Each deep breath felt normal, but I had to be breathing like a hummingbird. Even my thoughts felt sped up far beyond normal, allowing me to consider these questions in the fraction of an eyeblink I needed to cover the distance.

But I was closing on Smashface.

A frozen manic glee distorted Bill's face, his fury-twisted lips and gleaming teeth even uglier in my languid world.

If I hit Smashface straight on, I'd impale him on the flamethrower.

I tucked my head to one side and did an old-fashioned shoulder tackle into Smashface's flank.

The impact wrenched Smashface partway into my accelerated world. His hands flew up, his back arching, arms and legs flying away, and he spun to the side, away from Bill's puttermobile and the flamethrower.

Abrupt, rabid hunger stabbed my stomach. The world quivered and lurched around me. The melon had given me energy, but the burst of speed burned through it too quickly. My feet became incredibly massive and clumsy, as if I waded through knee-deep molasses. I tasted hot metal at the back of my throat, and my heart spasmed and jittered in my chest.

I'd started the charge to keep Bill from blowing us all into our own local Hell.

But now I had too much momentum to stop.

Smashface lazily spun in slow-motion, arms and legs trailing back.

The overdrive switched off as instantly as it began. The world raced back to full speed, leaving me helplessly out of control, moving too fast for my mind to understand. My legs spun and skipped beneath me, bouncing across the concrete. I wobbled and weaved, trying to get my feet in front of me to seize my balance, but instead tumbled to the pavement.

I wrenched my hands around, trying to catch myself on my forearms rather than my palms. Asphalt scraped across the inside of my left forearm, shredding my skin, but the crash of my right hand against the asphalt sent a gut-twisting snap echoing up that arm. I bounced off the road, struck the broken ribs sparking too much pain to scream, rolled over my shoulders, and logrolled another couple yards before coming to an exhausted, panting halt.

I needed a breath to organize myself, to find the ground and sky through my dizziness. Tiny pebbles from the road riddled my scraped, bloody, exposed arms and legs. Even the skin protected by my shredded shorts and shirt was battered and bloody. But my right wrist radiated a ghastly pulsing agony through my every nerve, overriding everything but the pain of breathing.

Smashface lay a few yards behind me. He'd come down face-first on the asphalt.

His deformed skull had acquired a whole new shape.

From his car Bill shrieked "Get out of there! I have this! I have this!"

I made myself look back towards the dregs.

Nine of them.

A chubby man in shorts and Hawaiian shirt, unharmed but with vacant eyes.

A teenage girl in a bloody beach cover-up, the handle of a kitchen knife protruding from one shattered eye socket.

A skinny, heavily tanned lady with bright red hair and a slack face, wearing a flouncy, blue, flowered dress, somehow balancing on high heels.

A gaunt old man in jeans and a flannel shirt, one hand burned away, head half chopped away at an erratic angle, maybe by a band saw. I'd seen this one before, hanging around Woodward's crew when Eric and I rescued Cuddles.

A short-haired college boy in blue dress pants, a white shirt, and a blue-and-white-plaid silk tie, drooling from one corner of his mouth, sticking by a brown-skinned girl about his same age in matching blue slacks and white blouse.

A chubby matron in jeans and a short-sleeve, pink T-shirt that bore a great big flower picked out in sparkling crystals.

Two Backs in the middle.

Wormface, playing acidic tail gunner behind them.

Plus Smashface, sprawled unmoving across the curb to one side.

The nine standing simultaneously raised their right feet and stepped forward.

"Get out!" Bill shrieked.

Somewhere behind me, tires screeched. Car doors slammed.

I scrabbled at the ground, struggling to get my legs beneath me. No—get one knee up. Then the other. Ignore the screaming pain from the right wrist. Lurch forward—there.

I'd barely touched the curb when the blistering rage of the flamethrower erupted behind me. I raised my hands as if to ward off the volcano of heat behind me. My skin instantly dried out, wet blood growing sticky as I staggered across the grass easement away from the conflagration.

The smooth gray trunk of a maple tree caught me before I could fall, panting, cradling my doubly maimed right hand to my chest with a pain too precious to share. My lungs ached for air. Knives of hunger stabbed my stomach. Every muscle shook with strain and exhaustion. That burst of speed hadn't only burned up any energy I'd gotten from the melon, it had taken all my usual reserves with it.

Behind me, the torrent of flame continued. I raised my left hand to shade my eyes, but couldn't see the dregs through the coursing flame.

"Bill!" I screamed. "One-second bursts!"

The flamethrower bellowed for another half second, then cut off.

The first thing I noticed was the flame burning on the hood of Bill's puttermobile. He'd held the flamethrower out the window like a drive-by shooter, pouring the flame right at the dregs—and maybe half the gel had sprayed the hood of his car. Flames and white smoke coursed up from the hood towards the sky.

Two of the dregs were thrashing columns of fire, totally drenched with incendiary gel. Holding the flamethrower out the window and firing straight ahead meant that Bill's wild spray had lacked the flexibility to hit the old guy with half a head, the cute college couple, Two Backs, or the flowery matron. The woman in high heels had grotesque red blisters over half her body.

And the line had shielded the most deadly of all, Wormface, from the flame.

The remaining dregs screamed. Not like Two Backs' synchronized shrieking—this was half a dozen separate, agonized cries, as if every one of them had suffered a horribly painful wound.

"Bill!" I screamed. "Get out of that car!"

The screams cut off.

In perfect synchronization, the dregs turned to glare at me.

I retreated a step.

They advanced in lockstep.

With slow, inexorable paces, they walked towards me.

Chapter 68

CAUSTIC FLAMES billowed out from under the puttermobile's hood, stinking toxic black smears already streaking the white plume of smoke as flaming gel seeped under the hood and ignited the plastic within. In the driver's seat, Bill struggled with the tangled hoses of the stolen flamethrower.

A few yards up the road, seven empty shells that had once been eight human beings marched towards me in creepily perfect lockstep. Through the innumerable leaves and dangling melons of the willow tree on the corner behind them, I glimpsed Alice and Nat locked together, immobile.

Behind all of them, a sky blue puttermobile raced up the road. Ceren.

Wormface was in the back of the dregs. If hotheaded Ceren drove the puttermobile into him—

No. I did *not* want Ceren tangling with Wormface.

Running meant abandoning Alice to her private battle with Nat.

But I couldn't charge straight through to help Alice, either. Not through acidic Wormface.

I stepped further back onto the sidewalk, almost backing into the wide glass window of Frayville Bay Souvenirs, then turned and bolted south.

Behind me, a sudden clatter of feet as the dregs broke out in a run.

I hurt everywhere. I'd gotten kicked and punched and almost crushed by Two Backs, crashed at twenty or thirty miles an hour into the pavement, and accumulated bruises and contusions everywhere. My right wrist pulsed with my heartbeat, the broken bones inside it grating against each other with every running step, blood still oozing from the bites, making my arm both slippery and sticky simultaneously. I cradled it against my breastbone and ran, chest heaving and pushing my feet as hard as I could.

It was like finishing a marathon and then having to sprint for another mile. I had nothing left. No reserves. Nothing.

With distance, I might have a plan.

Behind me, trapped in the burning puttermobile, Bill shouted wordlessly.

I glanced over my shoulder to see all seven dregs following me in lockstep, ignoring the inferno.

I couldn't untangle Bill from his car—all I could do was lure the dregs away so he could get himself out.

I ran past the souvenir shop, the Frayville Bakery with the shattered front window and the glass display counters of desiccated donuts, across Horse Stall Lane towards the day care, between the few cars parked alongside the road and the businesses, dregs trailing behind me single file through that narrow passage.

My chest ached, and my throat burned drier and drier with each step.

I reached a huge pickup truck sporting a monstrous plow with the State of Michigan Department of Natural Resources logo on the side, parked on the corner. *Who got this beast out of storage?*

The massive bulk of a black-and-white Rottweiler hurtled itself against the pickup's rolled-up windows.

Cuddles.

Eric had picked up this truck, and now Cuddles was going mad trying to reach the dregs chasing me.

For a split second I pondered opening the door and freeing the dog to help me—but there wasn't time.

Run.

Get distance. Make a plan.

And in that second, the plan appeared.

Saint Michael's was less than a block south.

I'd lead the dregs right into the church.

Acceptance waited for me there.

I'd *make* them take sides.

I passed the back of the truck, and had gone another dozen steps before realizing what I'd seen.

Eric, his massive body crouched absurdly behind the truck's tailgate.

With a great big round-bladed shovel in his hands.

I'd warned Eric about flamethrowers in tight quarters this morning, but at the moment, I'd be thrilled if he blew up the truck and the building both, if it kept Wormface's acid touch away from him.

I tried to turn around and keep running. Tried to shout "Don't!" even as I gasped through battered ribs for more air, and succeeded only in stumbling a few steps forward.

Somehow, the skinny lady in high heels led the charge down the sidewalk, between the parked cars and the white brick day care. She'd almost reached the back of the truck when Eric leaped to his feet, raising the shovel blade to meet her face.

High Heels smashed face-first into the back side of the shovel blade and toppled backwards, crashing into College Boy. The pileup escalated, all six of them cascading together into a single massive knot on the sidewalk.

Wormface, trailing at the back, came to a stop a few feet short of the mess, in front of the truck.

I staggered to a halt and turned back.

Eric shook the shovel at Wormface. "Come on, you piece of shit. Come on!"

The tangle of dregs thrashed chaotically, arms and legs kicking in random spasms, then as one, stilled and lay limp.

Standing behind them, Wormface shifted his stance. All of a sudden he seemed…less mechanical? The tendrils of Wormface's head twitched and shuddered, extending a little near the bottom, bulging out in the middle, sinking in a couple spots above—

A face.

Wormface used the slithering tendrils to create a repulsive caricature of a face.

A face with a great big smile.

Danger had shifted his attention onto Wormface, putting all his focus into one dreg.

What kind of person would use that to taunt us?

Eric hefted the shovel. "Come on, you!"

Wormface raised an arm dramatically. The worms of his extended hand lashed and thrashed.

I hopped up the truck's tailgate. As I'd hoped, he'd thrown a few of his tools back there. Eric's flamethrower sat near the driver's side tire, secured with a loosely tied chain.

My shaking, bloody fingers scrabbled at the steel links.

Cuddles barked frantically.

The chain came free. I used my left hand to shrug the right shoulder strap on, hefting the weighty tank onto my back. The air already carried a veil of black ash and the stink of burning plastic, and I was about to add to it.

I whirled, flamethrower tank held to my body with a single shoulder strap, my right arm fumbling for the second strap.

Wormface stood where he had before, separated from Eric by the massive pickup and a morass of unmoving, broken dregs.

Eric, holding his position by the tailgate, shifted his eyes just enough to catch me struggling with the flamethrower. "Go around," he grumbled. "Burn this bastard."

Wormface's hand rotated, spinning like the pole of a merry-go-round.

A thin gray-black line shot from Wormface's outstretched hand towards Eric's.

The line twitched, rippling through the air like a spray of water—

—and circled Eric's throat.

Eric's eyes bulged.

He tried to scream.

Nothing came out.

"Eric!" I reached for the flamethrower nozzle, but it was on the side I hadn't shouldered yet. Snarling, I wrenched the tank onto my back, heedless of the surge of pain in my chewed and broken wrist.

The ring around Eric's neck flashed bright red. Blood gushed down his chest, his shoulders, his back, steaming and sizzling from Wormface's acid tendril.

Eric jerked the shovel up, into the line.

The shovel bounced back off, twanging the line like piano wire.

Wormface jerked forward at the impact, but Eric's back arched like a bow. He dropped the shovel to scrabble at his neck, fingers trying to grab the tendril but coming away with only blood.

The flamethrower nozzle was on my right side, perfectly positioned for my maimed right hand to grab it. I reached my left around to clumsily snatch it from its holster, chomped my teeth on the brand-new nozzle's protective plastic cap, and used my right forearm to twirl the knobs, jamming the valves wide open.

Eric shuddered and danced on his feet. The deep brown skin of his face faded towards gray. The white of bone peeked through the blood of his neck.

The pain of wrenching the weapon around made me screech, but I turned it into a scream of rage and swung the flamethrower nozzle one-handed to Wormface.

The torrent of blood had reached Eric's belt.

A geyser of orange-white flame burst forth from the nozzle.

The flame bounced off the day care center's brick wall, channeled between Wormface and the huge truck. I'd warned Eric about flamethrowers in tight quarters just that morning, and now heat splashed back at me, a sudden baking shock.

Wormface tumbled backwards, covered in flames from the waist up.

The tendril to Eric snapped with the liquid *pop* of a bad fart.

Well beneath the flames, the tangled mass of dregs lying on the sidewalk instantly screamed, screeched, and flailed.

Observation and supposition abruptly coalesced into knowledge.

I understood how to deal with the dregs.

I knew how to master Danger, whoever he was.

Eric's head tumbled from his body and rolled out into the street.

Chapter 69

ERIC'S DECAPITATED but upright body sagged to its knees, then fell towards the street, neck still steaming from Wormface's acid tentacle. I glimpsed white bone and hollow cartilage through pulsing blood.

I froze, balanced on the pickup's bed, ignoring the reeking flamethrower gel burning into the brick wall only a few feet away. If the huge pickup wasn't already burning, those flames might set it off. The dregs screaming and thrashing on the sidewalk weren't burning yet, maybe some gel had splashed down that far, but they weren't living candles, yet. A voice in the back of my head screamed that I needed those dregs, that I couldn't let them burn.

But I only had eyes for Eric's body.

Whether I was Kevin Holtzmann or not, a cop or a copy, Eric had been my co-worker for weeks now.

No—he'd been my friend. My best friend.

And I'd talked him through his own shock and horror yesterday. I'd convinced him to come out and join the world, to not let his change in skin color stop him.

Because of me, he'd been here.

Eric had died fighting for me.

My heart filled my trembling throat. The fire, the hot flamethrower in my clumsy left hand, the screaming pain of my shattered wrist, all of that seemed unimportant.

I stared without seeing as the flame-topped candle of Wormface staggered into the street and fell, face-first onto the road.

Compared to the horror of losing Sheila and Julie, and the whole world with them, the death of a single friend shouldn't have hit me like that. No, not a single friend—Jack was dead too. I'd liked the guy, even if I didn't know him that well.

But standing there, beaten and battered and bruised and bloody, my soul misfired. Again. Too many shocks in one day. I couldn't even make myself care that the dregs were dragging themselves out from under the flames.

"Kevin!" someone behind me shouted, irritated.

I flooded back into myself with a jump.

Veronica Boxer stood behind me, ring-covered hands raised as if to catch me. "Kevin, are you all right?"

A cluster of people stood behind her, mostly bigger men, dressed in everything from white shirts and ties to cutoff blue jeans. A couple tough-looking women and one petite college girl stood with them. Pendleton stood in the rear, face in a scowl and arms crossed over his massive gut. Scrawny Otto was on the side, seemingly recovered from the gunshot Woodward's men had put in his shoulder.

I blinked, trying to make myself think.

"You were right," Boxer said, climbing up onto the truck bumper. "We heard the chaos and came to help. Let us get you down. Tell us what's happening."

Boxer reaching to stabilize me did what nothing else could. I jerked away from her touch, Acceptance's touch. "I'm okay."

Boxer hopped back down, hands still raised to catch me if I fell.

I shakily clambered down from the truck, hissing with pain as the short hop to the concrete jarred my wrist. My knees hurt, too—I must have bruised them in the tumble.

I'd planned to run the block to Saint Michael's, and dump the dregs on the members of Acceptance. And here they'd made the right decision, and come to help.

"What's going on?" Boxer said.

The entire crowd behind her looked calmly at me, ready to accept anything I said.

With a shuddering breath, I looked around. "Flamethrower," I said, pointing at Bill's burning car. The flames hadn't spread much beyond the puttermobile's engine, but the smoke had turned rich toxic black. "In the car. Fire hits it, lose half a block. Town'll burn."

Without a word, two of the taller, lankier men immediately split off from the crowd and dashed towards the car.

In the distance, an approaching siren warbled. Fred and Harry in the fire truck.

Amongst the dregs, the college kids and High Heels had managed to crawl out from beneath the fire and continued on south, walking calmly as if hoping I wouldn't notice. Two Backs was just extracting itself, pulling itself out of the tangle on its front hooves. Becky's hair was scorched, and ugly red blisters covered her back.

"The dregs," I said. "Don't kill them—catch them. Push them around, make them dizzy. Confuse them. The ones still on the ground, pull them out and spin them, too."

Boxer looked puzzled.

"Danger's controlling them," I snapped. "They act together, as a group. But hit one with a flamethrower, they all scream. They all feel the pain of one. Plus, he's only got so much attention to go around. If we can make them dizzy, overload them—"

The crowd behind Boxer split into knots of two and three people. They didn't do any of the usual milling about to pair up you'd expect. Without any false starts or confusion, each cluster darted towards one of the dregs.

The uncanny coordination sent a chill down my spine. I licked my lips. "Don't knock them out, unconscious people aren't confused. Are there any more of you around?"

"At Saint Michaels, with some of the people who fled Jack's," Boxer said. "We're those willing and most able to fight."

I didn't want to know how that tiny girl fought. "There's a red van around here." I glanced wildly around. "Send the others to find it. Cars, bikes, whatever. Tell me where it is."

Boxer nodded. "Done."

"Don't approach it. Danger might have—probably has got weapons."

One of Acceptance's bigger men grabbed High Heels' shoulder and spun her around. Behind her, the woman he'd partnered with caught her arms and gave her a push, making High Heels stumble back towards her partner.

"That's it," I shouted. "Don't have to hurt them."

Pushing people around is hard work. They couldn't keep it up for long. "Find Danger," I said, half to myself, looking up towards Jack's.

One of men at the burning puttermobile had yanked his shirt over his nose and mouth to block out a little of the thick, stinking black smoke. He'd already wrenched open the puttermobile's passenger door and was hauling out the flamethrower, using his partner's shirt like a makeshift mitten to protect him from the smoking-hot flamethrower tank, the drab gray paint already discolored to black. The man who'd donated his shirt was stripping off his pants, leaving him clad in socks and bright yellow boxer shorts. As the first guy pulled the flamethrower a few feet from the car, the second stuffed one pant leg through a loop in the weapon's metal frame. The first man fell away, clutching his shirt-covered hand and coughing as he staggered to collapse on the lawn. The second used his pants to slowly drag the scorched, heat-damaged flamethrower towards the side street, keeping it on the concrete, closely watching the trailing hoses.

Flames burst from the puttermobile's open passenger door.

"Just in time," I said. "Keep on them." I hauled in a deep breath and started trotting back towards Jack's.

Boxer followed. "Where are you going?"

"A dreg has Alice treed."

"I'm coming with."

I didn't have breath to argue. Besides, if Acceptance found this Danger asshole, I needed to know.

We passed the burning heap that had been Wormface. His unmoving calves and feet protruded from the flames, shriveling as they charred to red and black. The stench of burning flesh with acid overtones knotted my guts.

The flamethrower bounced on my back as I trotted, its bulk slamming my spine and hips with each step and aggravating my bruises. The hip belt would stabilize the tank, but I couldn't fasten the belt with a broken wrist. And I sure wasn't going to let Boxer put it on me. I didn't like touching anyone, let alone inviting Acceptance any closer than I needed to.

Once I got around the puttermobile pyre, I almost tripped over my own feet in surprise.

In front of Jack's, my tiny blue puttermobile was parked on the sidewalk under the willow.

Bar stools and chairs sat randomly on the sidewalk and grassy easement and edge of the road, some lying on their side as if dropped.

Woodward's thugs were clustered around the tree and the car. One of the taller men, in big wafflestomper boots, clomped on the puttermobile's roof, concealed from the waist up by the willow's drooping leaves and melons.

I didn't see any sign of Alice. Or Ceren. Ceren didn't worry me as much, though—at least, not in the same way.

"Alice!" I shouted.

Faces turned to me, then glanced back. Some of the men on the sidewalk shifted and shuffled.

Tiny Alice slipped out between two of them. "Kevin!"

Ceren appeared immediately behind Alice.

Somehow, my trot turned into a run, heedless of the flamethrower bouncing on my spine, my near-terminal road rash, my countless bruises and contusions.

Alice came dashing up like she was going to give me a hug, then her nose wrinkled with revulsion and she skidded to a halt. "Kevin, what—did you get killed? Again?"

"Are you all right?"

"I'm fine. Nat's harmless."

Ceren arrived a heartbeat later. "Kevin!"

Alice looked me up and down. "You look like someone dragged you behind a car."

"Tell you later. What happened?"

Alice lowered her voice. "When Teresa—" She suddenly looked nervous, and swallowed. "I remembered how Teresa went after me." Alice glanced worriedly over her shoulder. I followed her gaze.

"I got the car down here," Ceren said, "just as you burned Wormface. So I went to help get Alice down."

Behind my girls, Woodward's men were helping Nat Reamer out of the tree and down onto the cruiser's hood.

Even in the willow's shade, the bright June sunlight reflecting off buildings and cars and everything else silhouetted Nat's gaunt limbs and chubby gut through the filmy nightdress. The men handled her with deference and care.

Nat had one hand clutched around the nightdress, as if holding it closer could protect her modesty. Embarrassment flushed her cheeks. Even from here I could hear her say, "I'm fine. Fine, I tell you, young man."

Will, the man with a bandage over the eye he'd lost to Eric's Cuddles, came out of Jack's holding a huge flannel jacket. "Not right for the weather," he said, handing it up to Nat, "but it's the best I could find."

Dancing from foot to foot on the hot car hood, Nat snatched the shirt from Will. "It's perfect, young man."

I stared at Nat, then at Alice.

Alice looked as red as Nat. "I could feel her hurts," she whispered. "She had this sharp piece of bone, like, sticking in her brain. You healed that gunshot, so I kinda…told it to go back."

I stared at Alice.

Beside me, Boxer gave a low whistle.

Then I flung both my arms around Alice and hugged her into my chest. "That is amazing," I said through the hiss of pain from my broken wrist and the burn of broken ribs.

Alice patted the flamethrower, then my side. "Mmmph!"

I released her instantly. "Sorry."

"You smell like a dirty barbeque," Ceren said.

"Not that good," I said. "Alice, that's great." Fears I hadn't dared think about evaporated. Maybe we changed with our self-image—but a head injury, like Nat had suffered, like all—most—of the people Danger commanded had suffered, would turn us into shells of ourselves, empty bodies.

But Alice could heal them.

"Listen," Alice said.

"That's wonderful," I said. "All those people—"

"Listen!" Alice shouted.

I stopped, surprised.

"Danger," she said quickly. "I saw him, in Nat's head. Two blocks north, on Everglades, right off Main. In a big red van."

Chapter 70

TWO OF Woodward's men lounged against the puttermobile as I lumbered up, the smoking flamethrower bouncing on my back and my girls trailing right behind them. "Clear a path!" I shouted. "Gotta go!"

The men stared at me, their hostility towards me softened but still charged from the attacks. "We got this," Will said.

I shook my head and pointed with my unbroken hand. "Dregs," I said. "Down there, past the car fire. Don't hurt them, but keep them busy." I glanced back at Boxer. "Tell them." To Will, I said, a little louder, "Take turns, it's hard work. Keep them dizzy, stumbling around, till I come back. Confuse them."

Beside me, Alice opened her mouth but said nothing.

I waited a beat for her, then shouted "*Don't* hurt them!"

"What are you making all this fuss for, young man?" Nat Reamer demanded. The flannel shirt she wore over her nightdress hung to her bony knees and hung around her with enough room for four more old ladies.

"No time," I said. I used my left hand to yank the puttermobile's trunk open and pivoted to dump the flamethrower off my shoulders. The pain of sliding my maimed wrist through the shoulder strap made me gasp, but even as my vision turned a little pale I slammed the trunk shut with my good hand. The puttermobile's rear end sagged with the weight.

"'S a good question," said one of Woodward's men, the good old boy with the truly impressive beer gut.

"Look." I glanced at the men. "You help keep those poor bastards tied up for a few minutes, I can bring in the guy responsible for all this. But I gotta move *now*." Cradling my right hand to my chest, trying to ignore busted bones ends grating against each other, I levered the puttermobile's front passenger door open with my left. "I'll tell you everything when I'm back, but he's gonna get away."

Beer Gut studied me for a beat before Woodward stepped in front. "Come on, gentlemen. It's our civic duty."

I spied the serving bowl of sliced melon I'd dropped at the corner, only a few minutes ago. Most of the melon had spilled out across the lawn, but I gritted my teeth, staggered forward, and scooped a few slices back into the bowl. Seizing the bowl with my left hand, I stumbled back to the car. "Ceren!"

Ceren looked up from Nat. "Yeah?"

I jerked my head at the puttermobile. "You're driving. Broken wrist."

Ceren's eyebrows shot up, but she dashed towards me without hesitation.

"North on Main," I said, swinging my legs into the car. The hot vinyl seat triggered a prickly burn in the road rash along the back of my thighs and my back. "Right off Everglades. Go, go. Red van. Go!"

Ceren started the puttermobile, glanced at the clot of men dissipating in front of us, and put us into reverse.

The puttermobile was not the right vehicle for a chase. The cruiser could run Danger down like a raccoon, leave him a flat smear on the asphalt. A puttermobile wheezed going uphill.

But it was what we had.

Feet braced on the floorboards, I dug into the serving bowl with my left hand and slid a slab of melon up to the edge. The rich, meaty fruit tasted fantastic, the juice seeming to soak into my parched mouth and desert throat. *My wrist*, I thought. *It's healing. It's growing back together. The bleeding is stopping. Quickly.* Now. I concentrated on remembering how Absolute had changed form, right in front of me, up at the mall. *This is fuel, food, medicine. Those bones are knitting together, like new. Moving into place. No, better than they were. Solid. Unbreakable. Invulnerable.*

By the time I choked down the second slice, spots of dirt and all, barely chewing, my wrist's pulsing pain had faded to a million pinprick aches. I didn't dare try it, instead snarfing the third and last slice from the bowl just as we reached Everglade Street. Ceren took the right turn a little too fast, making me tense my legs to pin my bruised back against the seat.

Everglade Street lay exposed before us. The old twentieth-century apartment building on the left, converted to senior condos. Cookie-cutter Cape Cods on the right.

But no red van.

I gritted my teeth. "Dammit!"

Ceren stomped on the brake. I threw my left hand up to the dashboard to catch myself.

She was shoving the car into reverse again, staring in the rearview mirror. "Right off Main," she snarled, "or *right off* Main?"

I looked over my shoulder.

Behind us, on the other side of Main, maybe twenty feet down Everglades, sat a red van. The van had an extra high roof, obviously for some sort of cargo. It had extra-wide side view mirrors on metal frames like wings, plus a round mirror mounted at the rear corner so the driver could back up easily.

Just as obviously, gasoline or diesel powered. The van could outrace the puttermobile, even if we had a tailwind and a jetpack.

Ceren reversed the puttermobile onto Main.

The van started rolling away.

Ceren had her fingers self-consciously looped around the steering wheel, steering with the edges of her hands against the crossbar, obviously fearing her grip might tear the wheel off the car. Sweat beaded on her forehead.

Everglade is one of those narrow residential streets where if someone parks at the curb, two more cars can pass it if they're very careful. The puttermobile couldn't possibly do a U-turn. I itched to tell her to veer into the condo parking lot and put the car in forward, or grab the wheel, or tell her to stomp on the accelerator. Instead, I forced a deep breath and said, "You got this, kid. You got this."

Ceren said nothing, but I was almost certain I heard her teeth grinding together.

She took the corner onto Main too quickly again, this time in reverse, then slammed the cruiser into forward and punched it down Everglades.

The red van lurched into motion, raising a haze of drifting green seed pods from the asphalt.

Ceren pushed the accelerator to the floor, and we buzzed after Danger.

Chapter 71

"DON'T RAM it," I told Ceren. "Not yet." What was I going to do, talk her through a PIT maneuver to take out a car? The puttermobile didn't have the mass to knock Danger's massive red van off the road.

The van's engine roared—diesel, almost certainly. The puttermobile didn't have nearly that kind of power.

If the van sped away, maybe I could jump out and supercharge myself again. Run down the road. Outrace the puttermobile. Leap through the air, grab the van's bumper, and wrench it to a halt.

A bit of melon juice stuck to the bowl in my lap. I ran the fingers of my left hand through the drying syrup and sucked them clean.

But hurt as I was, my body probably had all it could do just keeping me vaguely functional, even with the meager slices of super-melon I'd scrounged.

"Look," Ceren said.

The van wobbled close to one curb, jerked back into the road, and spasmed back, as if the driver was too drunk to stand.

"The dregs," I said. "Their dizziness, it's getting to him."

I could imagine the faceless Danger, crouched behind the wheel, fighting the nausea of half a dozen inner ears. He'd connected himself to a bunch of bodies with broken brains, dominating them by…what? His will? Or had he just grabbed them and started using them?

But now, he drove as if he'd drunk a gallon of whiskey.

Too much dizziness, pouring into his head.

The van's engine roared. The big tires shrieked, and the red van lurched around a corner.

Ceren followed. "No you don't, shithead."

"Easy, Ceren," I said, bracing myself to keep from tipping into her. The top of my head pressed the puttermobile's tight, low ceiling. "Don't let this bastard rattle you."

"I'll show him rattled," Ceren spat.

An antique Caddy growled up behind us, its gleaming metal flecked white paint and gold chrome brilliant in the shards of sunlight seeping through the trees. Turning my head, I saw Pendleton's rust-bucket pickup lumbering up behind it.

I muttered. "Go around, cut him off."

"How?" Ceren shouted.

"Not you." I jerked my head back. "Acceptance sent the cavalry, and they're following us."

"Idiots," Ceren said.

Rumbling forward, the red van sideswiped a battered family sedan. Metal tore, the screech making me grit my teeth.

The sedan's driver's side mirror spun through the air.

Ceren yanked the wheel to avoid it.

With the sudden jerk, the puttermobile's display flashed red. Safety features, chiding the driver.

"I know," Ceren shouted, wrenching the wheel straight again.

The van's passenger-side running board bounced off the concrete, making Ceren swerve again.

"Not so rough," I said.

"I know!"

The van had slowed with the impact, weaving towards the far side of the road. Just before the wheels would have kissed the concrete curb, it swerved vaguely straight again. The diesel engine surged.

I'd been telling everyone guns were useless. I'd given up carrying one myself. And now, I desperately wished for a handgun to shoot out a tire.

I glanced at the speedometer. Twenty-nine miles an hour. Thirty.

Ceren edged the puttermobile towards the van's rear bumper.

"Don't ram it," I said quickly.

"I know," she said. "I know, I know!"

Sooner or later, Danger would deal with the dizziness sifting into him. Maybe he'd disconnect himself from his dregs, or find a way to cope with it. Maybe he'd just floor it and drive like a maniac.

Or maybe he'd crash the van.

All things being equal, I'd rather take Danger alive.

If I wanted to catch him, we needed to do it quickly.

Another intersection ahead.

The van's flank kissed a parked puttermobile. Plastic shattered in an ear-splitting hail of yellow shards, spraying across the grassy easement and sidewalk. The van swerved, wobbled, and wrenched sideways onto Lagrange Road, running towards the lake.

"This is it," I said. "We move now."

Chapter 72

RESIDENCE-LINED Lagrange Road runs perpendicular to Main Street, one way straight down to the lake and the other out to the now-buried freeway.

Most importantly, it was four lanes of dust-swept, empty concrete.

The red cargo van swerved and quivered as the driver fought the steering wheel and his externally imposed dizziness, but wobbled right around the double yellow line.

"When I thump twice, get up beside him," I said. "On the driver's side."

"How?" Ceren said. "He's weaving all over."

"Guts," I said. My right wrist didn't hurt at all, so I reached out my open window to seize the roof—

—and couldn't grab it.

My wrist was as flexible as a concrete pillar. The fingers worked, and by making a fist I could flex the back of my hand, but the wrist itself felt as if I wore a cast-iron brace. The muscles tightened, but the underlying bones didn't move.

I'd concentrated on making my wrist unbreakable.

Apparently flexibility is fragility.

I swore, reached up, and grabbed the puttermobile's slick plastic roof with my left hand.

"You're insane!" Ceren said.

"Just get me up by him," I said. "When I pull out, pull away."

And hoisted myself up to sit on the windowsill.

Twenty-five miles an hour doesn't seem like much when you're tucked safely inside a puttermobile, watching the expensive cars stream past you in the next lane over. When your rear end is hanging a yard above the asphalt ripping by, the wind tosses your hair straight back and roars in your ears, and your only handgrip is the tiny edge of weather-stripping where the windshield meets the roof, it's plenty fast enough.

I already had a bad case of road rash on my bare arms and shins. If I fell, I'd lose a bunch of meat with it.

The red van swerved left, then right. Dizziness? Or had Danger watched me climb out here?

I gritted my teeth, ignored the frenetic survival instinct punching me in the gut for attention, and squeezed one leg out of the puttermobile.

If I straightened the dangling leg, I'd hit asphalt. Instead, I held the leg up as if I had an invisible stirrup, and clamped the door between my thighs for a little extra balance.

I made a fist and smacked my immobile wrist against the roof, twice.

The puttermobile surged forward, pushing me back against the rear of the window frame. My guts knotted and my fingers dug more tightly into the tenuous edge of weather-stripping. I reached into the passenger compartment with the half-petrified hand and snatched at the meager slope where the ceiling curved down to the door.

The van weaved right.

The puttermobile surged up right behind the van's rear tire. The wall of steel slid into place a couple yards away, a looming threat.

I heard a distant shout, the words dissolved in wind.

The van jerked towards us.

Suddenly I felt even more exposed. If Danger sideswiped us, I'd get crushed between the van's body and the puttermobile's plastic frame. The puttermobile's roof, now digging into my ribs, would slice me in half. I imagined the puttermobile spinning into the curb, Ceren screaming, two halves of my body sailing through the air to be crushed beneath tires.

But the van weaved away.

Fear, I thought. Boxer had said that Acceptance had sensed fear.

And the only mind involved in the attacks was Danger's.

The thought gave me confidence.

Danger hadn't attacked directly, but only through remote-controlled puppets.

He'd left notes.

He hid behind a fake name.

Danger…was a coward.

"Go!" I shouted. "Right up by the driver's door!"

Ceren floored it.

The van's engine gave a little burst of speed, but jerked and wobbled with the energy. Danger was at his limits.

Inch by inch, we crept forward.

"Danger!" I shouted. "Pull over! It's not worth it!"

The van twitched towards us.

I grimaced. An image of the puttermobile roof slicing through my ribs flashed through me.

But the van lurched back away, veering towards the curb as if trying to get away.

Ceren kept the accelerator down and smoothly followed.

The driver's side door crept closer, the bottom of the window even with the top of my head.

I peered at the van's side-view mirror on its metal frame, trying to see Danger's face, but only glimpsed the van's white interior ceiling.

Asphalt flashed beneath my dangling foot.

I clamped my thighs harder. Sweat soaked the leg of my shorts inside the car, but the wind blew the outside leg desert dry.

"Danger!" I shouted at the top of my voice. "Let's talk this out! Stop the van!"

Two empty lanes streamed past the far side of the puttermobile. Ceren had Danger pinned right up against the curb, as close as his wobbling nausea permitted.

Forget Danger's fear. If the van kissed the curb, it would bounce straight into me.

Another breath, and I reached out to grab the iron frame of the extended side-view mirror. That wrist couldn't bend, but the fingers closed around the aluminum shaft and clamped tight.

I relaxed my legs and swung the outside foot out onto the thin running board.

A heave, and my weight was on the van.

I seized the mirror with my other hand and straightened, pulling my leg out of the puttermobile.

My foot had barely left the puttermobile when Ceren swerved away, putting blessed distance between us.

I straightened my legs to get my first look at Danger.

Danny Gervais, Woodward's right-hand man, hunched behind the wheel, his face blotchy green and white. Vomit covered his chin and his shirt, but he still glared hateful death at me.

"It's over, Danny," I shouted above the wind.

The puttermobile's horn tooted.

I looked up.

About a hundred yards ahead, three cars sat blocking the road.

Chapter 73

FRUSTRATED FURY twisted Danny's features. Dry heaves spasmed up his chest.

Wind streamed past me. I gripped the side-view mirror more tightly, wishing my toes could somehow dig into the running board. The asphalt whizzing past beneath and behind me crowded my awareness.

Ahead, people scuttled from the makeshift roadblock, one of them an older man hobbling with his cane. I remembered him from when Eric and I had rescued Cuddles.

Acceptance.

They'd paralleled the chase on Main Street, and seized a chance to block Danger in.

I'd asked for their help.

They'd decided to give it.

Danny screamed in frustration.

The van surged forward.

Copper fear pounded in the back of my throat. In the rush to get in place before Danny arrived, Acceptance had parked the cars willy-nilly. With some speed, maybe Danny could ram the van through them—but I'd certainly be crushed and flung away.

The diesel roared.

No time to think. No time to talk.

I raised my half-frozen arm, curled the fingers into a fist, and punched Danny in the temple.

The van sluiced sideways, pressing me against the door, but the motor's roar faded. Danny rocked with the hit, turning back towards me, mouth twisted in a furious snarl.

I punched at Danny again, but he swung his head back.

My fist brushed his cheek and went past.

The wind whipped away Danny's shouted words.

I yanked my hand back—not out of the car, but into the steering wheel.

Seized the hot vinyl.

And wrenched.

Danny's fingers, slackened by my blows to his head, slipped away.

I spun the wheel.

The van's front tires squealed.

The van spun sideways.

I wouldn't survive ramming the roadblock—but I *might* survive a crash.

Danny screamed again, his hands grabbing at the wheel.

My shoulder crashed against the side-view mirror as the van slowed—Danny had stomped the brake.

But my harsh turn had already lifted the tires beneath me away from the concrete.

The van swerved in a tight curve, spinning towards the curb.

Slowing, but not enough.

Steel shifted beneath me.

The asphalt receded as the van started to tip.

Then the front tires punched the curb.

The side-view mirror clubbed me.

My grips wrenched away. My feet left the running board.

Open air, everywhere around me.

Soaring free.

A peaceful moment, shattered when the hard ground smashed into me.

Chapter 74

FOR A while I lay on dry, spiky grass, distantly contemplating my aches.

I only thought everything had hurt before. My teeth felt loose, and I tasted blood. My ribs felt like someone had played them like a xylophone, with ball-peen hammers. My legs and arms all lay at weird angles.

And through all that, the sound of Ceren saying "fuck" over and over again.

I needed a nap. After a sauna. After a massage. After an hour in a hot tub, and a nice steak, and a bucket of prescription painkillers.

With a deep groan, I hoisted my eyelids.

The dry, spiky grass dug into my cheek and filled half my vision. A close-up knee filled the other half.

"And how is our young action hero?" someone asked.

"Kevin!" Ceren said. "Are you okay?"

I shifted to untangle my knot of limbs. Gravity claimed me, and I rolled onto my back, my arms and legs sprawling. Nothing was broken, at least. But my joints felt as though I'd been through an earthquake simulator.

The knee had belonged to Ceren, who leaned over me. She looked ready to punch…anyone, really. "Kevin!"

I worked my mouth. "I'm okay."

"You were going, like, fifteen miles an hour."

"Oh, good." I slowly flexed my fingers. My voice worked slowly enough that I had to take a breath every few words. "I was afraid…I might not be going fast enough…to complete my road rash collection."

Ceren thumped my shoulder with a loose fist. "You could have died!"

I grimaced. "If you punch me again, I might."

Low discussions nearby made me turn my head.

The van's front tires had bounced over the curb onto the grassy easement, over the sidewalk, and onto the lawn, but the van didn't have enough speed left for the back tires to hop after them. Pendleton's rust-bucket pickup sat right behind the van, blocking it from going into reverse. A couple more cars sat close around.

Danny Gervais knelt hands and knees on the grass, retching.

Half a dozen people stood around him, all members of Acceptance. Rick, the teenage surfer wannabe with the half-shaved head. The elderly gentleman with his cane. A couple other faces I knew but had no names for.

I shifted again, trying to get my elbow under me.

"Hang on," Ceren said. "You stay there."

"I'm okay," I said.

"Bullshit."

Ceren's clenched jaw shook. I needed a moment to realize she looked perilously close to crying.

She'd never forgive me for seeing her bawl. "Listen," I whispered. "That's Danger. After this, I'm going to bed for a week, but right now, in front of him—help me up."

Ceren gritted her teeth. I knew Ceren well enough that she'd believe my reason all the way down to in her bones.

I hissed and groaned as I moved bruises and contusions with scraps of muscle and bone around them, but in a moment I was on my feet. Ceren flanked me, arms at her side, ready to punch someone or catch me. Whatever.

I shuffled over towards the knot of people by the van. "Danny."

Danny shuddered.

"Rick," I said. "Any more trouble?"

"It's all cool, dude." Rick's voice, with a hard edge completely alien to his easygoing nature, told me that the fighting might be over, but that the ass-kicking hadn't yet started.

Kipuka Blues

"Listen to me, Danny," I said. "You have your dregs stand down. If they so much as twitch, I will jam a flamethrower nozzle down your throat and pull the trigger." I glanced back at Rick. "Can your crew get him back to Jack's? No—where the dregs are, that's better."

The older gentleman said, "We would be most pleased to help." He didn't sound pleased.

"Good. Ceren," I said. "Get the car."

Ceren studied me, and seemed to decide I wasn't going to topple like a stack of blocks.

Nevertheless, I stood very still while she fetched the puttermobile.

"We'll meet you there," I called to the people hoisting Danny into the back of Pendleton's pickup.

Ceren held the passenger door for me.

I collapsed gratefully into the warm plastic seat. "The dregs, please."

"Yes, boss," she said. "And that's two weeks you're down for."

By the time we pulled up in front of the fight, I'd put it all together.

Chapter 75

A FEW minutes of quiet and a chance to actually catch my breath didn't reinvigorate me. But they gave me a chance to push the abraded skin, countless bruises, aching ribs, and throbbing jaw, knees, and elbows away. A moment of quiet cleared my mind.

We got back to Main Street, where Ceren smoothly steered around the fire truck flashing near Eric's big pickup and pulled to a stop. Fred and Harry sprayed extinguishers of chemical foam on the smoldering remnants of Bill's puttermobile. To my surprise, Bill stood behind them, holding a pressurized but closed hose ready for them.

The fire crew had arrived before Eric's giant pickup caught. Foam oozed down the wall I'd splashed with gel. Poor Cuddles sat behind the driver's wheel, nose pressed hard against the window, desperate for a glimpse of Eric.

My heart panged. I'd get more than a glimpse of Eric's body, once the day was through.

Woodward's good old boys stood intermingled with some of the Acceptance crew, exhaustedly pushing and spinning Frayville's dregs between them. Two big guys gingerly manhandled the woman in the blue dress and high heels, trying to keep her spinning and stumbling. One reached to shove her, accidentally squashed her boob, and jerked his hand back. His partner heaved her shoulders, letting him try again. Two of Acceptance's women handled the college girl, saving the men the embarrassment.

Two Backs lay upended, with five of the biggest men and the petite woman surrounding them. They seized Two Backs' sprawling, flailing limbs and wrenched them to the left, keeping Two Backs spinning counterclockwise. Two Backs thrashed, trying to bite with Becky and Paul's teeth. One of the men staggered back, red face drenched with sweat and chest heaving, and a slightly less exhausted man took his place.

Others stood nearby, faces red and hands on knees, trying to catch their breath before rotating in again.

More people had appeared. People who had fled the attack on Jack's had come back, carrying everything from baseball bats to shotguns. One of the teenagers, Mack, had somewhere found an old-fashioned scythe that stood taller than him, the blade mostly rust and its curved handle so elderly that the wood's grain had deepened to canals. He held it at the ready near the group surrounding Two Backs, poised to sweep the heavy blade down.

Woodward himself stood near his resting guys, watching the spinning dances. It didn't surprise me to see that Woodward hadn't even stripped off his suit coat, perfectly comfortable to supervise sweat-free.

Ceren had barely stopped when I swung the door open. "We got him! Stop pushing."

People staggered back from the dregs, gasping. The two good old boys who'd been pushing High Heels around stumbled away, holding their arms in front of themselves defensively, while trying to shake out the knots in their shoulders.

Two Backs spun another few degrees, then lay still.

High Heels staggered a few steps, then fell against the glass window of the resale shop, bounced off, tumbled to the ground, and lay still. The college kids and Flower Shirt weaved and staggered a few steps before hitting the ground and lying flat. Weirdly, the old man with half

Kipuka Blues

a head stopped moving almost instantly, merely standing in place.

Seems you need a head to get dizzy.

Pendleton's pickup pulled up right behind the puttermobile, Rick behind the wheel.

I limped around to the tailgate, nodding at the four people sitting up in the back. "Let me present the man who tried to massacre everyone at Jack's tonight. Who *did* kill Jack, and Eric, and Kenny, and probably more. The man controlling these poor dregs." I gathered my strength, grabbed the tailgate handle, and pulled.

The tailgate didn't even groan. Petrified with rust.

I grimaced, ears turning red with embarrassment rather than pain. "Uh…"

The elderly man, his cane standing tall by his head, said "One moment, if you would."

Rick trotted around, hopped onto the bumper, and climbed in the back.

Seconds later, Rick and a burly man with a ridiculous walrus mustache heaved Danny out of the pickup and spilled him on the ground.

Danny was still twitching and dry heaving. We'd stopped spinning his dregs, but he'd need a while to get over that much dizziness.

The crowd's attention focused on Danny and I. Teenagers, Woodward's men, the members of Acceptance, even the two young men who'd been necking in the back of Jack's. I glimpsed Frost and Langley near the edge with their cluster of friends.

The closest one of Woodward's men, Will with his bandaged eye, spoke first. "Danny?"

The concentrated stares of a hundred pairs of eyes sent twitches of embarrassment through me. I let the embarrassment argue with my bloody scrapes and wrenched muscles—the sooner I finished this, the sooner I could go clean the blood off of me and pick bits of road out of my scrapes, see just how badly I was injured. And the sooner I could go find poor Eric and take care of him, properly.

I tried to talk, but the crowd's rising babble drowned my voice. I took a deep breath and shouted, "The person controlling the dregs called himself Danger. Or, *Dan Ger*vais."

"What's wrong with him?" someone shouted.

"He's dizzy," I said. "The dr—those shells of people that you've been spinning and shoving? He's feeling all of that. Because he's connected to them. Like Acceptance. Danny used them like meat puppets."

I couldn't make myself say, *like Absolute used us.*

From the ugly, low murmur that ran through the crowd, they heard those words anyway.

Sudden, fresh anger filled me, drowning my exhaustion. "You sent dregs to kill me and my girls," I shouted at Danny. "I stood up to you about Cuddles, and you sent them to burn down our home."

I hadn't noticed Ceren climbing out of the car. Suddenly she charged forward and aimed a brutal kick at Danny's gut. "You son of a bitch!"

Danny crumpled around his belly and slid three feet, trailing a sudden surge of bright yellow-green vomit.

I leapt to grab Ceren's shoulders before she could charge after him. "Not like that!" I shouted. "Not like that."

Ceren trembled. She looked at my bloody, bruised hands on her shoulders.

I kept my gentle grip. I didn't squeeze. I *couldn't* stop her—she could break my arms with a sneeze.

Ceren took a deep breath. She shook my hands off her shoulders, but stood there, eyes burning into Danny.

Danny tried to moan, doubled around his stomach.

"What was it you said, Danny?" I said. "'We don't have a lot of time to get organized,' wasn't it? And there was 'we're not lazing around like some useless people,' something like that?"

Danny's head sagged.

"When I killed Suit—the shell of a person that he'd used to burn down Ceren's home, he kidnapped Nat Reamer and another brain-damaged woman. Added them to his collection."

Danny wheezed.

"The dregs don't have minds," I said loudly. "Connecting to people—it isn't hard. Veronica Boxer did it without thinking. So have others. So Danny touched them. Connected to them. Used them. And when he did, when he gave them commands, they felt everything he felt."

From her place in the front row of the ring of people surrounding us, Veronica Boxer raised her chin in understanding.

I released Ceren and went to stand over Danny, trying to stand tall despite my battered body.

As a police officer, I'd dealt with hundreds of violent people. I'd arrested killers, rapists, arsonists, too many drunks. I'd caught serial criminals who had committed atrocities that kept me awake at night. But I'd never faced someone who'd deliberately targeted me and my family. Standing over Danny, I felt a sudden burn of cold fury in the marrow of my bones, so strong that I couldn't hold still.

We had no law.

No court. No judge.

With Eric dead, I was the only one with the flamethrower.

Danny groaned and shifted.

Woodward took a step forward—when people had approached me, he kept pace so no one could usurp his place in the front. "Danny." Woodward's hands hung limp at his side. "Danny, why did you do it?"

Danny rolled onto his back and forced in a deep breath. "Don't you even try to pin this on me, you bastard!"

Chapter 76

"HOLD ON now," Woodward shouted. "I did *not* tell you to attack anyone! I had nothing to do with this."

Lying on his back on the asphalt of Main Street, Danny Gervais squinted against the evening June sky but still glared at the bulky Woodward. On his face, anger fought nausea to a draw.

"You said," Danny gasped, "you said at the next disaster, we'd move. We'd be in charge."

"I did not tell you to create that disaster!" Woodward shouted.

Danny tried to sit up, but Ceren's sneaker to his gut had put him down hard. "You said, 'Will no one,'" he wheezed, "'ditch this annoying priest?'"

Woodward's face turned white for a moment before sudden anger blossomed red in his cheeks. "I did not say that!"

"It's 'will no one rid me of this meddlesome priest,'" someone said.

The crowd surrounding us seemed to ring us more tightly. Despite the clear sky and bright sun, the quiet muttering seemed to turn everything darker.

Woodward looked around. "I said that someone had to be ready when things went wrong! Someone has to be ready to deal with disasters."

"What," I said. "Like the world ending?"

Woodward wheeled on me. "Yes! We still have a chance now."

"And you did so well the first time, protecting us—the human race—from Absolute."

"Nothing anybody did could have stopped Absolute!" Woodward shouted, his voice rough and even a little pleading.

I deliberately lowered my voice, trying to sound as calm as possible. "This isn't about you, Woodward." I looked down at Danny, then back up at Woodward. "I saw your face when I hauled Danny out. You were shocked."

Woodward took half a step back, like I'd slapped him.

"I don't think you ordered this little creep to attack people. You had no clue Danny did any of this."

My support seemed to deflate Woodward, but he rallied magnificently. "Yes. That's right. Yes, yes, I did *not* know."

"At dinner a few nights ago," I said, "Danny heard me tell my girls about the house we were going to look at the next morning. He had a couple of his….his *puppets* meet us there. One of them had a gun." I looked at Will, who now split his time between gaping at Danny and giving occasional glances at Woodward. "After Eric and I caught the dog and left, what did Danny do?"

"We picked up," Will said slowly. "Sat down, had lunch."

"Did Danny say anything?" I said.

"He just sat there," the guy with the big beer gut shouted. "Sat up against a tree. Had his eyes closed."

"We showed Danny up," I said. "We pissed him off even more. He was steering." I nodded, showing the crowd I believed what I heard. My voice rose. "Steering his puppets to *burn down our house*."

Ceren's fists were tight. Her eyes didn't leave Danny's face.

"I'm disappointed, Danny," Woodward said firmly. "I suppose I—we will need to do something about you."

I whirled to Woodward, shoving a finger on my petrified wrist under his nose. "You do *not* get to take charge here!"

"Someone has to," Woodward said, his tone aggrieved and sad, as if the slow student couldn't quite comprehend that two plus two really did equal four.

"You just admitted it!" I snapped. "You're only waiting around for a disaster to hit so you can take charge!"

"I was *preparing* for disaster!" Woodward shouted. "If we had a big fire, or ran out of food, or got attacked from outside, you'd be begging someone to handle it!"

"But it's not about helping people for you!" I roared. "As long as you're in charge, the big man, you couldn't care less about everyone else. We all saw how much you loved being in charge, back in the day. Back when Building the Future made you a big man. And you've been waiting to slip back into that!"

"Someone has to be ready when Absolute comes for us!" Woodward shouted.

"How will this time be any different from the last?" I said, my voice coming back down. "When you said there was nothing anyone could do last time? What special wisdom do you have now?"

"We have to fight!" Woodward said.

"And so you get help," I said, more slowly, but loudly enough for people to hear. "Your right-hand man is so afraid, so terrified, he'll do anything. He had one of his dregs crack an old lady's skull and write 'number one' next to her, just so people would be almost as afraid as he is."

"I did not tell him to do that!" Woodward shouted.

"But you fed his fear." I raised my voice. "And I, for one, am sick of being afraid!"

Next to Woodward, one-eyed Will put a beefy hand on the shoulder of Woodward's expensive suit. "Boss," he said in a quiet voice. "Boss, we like you. And you're right. We all know that." He glanced at Danny. "But maybe right now ain't the time. Once we *all* deal with Danny, maybe we take it up again."

Woodward's jaw dropped open. He turned to stare at Will, then slowly studied the crowd around us.

A wall of hostile gazes met his.

Woodward's attention turned to Danny, lying sprawled at my feet.

Danny breathed a little more easily, but his hands still held his midriff.

Staring at Danny, Woodward took a step forward.

Danny's eyes widened.

I moved to intercept Woodward, holding up my hands. "Hang on."

Woodward's glare turned on me. I saw something broken behind his eyes.

Woodward had his shell of competence over a world of pain.

And I'd just shattered that.

"You!" he shouted. "You've ruined—everything!"

I didn't even see his wild punch coming. Pain exploded on the left side of my jaw.

Everything spun around me, right up until the asphalt rose to meet my face.

Chapter 77

EVERYTHING SEEMED distant and gray.

Shouting, somewhere on the other side of the planet. The *far* other side of the planet.

Everything swam and oozed around me for a second or two before snapping back into razor focus.

I lay facedown on burning-hot asphalt, with something sharp and stabby digging into my cheek as a bonus. Near my head, Alice murmured, "Come on, Kevin. Wake up."

The angry voices surrounding us almost drowned her out, countless burning words combining into a growl just short of fury.

I put my abraded hands on the asphalt and heaved myself to all fours, then to my knees. Brushing at my cheek flicked a tiny pebble to the ground.

Someone said, "Here, let me help. Brad, give us a hand." Hands grabbed my biceps and helped me to my feet. I didn't know the people who'd helped me up, but I nodded my thanks.

The four biggest men from Acceptance, faces brutal, surrounded Danny. Danny sat on his rump, hugging his knees to his chest. His white face gleamed with sweat, and his eyes flashed between his guards' faces and the crowd.

Woodward lay on the ground by Danny, sprawled spread-eagle like a cartoon character who'd fallen off a cliff. Ceren sat on his back.

Around us, the crowd had moved in. I saw a lot of tight faces and shoulders, with clenched fists and flashing eyes glaring between Danny and Woodward. I didn't need my police training to know the crowd was one hard word away from a lynch mob. Alice almost huddled up to me, casting nervous glances everywhere.

The people who'd helped me up released my shoulders. I weaved on my feet, but managed to keep my balance. Exhaustion burned in every muscle, and I hurt from scraping the road and fighting dregs and falling off a slow-moving van and even from Woodward's well-placed hook to the side of my jaw. My mouth tasted of rusty blood, sticky willow melon, and hints of puke.

I looked at Woodward. Ceren had squeezed the air out of him, and while he twitched and scraped the ground to escape, she had her legs braced widely enough that he couldn't possibly get away, let alone slug me again.

I really wanted to sit down. Stagger the few yards to the puttermobile. Open a door. Sink into the seat. The rough cloth would feel like down. Let the crowd carry out the rough justice. It wasn't the right thing to do—but who was I to declare what was right and wrong? Who would we take this to?

And closing my eyes for a few minutes would feel *so* good.

If Alice hadn't been watching me, I might have.

Instead, I pulled in a breath deep enough to make my abused ribs creak in protest. What was I going to say?

"People!" I shouted. Groaned.

The couple folks near me looked my way, but the rest of the crowd kept talking. If anything, the words were growing more and more angry.

"People!" Raising my voice felt like lifting a forty-pound bag of rock salt.

Ceren bent to say something in Woodward's ear. She shifted her weight, kneeling with one foot on the ground and the other knee in the middle of Woodward's back. She shouted, "Hey!"

The bellow was loud enough that I flinched back and had to fight the instinct to clamp my hands over my ears.

The people nearest her recoiled, bouncing off the people behind them. The closest angry conversations shattered into surprise and befuddlement.

Ceren took a deep breath and shouted again, this time louder. "Listen up!"

This time I did wince and tucked my head down closer to my shoulders. Alice clapped her hands over her ears, but too late to protect them.

Ceren nodded at me.

"Everyone," I shouted. "You've got reason to be angry. We all do. This isn't the way, though. You know that. You know it. Even if the rules have changed, you know it's not right to string people up and hang them."

Ceren's face clouded.

"We aren't a mob," I said. "This isn't the Old West or the KKK. We don't lynch people."

"Hanging's too good for them," said a man peering over the shoulders of those in front of him. "And it wouldn't work. We'll have to burn them."

A lot of folks in the crowd shouted agreement.

"This is important!" I shouted. "What we decide here is vital! What we do today determines who we are, who we become! Do we have judges, and trials, and all the things that make people civilized? Or do we just put people to the torch?"

"We don't have a judge," someone else called. "Or laws!"

"Maybe it's time we did," I said. "Or maybe we break apart. Maybe a year from now the Sand River families and the Orchards folks are at war. But I think we're better than that. Once we start lynching people, no matter how much they might deserve it, it's too hard to stop. Too easy to see mob justice as the only way."

I put my hand down towards Danny. "Yeah, Gervais hurt us. But Woodward just didn't know. And he tried to get us ready for whatever happens next." I couldn't believe I was saying this. "You going to lynch him for that?"

A low murmur ran through the crowd.

To my side, the crowd shifted. Someone was fighting their way up from the back, and using elbows to do it. As the front split, I heard a muttered "S'cuse me…pardon me." A lanky man in blue jeans and T-shirt stumbled free, arms and legs swinging like an overly limber doll.

Ian Reamer. The recent days had put fresh lines of worry into his face. Despite what I assumed to be regular bathing, old motor oil had seeped into the lines and the pores of his face, making sure he never looked quite clean. Working with engines does that to you.

"Hey," Reamer shouted. "Listen up a minute."

Reamer glanced at me, then back at the crowd. "Holtzmann's right."

I leaned back in surprise.

"Everybody knows I don't like Holtzmann. And he don't like me." Reamer tried to stand up straighter. "We've had our problems. But the sanctimonious bastard always does the right thing. He doesn't like me—doesn't like what I done—done before—but he helped me." Reamer's voice caught. "My mom was hurt. Hurt bad. Kidnapped. Holtzmann got her back—and got her healed."

I opened my mouth to protest, but Reamer marched on. Battered as I was, I didn't have the energy to stop someone from saying something nice about me for a chance.

"He does the right thing, and he's busted his ass doing it ever since we all—we all got here." Reamer pointed a bony, oil-stained finger in my direction. "I mean, look at him! He's damn near killed himself to catch this guy."

Reamer paused a breath, then shouted even louder.

"I say we put him in charge."

Oh, hell no.

People turned to each other, talking in low voices.

"Hold on, people," I said, but nobody seemed to hear me. "Hold on!"

"What do you folks say?" Reamer shouted. "Kevin. Ke-vin."

A second person, in the back of the crowd, joined Reamer's chant. Then a third, a fourth. A fifth.

Too many to count.

As Ceren would say: *fuck*.

Chapter 78

I JERKED my hands up over my head, desperately waving for attention over the massed people shouting my name. My stomach clenched at the idea of becoming the boss—I didn't want the job; I couldn't do the job; I sure as hell didn't *deserve* the job.

But Alice and Ceren were right there in front, chanting my name along with the crowd.

I'd face Two Backs with a toothbrush before I took the job.

What was wrong with people, demanding I become—what? Mayor? King? Warlord?

Right in the middle of Main Street, on a hot sunny June day, amidst a knot of my neighbors, everything was going to hell. I could almost smell their passion over the smoldering shell of Bill's puttermobile.

Not everyone had joined in the shouts of approval, though. The members of Acceptance that I recognized all stood still and calm, neither pushing for me or objecting. I glimpsed Langley and Frost through the crowd. Langley seemed dispassionate, but a frown twisted Frost's smooth face.

I shouted for calm.

The crowd ignored me.

I jumped up and down, waving my arms, but their cheers drowned my bellows.

Finally I shouldered my way through the crowd, ignoring the hands clapping my bruised back. Near the rear of the crowd I saw more disapproving faces, some glaring angrily at me as I weaseled towards the massive pickup parked on the side of the road.

I gritted my teeth as the fresh scabs on my arms and legs cracked and oozed as I clambered up into the truck bed. The summer heat reflected by the metal bed didn't help either. At least the huge open-bed pickup didn't even quiver as I tromped back and forth, trying to get people to stop chanting my name.

The crowd was bigger than I thought—maybe a hundred fifty, two hundred? More than I'd seen in Frayville since Alice dragged me out of Kevin's home. From my elevated vantage, the pro-Kevin contingent seemed to be about half the crowd, perhaps a little more.

For a heartbeat I considered taking charge. Woodward was right about that. Someone had to do it.

That someone wasn't me.

But didn't everyone secretly want to be in charge? Deep down, didn't we want to tell people what to do?

If I'd been twenty years younger, I might have gone for it.

But I knew better. Negotiations among a family are hard enough. I might have caught Danger, but that was a momentary victory. Tomorrow, I'd be just another person, just as likely to screw up.

Finally I stood on the pickup bed, amidst shovels and rakes and a couple of machetes, holding my upraised arms palm-down and making quieting motions. The chanting trickled away until every face was watching me. I caught Frost staring at me, her face as cold as her name.

"Don't you dare!" someone shouted from the back.

Jeering broke out. The middle of the crowd rippled. I picked out a couple men pushing at each other, just short of a fistfight. Bystanders pulled the two men apart, but the crowd seethed uneasily. Low murmurings threatened to turn into shouting matches.

These people weren't my friends and neighbors anymore, probably never had been, even if they'd managed to partly unite in a stupid gesture. They were a mob. A mob that threatened to detonate. If I couldn't calm them, if I couldn't do something that satisfied enough people, Frayville would tear itself apart.

In my name.

"Elections!" I shouted.

People who had been glaring at each other turned back to me.

"Look, people," I said loudly. "I am—I was, was, a cop. That's all. And I'm smart enough to know that I can't run this town. I shouldn't run this town. But for all his flaws, Woodward was right about one thing. We need someone in charge for times like this. I think it's time we held elections. I will *not* run, but I'll volunteer to proctor them."

"Boo!" Reamer shouted.

"We are not a kingdom!" I bellowed.

People turned back towards me. I immediately felt the power of hundreds of focused eyes, waiting on me. Some giving me a chance, others awaiting my commands.

My mental wheels spun almost out of control. "So...so, we're voting for a town council. Four people, a mayor."

"Kevin for mayor!" Ceren shouted.

Damn it, Ceren, knock it off!

"I'm *not* running!" I shouted back. "I'm neutral. I'm not endorsing anyone, I'm not rejecting anyone or campaigning against anyone. If councilors or the mayor want me to be some kind of sheriff, they can talk to me after they're elected. But I'm not running."

Frost's face lost some of its rigor. She had no reason to like me either—she'd told me the truth, as she'd known it, and I'd detonated, nearly taking her with me. But her gaze met mine. After a moment, she nodded slightly and looked away.

"Okay," one-eyed Will shouted. "In that case, I'm running. Who else?"

"Nominations in a week," I said. "Elections a week after that. Spread the word—I'm sure there's more people out there."

"Where?" Will shouted.

I glanced around nervously, feeling my hold on the crowd evaporating. "Look, folks, I'm making this up as I go along."

A small chuckle rippled through the crowd.

I raised a leg to show off the freshly oozing road-rash scabs covering my shin and thigh. "I'll figure a place, post a sign up at Jack's in a couple days, okay? Right now, I just want a bucket of aspirin and a ten-hour nap."

"What about Danny?" Will shouted.

"Let the council figure it out," I said. "That's what we're electing them for. We just need to keep him and a couple other people where we can keep an eye on them until then." I studied the crowd. "Has anyone seen Bill? Teenager Bill?"

"He's over here," shouted Harry the apprentice firefighter from behind me.

I turned.

Bill stood next to the firefighters. Soot covered his face. His shorts and T-shirt were filthy, but he defiantly stared at me, chin up, daring me to arrest him.

The kid had killed Keith Gifford. Had killed a bully.

He'd stolen a flamethrower.

And when things went bad, when he'd heard hell arriving, he'd come back to help.

"I don't want to lock you up." My voice had been one of the few parts of me that felt okay after this afternoon, but all this shouting was making me feel hoarse. I spoke just loudly enough for my voice to carry. "But you need to stay with someone. Let's call it parole. Any volunteers?"

Nobody said anything for a moment.

Beside Bill, Fred raised his head. "We'll take him."

"Aren't you busy with fire watch?" I said.

"Yep. Too busy. A third set of eyes will help."

I nodded. "The fire crew's still short-handed. If you're adding Bill, you really need more people too."

"Hey!" someone shouted. "I'll do it."

Another teenager came shuffling out of the crowd. Black hair hung over his right eye, but the left side of his head was shaved to gleaming scalp. Sunlight glinted off the silver rings in his nose and left ear.

"Rick," I said. One of Acceptance's people.

"I got this," Rick said.

"Are you up for it?" I asked.

Rick grinned. "I can't just hang around and look awesome all the time, dude. And I can spread the word if things go really bad." His voice dropped to a stage whisper. "Besides, the girls all love them a firefighter."

That surfer talk went out of fashion twenty years before you were born, kid. I looked back at Fred, who studied Rick dubiously but finally offered a grudging half-nod.

Rick whooped and bounced over to the firefighters.

"Then Danny," I said, a little more loudly.

Danny Gervais sat on the asphalt, legs folded up to his chest. The four big guys from Acceptance who stood around him, half watching Danny and half guarding him, shifted a sliver of their attention to me.

"You killed Jack. I watched you do it. And you burned down Ceren's house. You hurt people, and you kept hurting people, all so you could have someone you liked in charge of us." I shook my head. "The council might parole you. I won't."

I glanced down at Veronica Boxer, who had somehow made it to the front. "If we put him in a jail cell, can you watch him?"

"We're spread thin," Boxer said. "We could help, but we can't do it on our own."

A hand went up in the middle of the crowd. "You know," Will said, the bandage over his missing eye gleaming white, "I think me and my buddies could help out."

"You hung out with him," I said.

"Yeah, and he jerked us around!" Will dropped his hand. "We trusted him, and the bastard lied to us." Angry cries from other men who'd followed Woodward echoed him. "Trust me on this one. He won't get away."

I glanced back at Boxer, then at Will. "Why don't you two get together and work out a schedule?"

Will stormed over to Danny, seized his arm, and yanked him to his feet. "Oh, we'll make a schedule, all right." Danny's eyes looked huge, and he couldn't look away from Will's fury.

"The council needs to decide what to do with him!" I said. "Trial, I don't know. Something. You just keep him restrained until then."

"He'll make it to trial just fine," Will said.

Danny seemed to shrivel under Will's too-wide smile.

"What about the dregs?" Boxer said.

"Alice, you still here?" I shouted.

A hand popped up above the crowd, then disappeared.

"Let's park those poor people somewhere," I said. "Reamer, I didn't save your mom. Alice did."

"Then thank her for me," Reamer said.

"She's right there, thank her yourself."

I looked around. "Okay, people, show's over. Anyone who can should stay and help clean up this mess. Me," I sighed in a sudden wash of fatigue, "I need a nap. Shoo! Shoo!"

Not that I was going to get one.

Chapter 79

I CLIMBED out of the truck bed, groaning almost continuously at my bruises and scrapes. My unmoving right wrist felt like a club weighing down the end of my arm. The sunlight burned nails of pain into my head. I felt parched and tired and, despite the crowd chanting my name only moments before, very much alone.

Letting Reamer's proclamation to declare me a czar succeed might have gotten me to bed faster. But it was the wrong thing to do.

And for as mistaken as he was about the idea of putting me in charge, that bastard Reamer was right about one thing. I will try to do what I think is the right thing.

Dammit.

The crowd slowly broke up into dozens of small conversations as people discussed what to do. The men who had been Woodward's army stood in a cluster around Danny, with stern faces and unpleasant demeanors. The four men from Acceptance had retreated a bit to let Will and another man support Danny. Discussions seemed to be going quickly but politely.

Woodward still lay on the ground. Ceren knelt with one knee in the small of his back. From here, his face gleamed. Ceren caught my gaze and gave a quick, savage smile.

Alice met me as my feet touched the asphalt, her arm slipping easily around my waist, her shoulder fitting under my arm. An observer might have thought *she* was the one leaning on me. "Are you okay? I mean, will you be okay?"

My mouth tasted like slaughterhouse runoff. "Yeah. I'll be fine." I made myself smile. "Are you okay? I mean, after what you did with Nat Reamer? What did you do to her?"

Alice flushed. "I'm fine. I just…I remembered how it felt with Teresa—you know, when she grabbed me?"

I nodded.

Her voice dropped. "I did the same thing to Mrs. Reamer. I grabbed her like Teresa grabbed me."

I flinched. "Did it hurt you?"

Alice shook her head. "I felt her pain. She'd forgotten what it was like to feel herself. I don't think anyone can really feel themselves—you must get so used to it. But I felt her arthritis, her stomach—I don't know what that is in her stomach, but it doesn't feel good—and her head."

"What in her head? How did you do that?"

"She had…" Alice swallowed nervously. "There was this piece of her skull stuck in her brain," she whispered. "I told it to move out. It was like telling my own hand to make a fist. Then I told the brain to grow back together."

I looked to the back of the thinning crowd. Ian Reamer still stood there, a thin smile on his face as he held his mother's hand and listened to her talk. I couldn't make out her words from this distance, but Ian seemed fascinated. Ian looked away from Nat long enough to look death in Danny's direction, but quickly soothed himself and looked back to his mother.

"You healed her," I said quietly. The thought unnerved me. Alice had said that making that sort of connection wasn't hard. But living with the aftereffects might very well be. Just thinking of Teresa and Jesse's assault on me made a quiet voice in the back of my mind shriek in terror.

Alice nodded. "And when I was touching her, it was really easy to feel Danger. He just kind of, goaded them. Pushed them around. Made them afraid not to obey. But touching her, it's like I had better bandwidth and less latency. He was so slow; I just, like, kept slapping his face every time he did anything and he gave up."

"That is amazing. Really." I glanced back at the other dregs. As I'd instructed Danny, they stood in a line along the building. Two Backs lay on the sidewalk, resting all four legs and both arms. "Do you think you could help the others?"

Alice nodded. "I think so, yeah. I'm going to try. The guy with half a head, maybe not?"

"Don't try anything you can't handle. And hang on a second." I glanced around. "Hey, Reamer! Ian!"

Ian looked up.

I jerked my head at him.

Ian tucked his mom's hand in his arm and started towards me.

"I thought you didn't like this guy," Alice said.

"Can't stand him. But—hey, Reamer."

"Holtzmann." Reamer stood straight, and couldn't hide just a hint of joy behind the stern mask he'd put up.

"Detective," Nat Reamer said.

"This is Alice."

Nat smiled, the brightest, most genuine smile I'd seen on anyone more than six months old. "I know who she is."

"I owe you," Ian said. "I can't never repay you, but I'll try. Whatever you need."

"You can start," I said, "by watching Alice as she tries to help the other people. If she seems at all distressed, you yank her away from them."

Ian looked straight in my eye. "Count on me."

"Hey!" Alice said. "I can do this! I rescued myself, dammit!"

"You did it once, in an emergency," I said. "But I'm not taking any chances with you. You and Ceren are too important."

Alice blushed.

"Besides," I said, "if Ceren and I do all the cooking, it'll be canned ravioli three times a day."

"Thank you so much!" Alice said with mock indignation. "Just for that, you do get to do all the cooking."

"If you can help those people," I said, "you're on."

Alice walked towards the line of brain-damaged people.

I watched her go, a little sad and a little scared. Alice was heading into new territory now, where the human soul touched the alien.

I'd have to help Alice, as best I could.

Whatever that meant.

"Before you go, Nat," I said.

Nat and Ian stopped and looked quizzically at me.

"Who hit you?" I asked.

"You just said," Ian said.

I lowered my voice to a whisper. "It made sense, but—I guessed."

"You guessed right." Nat's face twisted into a scowl. "That pretentious little twerp that called himself Danger. Calling me old and useless." She glared at Danny, who was too busy gaping at his guards to notice. "Useless is having people guarding him. He wanted to take me away right then, add me to his gang, but Ian came home too soon."

She raised a bony, rheumatism-twisted fist and shouted at Danny. "Hanging's too good for you, I tell you. Too good!"

"You're exactly right," I said. "I'm glad Alice could help you."

Nat smiled. "Dear child."

"Come on, Mom," Ian said. "We don't want her to start without us."

"And Mister Reamer?" I said.

Ian stopped and raised his eyebrows.

"You try to crown me again, and I'll crown you. With a club."

He grinned. "This council you're setting up might not like that. Later."

I took a deep breath, trying to relax. Almost everyone looked at me as if they wanted to come bend my ear, but seeing me tired and slumped and battered and bloody changed their minds. Looking like a skin graft "before" picture probably helped some, too.

"Kevin!" Ceren said, just loud enough to be heard over the chatter surrounding us. She still knelt on top of Woodward.

I walked towards her, staggering only once and catching myself in one step.

"What about him?" she asked, bouncing her knee half an inch into Woodward's spine.

Woodward gasped with the impact. He lay still, arms and legs outstretched. His face was a scrawl of pain, lips tight and eyes closed. Tears ran down his face.

I'd expected Woodward to be defensive. To stand up for himself. Instead, he seemed a picture of misery—

"That's it," I said softly.

Ceren narrowed her eyebrows.

"It's okay, Ceren," I said softly. "You can let him up. He's not going anywhere."

Ceren shook her head once, slowly, but took her knee off the man's back and stood.

Woodward sucked in a great big breath as her weight lifted.

"This is what you do, isn't it?" I asked, kneeling by his head. "You know how to take charge. To deal with emergencies. You bull your way in, drag people together, and make things happen."

"You don't get it," hissed Woodward.

"Why do you think I watch out for people?" I said. "Kevin was a cop. That's all I know. So I what I do." I took a deep breath. "And as long as I'm busy, I don't have to think about—other things."

Woodward made an obvious effort to steady his breathing. It didn't work all that well.

"So you want to be in charge. Same thing as me trying to be a cop. I get it. It's not going to happen, but I get it."

Woodward squeezed his eyes shut.

"You know how to organize things," I said. "And we're going to need that. The council's going to need that. You want to be in charge? Run for it, fair and square."

"After this?" Woodward wiped his face and raised himself to his hands and knees. "Kid, you wrestle like a Great Lakes freighter—I went straight down, wasn't coming back up." His voice had lost its usual mellifluous lilt, instead weaving around as if he was a little drunk.

"Take a swing at Kevin again," Ceren said, "or anyone in my family, and you'll find yourself on the *bottom* of the lake."

Her family. *My* family. My heart lifted a little.

Woodward took another breath, this one a little less shaky. But when he opened his eyes, he looked completely lost.

"You have skills," I said. "Maybe you're a clerk instead of the boss—but it needs doing."

Woodward shook his head. "After Danny? Damn fool ruined me. Nobody'll trust me, ever again."

"Then start small." I glanced around the crowd. "Look, everybody knows you and I don't get along."

Woodward snorted. "I told my guys you were the biggest threat to taking charge. And you are. Were. Did."

"So, you can play my auditor." My stomach lurched unhappily as my brain caught up to my mouth.

"Auditor?" Woodward snorted. "What are you doing, wasting taxpayers' money?"

Yeah, Kevin, what are you doing?

But Woodward had skills. Organizing things is a skill, and Frayville needed every skill its people could offer.

And I couldn't turn my back on his sincere, too-human pain.

"I'm running an election," I said. "I don't want anyone accusing me of rigging it. You double-check my work, help count the votes. Read the rules before I put them up, see the weak spots. Make it easy, but watertight. Because *nobody's* going to accuse the two of *us* of conspiring to fix the vote."

Woodward chewed the thought over for a second.

My stupid instinct to help people, getting the better of me again. "Well?"

Woodward gave a slow nod. "All right. I can do that."

At least it's only for two weeks. "Do it well, maybe the council will ask you to take something on." I slowly rolled my shoulders, trying to work the bruises out before they petrified. "One thing, though. I don't want anyone working the election to run, or endorse people, or talk against someone. We've got to stay impartial. Think you can do that?"

Woodward scowled. "Yeah."

That'll keep him from putting up a puppet candidate. Or slow him down, at least. "I'll talk to you later."

Ceren came to my side as I walked back towards the oversized pickup. "You all right, roomie?"

"I will be."

"Let's get you home."

"One thing to do first," I said.

"Let other people clean up. You've done enough."

I shook my head. "I have to take care of Eric."

Ceren's voice got quiet. "Oh."

"Why don't you go help Alice?" I said.

Ceren shook her head. "Alice has other people watching her."

Across the road, Alice had lifted her hands to the college girl's temples. Ian Reamer stood nearby, hands raised, ready to leap and knock her away from the girl. The gay guys I'd seen making out at Jack's an hour or a lifetime ago stood on Alice's other side, ready to catch her and Ian alike.

Veronica Boxer stood beside Nat Reamer, watching intently.

I wondered just how much Acceptance saw.

How much they knew.

At least, when everything had gone to hell, they'd come out to help.

Ceren walked beside me, head down. Her passion had faded, leaving her looking a little lost.

"You know, Ceren," I said, "there's a term, a phrase, for people who keep jumping to attack bad guys, who keep putting themselves in the middle of trouble."

"I know you're trying to protect us," Ceren said. "You don't want us getting hurt. But it's too late for that. I'm not going to stand aside and let some asshole hurt you, or hurt Alice." Her voice softened as we approached Eric's decapitated body. "Or Jack, what happened to him—I've got to try to stop that. I've just got to."

"The phrase," I continued as if she hadn't interrupted, "is *police officer*."

She stopped still.

I stopped as well, painfully swiveling to look in her face.

"And if you're going to go around playing cops and horrible alien mutant robbers, it's best you do it with someone who knows what they're doing. On the cop part, at least. Not the mutant thing, 'cause I don't have a clue there."

Ceren took one long step forward and gave me a hug, tucking her head easily under my chin.

She was gentle, but my broken ribs stabbed into my side. Even the intact ribs creaked. Her touch loosened my heart, but I couldn't help the groan as my bruises and contusions complained.

"Oh!" Ceren let go and skipped back half a step. "I'm sorry."

I spread my arms to balance myself and ease my breathing. "Lesson one: don't squeeze broken ribs."

"I *said* I'm sorry."

"There's another word for someone who keeps throwing themselves into harm's way for other people," I said. "It's 'idiot.' Get used to hearing that one a lot."

"With such a good role model," Ceren said, her voice very matter-of-fact, "I'm sure I'll get that down perfect."

"I'm sure you will."

Ceren bit her lip, suddenly uncertain. "And really—it's Karen."

"Excuse me?"

"My mom—my mom named me Karen, she gave me Karen. I got to junior high, we had so many Karens, I changed it."

I smiled. "Pleased to meet you, Karen."

We got to the oversized pickup truck, and my tentative smile evaporated.

Eric's decapitated corpse, tumbled on its side, cooled behind the rear bumper. His hands still held the severed shovel handle. Inside the cab, Cuddles the Rottie sat with her nose pressed up against the rear window, whining loudly.

My throat knotted. "Why don't you let Cuddles out?"

Ceren straightened her shoulders, pushing away her own trembling. "Sure."

Eric's head had rolled beneath the truck. It lay ear-down, facing the road. I painfully eased myself to my knees, then lay on my side. I could have grabbed his hair and dragged him out. Instead, I put one hand on the crown of his skull and the other at the back, and gently lifted him out into the light.

I knelt behind the truck, cradling his head in my hands, looking into the eternally surprised face. Eric's eyes were open, the pupils expanded in death. The stump was scorched black and red across skin and throat and bone, right across the Adam's apple. I'd seen a dozen bloodless bodies before, but Eric's blanched brown skin dragged me down like no other before it.

"I am so sorry," I said quietly. "I'd be dead without you. You deserved better."

Eric's head twitched.

I spasmed, launching the head away from me and toppling onto my butt. "Fuck!"

Eric's head hit the asphalt and bounced into the gutter. Half a turn, and it rolled to a stop.

My heart hammered hard enough to twitch my broken ribs. Fresh sweat broke out everywhere, mingling with the blood.

Years of police service had taught me that severed heads don't move.

"What?" Ceren said behind me.

Shaking with adrenaline, but no longer feeling my own numerous pains, I dragged myself to the curb and cautiously lifted Eric's head.

The head hung still for a moment, then gave a little twitch.

His tongue clicked against the roof of his mouth.

Tock-tock-tock.

Tock.

Tock.

Tock.
Tock-tock-tock.
Morse code.
SOS.
My fragile calm dissolved.
We're not dead until we decide we're dead.
"Ceren!" I shouted, voice ragged. "A melon! Now!"

Shaking, I brought Eric's head back to his body. I used my foot to gently roll the decapitated corpse onto its back, arms akimbo.

I lined Eric's head up with the body's oozing stump. Matched the stump of bone protruding from the base of the skull up with the bony socket. Lined up the two ends of the severed esophagus. And brought head to body.

The flesh of the severed stumps twitched at the contact.

Chapter 80

THE SUN had dropped behind the row of stores on the far side of the street, offering us a scrap of blessed shade. Bill's puttermobile had burned out, but the stink still filled the air despite the faint breeze that had risen as the sun disappeared.

I still felt exhausted and hungry and generally horrible, with broken bones and freshly cracked, oozing scabs and who knows what trashed inside me. Adrenaline had eaten my strength. I was content to sit on the concrete curb, its stored heat baking my buttocks, my club-wristed hand in the grass to support me as my stomach growled.

We sat behind the huge pickup truck with the ridiculously massive plow. Now that I had time to think, I recognized it. Fire crews used it clear roads after forest fires. With the solid tires and over-torqued trans, it could plow a path out of Frayville, right out of the kipuka. While I'd been having my breakdown, Eric had fetched it.

Eric.

My blank shock had passed, but I still couldn't take my eyes off him.

Ceren—*Karen*—brought a sixth melon from the nearby willow, hefted the machete she'd found in the bed of Eric's giant pickup, and hacked it into eight chunks with a little too much glee.

Kipuka Blues

Eric picked up the last chunk of the previous melon and chomped into it, eating the rind as well as the succulent meat. If I felt like I'd been on the wrong side of an auto-pedestrian collision, Eric looked like he'd lost a heated argument with a train. Black acid burns ringed his neck, and the skin hadn't yet grown to cover twitching sinews and muscle tissues as they grew together. His brown skin still had a pallor I associated only with the dead.

But he sat on the curb beside me. Cuddles sat behind him, propping him upright. And Eric's eyes twitched with recognition.

And after he'd eaten the first melon, he'd managed one word: "Thanks."

Ceren stepped back, machete blade across her body, and watched Eric tear into the first chunk of the sixth melon.

Eric swallowed, mouth moving a little more freely than it had just moments before. "More." He jammed the next slab of melon between his teeth as if the word had robbed him of valuable eating time.

Ceren nodded. "It's all-you-can-eat tonight, don't worry."

Eric grunted and gave a little nod.

Eric had devoured half of that melon before Ceren came back, this time carrying two. "A piece of one of these is for Kevin."

"I'll be okay," I said.

Eric grunted.

Ceren said, "You look like hell, Kevin. Yeah, okay, Eric looks like hell in a blender, but still." She hefted the machete. "Eat a piece, or I'll chop bits off you until you do."

Eric thrust a chunk at me, reaching for another slab with his other hand.

"'Hell in a blender?'" I said. "What does that even mean?"

"You said to save the f-bomb for when I needed it," Ceren said. "Like when your buddy's severed head comes alive in your hands, I guess."

I raised my working hand. "Fine, fine. And that was a fully justified f-bomb. Just so you know."

The fruit's meaty, succulent flavor felt wonderful on my tongue. The dried blood on my teeth added its own copper-iron taste. Hunger claimed me, and I devoured the eighth-melon just as savagely as Eric.

I was licking my fingers when someone said, "Holtzmann?"

I looked up.

Frost and Langley stood in the empty street, just beyond the pickup.

Langley rolled her gaze over both of us. "I've seen better-looking corpses," Langley said. "In geological digs."

Eric snorted a laugh around a mouthful of melon.

I made myself smile. It hurt less than I expected, as if my cheeks had directly absorbed the melon juice and used it to heal. Maybe they had. "They probably felt better than us, too."

Frost jerked a thumb down the street. "That girl's with you?"

Alice sat on her knees next to College Boy, Reamer hovering over her. The girl she'd helped first was sitting up, alert and conscious and aware. And crying. I'd overheard scraps of their conversation, something about a deliberate drug overdose. A post-Absolute suicide pact.

Drugs hadn't occurred to me.

Then again, neither had eating my gun.

"Yeah," I said.

Frost nodded. "That's…impressive. I'd like to talk to her when she's done."

"I'm sure she won't mind."

Skin had started to grow across Eric's neck, and a hint of color oozed back into his face.

Keeping half an eye on Eric, I reached for another slab of melon. He didn't object.

"And when you're done," Frost said to Eric, "I'd like to talk to you. About—" She waved her hand. "This. What happened. I'm a biologist. I'm trying to make a rational theory about us."

Langley coughed into her fist.

Frost shook her head. "Fine, fine! *Vaguely* rational."

Eric nodded, mumbling something around a mouthful of melon. Juice ran down from the corners of his mouth, making his blood-soaked shirt even more sticky.

"Listen," I said. "Doctor Frost. I'm sorry."

Frost met my eyes, neither encouraging nor rejecting.

I swallowed. "You told me the best truth you knew earlier. I took it badly. I'm sorry. I wasn't prepared to hear that, but you don't deserve—"

My breath caught.

Kevin did something terrible. To save Julie and Sheila from Absolute.

I wish he hadn't. But he did.

Now I have to live with what he did.

And I had too much to do to fall apart now.

Just the thought of what Frost had said had been enough to destabilize me.

But I remembered dying. I remembered Absolute's thorns plunging into me. I remembered Kevin's consciousness winking out.

Frost had her reasons for believing what she believed. She probably had some mental need to believe she was still the same person.

I wouldn't try to prove her wrong.

I wouldn't take that away from her.

I needed a moment to steady myself. "It's my problem. Not yours."

Frost watched me calmly for a moment, then her expression softened. "I understand," she said. "Apology accepted. These days, every dog gets one bite."

Behind Eric, Cuddles *woofed* and wagged her stump of a tail.

Langley burst out into deep, sincere belly laughter.

I couldn't help smiling. "You already got your bite, Cuddles."

The dog grinned at me, tongue lolling.

Just how smart was a dog made of alien stuff, anyway?

"Holtzmann!" someone shouted from up the road.

I shook my head and bit off another chunk of the melon in my hand. With my petrified hand, I grabbed the rear bumper and levered myself upright.

The guy with the huge beer gut lumbered down the street at what was probably the closest thing to a trot he could manage. "Holtzmann! You down here?"

"Yeah," I said loudly. My throat ached from all the shouting. *And the screaming. Don't forget the screaming.* "Do *not* tell me everything's gone bad again."

Beer Belly slowed as quickly as his massive inertia let him. "You want to see this. Before word gets around."

I bit back any number of sarcastic remarks. I had a bit of détente with the veterans of Woodward's army, and I wanted to keep it. "Cer—*Karen*, can you keep at this?"

"Ceren's fine. Sure." She dropped two more melons at Eric's feet and hoisted the machete. "Take another chunk with you, though."

I didn't argue. If Beer Belly wanted me to move more than ten feet, I needed a boost.

Beer Belly watched me gimp towards him, shaking his head. "You need a ride, dude?"

"Nah, if I don't move now I won't walk at all tomorrow." At least my breathing had finally eased—apparently my body had decided that the busted ribs were more important than my mutant wrist.

I concentrated on putting one foot in front of the other as we slogged past the burned-out shell of Bill's puttermobile, Beer Belly keeping a careful eye on me the whole way as if he expected to catch me and throw me over his shoulder at any second. The physical effort gave me time to drag my thoughts together.

Maybe we were the whole world.

But we'd figured out how to survive, even things like brain damage.

And decapitation.

Danny had tried to terrorize us, so his gang could seize control. We knew what an army of dregs looked like now. And now that Acceptance knew what that felt like, we'd have warning if anyone tried. With Alice's discovery, even the dregs had hope.

I didn't know why Absolute had broken into Legacy and stolen hard drives. But the fact that it had meant that Absolute needed something from us.

And if we were the whole world, Absolute was in here with us.

We were learning.

And we could find it.

I eventually found enough breath to gasp, "I don't think… we've been introduced."

Beer Belly flashed a big broad smile. "Name's Rick, dude."

I recognized that smile, but not on that face. "You aren't related to the skateboard kid?"

Rick's smile grew a little sad. "He's my son."

I nodded. "Good kid."

"Thanks." Rick looked away.

Rick Junior was part of Acceptance. How would I have felt if Julie had come through—had been *copied*, like me? Or Sheila? And decided she couldn't live, and fallen into Acceptance's waiting arms? Alive, but forever changed?

The mere thought made the last bite of melon bitter.

Lights spilled out the open door of Jack's, silhouetting the people standing in the doorway. I glimpsed more people past them, all standing still, as if they were in church. Or attending a funeral. Jack's body was missing from the front—had they brought him inside? Laid him out? And what was that hissing, crackly noise—running water?

Rick raised his voice. "Come on, folks. Let the sheriff in."

Faces turned towards us. People silently shuffled aside.

Trepidation knotted my throat. What was wrong? The stink of an abandoned dinner and cooling blood spilled by the gallon coursed out the front door. Why was everyone standing so still?

I didn't want to go in.

But I followed Rick's broad back into Jack's.

Maybe thirty people stood around the room. Nobody sat at the varnished wooden tables. Nobody picked at the abandoned dinner. Despite both doors being propped open, the room reeked of a stomach-knotting mix of blood and corpse and cordite.

Kenny still lay in front of the bar, attached to the twitching bodies of the two women who'd attacked. The sight made me even sadder. If they'd lived a little longer, if Danny Gervais hadn't used them as weapons, maybe Alice could have helped them. If restoring thought to someone who'd decided to die was "helping."

Nobody moved. People hardly breathed.

The crackle came from behind the bar.

I froze, transfixed.

Eric's radio was at maximum volume. The tinny speaker buzzed.

But the frequency counter was frozen in place. The shifting weather, the fading day—something had changed. We were getting something.

Ordered sound emerged from the static. A haunting keyboard melody, attenuated by distance and radiation and who knew what else, in the hundreds or thousands of miles between us.

The slow, simple tune ripped open old memories. "I know this," I said quietly.

Rick looked at me.

"It's an old Pink Floyd song," I said. I couldn't keep myself from timing my words to fit with the imminent vocals.

"It's called: 'Is There Anybody Out There?'"

About the Author

The author of over 30 books, Michael Warren Lucas lives in Detroit, Michigan, with his wife and pet rats. He practices martial arts and is busy writing the next Immortal Clay novel.

Never miss his new releases! Join his mailing list at:

https://www.michaelwarrenlucas.com.

Printed in Poland
by Amazon Fulfillment
Poland Sp. z o.o., Wrocław